RED & LOWERING
Sky

RED & LOWERING
Sky

LYNN MORRIS

GRAND RAPIDS, MICHIGAN 49530 USA

Red and Lowering Sky
Copyright © 2004 by Lynn Morris

Requests for information should be addressed to:

Zondervan, *Grand Rapids, Michigan 49530*

Library of Congress Cataloging-in-Publication Data

Morris, Lynn.
    Red and lowering sky / Lynn Morris.
      p. cm.
    ISBN 0-310-22798-4
      1. Americans—Samoan Islands—Fiction. 2. Samoan Islands—Fiction.
3. Single fathers—Fiction. 4. Missionaries—Fiction. 5. Ambassadors—Fiction.
6. Hurricanes—Fiction. 7. Widowers—Fiction. I. Title.
PS3563.O874439 R43 2004
813'.54—dc22

                                       2003024445

Published in association with the literary agency of Alive Communications, Inc., 7680 Goddard Street, Suite 200, Colorado Springs, CO 80920.

Interior design by Beth Shagene

Printed in the United States of America

04 05 06 07 08 09 10 /❖ DC/ 10 9 8 7 6 5 4 3 2 1

The Pharisees also with the Sadducees came,
and tempting
desired him that he would shew them a sign from heaven.
He answered and said unto them,
When it is evening, ye say, It will be fair weather:
for the sky is red.
And in the morning, It will be foul weather today:
for the sky is red and lowring.
O ye hypocrites, ye can discern the face of the sky;
but can ye not discern the signs of the times?

Matthew 16:1–3

Contents

Part III: As the Sparks Fly Upward

Part IV: The Doors of the Sea

RED & LOWERING Sky

PART I

Days of Shadow

For we are but of yesterday,
and know nothing,
because our days upon earth are a shadow.

Bildad the Shuhite to Job, 8:9

Monday's child is fair of face,
Tuesday's child is full of grace,
Wednesday's child is full of woe,
Thursday's child has far to go,
Friday's child is loving and giving,
Saturday's child works hard for its living.
But the child that's born on the Sabbath day,
Is bonny and blithe, and good and gay.

"A Week of Birthdays," *Mother Goose*

Infernal Creatures

"Miss Livingstone, the Misses Carrolltons have come to call."
Trista turned to the door, where the Livingstones' butler, Rokeby, stood, left eyebrow arched high with elegant English disdain. He was wearing a leather apron and had dirty hands; he had obviously been polishing the silver.

But before Trista could respond, Charmaine and Colette Carrollton brushed by him, Charmaine pouting and Colette rolling her eyes. "Oh, Rokeby, that was just no fun at all," Charmaine grumbled.

"Your pardon, miss, I'm sure," Rokeby said with a mocking bow and glided away.

"He knows which of us is which," Charmaine said, throwing herself down on the small bed. "He's just too uppity to say it."

It was very easy to tell the Carrollton twins apart, though they were identical—perfectly identical—twins. Both were short and curvaceous, with glossy black hair and dark eyes and the same gamine heart-shaped face. But even when they were standing perfectly still and quiet, even in photographs when they were suitably grave for the solemn event, it was clear that Colette was the more mature and sober one, and Charmaine was flighty, mischievous, and flirtatious. Trista had never been able to figure out if it was because Colette's expression had grace and dignity or if it was because Charmaine's eyes sparkled as if she were about to have a fit of the giggles. Or both.

"Well, I expect it's your own fault this time," Trista said, turning back to arranging her dried eucalyptus. "It's really beneath him to answer the door since we're not formally receiving calls yet. What did you do, make poor Susie run him to ground?"

"Of course she did," Colette answered, settling herself on the edge of the single straight-backed Windsor chair. "And it's because of her silliness that he won't announce me properly."

"I honestly think that Mother was right when she said that the women in this town only come to adore Rokeby, not to call on us," Trista said dryly.

The twins exchanged a quick look of satisfaction and relief. Trista had not made the slightest mention of her mother in the year after her death. Phoebe Racine Dodge Livingstone had died on March 30, 1887. It had seemed that the one-year anniversary of her death had been a milestone for Trista, for she had begun to speak of her mother in this sort of offhand manner just last month, though only rarely.

Charmaine then said, "Oh, Colette, stop your complaining. You'd think you were an elderly matron. You're only eighteen minutes older than me—"

"Than I," Colette said.

"—than I and in any case, it would seem that old Rokeby would be glad to be called away from scrubbing the flagstones or scouring pots or whatever he was doing," Charmaine finished triumphantly. In her mind she had scored a point.

"Excuse me," Trista said, stepping back to view her arrangement with a critical eye, "but do I understand that all this contention is because Rokeby has made a mistake in butler etiquette? Impossible."

"I'm the eldest daughter," Colette maintained with unusual vehemence. "He's supposed to announce me as 'Miss Carrollton' and her as 'Miss Charmaine Carrollton.' Everyone knows that."

"At the risk of repeating myself, I must remind you that we're not receiving callers, that Rokeby was busy in the kitchen polishing the silver, and that Susie is perfectly capable of opening the front door to let people in who know very well that we are not receiving callers." Somehow the eucalyptus just wasn't flowing right; it looked haphazard. "Does this look all bunchy to you?"

"Yes," Colette said.

"No," Charmaine said. "Oh, how I love Rokeby. He's so—so—aristocratic. He must, he simply must have royal blood. Oh—do you think maybe that he's actually French? A count or something? A duke? And that he had to flee the guillotine, in disguise as a butler during the Bloody Revolution?"

"Since the French Revolution began in 1789, and this is 1888, that would make him over one hundred years old," Colette observed.

"And he would be much more offended for you to think he was French than if you think he's a hundred and twenty years old," Trista said, frowning and snatching the whole bunch of eucalyptus out of the brass pot to start all over again.

"Oh, you two think you're so smart," Charmaine grumbled.

"It's very difficult not to think so during conversations with you, Charmaine," Colette said with clear affection.

"What? Oh, never mind, I just know you said something clever. Trista"—Charmaine looked around with sudden surprise—"isn't this Merritt's room? Whyever are you cleaning Merritt's room? And by the way, you look like a scullery maid. Your apron is dirty."

"She doesn't look like a scullery maid, Charmaine," Colette said. "A governess, maybe."

Trista was small, barely over five feet tall, with a wispy waist and delicate frame. She had lovely red-gold hair, a welcome inheritance from her father's side of the family, with mysterious hazel eyes that sometimes looked smoky brown and sometimes a clear pine green. Her face was heart-shaped, with a small but well-shaped mouth, thin nose, and straight thin brows. She was not extraordinarily pretty, nor was she plain. At first glance she looked the type of girl to be shy, like a small bird, for she was so tiny and seemed fragile. But her direct, assessing gaze and her poise, unusual for a girl of nineteen, were what made her notable in the company of her more flamboyant friends such as the Carrollton twins.

Trista turned to answer, "Yes, Charmaine, I know I look drab in drab colors, but we are in half-mourning, you know, and I flatly refuse to wear that putrid lavender that ancient matrons wear for years. And yes, this is Merritt's room. I've put him back in the schoolroom, for McKean has said that he'll stay here at The Cedars for a while when he returns, instead of in his flat in town."

"McKean's coming home?" Charmaine exclaimed. "When?"

"The SS *Golden Phoenix* docked in Baltimore yesterday," Trista said with a sigh, knowing that she'd get no more sensible conversation out of Charmaine—if it could be called that—for the rest of the afternoon, only gushings and vaporings over her elder brother. Even sensible Colette's eyes sparkled. "They decided to ride in. McKean's telegraph said they couldn't stand another train or carriage or ship or boat. So I think they should be home late this evening."

"McKean! McKean's coming home! Why didn't you say so, Trista?" Charmaine cried, bounding up and turning to smooth the down comforter she'd mussed while lolling on the bed. "And just look at that window, it's positively filthy!"

She hurried to the door, leaned out and shrieked, "Mrs. Cross! Mrs. Cross! Oh, here, Elspeth, bring some hot water, vinegar, and clean rags right now. This room is shameful, girl, for shame!" The Carrolltons were practically family, and as such, the servants knew not to pay much attention to Charmaine. Elspeth, the stocky, cheerful upstairs maid, glanced cautiously at Trista.

"Never mind, Elspeth, it's just a tiny smudge on the window," Trista said. "I can clean it with my apron."

"Yes, miss." She bobbed and disappeared in a great hurry.

"Why didn't you tell me McKean's coming home?" Charmaine said, hurrying to check her face and hair in the small shaving mirror on the chest.

"Because I thought you knew since your own brother is with him, and I'm certain Endecott telegraphed your parents when they arrived, just as McKean did," Trista said patiently, scrubbing the tiny smear on the window with a corner of her apron.

"Oh, bother Endecott, he's such a—such a—big-brotherly old thing," Charmaine said. "I thought they weren't coming back until next month."

Trista's elder brother, McKean, and the eldest Carrollton son, Endecott, had been best friends all their lives, they and Vaughn Pascal. The Livingstone, the Carrollton, and the Pascal families were all close friends, since their fathers had been partners in a thriving law practice for almost twenty-five years. Their children had all grown up together, and they were neighbors.

Evangeline Carrollton and Bettina Pascal and Phoebe Livingstone had been best friends their entire married lives. When Phoebe had died in March 1887, it had devastated the Pascal and Carrollton families almost as much as it had the Livingstones. Almost, but of course not quite. Though Phoebe had been dead for over a year, Stockton Livingstone was still living much in seclusion, still in private mourning, not yet rejoining his life. That was why the Livingstones were still not giving or receiving calls, that most important bulwark of Washington, D.C., society. That was why Trista Livingstone, at nineteen years of age, was still wearing half-mourning, why she felt constant helplessness in the face of her father's pain, why she felt such terrible uncertainty in her role as surrogate mother to her four younger brothers and sisters, and why she was so very glad that McKean was coming home. He was the only person in the world who could help her. He might even be able to help her father heal.

McKean was like that—capable, confident, sure of himself and of his place in the world. He was also reckless, brash, restless, and something of a rake, but that only added to his rough charm. And that was why Charmaine Carrollton was hopelessly in love with him, or so she often insisted, but in fact McKean was a favorite with ladies, all ladies, young awkward twelve-year-olds, ancient society doyennes, maidservants young and old, all of Trista's and her younger sister Lorna's friends, stiff and pretentious senators' wives—it didn't matter. McKean was dashing and women adored him.

Trista came out of her reverie—the smear had long since disappeared and the window was squeaking in protest—and went back to the Federal worktable in the corner to wrestle with the eucalyptus. She had missed her friends' last few words and now dutifully attended again.

"—from Cherbourg, you ninny," Colette was saying. "In France."

"But I thought that everyone went to London on the Grand Tour, so I just assumed they'd take ship from there," Charmaine said stubbornly.

"They didn't go to London, they didn't go anywhere in England," Colette said. "They were on the European continent, Charmaine. Paris, Vienna, St. Petersburg. Because they only had six months. So they sailed to St. Petersburg first, and then came back to Vienna, then Paris, then Cherbourg. Which is on the sea. To get the return ship home."

"Well, I don't understand why they didn't go to London—it is the Season you know, and there it is, so close," Charmaine argued.

"So close? Charmaine, it's all the way across the English Channel and all the way up the River Thames!"

"It is? Oh yes, yes, I forgot London's not actually in Europe. Oh, and don't you two exchange those looks. We're just alike, Colette, and I'm as smart as you, I'm just not so unbearably pretentious about it." Charmaine theatrically fell onto the bed and then threw herself back, her arms over her head. "Oh, just think, McKean's actually going to be sleeping—"

"Charmaine! Really!" Colette was appalled.

"You are the silliest creature," Trista said. "It's just my brother, with his hair uncombed and his dusty boots and silly jokes. Get up right now, Charmaine, I've plumped that down comforter way too many times already."

Charmaine rose, the picture of injured dignity. "You have no idea of the deep affection, the esteem, that I hold for McKean, Trista, and I'm sure that he feels the same for me. He's just young and young gentlemen must be allowed to sow their wild oats, as they say, but when he wants to settle down with a mature, discerning, caring woman he'll see how well suited we are."

"Discern this, sister dear," Colette said with a rare giggle. "You've busted your bustle. Again."

"Oh no, no!" Charmaine wailed. "And this is one of those new Langtry bustles with springs! It's supposed to retain that elegantly correct Parisian shape."

Colette and Trista could barely hear her wail, they were laughing so hard. Charmaine was turning to try to see the damage, but the effect was something of a puppy chasing its tail. When she turned, the collapsed bustle, of course, whisked around and disappeared.

"Oh, oh, Charmaine—wise, mature woman of the world—if McKean only knew—" Colette choked.

"Knew what?" he said from the doorway, grinning.

"McKean!" Trista ran and jumped, for she was so tiny and McKean was over six feet tall. He picked her up, whirled her around once, kissed her cheek with a loud smack, and set her down. With his arm still around her waist he said, "C and C, you're here! What are you doing in my bedroom? And Charmaine, that's an interesting new fashion. Let me guess—the new soup tureen bustle? Didn't see many like that in Paris."

"Oh! You—you're so—you're such a—a—grubby, silly little boy!" Charmaine blustered and then backed out of the room in an odd crablike sideways shuffle.

"That's not what you said—" Colette began with wide-eyed innocence.

"Do shut up, Colette," Charmaine said. "If you will step aside, you great clomping boor, and let me by."

"Sure, Char," he said, bowing in a courtly manner as she practically ran into Trista's room. It was a major endeavor to undress and then reshape a big inside-out bustle.

"She collapsed it," Trista explained, rather unnecessarily.

"Tough break," McKean said sympathetically. "Colette, you look as lovely and graceful and uncollapsed as ever."

"Thank you," Colette said calmly. "It's good to see you, McKean. It was a long ride, I see."

"Yeah, I really am grubby, huh? I thought I'd come up and clean up a little before making my entrance; didn't know there'd be a parcel of females in my room. Beautiful, lovely, welcome females, of course."

He threw some rather worn saddlebags on the spotless, much-plumped bed and ran his hands over his head. His hair, thick and unfashionably short, with a tendency to be spiky, was dusty. He was dressed the way he always dressed for long hard rides—denim jeans, soft leather riding boots, a plain white linen shirt, no waistcoat. McKean was not actually a handsome man; he was more rugged-looking. Even though he was just now twenty-four, his face was weathered, with deep smile creases and sun-squint lines at the corners of his eyes. He always had a deep tan, more akin to a laborer's or sailor's than to a fine gentleman's, and his hair was usually bleached out to a whitish blond. He was tall and athletic, with a little bit of a rough edge about him—though his dark blue eyes were warm and his lips were full and well-formed, both were somewhat jarring in that tough face.

"That stuff smells good. I always forget what it is but I like it," he told Trista, stretching high. He could touch the sloping ceiling with his fingertips.

"Eucalyptus. Oh, McKean, I'm so glad you're home, I don't care if you are grubby," Trista said. "Have you seen anyone else yet?"

"No, like I said, I just—"

"Good heavens," Colette said, jumping up from her chair. "What is it?"

It was a spectacular ruckus, obviously coming from downstairs, obviously from the kitchen: women's terrified screams, the clang of crashing copper pans, crockery breaking.

McKean ran downstairs, followed by Trista and Colette, who unceremoniously picked up their skirts so they could follow McKean's long strides. Charmaine appeared, properly bustled again, demanding breathlessly, "What is it? A fire? Murderers? Robbers? What is it, McKean?"

He didn't answer as the four of them ran down the stairs, bowling around the great carved banister, through the long back hall to the kitchen. The four of them burst in together.

Mrs. Cross the housekeeper was shrieking and whirling around in a desperate manner, while Mrs. Trimble the cook was down on her hands and knees, crawling around, shouting, "It's all right, it's all right, Mrs. Cross, it's not on you, not now—"

Also down on the floor, flat on his belly, was twelve-year-old Merritt Fielden Livingstone, bane of all servants' existence, and a sore trial to his older sister, Trista, who tried all day every day to keep him out of mischief and keep him healthy. Right now he was halfway under the great oak worktable, saying something, but it was muffled and just sounded like "Oomph—mit hrrr—whoomph—"

Susie the parlormaid came running in, eyes wild, and shrieked, "Oh, Lord save us, Master Merritt, is it snakes again?"

"Snakes!" Colette and Charmaine screeched together, and Charmaine got a death grip on McKean, who tried unsuccessfully to disentangle himself and reassure Mrs. Cross at the same time.

"Calm down, calm down, Mrs. Cross, there's nothing on you. Diggers, what is it? And how many?"

Merritt popped up, grinning with delight. "McKean! Hi! I didn't know you were home yet!"

Mrs. Cross did stop whirling like a mad dervish and pressed both hands to her ample bosom. "Oh, I'll have an apoplexy! That boy will be the death of me—"

"Is it snakes? Merritt, it's not snakes, is it?" Colette pleaded, now perched, rather precariously, on a three-legged stool, with her skirts hiked all the way up to her knees.

"Naw, it's just skinks," Merritt said with disdain. "I just wanted to show them to Mrs. Trimble."

"Skinks! What is a skink! Tell me what a skink is!" Charmaine screamed hysterically, clinging like death to McKean.

"It's just Rosalie and her babies, and you're scaring them. Oomp—rumph—" Merritt said, squirming underneath the table again.

"*We're* scaring *them!*" Mrs. Cross said, picking up a long-handled wooden spoon with murder in her eyes, and taking a step toward Merritt's still-visible lower half.

"Wait—" McKean and Trista said together.

Unfortunately, Rosalie, the biggest, fattest, slimiest-looking lizard that Trista had ever seen, at this point saw fit to attack Mrs. Cross, running out from underneath the table, her mouth opened wide, right to the housekeeper's shiny half boots. Mrs. Cross screamed again, dropped the wooden spoon, whirled, and ran to cower against the far wall. McKean finally pushed Charmaine away, grabbed a bowl, and upended it over the lizard. Mrs. Trimble made a grab for a smaller lizard that was trying to sneak by behind McKean's back and managed to capture it.

"Oh, oh, how can you bear it, Mrs. Trimble?" Charmaine said, now clinging to Trista. "I would faint, I just know I would, I may anyway!"

"Please don't, we're all too busy," Colette snapped.

"Oh yes, you're really busy, teetering up on that stool," Charmaine said, straightening indignantly. "And McKean can see your bloomers!"

"Do be quiet, Charmaine, McKean doesn't care about Colette's bloomers," Trista said, leading her to a high stool stowed in the corner. "Here, sit up there and be quiet."

Trista, McKean, and Mrs. Trimble flattened themselves on the floor at the other three sides of the big table, surrounding the lizards, as it were. "How many more, Diggers?" McKean asked.

"Oo—eenk," Merritt answered.

"Twenty-three? Did he say twenty-three?" Charmaine wailed.

"Master Merritt, I am going to whale you, I mean literally whale the tar out of you," Mrs. Cross said.

The ancient oak door at the back of the kitchen creaked slowly open, revealing a strong bolt of afternoon sunlight and a little blonde girl with wide blue eyes. "Hullo, everyone. Is it the skinks? Uncle Jumbo's in the garden."

"No, no, Dolly, you'll let them out!" Merritt said, wiggling out from under the table.

"Please! Please let them out!" Charmaine said. "Open the door, Dolly! Wider! Shoo, shoo!"

"I've got one, Diggers," McKean said conversationally. "Slippery little sods, aren't they?"

Trista suddenly sat up straight. "Dolly. Dolly, what did you say?"

"I said Uncle Jumbo's in the garden." Dolly was clearly pleased. Such cool amusement in the eyes of a five-year-old girl was unsettling.

"What—what's an Uncle Jumbo?" Charmaine asked.

Now, skinks or not, loads of lizards or not, Mrs. Cross rounded the table to loom over McKean's prone body, waving the wooden spoon. "Mr. McKean, you had better not have brought back any elephants or anteaters or other infernal creatures from those nether lands!"

McKean looked up with righteous indignation. "I didn't, Cross! Honest!"

"No, he didn't," Trista said, sighing as she rose and tried to dust herself off. "Uncle Jumbo's not a creature, he's a person. Where is he, Dolly?"

"In the dollhouse. With Penn," she answered, delight growing in her eyes.

"Well, I suppose—" Trista began, but Rokeby appeared at the door leading into the hallway, in full splendor now—black coat, waistcoat, perfect tie, white gloves.

"Miss Livingstone," he said, bowing slightly, "the first lady is calling."

"Thank you, Rokeby. Where have you put her?" Trista asked.

"I have not put her anywhere, since she is neither a chess piece nor an errant house cat," Rokeby replied, staring very hard at Colette, who blushed and let down her skirts. "She is waiting for you in the morning room, and I took the liberty of telling her you would be with her directly. Directly, miss."

"Yes, Rokeby," Trista said meekly and scooted out.

Rokeby looked around the room, eyebrow at full tilt. Everyone was still frozen.

Dolly said conversationally, "The president's out in the garden, Rokeby. With Penn."

"Very well," he said calmly, "I shall go suggest that Mr. Livingstone join them. And then I'll hurry and return and offer my services, as they are so clearly needed here." He marched out.

"Rokeby always makes me feel like a—like a naughty little boy," McKean said.

"Now why would that be, I wonder," Mrs. Cross snapped.

McKean rolled his eyes—he was facing away from her—as he was struggling to get to his feet, for he had a tiny wiggly lizard in each hand and couldn't use his hands without squishing them. Colette collected herself before Charmaine could, jumping down and hurrying to help him up, surreptitiously making a face at her sister over his head.

"Wait—" Charmaine said, but it was too late. McKean was upright, and she was still mindful of the skinks.

"Hullo, McKean," Dolly said a little shyly, throwing her head up to look at him. Only with her eldest brother did she ever seem to be a doll-like child.

"Hi, Dolly dear," he said. "And what's this about calling the president 'Uncle Jumbo'?"

"He said that we might—Penn and I, you see, because we're still children. He said that his nieces and nephews call him that, and that he'd like it if Penn and I did," Dolly explained as McKean and Merritt, also now upright, carefully collected Rosalie and her four babies and put them into a pot with a lid. The women scattered to the far corners of the room again, except for the courageous Mrs. Trimble, who started sweeping up the broken crockery.

"He did, huh? Okay, Diggers, is that the last? Scoot along, then—oh no, buddy, I don't think you'd better set them free in the greenhouse," McKean said, grabbing Merritt's shoulders and turning him. Merritt was headed to the door that led into the greenhouse, which led into the conservatory, which led into the dining room. "I can foresee great tragedies arising from that course of action," McKean added gravely. "They'll be fine out in the garden."

"Not the kitchen garden!" Mrs. Cross warned, waving her wooden spoon again.

"No, no, 'course not," McKean said quickly.

"Aw, McKean," Merritt said. "They're just skinks. Rosalie and her little babies."

"So we all have seen. Come on, I'll show you a good place out under the pergola," McKean said, slapping him on the shoulder. They started out the back door and as they passed Dolly, her face fell. McKean stopped, turned, and said, "Well? Aren't you coming, Dolly? I know—how 'bout piggyback? You too big for that now?"

"No, McKean, I'm not too big for that," she answered solemnly.

"Hop on, then. Bye, ladies!" he said, after Dolly had settled on his back and secured skinny arms around his neck.

"Oh, I am so in love with that man," Charmaine said.

Colette, frowning prodigiously, turned to Mrs. Trimble. "Excuse me. Did he say—the president? Of the United States?"

Evildoers

The twenty-second president of the United States, Stephen Grover Cleveland, knelt into a rifleman's stance, threw the wooden stick up to his shoulder, closed his left eye, and took careful aim. "Ka-whoom!" he thundered, to almost-four-year-old Penn Livingstone's satisfaction. It was a much more satisfying rifle noise than when grown-ups simply said bang.

"Did you get him?" Penn asked from his own stance at the other dollhouse window, sighting down his own carved stick.

"I'm not sure. Might have just winged him."

"I'll get him," Penn said with assurance. "There he is, that ol'—uh—what was he, Uncle Jumbo?"

"A thieving, murdering journalist," Mr. Cleveland answered.

"See his big ol' fat head. Ka-whoom! Got 'im!"

"Good, good shooting, Penn," Mr. Cleveland said, reaching across the room—it was only six feet wide—to offer Penn a congratulatory handshake. Penn stood up to receive it manfully, though Mr. Cleveland could not return the gesture. He was a big man, with a barrel chest and enormous shoulders, and his bulk quite overwhelmed the dollhouse.

"Trista says you're not 'posed to shoot people," Penn said gravely. "But I think if the president says so, then it must be you can."

"So they tell me. Though I'm not too sure it's all right even then. But then again, I'm of the opinion that journalists are fair game."

"Me, too," Penn agreed. "What's a journamiss?"

"They're evil. That's why I'm very grateful that you let me hide in your fort from that one."

Penn's blue eyes grew very round. "Are you scairt?"

"Not now, not with such an excellent sharpshooter to bag them for me."

Penn nodded, accepting it as his due, and knelt again, sighting out into the garden. "I'll keep watch, Uncle Jumbo."

"Good, good," Mr. Cleveland said absently. He, too, was searching out the window for more evildoers.

"There's Papa," Penn said dispiritedly. "He'll make you quit playing, won't he?"

"I expect he will. I don't get to play much at all, you know."

"Guess presidents don't much," Penn said sympathetically. "But if you can come back sometimes, we'll bag some more journamiss."

"You may be sure that if I get to come back they'll be stalking me," Mr. Cleveland said, half-stooping, half-crawling through the tiny door. "And I'll expect you to make short work of 'em, Penn. Hello, Stockton. Are they gone?"

"Yes, sir, Mr. President, my overseer and a couple of the stable boys are escorting them off the grounds." Stockton Livingstone gave Mr. Cleveland a hand and then stooped to peer through Penn's window. "Penn, have you been taking care of Mr. Cleveland?"

"Yes, sir, he only winged that evil ol' journamiss, but I bagged him," Penn bragged.

"You did?" Stockton said, amused.

"Bagged him but good," Mr. Cleveland said. "Thanks, Penn."

"Welcome, Uncle Jumbo."

"Mr. Cleveland, could I interest you in some cold lemonade?" Stockton asked, motioning back toward the house, which could barely be seen through the hedges and thick clumps of flowers and decorative grasses. The dollhouse was in the English country garden, which was something of a genteel wilderness, with only small dirt footpaths threading through the flower beds and stands of old beeches and ash trees. In fact the entire fourteen-acre grounds of The Cedars were only subtly sculpted into different informal gardens. Phoebe Livingstone had preferred to keep the grounds as close to the woodlands they had always been, merely trimming a little here and there, adding footpaths to the old bridle paths, nestling the pergola, parterres, gazebos, dollhouse, and teahouse very inconspicuously in the woodland setting. Only the garden that contained the two-hundred-year-old cedars of Lebanon was formal in presentation, with a fountain and close-clipped geometrical beds of herbs framing the two graceful trees.

Taking out an enormous handkerchief, President Cleveland mopped his forehead. "Cold lemonade sounds just right, Stockton. Those sneaky fellows followed me right out through the garden and never once thought of the dollhouse. Can't imagine why," he said, laughing his low rumble. "It was a tight fit, but not totally impossible."

"I expect they couldn't imagine that you would go to such lengths to avoid them."

"Nosy interfering dogs," Cleveland growled. "I'd ride a razor-back hog bareback through a briar patch to get away from them. And so would Frank."

Stockton couldn't help chuckling. "Sir, I do doubt that."

Mr. Cleveland grinned. "Well, maybe not Frank. But I would, I truly would."

The press had been particular tormentors of President Cleveland and his first lady, the young and lovely Frances Folsom Cleveland, whose close friends called her Frank. Ever since they had had their wedding in the executive mansion in June of 1886, when the forty-nine-year-old president had married his deceased law partner's daughter when she was just twenty-one years of age, the journalists had been so intrusive, so obnoxious, that Grover Cleveland had made one of the most sweeping denunciations ever made against the press: "I don't think there ever was a time when newspaper lying was so general and mean as the present, and there never was a country under the sun where it flourished as it does in this."

"I do apologize, Mr. President," Stockton said as they crossed the little dirt path through the kitchen garden so as to come in the back door into the greenhouse. "If I had known you were coming, I certainly would have sent Kruger down to the road to escort you to the house and to keep them off the property."

"Never mind, never mind," Cleveland said, waving one beefy hand. "For some reason, it seemed that Frank didn't mind too badly this time. Said something about a call on the Livingstones' being in the papers might not be a bad idea. You know what that's all about?"

Stockton had an odd, vaguely guilty look on his face. He was an attractive man, an older version of McKean, with rugged features and midnight blue eyes, thick straight sandy reddish hair, tall and athletic like his son. But he had a much calmer, gentler persona than did McKean, and for months now he had looked older and more careworn. "Perhaps," he said with some reluctance. "We haven't come out of mourning yet, and I suppose Mrs. Cleveland thinks it's time. Once the newspapers publish her call, the carriages will be lined up at the door again."

"I see. It has been over a year, my friend. Frank usually is pretty sharp about these things."

Stockton managed a small smile. "Yes, she is."

"Well, I'm not here for tea and ladyfingers," Cleveland said stoutly. "Guess you know that, don't you, Stockton?"

"Yes, sir." He opened the glass door of the greenhouse and courteously stood aside to let the president go in first. "This goes right through into the conservatory, sir. If you'll excuse me, I'll lead."

"Lead on. Lovely greenhouse, Stockton. Are those orchids? They are, aren't they? I heard they were the devil to raise, or grow, or whatever you call it."

"Yes, sir, they are orchids, and they are difficult, I understand. Phoebe—Phoebe loved them dearly, and my son Merritt—you know Merritt, my twelve-year-old?—could make a fencepost bloom."

"Can he?" Mr. Cleveland said with interest. "Unusual occupation for a boy."

"Yes, he has several—many—unusual occupations," Stockton said, finally reaching the door into the conservatory. Ten years ago Stockton had built these graceful additions to the house: The all-glass greenhouse that spanned the back half of the house and neatly provided a cover for the outside walkway from the kitchen to the dining room—an outside path that was the bane of the servants since Stockton's great-great-great-grandfather had built The Cedars in 1762. On the east end of the house Stockton had built Phoebe an immense conservatory, extending the frontage of the house in mellowed red brick, but the east end of the new room was a long sweep of floor-to-ceiling French doors. No back wall separated the conservatory from the greenhouse, only a decorative wooden lattice with an arched opening.

The conservatory had almost as many plants as the greenhouse, and even had lemon and lime trees in pots, shading a nook of white lacy iron furniture with big cushions and pillows. Rokeby was there, hovering over a round table with two cushioned chairs, arranging a tray with a crystal pitcher of lemonade, condensation running coolly down the sides, and two tall glasses. As the men sat, Mr. Cleveland fanning himself with his handkerchief, Rokeby asked, "Will there be anything else, Mr. Livingstone?"

"No, thank you, Rokeby."

"Miss Livingstone has ordered tea in the parlor in half an hour," Rokeby said. "Perhaps you and Mr. Cleveland will join her and the first lady?"

"If I haven't had sunstroke by then," Cleveland answered. The May afternoon had grown very warm and his face was red.

"We'll be honored to join the ladies then, Rokeby," Stockton answered, eyeing the president cautiously. Rokeby bowed and slipped out.

Mr. Cleveland drank thirstily and Stockton poured him another glass. Mr. Cleveland nodded, settled back in his chair, and regarded Stockton somberly. "Stockton, I need you," he said bluntly. "I don't know about all this etiquette of calls and mourning periods and such, and I don't want to commit some great blunder and offend you or intrude on you. It's just the plain truth. I need your help."

Stockton nodded, his face giving nothing away. "I did understand this wasn't a social call, sir."

Cleveland leaned up and spoke earnestly. "I need you to come back to work, Stockton. Can you? Are you ready?"

Frowning, Stockton gazed off into a far distance. "I don't know. To be perfectly honest, sir, I haven't thought much about it. No man is indispensable, and I've always believed that the European Desk is the best department in the Foreign Office—with or without me."

"Not true," Cleveland argued. "You've left a big hole, Stockton, and just now the trouble's brewing right in the very hole you have left."

Stockton grimaced. "It's Samoa, isn't it?"

"It surely is."

"But Harold Marsh Sewall is a good man, young, but capable and fully able to handle the Samoans."

"I agree. But it's not the Samoans that need handling. It's the Germans. And no one can handle those prickly, proud, overbearing Prussians as well as you can. No, don't protest, you know it's the truth, and false modesty is a vice as surely as is false pride, or so Frank tells me."

Stockton replied, "Yes, I suppose that is true, sir, so I will admit that I have had the most experience with the Prussians, and in the years I've spent studying Bismarck I have come to some understanding of him and the nature of German culture."

"Yes, and that's more than the rest of us can say. I just can't get on their program, and that's why I have such skillful foreign officers anyway—like you. In this Samoan brew, we've got the German navy, the British navy, and now our navy. There's that bothersome German firm buying up the country. There's all the consuls and vice-consuls, and that's not to mention the poor Samoans with their little tribal chiefs here, there, and yonder."

"But Sewall has been managing just fine, hasn't he? I haven't been reading his dispatches, but I have been reading the newspapers, and so far it seems like a lot of posturing and prancing about over a three-mile stretch of beach. And the coaling station at Pago Pago is secure, isn't it, sir? It's my understanding that this little dustup is taking place on the western island, not on Tutuila, where our station is."

"That's right. They're all like busy little ants at Apia, on Upolu. And yes, Pago Pago is secure, and actually it's a much better bay than Apia, which is a dangerous little lagoon, really, ringed by coral reefs. But the problem is that the Germans are really coming it high hat, you know, overrunning the place, and the natives don't like it and neither do I."

"Again, sir, I think Mr. Sewall is fully capable of handling the situation. However, if you wish, I'll come back and read through the dispatches and meet with Secretary Bayard and see if I might offer any helpful suggestions."

The president shook his leonine head. "That's not what I need, Stockton, because Sewall's coming back to Washington. He wants to update me personally, and also he wants to address Congress on the situation, which is getting trickier by the minute."

"He is? Do you have a vice-consul there?"

"No, I don't."

"But, sir—sir, you can't mean you want me to go to Samoa?" Stockton asked, astounded.

"That's exactly what I mean," Cleveland said, drawing himself up to his full height, imposing even when he was seated. His big mustache bristled. "I can be as stubborn as a general's old bulldog when I want. And why all this missish shock, Stockton? It's a paradise, they tell me. Even better than the Hawaiian Islands."

"Yes, that's true," Stockton agreed. "The islands are bountiful, the climate is mild, the weather usually agreeable. And generally, of all the Polynesian peoples, the Samoans are the gentlest, the most devout Christians, though they do prefer a simple life: *fa'a Samoa*, 'the ways of our fathers.'"

Cleveland stared at him. "Great heavens, Stockton, you speak Samoan, too?"

Stockton Livingstone, among his other talents, had a rare gift for languages. He spoke French, Latin, and Greek, of course, the staples of learned gentlemen's education, but Stockton had also taught himself Spanish, Italian, and German, and was currently working on Russian.

"No, sir, not exactly. I've just picked up some phrases from a—family friend that lived in Samoa. He died not long after—" He stopped, cleared his throat, and finished with some difficulty. "About a month before Phoebe passed away. Anyway, we had kept up a correspondence for many years and I picked up some of the simple phrases from his letters."

Cleveland eyed him shrewdly. "He was a missionary?"

"Yes, sir."

"One of your secret philanthropies, Stockton?"

"My father helped sponsor him, sir," Stockton answered evenly. "As I said, he was an old friend of the family. Actually, his wife was a distant, a very distant connection. She was Scottish and her mother's maiden name was Livingstone."

"I see," Grover Cleveland said knowingly. They were silent for a while, a silence heavy with memories for the both of them.

Grover Cleveland's father, Richard Cleveland, had attended Yale with Stockton's father, John Edward Livingstone. The two were unlikely friends. John Ed Livingstone was very wealthy and was included in the circles of the old landed families, while Richard Cleveland's family was not nearly of such note. But somehow they had become close—it was unclear from their correspondence—and John Ed had kept up with Richard Cleveland's career as a Presbyterian minister, his moves from place to place, and his large family.

When Richard Cleveland had died unexpectedly in 1853, leaving a widow with four children still too young to work, John Ed had given Ann Neal Cleveland a small stipend until 1855.

Then eighteen-year-old Grover Cleveland had written to John Ed, thanking him for his generosity, but assuring him that he and his brothers were in better positions to help their mother now and the loans would no longer be necessary. In addition, young Grover took it upon himself to repay John Ed. It took him nine years.

Stockton's father had never meant for the money to be a loan; it was meant as a gift. But John Ed had approved of the young Grover Cleveland's scrupulous honor.

Stockton had not found out about any of this until after his father's death in 1866 when he had gone through his father's myriad papers and correspondence. He had no idea who Grover Cleveland was then, for he had been fighting for the last four years for the Confederacy in the Great War, and didn't know the young assistant district attorney of Erie County, New York.

Grover Cleveland had come to John Edward Livingstone's funeral, which was the first time Stockton met him. He remembered thanking Mr. Cleveland for coming. Grover Cleveland had said, "Your father did my family a very great service, Mr. Livingstone," and by that time Stockton was in such deep mourning that he had quite forgotten who Grover Cleveland was and had no idea what he was talking about. In fact, there were many, many people at John Ed's funeral who said much the same thing; and Stockton had found numerous charities, both public and personal, that his father had supported all his life. Stockton could hardly remember all the names.

When President Grover Cleveland had approached Stockton for an appointment to the Foreign Office, he had said, "You are the only man to whom I truly owe a great debt who has not approached me, either directly or indirectly, for an appointment."

Stockton was genuinely surprised. "Sir, you owe me nothing. It was my father who was your father's friend, and he only did his duty as a friend should. It would never occur to me to extract some sort of repayment for my father's loyalty to his friends."

Grover Cleveland had a rock-solid honesty and could readily recognize it (and the lack of it) in others. "Yes, I can see how that would never occur to you, Mr. Livingstone, but I can assure you that it has occurred to everyone I or my father or mother or great-great-aunt Tildie ever knew, and with much less claim to it. So what would you like? Ambassadorship to Paris? London?"

But on that horrible gray grizzly day in 1866 at the Oak Hill Cemetery, Stockton Lee Livingstone hadn't even known who Grover Cleveland was. Oddly enough, Phoebe had; Stockton had found out later that his wife's family, the Dodges of New York, had distant connections to the Clevelands. But even if they hadn't been relatives, Phoebe would have known the promising young lawyer. Phoebe knew everyone—

Stockton came back to the present with a sharp pang, a stab of grief so familiar that he was often more surprised at its absence than its onset. The president was watching him with narrowed eyes. Stockton met his shrewd gaze with sudden weariness.

After long moments Mr. Cleveland said blandly, "So you already know about Samoa and Samoans, you're the only one in the European Desk who can think like a Prussian, and you're long past due for a change, Stockton. Go to Samoa for me. It will do you a world of good."

"But I can't leave my children," Stockton argued. "Especially not now, now that Phoebe—since their mother is—has passed away."

"Take 'em with you. Be good for them. The United States of America will even pay, though I know you don't need the money."

"But my youngest is not quite four years old."

"I know, I have had the pleasure of making Penn's acquaintance," Cleveland said with a hint of a smile. "And I know Dolly, too, and they're both fine children, full of spit and vinegar, even the little girl. I like children," he said wistfully. It was jarring in so forceful and stern a man. "I liked both of them. Anyway, they seem like the kind of children that would much rather have an adventure at the ends of the earth than play in a dollhouse, no matter how fine.

Besides, haven't you always carted your children around on your travels?"

Stockton stared at him, bemused. "Well, yes, we did. Phoebe and I always took the children to Europe. But, sir, surely this situation in Samoa is different—maybe even dangerous. There is, after all, a lot of artillery in that little bay."

Cleveland shrugged. "Always a chance with those bloody-minded Prussians, I guess, but the very reason I want to send you—and the reason I'm sure that any explosive developments will be defused—is because you're the man that can do it. And as we said, Stockton, this little brouhaha is small and localized. That one three-mile strip of beach is the only hot spot and it's still only lukewarm. As you said, it's mostly just pointy-headed Germans strutting about talking too loudly and too much."

Stockton took a sip of lemonade. "When is Sewall coming back?"

"When I say he can, which will be when you say you'll go."

"May I have some time to consider it?"

"How much time?"

"I don't know, sir." The weariness and lassitude were now clear in Stockton's voice. "I will consider it, that's all I can promise right now."

The president nodded. "Of course you can take the time, but I hope you'll do this for me, Stockton. I'd like to send word to Sewall soon. It takes about a month, you know, to get word to the South Pacific."

"Thank you, sir, you will certainly have my answer as soon as I can possibly give it."

"Good. As long as it's the right one. Now for some really tough talk," he said sternly. "What's all this I hear about Miss Lorna's Debutante's Ball?"

The Stately Old Dance

*T*rista steadied herself before going into the morning room. She was a little breathless, for Rokeby had dispatched Elspeth to brush, straighten, and primp her, and Elspeth could be very businesslike and brusque in societal emergencies.

But it was not just the shock of the first lady's call, nor the fact that Trista had been wallowing on the flagstone kitchen floor wrestling with baby skinks when it occurred, nor even the fact that it had been over a year since there had been a formal caller at The Cedars and Trista, having grown rustic, was desperately trying to recall the particular etiquette.

It was because Rokeby had put—hastily Trista corrected herself—had shown Mrs. Cleveland into the morning room. She knew he had done it on purpose, for callers were always received in the more formal parlor. It was obvious to the whole household that the morning room had been avoided since Phoebe's death, and though Rokeby never commented on family intimacies, Trista understood that he was making a point.

It was a lovely room, rather less formal than the parlor or sitting room. It was the only receiving room in the house that faced south, with the medieval spires of Georgetown University to the west, parklands to the east, and Georgetown proper far below, the somewhat grubby old port town softened and refined by height and distance.

But more than any room in the great house of The Cedars, the morning room echoed with her mother's laughter, the sweetness of her clear soprano voice, the delicious memories of so many evenings of music and, of course, dancing. Phoebe had loved dancing and not just at balls. She had taught all of them, even Merritt, how to dance, and not just waltzes and the polka. She taught them the quadrille, the cotillion, the Sir Roger de Coverly, all of the old country assembly dances, even the minuet. As she neared the door, Trista could vividly recall the solemn line of Livingstones—her father, her mother, McKean, Lorna, Merritt, and herself—slowly walking through the intricacies of the stately old dance, and then collapsing in laughter when someone walked the wrong way, which invariably happened.

It wasn't that she hadn't been in the morning room, for of course it was cleaned every day and aired three times a week, and Trista had been in it many times to check it. But she had never sat down in it, never played the Steinway grand piano that her father had given her mother for her last birthday, had never paused to look out the tall windows. And the family no longer met every morning, as they had when Phoebe Livingstone had been alive and had been their anchor, and prayed with all the servants dutifully attending.

When Mother was alive, Trista thought dully. Now, blessedly, the raw pain of loss had dulled to something like an old bruise—not a constant grievous ache, but an occasional kind of tenderness if the grief was somehow bumped. Trista hoped that receiving her first caller as mistress of The Cedars in this room would not bump that bruise.

With determination she smiled and went into the morning room. "Mrs. Cleveland, please forgive me for keeping you waiting," Trista said a little breathlessly. "How good it is to see you again."

Francis Folsom Cleveland turned from the window and smiled. She was twenty-three years old now, slim and graceful, and her smile was of such warmth and kindness that it transformed her prettiness into deep beauty. "Trista, hello. You are looking very well, and I'm so happy to see it."

She grasped Trista's hands briefly, and they sat down together on the sofa. Trista was a little tentative, for the first lady had been her mother's friend, even though Frances was much closer in age to Trista, who was nineteen. But Mrs. Cleveland had always been warm to Trista—indeed, to all of the Livingstone children—and so Trista was not so nervous as she might have been with some other doyennes of Washington society.

"As I said, you look very well," Mrs. Cleveland said, searching Trista's face. "Are you well?"

"Yes, ma'am, I thank you."

"And your father?"

"He is in good health, ma'am," Trista answered, dropping her eyes. "I'm sure he'll be so glad to see you and the president."

"I hope so," Mrs. Cleveland said gently. "We've missed him a great deal. And I don't just mean the Foreign Office. Mr. Cleveland depends on him, of course, but we've also missed his company, and also yours and your charming brother's. Your seclusion has created quite a void in the social scene, Trista."

Trista gazed, rather helplessly, around the room. It was a glowing room, with heavy walnut chairs covered in red toile de Jouy, a scattering of colorful dhurrie rugs on the polished oak floor, for Phoebe had refused to have it carpeted, both for acoustics and for dancing. The walls were painted a deep warm gold. Two massive Italian landscapes in heavy gold frames brooded above the piano; Lorna's violin and her father's violoncello, in their black leather cases, leaned against the piano bench, untouched for—

"It's been over a year, Trista," Frances said in a low voice. "Mr. Cleveland and I, and all of your friends, are growing concerned."

Trista frowned, unsure how to respond. "That's very kind of you, ma'am," she finally said hesitantly. "But we're fine, really. I'm sure my father will be rejoining the Foreign Office soon."

"I'm sure he will," Mrs. Cleveland said, her dark eyes lighting with a hint of mischief. "My husband can be very insistent when he gets his mind set on something."

"Yes, ma'am, he can be very persuasive," Trista meekly agreed.

"Stubborn and dogged, you mean?"

"Oh no, ma'am, I would never say anything like that about the president," Trista said quickly.

"Your mother would have," Frances said lightly, but she was watching Trista very closely.

Trista managed a genuine smile. "Yes, ma'am, she certainly would have. Oh, but—you mean she did? Say something like that, to the president?"

"Only once, to my knowledge, about the railroads' and ranchers' public land grants, you know," Frances said. "To the best of my recollection she told Mr. Cleveland that he had better get his bulldog bite right into it and get it under control."

"Oh, dear," Trista said helplessly. She was not very much like her mother.

"He laughed," Francis reassured her. "Phoebe amused him very much. Now I must know about the rest of the family. I understand McKean is coming home? When does he arrive, do you know yet?"

"Oh, he's already here, ma'am. He arrived just a little while ago."

"Good," Mrs. Cleveland said with satisfaction. "He's in time for my dinner on Friday. I'll send you cards of invitation, of course, but please go ahead and tell McKean I'll expect him to attend. And you, Trista, and your father. It's a small dinner at Oak View for friends, not affairs of state."

"That's so kind of you, Mrs. Cleveland," Trista said, already wondering if her father would go. Suddenly and surprisingly Trista's heart surged at the thought of finally getting out again, of parties and balls and dinners, of the endless but absorbing talk of American politics and world affairs. But she thought that her father might not be ready yet.

Frances was watching her, a slight smile playing on her lips. "As we've already discussed, I'm certain that Mr. Cleveland will persuade your father to come."

"I'm sure he will, ma'am, and I—I'm very grateful to you," Trista said awkwardly.

"No, no, Trista, I'm not doing any charitable work, dear. I loved your mother and miss her, and I do worry about all of you. I hope you understand that our duties never allow us to spend as much time with your family as Grover and I would like, and we haven't wanted to intrude on you for we always have such a circus following us," she finished with the most delicate of distaste.

"Yes, I heard that Kruger was dispatching the journalists with his usual efficiency," Trista said with a smile.

Frances's gentle brown eyes sharpened suddenly. "So Kruger is still with you?"

Redmond Kruger, the overseer of The Cedars, had been riding with Phoebe the day she was killed. He was a young German, with blond hair and blue eyes and a steely jaw and broad shoulders, and had been with the Livingstones for seven years.

"Why, of course he is," Trista said with surprise. "It wasn't at all his fault, you know. There was absolutely nothing he could have done. There was nothing anyone could have done."

"Yes, of course," Frances said a little too quickly. Trista was noticeably mystified by the odd timbre of the conversation. She had no idea—none of them had any idea—that one of Stockton Livingstone's jealous rivals in the Foreign Office, along with his rather shrewish wife, had started a rumor that Phoebe had been having an affair with the handsome young German.

Gossip in Washington, D.C., was rampant, as it always had been and always would be. But due to the gentle influence of the first lady, some refinement of the ancient art had had to be contrived. Mrs. James Andersen, whose husband was in the Foreign Office on the Scandinavian Desk, had introduced a new method of transmitting rumors.

She and her two widowed sisters, who lived with the Andersens, made a point to discuss juicy gossip in front of the servants. This infallible if somewhat amorphous line of communication worked admirably, for the servants transferred it to the servants of the other important houses, and eventually the mistress of the house would hear it all, for it was an established rule that the mistress must always be aware of the talk in the servants' quarters so as to effectively manage the household.

Then, in quasipublic gatherings such as state dinners or levees or the most popular salons, oblique mention of the topic du jour would be made, and those in on the pipeline would exchange meaningful nods. For instance, when the rumor had circulated that Mrs. Dean Lang, an elderly Congressman's wife, was drinking, at one of the first lady's teas as they were discussing tariffs Mrs. James Andersen had said, "I understand that Mrs. Congressman Lang cannot possibly support foreign tariffs any longer and has persuaded Congressman Lang to change his posture on the issue. She is especially sympathetic to Canada, I believe." Mrs. Lang was said to particularly enjoy Canadian blended whisky; and several of the ladies exchanged heavy-lidded glances and nods, like wise old owls.

Frances Cleveland, once she became aware of this spider's web, shamelessly set her maid to spying, and in the most professional manner made her repeat all of the gossip to her. In this way she could—always with grace and tact—divert even the most vague innuendoes, at least in her presence.

Mrs. James Andersen had told her sisters during tea with two maids in attendance that it was well known in town that Redmond Kruger and Phoebe Livingstone had often rendezvoused at the old stone fisherman's cottage by Rock Creek, a faraway, tucked-in corner of Livingstone land, and they had left it too late that afternoon. They had ridden pell-mell back, running from a storm, but they had been caught. Lightning had struck right next to Phoebe's high-spirited thoroughbred, Paladin, and he had thrown her and she had died instantly, and the storm had broken over the two of them like the wrath of God.

So Mrs. Andersen had said, and so it had been whispered around and around the vicious little circles of fair-weather friends in the capital city. Frances wondered for a moment if the Livingstones' servants had heard, and was certain that they must have. But obviously

Trista had not, and of course Frances would never in her darkest dream repeat anything of such an ugly nature, not even to provide her friends with warning.

Since Frances Cleveland was a woman of great poise she quickly recovered, all of this running through her mind in the space of a few seconds. "Now, Trista, I do have an ulterior motive for calling just now, I must confess," she said lightly. "I believe Lorna is turning sixteen this year?"

"Yes, ma'am, her birthday is in December."

"And I know that your mother had planned to give her a debut this spring, though she isn't quite sixteen."

"She did? I—I didn't know."

"Yes, she did." Frances reached over and took Trista's hand. "And since she's gone, Trista, I would like to be Lorna's patron and sponsor her debut."

"You—you would?" Trista was astonished. The first lady was required to weave an intricacy of social connections in the highly charged atmosphere of Washington; showing particular favoritism to a debutante would make all sorts of petty jealousies rear their ugly heads, from her father's political enemies to envious matrons to indignant family matriarchs to bloodthirsty Republicans. Surely, if the first lady was the patron of one debutante, she would be asked, even demanded, to sponsor two or three hundred more.

"It's such a little thing, but I do feel it's something I can do that Phoebe would have appreciated," Frances said softly. "No—truly, since I know very well that she is in heaven, I believe she appreciates it now."

"*I* certainly would, Mrs. Cleveland," Trista said sincerely. "And it would help my father—and—oh, Lorna will be simply unbearable!"

"I doubt that," Frances said with a small smile.

"No, no, she's not like that, but—gracious, we haven't anything to wear! I haven't even started on Lorna's wardrobe for a debut, much less for the season!" Trista said, dismayed.

"You might not need as much as you think," Frances said, again mysteriously. "Anyway, I would very much like to give Lorna's ball next month."

"Oh, dear," Trista mumbled, thinking of the mounds of clothes that Lorna—and she—would need.

"Oh, nonsense, Trista, you're perfectly capable of hounding poor Madam Trevor to distraction, just as Phoebe was. I've never seen you or your mother want for lack of beautiful gowns. And anyway, I must have Lorna's ball soon, before McKean goes off into the blue again. I shall insist that he and Vaughn Pascal and Endecott Carrollton attend, so that all the young ladies will be happy. And some of the old ones, too," she finished with a touch of mischief.

"Yes, they will. McKean does flirt so outrageously." Trista sighed. "But honestly, Mrs. Cleveland, I don't think that McKean is planning to leave again until July or perhaps August."

"No?" she said lightly. "We'll see. Now where is that wonderful Rokeby with tea? I vow that he makes the best tea in Washington. Oh, how I wish I could have Rokeby at the executive mansion, but then again I know that every one of your acquaintances has tried to steal him, and I should probably have no better luck. Anyway, Trista, do ask Lorna to join us. I want to see her again, and we'll have fun planning her ball. Then later, when we talk to your father, perhaps you and I can remind him," she said, suddenly somber, "of the importance of coming out into the world to be with friends."

"So now I'll probably never come out." Lorna Yvonne Livingstone groaned. "It's as if Trista's deaf and dumb on the subject. She had such a debut, with your sisters and Roxanna Pascal, it's just not fair!"

Lorna's best and lifelong friend, Simone Carrollton, regarded Lorna cautiously. She had stuck with Lorna all through the long last horrible year, helplessly watching Lorna's suffering. It seemed—outwardly at least—that Lorna had been more devastated than any of the other children at their mother's death. Simone, at sixteen, had had no idea how to help Lorna, but then she did seem to be some sort of comfort to her, though she rarely said a word. It had occurred to Simone once that she was much like Job's friends Eliphaz, Bildad, and Zophar, who had, after all, sat with their friend for seven days and seven nights, mourning with him without saying a single word. It was only after they started talking that things went sort of downhill—again—for poor Job.

And so it had seemed to Simone that the rare times she tried to talk to Lorna, tried to soothe her little temper fits or cheer her melancholy, that Lorna often took offense. And so Simone mostly just listened, and rarely responded when Lorna was upset. Now, however, Lorna was watching her expectantly, so Simone said calmly, "I'm sure if you and Trista speak to your father he'll make some arrangements, Lorna."

"Father's like a ghost," Lorna said forlornly. "I hardly ever see him except sometimes at dinner."

"Then ask him at dinner," Simone said pragmatically.

"Oh, you just don't understand, no one does!" Lorna cried, snatching up a lacy pillow and hugging it. She was seated cross-legged on her bed, but even in that unladylike position she had a particular feline grace.

Lorna was the beauty of the family, much like Phoebe, except that Lorna's features were even more perfectly sculpted than her mother's. Her nose was tiny and straight, her mouth a perfect full cupid's bow, her hair even more silvery than Phoebe's true light blonde, her dark eyes giving her an exotic look with her light hair and pale, fine complexion. She was not as tiny as her sister Trista, but she was fine-boned and slender. At the tender age of thirteen she had managed to overcome childish awkwardness and become graceful, even elegant. Now, at fifteen and a half, she could easily hold her own against many older, more accomplished girls.

Simone Carrollton was rather lumpish and stolid compared to Lorna—and compared to her older sisters, Charmaine and Colette. She was sixteen now and was only just beginning to lose her baby fat.

She had the same glossy black hair and dark eyes as her sisters and mother, but she had none of their vivacity. Certainly Lorna had always made her look like an ugly duckling in comparison, but because they had been friends since they were toddlers, Lorna never seemed to be aware of the fact, and Simone had fought and conquered her feelings of inadequacy quite successfully. She was a taciturn and practical sort of girl, while Lorna was passionate and dreamy, but somehow the two of them had always had the most unusual, almost supernatural, rapport.

Now she said softly, "Lorna dear, as I've said a hundred times, I know I can't possibly imagine what it's like for you. I've even tried, you know, to picture what it would be like if"—she took a deep breath and plunged in—"if my mother died. And I can't. Somehow one's mind just refuses to contemplate it. I'm so sorry for you. Just tell me how I can help you, what I can do for you. I'd do anything, you know."

Lorna nodded. "I know. I know you would, Simmy. I wish I could think of something you could do for me. I just feel so— colorless. So gray, so bland. Do you know what I mean?"

"Yes, I do," Simone answered dryly. "I often feel gray. Perfectly colorless. Even invisible. Especially around Colette and Charmaine. Good heavens, what's that?"

At this time they heard a vague din from downstairs—Lorna's room was heavily carpeted and the thick oak door was closed—and then they heard several people thundering down the stairs. "Is that my sisters and Trista?" Simone asked disbelievingly. "They sound like a herd of bison."

Lorna giggled in spite of her low spirits. Just lately she had seemed, more often, to come out of her deep gloom and become restless with her family's solitude. "They do, don't they? Oh, it's probably just Merritt causing havoc down in the kitchen. You know him, he's always doing some sort of experiment with his nasty chemicals or repotting ragweed in the soup tureens or something."

"And the snakes," Simone said with a shiver. "I'll never forget the snakes." Almost two years ago, Merritt had found that a young garter snake was coming into the kitchen through a crack in the kitchen floor where the old mud grouting had dissolved between two flagstones against the wall. In the winter she had snuggled down behind the oven, hibernating in the warmth, and Merritt had named her Maybelle and had sneaked down every night to feed her beetles and grubs. When spring came she had obviously gone out a-Maying, for she came back to her little nest—by this time Merritt had made her a small bed with soft dried winter wheat—to have her babies, nineteen of them.

The Livingstone house, when all the little Maybelle children came out exploring that afternoon, had naturally been in an uproar, with the Carrolltons and the Pascals in for tea and an evening of music and dancing. It had taken until almost ten o'clock for all of the snakes to be rounded up, for Maybelle to be captured without harm, and for the men to take them back to the fertile grasslands by the back pond to set them free.

Lorna laughed, a sweet silvery sound that was eerily just like her mother's, although she was unaware of it. "Oh, that was a night! Wasn't it, Simmy? We were all so tumbled around and busy and running about and the maids shrieking and Mrs. Cross chasing Merritt with that great wooden spoon. We all had to have supper so late, and then we danced and danced, even Merritt got to stay up and dance because Mother felt so sorry for him after Mrs. Cross paddled him so!"

"She hardly touched him, she never does, though she talks as if she's going to seize him up to the grating and flog him," Simone said disdainfully. "I could have, I swear I could have, the little beast."

"Oh, they were just little babies," Lorna said, her dark eyes dancing now. "I thought they were cute, in a creepy sort of way."

Simone shook her head. Lorna's kaleidoscopic personality was jolting sometimes, even to Simone, who knew her so well. She seemed the very opposite of the sort of girl who would find snakes—tiny, wriggling, sickeningly quick little reptiles—to be cute, even creepy-cute. Simone herself, along with her sisters and her mother, had been terrified. Phoebe, Lorna, and Trista had laughed and had even tried to help the men catch them, though they were all three giggling so much that they had been of little help. They all had a sort of courage and solid self-confidence that was found much more often in men than in women, particularly young girls. Simone admired this exceedingly in the Livingstone women.

Now she simply agreed with Lorna. "Yes, it was fun. The late supper and the music and dancing at least."

Lorna nodded, then went to the window and pulled aside the curtains. "Dancing," she said in a low voice. "We haven't danced for so long."

Simone glanced at the mandolin in the corner, the centerpiece of a tableau made up of dried white baby's breath in a white ceramic pot, a white velvet footstool, and a French doll clothed in filmy white lace. All of Lorna's room was white: the sheets, the duvet, the curtains, swags of wall coverings, cast-iron mantel, carpet, and ceiling, and the furniture was upholstered in white velvet. Phoebe had indulged this madness just before she died, Simone remembered. Lorna had insisted that she must have a white lace and velvet room, and since she was so much indulged by her parents, and even her brothers and sisters, she had gotten it. It had caused untold dismay for the maidservants, who had to spend twice as long dusting the fine grit that continually emanated from the gas lamps on the acres of white lace and velvet than they did any other room in the house. But Lorna had loved it.

The only thing that hadn't been white in the room was her beloved mandolin that McKean had bought her in New York for her thirteenth birthday. It had been in that same corner when Phoebe was alive, and Lorna played it every day for sheer enjoyment; it was a true release after her stringent practice on the piano and flute and particularly the violin.

But a month after Phoebe's death Lorna had made one of the gardeners paint the mandolin solid white, which had, of course, ruined it, and then she had placed it in the aesthetically pleasing but sterile arrangement in the corner. As far as Simone knew Lorna had never touched it again.

"Have you been playing at all, Lorna?" Simone asked, frowning.

"No," she answered shortly, her back stiffening.

"You haven't even been playing your violin?" Simone blurted out. Lorna was a musical prodigy—she could play any instrument after only a short familiarity, and she was a pure genius on the violin, her greatest love. Simone was shocked that she hadn't noticed this great chasm in her friend's life.

"But—when you left the academy I thought that your father engaged a music teacher for you," Simone went on in a small voice. Lorna, along with Simone and ten other young ladies of good family, had been at Miss Darlene's Select Seminary for Young Ladies in nearby Somerset, a boarding school of good reputation among the old families of Georgetown. Lorna had not returned for the six weeks remaining of the academic year after her mother's death in March 1887, but she had returned the following September—for a little less than two weeks. She had not been able to stay away from her family.

"He did, but I just didn't want to pursue it," Lorna said shortly. Her mother had always been her music teacher. "I haven't even set foot in the morning room since—since—" She choked a little and her slim shoulders sagged. Simone felt awkward and couldn't make up her mind whether to go to Lorna or just to stay quiet. Lorna solved it herself as she straightened again, whirled, and grabbed up the pillow to hug it as she sat cross-legged on the bed again with her easy grace.

"Oh, Simmy, I just feel so restless, so tired of the same day after day after day, with nothing to look forward to, nothing exciting ahead! I wish, I wish somehow I could—run away, do something daring, go somewhere exotic, like McKean and Vaughn and Endecott!"

"Well, you'll have to come out first," Simone said with her usual practicality. "And listen, Lorna, I have an idea about that. Why don't we talk to my mother? I know she'd be so glad to be your patron, and maybe you could debut at the Georgetown Ladies' Society Spring

Cotillion. It's in two weeks, but my mother could manage it, I know. And then you could be presented at the Georgetown Bachelor's Gala in June."

Lorna's woeful face lit up. "Do you think so? Even though I won't be sixteen until December? Oh, how I hate having a December birthday! It's made my years all wrong, and besides I never get good birthday presents or parties because everyone is all taken up with Christmas. Anyway, do you think that your mother would sponsor me?"

"I think she would," Simone answered tentatively. "It does seem cruel to make you miss this season, and then when you turn sixteen it's so long until the next season. Anyway, we can ask her."

"Oh, if Father would only—" A quiet knock sounded on her door. "Yes, come in," she called.

Rokeby opened the door and grandly announced, "Miss Lorna, the first lady is calling and is in the morning room with Miss Livingstone. Mrs. Cleveland has asked that you join them."

Childish Things

Rokeby, who seemed to be in all the important places at all the right times when he was in his butler persona, met the merry and very muddy company as they tried to sneak back into the house through the kitchen door. Rosalie and her brood had been safely set free in a convenient clump of tall pampas grass by the pergola. Unfortunately McKean and Merritt had been obliged to crawl a little way to show Rosalie the way to freedom, as she had evidently become so attached to Merritt's warm jacket pocket that she showed definite signs of trying to return to her old home.

Penn had joyously joined them, as he had been skulking through the boxwood hedge to escape his latest guardian, poor old McElhenny, the head gardener. Penn had popped out of the hedge and jumped onto McKean, who sat suddenly sideways and did further injury to the seat of his denims, though Dolly had managed to keep her limpet's hold about his neck and remain safely piggybacked.

With a sniff Rokeby said, "No, sir, those boots will not do, not even in the kitchen. Remove them at once. In that state even the boot scraper won't be adequate."

"Yes, Rokeby," McKean said. It was amazing how childish Rokeby could make him feel, though the butler was only thirty-five and McKean was a full-grown man.

"I have stayed clean, Rokeby," Dolly said slyly from her grand height around McKean's neck.

"Prissy bloomers," Merritt muttered under his breath.

"Bloomers," Penn echoed. He even had mud caked in his shining silver hair.

Ignoring the boys Rokeby said, "So I see, Miss Dolly, and you at least are a good child. You may go on up to the schoolroom. I will bring you some cocoa as soon as I have dealt with this sad lot."

"But I wanted McKean to take tea with me," Dolly pleaded.

"Very well," Rokeby said, to McKean's bemusement. "Master Merritt, you are to go up and get out of those wet and filthy clothes this minute. Elspeth is already running a hot bath for you. Master Penn, you too are to be bathed, and though I have half a mind just to dunk you clothes and all into the horse trough, I will attend to your bath shortly. Meanwhile you just get your filthy little person up to Miss Wardwell's room."

"My luggage isn't here yet, Rokeby—" McKean began defensively.

"Sir, I already have your gray suit pressed and ready," Rokeby said sternly, "and hot water and towels in your room. I regret I cannot attend you, but I hope you can manage alone." His tone left much doubt of this.

"I can manage, thank you, Rokeby," he said, letting Dolly slide down onto the kitchen steps and sitting down on the bench so that he could remove his boots. He tried, angling up his long leg and tugging, but his high riding boots were almost impossible to remove in this posture.

"So I see," Rokeby said acidly as McKean grunted and strained. "I shall fetch a towel to place over them so that at least I won't be covered with mud from head to toe when I assist you."

"No American mud would dare stick to you," McKean muttered under his breath as Rokeby went back into the kitchen.

"I should hope not," floated back out the door.

Rokeby came back and the offending boots were removed, with no little effort. McKean, now in the kitchen in his stocking feet and feeling oddly vulnerable because of it, said uncertainly, "So I don't get to have tea with the grown-ups?"

"You may be surprised, sir," Rokeby said cryptically.

"But I haven't seen my father yet," McKean objected with a little more gumption.

Rokeby nodded, and though his icy expression hardly wavered, McKean could see the sympathy there. "Yes, sir, I know, but he is at present quite taken up with the president. By the time you and Miss Dolly finish your tea, I would imagine that Mr. and Mrs. Cleveland will have taken their leave and your father will be at liberty."

———————

Scrubbed and shining, McKean appeared at the schoolroom/nursery door in twenty minutes.

This was a lovely room, painted a creamy yellow, with big windows and filmy white curtains. Stretching the width of the house, it was long, with a ceiling low enough to be comfortable to children. At the far end were the small beds, hidden during the day by screens worked in colorful needlepoint by Phoebe and Trista and Lorna. At the other end was the schoolroom, with the blackboard and wooden table and Miss Wardwell's desk.

In the middle of the room was the play area with Penn's wooden horse, two wooden swords leaning against the wall, a box full of toy soldiers, a bookcase full of books, two adult-sized plump armchairs and three child-sized replicas gathered cozily around a low ottoman that also held a pile of large colorful books. The room smelled of lemon oil and chalk and paints, and McKean sniffed with appreciation.

Against the window was a tea table with two chairs, fine work in cherry wood by a local carpenter. The problem was that they were sized for Dolly, who was . . . doll-sized. She was standing expectantly by, smiling.

"Hullo, McKean, won't you come in and join me?" she said politely.

"My pleasure, ma'am," he said gravely. She sat down easily in the tiny chair. With only a slight hesitation McKean gingerly lowered his six-foot-two frame onto the other one, waiting for a disaster; but the set was very sturdy and there wasn't even a creak of protest. McKean was very glad they were armless chairs, for if they had had arms he might have gotten stuck. As it was, his knees almost came up to his chin.

"I like your tea table," McKean said. "Did Father get it for you?"

"Yes, for Christmas," she said with a hint of reproach. "We missed you."

"I missed you, too. But I brought presents enough to make up for it."

"Did you?" Her blue eyes shone.

"Yes, presents for Christmas, Boxing Day, New Year's, Easter, and because I felt guilty, lots of presents for everyone from all the wonderful places I visited."

She nodded, evidently accepting his guilt as a matter of course and gifts as his penance. "Father gave everyone lots and lots of gifts for Christmas," she said conversationally. "I expect he feels guilty, too."

McKean had not been able to figure out how to respond to this mature and insightful observation from his youngest sister—he had forgotten how very perplexing Dolly could be—or hadn't she been like that before he'd left? No, he remembered, she was a little four-year-old child then, with her red-gold curls and round blue eyes and thin face. Not this mysterious girl who looked like a baby doll and conversed like a young adult.

To his relief Rokeby came in then, and McKean was amused to see that he held one of the silver tea services, not the little nursery tray with the fat brown little teapot and crockery jugs. The enormous tray was bigger than the table, but he set it down and bowed to Dolly, as grand as if he were serving the first lady. "Will that be all, Miss Dolly?"

"Yes, thank you, Rokeby."

She stood up, critically looking over the tray. "Will you have China or Indian?" she asked politely.

McKean stifled a smile. The tray did have the oh-so-formal two pots, and Dolly had even known to say the traditional China, not Chinese. "Indian, please," he answered.

"Lemon or cream?"

"Uh—lemon, please."

"Sugar?"

"Two lumps. Please."

"I have to stand up, because the pots are so heavy," she told him, frowning a little. "But I wanted to learn how to pour like a lady, so Rokeby said I must learn with a good tea service."

"You're very elegant," he said as she placed his tea carefully in front of him, though of necessity it was still on the tray.

"Thank you. Marzipan?" It was Dolly's favorite.

McKean loathed it but because he was a gentleman he said, "Yes, thank you."

Dolly picked up a delicate saucer and the little tongs and placed two pieces of the candy on it, handing it to him so that he could balance it on his knee. Then she made her own tea—very heavy on the sugar and cream, McKean noticed—and delicately took two pieces of marzipan for herself. Finally she got seated again and crunched the candy thoughtfully.

"Where did you go, McKean?" she asked, not with reproof but with curiosity, he was relieved to see.

"Well, first we sailed to St. Petersburg—that's in Russia—and then we took the train to Vienna—that's in—"

"Austria," Dolly said mischievously. "And then to Paris, in France. I meant, what did you see?"

"Oh. I saw lots of wonderful things."

"Like what?"

He gave her a keen look, amazed that she really wanted to know. He had to keep reminding himself that she was only five years old. "In St. Petersburg I rode in open sleighs called *droshkies* in the snow, with a fur hat on, and piles of furs on my lap, and I bought a pair of boots, wonderful hand-stitched black leather boots that are as soft as kid."

"You always buy boots," Dolly scoffed.

"I know, I can't help it," McKean said wryly. "I have heard that some ladies buy lots and lots of shoes, more than they can possibly wear, and I think that I might have the same awful affliction. Only for boots."

Dolly nodded knowingly. "And did you see the Winter Palace?"

Surprised, McKean nodded. "As a matter of fact, I wrangled us an invitation there, through the American embassy. For a ball. They waltz differently. It was interesting."

"They do? Will you teach me?" she said eagerly.

"Uh—sure, Dolly," he said, hiding a smile as he pictured holding her up a full three feet off the ground and waltzing around.

"Good. Mother used to say that one went to St. Petersburg for the ballet, Vienna for the symphony, Paris for art, and New York for opera. So did you?"

"Why—yes, as a matter of fact we did," McKean answered. "Except for New York, we didn't go there."

"And did you bring playbills and programs?"

"I sure did, only they're with all with my luggage and stuff, so they're not here yet."

"But you'll show them to me and explain about everything?"

"I'll try, Dolly," he said. He was beginning to see that the nesting dolls, the *matryoshka,* he had brought her might not be quite the thing.

She cocked her head and considered him. "And did you have a gaggle of the demimonde hanging on your coattails?"

"What!" McKean said, dropping his saucer and his napkin and nearly upsetting the tea tray. "Dolly, where did you hear that—that word? That sentence?"

She looked unhappy and confused. "I—I didn't hear that sentence, that exact sentence. I heard Trista and Miss Wardwell talking in French, and Trista kept saying 'McKean' and 'demimonde,' so I looked it up. And first I'd heard Elspeth and Susie"—she was talking fast now, the words spilling out of her little button mouth—"and they said that you'd have a whole gaggle of those wicked foreign would-be ladies who were no better than they should be hanging on your coattails all 'round the Continent before you ever got home—"

"The devil they did," McKean growled. "And you remembered it? Every word?"

"I guess so," Dolly said, abashed.

McKean stared at her. "And you looked up *demimonde?* In the French dictionary?"

"Well—yes."

"I'm almost afraid to ask, but what did it say?"

"It—it said that—Mr. Alexandre Dumas fils—that means the son, you know, not the father, Mr. Alexandre Dumas père—had made up the word in 1855 and it meant half-class. *Demimonde,*" she pronounced anxiously, with a perfect French accent and cadence. "And so I thought that these ladies that Trista was talking about did not move in the best circles, as Miss Wardwell says, and so they must be those wicked foreign ladies who were no better than they should be."

"Good heavens," McKean managed, finally. "Child, if you value your life and freedom—and mine—and Trista's—you'd better not ever say anything about the demimonde or wicked foreign ladies to Father."

Solemnly she said, "I won't, McKean."

He frowned. "What else do you know that's going to give Miss Wardwell the vapors?"

She bit her bottom lip, puzzled. "I—I don't know. So many times I say things and all the grown-ups look funny, and I don't know what I've said. I can't figure it out."

McKean nodded sympathetically. She was, after all, still a child in understanding. Still, their entire teatime conversation had bothered McKean, long before her gaffe about the demimonde. It was obvious that Dolly was uncannily intelligent, and it made her odd, she perplexed adults, and she didn't know how *not* to do it.

"Look, Dolly, I'm going to talk to Father about your schooling. It sounds to me like we might need to consider some special tutors for you."

She looked troubled. "Do you mean because I'm odd?"

This echo of his thoughts jolted McKean, but he took the time to consider his answer instead of blurting out childish reassurances. Dolly deserved that much. Finally he said slowly, "You already know you're different from most five-year-olds, Dolly. It's not a bad thing, but I guess it must be confusing to you sometimes."

"It is, oh it is," she breathed.

"Just try not to worry too much about it," McKean said gently. "You're still a little dolly, you know, even though sometimes you know grown-up things."

She sighed and made a face. "I hate my name."

"Why?" McKean said, startled. "After all, you're named after a very great lady—"

"Dolley Madison, I know, I know, that's what Mother always said," she grumbled. "But she didn't even spell it like Mrs. Madison's, with an *e*, she spelled it like a dolly."

McKean grinned. "Sorry, but it does fit you, you know."

"Guess so." She was looking tired and cross now; it was almost three o'clock, and with the excitement of the day she had missed her nap.

McKean stood up and stretched; his legs were beginning to cramp. She looked up, dismayed. "You're not leaving, are you?"

She was so appealing that McKean couldn't bear to disappoint her. "No, I just thought I'd sit in this big ol' chair, 'cause my legs are starting to knot up." He settled in the big overstuffed armchair: heaven.

Dolly considered him gravely. "Do you think I could possibly sit on your lap?"

"Why, sure you can." Dolly hardly ever welcomed affection; he had seen her positively shrink away from it after their mother had died. But now she clambered up onto his lap, a bony little thing, light as a kitten. The room was warm, the smell of the still-hot tea heavy on the air, dust motes danced in the oblique golden rays through the windows. McKean yawned, which made Dolly yawn.

Quickly she said, "McKean?"

"Hmm?"

"Who's your favorite sister?"

"All of you."

"Is that true?"

"Yes, ma'am, cross my heart." He did.

She considered this for a long time. "I do believe you," she said slowly, "but you've never given me a nickname."

McKean gave everyone nicknames, and it was well understood in the family and among their close acquaintance that no one was allowed to use the nickname but McKean. He considered this. It was true, he hadn't ever nicknamed Dolly because she was, and he suspected always would be, more like a doll than anything. Finally he said, "Well, no, that's true, a sad neglect on my part. Let's see . . . what do you like best in the whole world to do?"

"Read," she said promptly.

"That's no good," he said, poking her side gently. "I can't nickname you 'Librarian.'"

"Or 'Bibliophile,'" she said, giggling.

By now McKean only felt a mild shock at her extensive vocabulary, and he was beginning to overcome it. "No, no, no, that doesn't suit you at all. Okay, how about this: What do you want to be when you're a grown-up lady? What do you want to do?"

She shifted slightly to sit upright and face him. "I want to do something important. I want to go exploring like you and learn everything about the world. And I want to help poor and starving and sick people, and—and—"

"Whoa," McKean said, holding up his hand. "That's a pretty tall order, but if anyone does all that, I imagine you will."

"Do you think so?" Her eyes shone.

"Yes. Now, let's see—explorer—very great lady—queen of the world—"

"I didn't say that." Dolly giggled.

"Oh, sorry. Anyway—I've got it. Let me tell you about a very great lady I read about in Voltaire named Lady Mary Wortley Montagu. She was beautiful, too. Like you. And she traveled to the mysterious east—"

"Where?" Dolly demanded.

"To Asia. Turkey, to be exact," McKean said, sighing. "Anyway, there she observed that the heathens had a sort of vaccine that helped prevent smallpox. So she had her son inoculated by this Turkish method—"

"What was it called? The method, I mean? And what year was this?"

"It was called variolation, which means—er—"

"I've been vaccinated, you know, McKean," she said impatiently. "And blood and dirt and things don't scare me."

"Okay, here goes then. You take a little bit of smallpox fluid from a blister, and then you prick it into your skin with a needle. And it gives you a slight case of smallpox, but after that you're immune. And I forget what year this was but it was long before we had the vaccine, so many, many people died of smallpox."

"But Lady Mary Wortley Montagu understood that this variolation—did I say it right?—this variolation would make you immune?"

"Yes, she did, and she took this method back to England and tried to make the doctors understand that it worked. And two princes of the royal blood were inoculated, and they lived and were immune. But the doctors didn't like this newfangled medicine, so they soon discredited it, though Lady Mary Wortley Montagu fought valiantly to make them have everyone inoculated," McKean finished.

"And she was a very great lady," Dolly breathed, settling back against McKean's chest again.

"She was. She was very courageous in the face of ridicule and even hostility—do you know what that means, oh forget it, in the face of hostility. By the grown-ups. Like you."

"And so you're going to give me a nickname after her?"

"Um-hmm."

"Are you going to call me Lady Mary?" she asked hopefully.

"Nope."

"Lady Montagu?" Hope was diminishing.

"Nope. 'Fraid it's got to be Wortley."

"Oh, dear." She sighed. "But it is better than nothing." She yawned, which made McKean yawn. "Even Wortley's better than Dolly . . ."

When Rokeby came to call McKean, they were both sound asleep.

PART II

Through the Dark Cloud

Is not God in the height of heaven?
And behold the height of the stars, how high they are!
And thou sayest, How doth God know?
Can he judge through the dark cloud?
Eliphaz the Temanite to Job, 22:12–13

Whenever the moon and stars are set,
Whenever the wind is high,
All night long in the dark and wet,
A man goes riding by . . .
"Windy Nights," A Child's Garden of Verses
Robert Louis Stevenson

Familial Duty

"Here you are," McKean said, cracking open the door of the morning room. He sauntered in and sprawled into an armchair.

"Yes, I am here," Trista agreed. "You're crunching."

"Mmm. Good apple. I missed luncheon."

"We noticed. That is, I noticed. Lorna snatched some plums and ran back up to her French dolls and fashion magazines, Merritt escaped after breakfast and no one's seen him since, Dolly was so sleepy she almost fell into her soup, and Penn was so cross that I sent him up with Miss Wardwell before he'd finished his sandwich."

McKean nodded. "We let the little ones stay up too late last night. But it was fun."

"Yes, it was. It's so, so good to have you back, McKean. We all missed you so much."

"You're just saying that because of the presents," he teased. McKean's gifts for the family, accumulated in the six months he had been trotting around the Continent, had arrived at seven o'clock the previous evening. Six large heavy boxes had held the treasures, which ranged from delicate dolls dressed in the latest French styles for Lorna, to a box of rocks accumulated manually by McKean from every province he set foot in for Merritt.

"True," Trista said, her eyes twinkling, "especially the rocks. I'm sure Vaughn and Endecott were thrilled to go on those little forays."

"Aw, you know Vaughn, he doesn't want to go outdoors unless he can shoot something. And E. C. kept asking me what kind of rocks I wanted, and I could never make him understand that they had to be *interesting* rocks, not just pretty rocks or rocks that were shaped like something or rocks with veins of gold in them. He just has no romance in his soul," he finished with a vehement crunch of his apple.

"Because he doesn't comprehend what makes a rock interesting?" Trista said, amused. "The callow, heartless youth."

"There it is," McKean agreed. "Say, what are you doing in here, just staring out the window and brooding?"

Trista sighed. "Trying to collect myself for morning calls."

"Yeah? You going to wear that?" McKean asked.

"I beg your pardon. This is a perfectly appropriate tea gown for receiving," Trista said, flustered. It was a flowing robe of dark gray Indian cashmere, belted at the waist, over a silvery gray gown of embroidered and flounced moiré. The high collar and bodice and cuffs were of white embroidery. The bustle was exactly the right size for afternoon, not quite as large as for evening wear.

"I know that," McKean said impatiently. "It's just so plain, Mab. You look like poor Jane Eyre in her one good merino. You should wear dramatic colors, not those drab governess things."

"Like that impossible cloth of gold you brought me from Vienna?" Trista said, her good humor restored. She could never stay angry with McKean; in fact, she knew of no one who could, including her father, who could be stern at times. "Wouldn't I be a vision, receiving calls in that? I'd look like Lucrezia Borgia or one of those awful Medici women, dressed to poison the next caller."

"Exactly," McKean said with satisfaction.

She glared at him, but then they laughed. "You're just awful, McKean. You truly are."

"So I hear. Anyway, what I came for was to get the dish on everyone. I wanted to talk to you before Father gets back, so start with him," McKean ordered.

"I suppose you've seen already," Trista said quietly. "Every day he's pretty much the same. Except today. I couldn't believe that he's gone into Washington. It's the first time that he's gone into town. He's gone to the law offices a few times, but did you know he hasn't even seen the new State, Navy, and War Building? Much less his own office."

McKean nodded somberly. "I thought he'd be better by now, Mab. But it seems as if he's about the same as when I left."

"Don't blame yourself, McKean. There's absolutely no reason to think that if you had stayed things would be any different."

"Maybe if I had gone on to work at the law offices," McKean said thoughtfully. "Or even jockeyed for an aide's position in the Foreign Office. In fact, Mr. Cleveland mentioned that to me when he first appointed Father."

"No," Trista said firmly. "You kept your end of the bargain—graduating magna cum laude from university and early at that. And then you stayed right here and attended to everything for so long after Mother died. You've earned the right to your life, McKean."

Phoebe, Stockton, and McKean did indeed have a bargain, with handshakes all around like gentlemen. McKean went to Georgetown University immediately out of Calvert Academy and proceeded to take an M.A. in the School of Arts and Sciences in two years as opposed to four, and then a three-year degree from the School of Law in two years, graduating with high honors, third and fourth in his classes. And then, according to the bargain, he was free for two years. He and Vaughn Pascal (who had barely scraped by with a four-year degree, second from last in his class) and Endecott Carrollton, who had just graduated magna cum laude from Yale, all took off for the Belgian Congo. Before they had been there three weeks Phoebe had died, and they had all come home.

McKean had stayed at The Cedars for six months, and then Stockton had insisted he go ahead and take the trip to Europe he and his friends had been planning since they were boys. It was a sign of how close McKean's friends were that Vaughn and Endecott had preferred to wait until McKean could go. Even as it was, because of McKean's family situation, they had only stayed six months instead of the year they had always planned.

Now he shrugged and said, "Maybe. But I'd like to think of something to do that might help Father. Think I'll stick around for a while instead of going to Barcelona in July. Too hot anyway. So. What about Lorna? She doing all right? Aside from this hysteria over her debut, I mean."

"Actually she's been better the last month and a half. You know, the anniversary of—well, you know, one year, seemed to be a kind of passage for me and for Lorna, too. Not that we still don't miss Mother horribly," Trista added quickly, "but it seemed that once that awful day was over, we sort of felt that we could start all over again."

McKean nodded with understanding. "I was in Vienna, you know, in March. I went to St. Stephen's Cathedral, and knelt and lit a candle and prayed."

"You did? You and your popery, Uncle Cash would be appalled," Trista teased.

"Let's don't tell him," McKean said. "He already thinks I'm an Inquisitor or a Jesuit assassin or something. Georgetown University's been there for a hundred and thirty years, you'd think he'd get over this obsession with it being a Catholic university. And telling him that I'm a staunch Presbyterian does not one whit of good."

"'Staunch' is a little strong for your leanings."

"I have no leanings," McKean said piously.

"I know, you politic Jesuit you," Trista teased.

"I give up," McKean said with an exaggerated sigh. "So how about Diggers? He looks good."

"He had a terrible bout around Christmas—it began on Boxing Day, actually, and that's why I think sometimes psychological stress brings it on. Then the usual early spring attack, which began on March 25 and lasted until April 10. And then he was fine on the eleventh, and he's been fine since."

Merritt, for all his high energy and constant activity, was sickly. He'd been subject to respiratory distresses ever since he was an infant. He was the only Livingstone who wasn't of sound and robust good health. Stockton and Phoebe had had a son between McKean and Trista who had died—not from ill health but from the heart-wrenching crib death when he was only seven days old.

"Boxing Day, huh," McKean said thoughtfully. "Funny how that was harder than Christmas."

"It was for me and Lorna—and I suppose Merritt—but Father seemed no worse than usual. And the little ones didn't really have a sense of it," Trista said. Phoebe had always had an enormous all-day party the day after Christmas, maintaining that it was such a boring, anticlimactic day anyway, and though it was a British tradition, for once John Bull had gotten something right.

"The little ones," McKean repeated. "I gotta talk to you about Dolly. But I can see Penn's right on target, the little beggar, I think he needs a turnkey instead of a nanny. Miss Wardwell ain't up to scratch, and I'm not sure a regiment would be, either. Did you know I caught that little whiff all the way down at the pond this morning when I was riding? I popped him right up and galloped him back pronto, meeting all the gardeners and stable boys beating the bushes on the way."

"I know, he's just like Maybelle's baby snakes, small and sly and slippery and quick. I could pinch his head. But, McKean, what about Dolly?"

"Have to talk to you about Wortley later," McKean said, pointing out the window with a denuded apple core. "The royal procession has begun." He hopped up and lurked at the side of the window to peek out. "Mrs. Julia Jane Van Vooren, with the poor pale daughter in tow. What's her name—I can't ever remember, one of those virtue names . . . is it Virtue? Virtue Van Vooren?"

"Oh, McKean, stop, it's Patience," Trista said, standing up and smoothing her dress, arranging her cuffs and flounces. "Who else?"

"Looks like Central Park on Sunday. Here we go, somebody in an unforgivable maroon barouche trying to jockey into position in front. Say, they have a right whip for a coachman, even though he couldn't quite beat out Madame Van Vooren. Oh, boy, Mab, are you in for it, it's the Gorgons."

"That's unkind, McKean, quite beneath you . . ." She couldn't maintain it and giggled. "They're not really repulsive like Medusa and Stheno and Euryale, and you know it. They're just—somber."

"Somber? All three of them look like they eat limestone and drink vinegar. Acid ain't in it—"

"No, it's not," Trista said, hurrying toward the door. "Limestone is basic, you great ninny." She stopped midstride. "Oh, horrors, what are the Gorgons'—I mean their names? Mrs. James Andersen, of course, but the two sisters . . ."

"Funny how it's easier to remember the Gorgons' names," McKean said unhelpfully, still peeking out the window. "Never mind, Mab, they're bailing; guess they didn't want to share with Her Majesty the Queen of the Washington Drawing Room."

"They'll just circle around for fifteen minutes and then come back," Trista said with desperation. "Do be quiet, I'll never remember the sisters from the introductions, they're too hard—oh, why don't I have Mother's book? Never mind, I'll just tell Rokeby to bring the card salver and leave it."

"He won't like that," McKean said absently. He was watching Mrs. Van Vooren and her daughter sweep up the walk with interest. "He says only common, vulgar persons ostentatiously display their cards in the room where they are receiving."

"Well, he'll just have to bear it." Trista gave a quick check in a gilt-framed mirror hung over the console table by the door. "I've got to go to the parlor before he catches—"

The door opened and of course it was Rokeby. "The parlor is just across the hall, Miss Livingstone, in case you need direction."

The doorbell jangled.

"Think I'll come with you," McKean said.

Trista turned and said suspiciously, "Why? Is some witless pretty young female calling?"

"No," McKean said in an injured tone. "I'll help you do the duties and protect you from the Gorgons."

Trista smiled. "Good. I can use some moral support. But I suppose I'll never get rid of any of them if you're there; they'll all stay and simper."

"What a revolting picture," McKean grumbled. "The Gorgons simpering." Rokeby gave him a glance more dire than usual, and blankly McKean stared down at the apple core he was clutching. Wordlessly Rokeby held out the silver card salver, and McKean deposited the now-wrinkled brown thing. Rokeby disappeared in the direction of the kitchen, holding it at arm's length as if it were emitting noxious gases.

"Besides, Mab," McKean said lightly, taking a casual stance leaning on the mantelpiece in the parlor, "you don't have to worry about me. Don't you know? That lot's after Father."

"What!" Trista said, jumping up with a jolt. "What?"

Rokeby opened the door. "Mrs. William Van Vooren, Miss Van Vooren are calling, Miss Livingstone."

"Deuce take it—oh, show them in, Rokeby," Trista blustered, settling herself on the very edge of the bloodred velvet sofa.

"Collect yourself, miss," Rokeby said coolly, stepping inside the room and closing the door soundlessly behind him. "Your color is much too high, it is unseemly."

"I think she looks pretty, all sparking and sizzling," McKean said lightly. "At least she doesn't look like she's out starving on the moors in her one good merino."

"Never mind, Rokeby, I'm fine," Trista said, relaxing the ramrod of her spine a little and taking a deep breath. "Show them in."

With one last narrow-eyed raking glance he nodded and again went out.

"You're joking, of course," Trista hissed in an undertone.

"Am not," McKean hissed back. "Father's prime game—"

"Mrs. Van Vooren, Miss Van Vooren," Trista said graciously. "How good of you to come."

Julia Jane Van Vooren was just the type of woman who intimidated Trista. She was a handsome woman with the sort of commanding presence that dominated a room. She had married William Van Vooren at twenty, when he was a sixty-two-year-old man, twice widowed. They had only been married for three years when he had died of influenza. That had been fifteen years ago, and evidently Mrs. Van Vooren had had no wish to remarry, for she had had many suitors. She was very wealthy and a fine-looking woman, but she seemed to be content to be one of the established old-family insiders, and presided over one of the most influential salons in Washington.

Her daughter—kind women inevitably said "poor Patience"— was very like her in looks, but not in manner. She was tall and fine-looking, but she seemed to be shy, though Trista had always thought that she was simply overshadowed and overpowered by her mother.

"Miss Livingstone, Mr. Livingstone, how good to see you, at last," Mrs. Van Vooren said in an attractive contralto, settling herself onto an armchair and motioning to her daughter to sit nearby. "Mr. Livingstone, I believe you have met my daughter, Miss Patience Van Vooren?"

McKean had no memory of being formally introduced to Miss Van Vooren, only vague recollections of a slender pale shadow following her mother at church. But he was a well-bred young man so he said, "Of course, Miss Van Vooren, it's a pleasure to see you again," with the very slight appropriate bow, which she returned with the very slight appropriate incline of her head.

"I'm happy to renew the acquaintance, sir, since it has been almost two years since we were introduced," she said in a surprisingly self-confident tone, eyeing him with amusement.

But McKean was not the kind of man that was easily ruffled, so he grinned engagingly at her. "Remiss of me, wasn't it? But then I have been traveling for a while, so perhaps I may be excused of too much negligence."

"We did see in the morning papers that you had returned, Mr. Livingstone," Mrs Van Vooren said, taking command. "You toured the Continent, I believe?"

"Actually, we went to St. Petersburg first, which of course isn't exactly the Continent. Then Vienna and Paris."

"Oh? And so you did not go to London, or travel in Italy?"

"No, ma'am. My friends and I decided to travel for only six months, and so each of us chose the one city we would most like to visit."

"Yes, you went with Vaughn Pascal and Endecott Carrollton, I knew," Mrs. Van Vooren said complacently.

Patience Van Vooren stared at McKean appraisingly. "Which did you choose? Which city?" Mrs. Van Vooren gave her daughter a distinctly disapproving look, but Patience had turned away to face McKean.

He looked a little surprised, but then he said mischievously, "Which do you think I chose, Miss Van Vooren?"

"I think . . . St. Petersburg. And Mr. Carrollton chose Vienna, and Mr. Pascal Paris."

"Perfect score," McKean said with a mock bow.

Trista, mindful of her social duties, put in, "It was hard for them to choose, for McKean was conscientious enough to limit his visit for the family's sake."

Mrs. Van Vooren had obviously been at a loss to recover this impertinent conversation of her daughter's, and now said briskly, "Devotion to familial duty is an admirable and rare trait in a young man. I'm sure your father is sensible of your esteem. And where is Mr. Livingstone, if I may ask? I had hoped that he might be receiving for a few days anyway, since you have just come out of mourning and are obliged to begin the social round anew."

Trista managed not to glance up at McKean when Mrs. Van Vooren asked after her father—wasting no time, she noted to herself with chagrin. "My father has gone into Washington for some consultation with the Foreign Office. I apologize for our lack of organization yet, Mrs. Van Vooren. I shall be sending notes with my cards in a few days. With the excitement of McKean coming home, and my father returning to work in Washington, I've been remiss."

Mrs. Van Vooren waved an imperious hand. "Of course, I'm sure the household has been mightily upset under the circumstances. And with the president and first lady calling so unexpectedly yesterday, I'm sure that you are quite at odds."

"We have recovered admirably," Trista said so mildly that Mrs. Van Vooren missed the irony.

"With my father being called to duty, I decided to stand in for him, poor substitute that I am," McKean said easily. "He was devastated that he was unavailable to receive today, but he did have some important matters to attend to."

"I'm sure," Mrs. Van Vooren said, nodding in a confidential manner. "Samoa, I take it?"

Trista was taken aback, but to her further surprise, McKean did not look surprised at all. Her father was generally concerned with Europe, and had not, as far as she knew, paid the least attention to the complex situation in the South Pacific island.

McKean said smoothly, "My father rarely discusses Foreign Office matters with us until he has a particular mission. At this time he is acting more in the manner of a consultant, rather than on active status."

Mrs. Van Vooren nodded again. "It's Samoa, I'm certain of that. It must be. With the Germans there causing so much trouble, Mr. Cleveland was bound to bring your father back. And oh, how Harmony Andersen is going to seethe! With your father's long absence James Andersen thought that he had secured your father's position at the European Desk. Of course, the man has never understood that his one and only recommendation for European consular service is that he can speak a sort of pidgin German that he learned, of all things, from a common German laborer, a baker in Pittsburgh."

"Is that so?" Trista said brightly. "What a coincidence. My father learned German from a German laborer, too—our overseer, Mr. Redmond Kruger. My father always said that though he learned the intellect of Prussians from language studies, he learned the mind of Prussians from conversing with Kruger. Kruger was in the Prussian army, you know, in the Iron Guard."

"I'm not surprised," Mrs. Van Vooren said with a calculating smile. "He cuts a fine figure, I'm sure, with all that Teutonic brawn and martial swagger. I understand that your mother engaged him for his knowledge of fine horseflesh?"

Trista replied, "Why—yes, that is true—er—at least, in the beginning. But then my father found him invaluable in managing the horses and stables, so—here he is. Still . . ." she finished lamely, wondering why on earth they were talking about their overseer.

Patience, whose eyes had dropped and cheeks had started burning as soon as Trista mentioned Kruger's name, suddenly jerked, said, "Oh!" and dropped her fan and her reticule, and knocked over her parasol, which was leaning against the chair. "Oh, please pardon me, but I just—just—felt—um—"

"Felt what, you silly child? Suddenly insane?" her mother snapped.

"Faint?" Trista suggested, mystified.

"Overpowered?" McKean suggested with a quick glance at Julia Jane Van Vooren.

"No . . . um . . . stick . . . pin . . . stuck," Patience blathered, her cheeks flaming. "Mother, I believe Angelina left a straight pin in my bodice, it's—sticking me. We must leave. To—um—unstick me." She fumbled helplessly with her accoutrements, and McKean knelt to gather up the tumbled articles.

"Well, of all the fuss over nothing, Patience, any lady of any mettle at all could hold her tongue and not wail over a little pin stick," Mrs. Van Vooren said, not moving so much as an inch. "I'm certain Miss Livingstone will be courteous enough to offer a private room where you might deal with this slight inconvenience."

"No, Mother, it would take entirely too long, and besides I am—um—sewn into—" She glanced at McKean, who had the awful cheek to wink at her, but she had the presence of mind to tilt her chin and say firmly, "No, it won't do. I'm afraid we must go home for Angelina to see about it."

Trista admired her exceedingly for this; it took some backbone to stand up to Julia Jane Van Vooren. Trista herself was by common courtesy obliged to say, "Of course one of our maids will be happy to assist you, Miss Van Vooren."

"You are kind, but no." She at last collected everything and stood up. "Mother?"

"Oh, very well, if you insist, but this shortened call is vexing," Mrs. Van Vooren grumbled. What she meant, Trista knew very well, was that she would certainly take her lost five minutes the next time. "I was not nearly finished talking to Miss Livingstone."

"Yes, I think we all understand that, Mother," Patience said with only the slightest hint of sarcasm. McKean's admiration for her grew by leaps and bounds. On the way to the door she said, "Miss Livingstone, we'll look forward to receiving your card. Have you set your at-home days yet?"

"Yes, on Tuesdays and Thursdays, just like my mother's," Trista said with real warmth. "I look forward to returning your call next week, Mrs. Van Vooren, Miss Van Vooren."

"I'll be here at The Cedars for a while, too," McKean added with particular attention to Miss Van Vooren. "Perhaps I'll assist my sister with her social duties and join her in receiving on—shall we say, Thursdays?"

"We'll keep that in mind, I'm sure, Mr. Livingstone," Mrs. Van Vooren said with an assessing look at him and her daughter. "And please do tell your father that I hope to see him soon."

"Without fail," McKean said gravely.

They finally ushered the Van Voorens out to Rokeby's charge, and hurried back to the parlor like two guilty schoolchildren. Shutting the door and leaning against it Trista said, "What in the world was that all about?"

"I don't know," McKean said grimly. "But I'm going to find out."

Trista stared at him. "Something about Kruger? Has he done something? Gotten in some kind of trouble? No, no, that's not possible. I would have known."

McKean paced for a few moments, his hands behind his back. "Look, Trista, something's making the rounds, you know what a big gossip Mrs. Van Vooren is—"

"I know, I just couldn't handle her as Mother always did," Trista said helplessly. "I can't duplicate that bone-chilling icy stare Mother had whenever anyone started gossiping to her. And always, if the bone-freezer didn't work, she would immediately start saying very nice things about whoever the person was talking about, only I couldn't think of any nice things to say about the Andersens. But how did we get talking about Kruger? Oh yes, the pidgin German. I sound like a blithering idiot, don't I?"

"Sorta." McKean paced another few steps forward, then back. "Look, Mab, something's up but I can't figure it right now, and I can see that this receiving callers thing is a lot more work than it looks like. Let's just get through this and I'll find out what that woman was on about later."

Trista took his hands. They were rough and scarred, not like a gentleman's at all. "Thank you so much for helping me, McKean. I honestly am not prepared for this."

He nodded and squeezed her hands, but gently, for they were frail little things in his grasp. "I get that, Mab, but you'll do fine. I'll give you covering fire when the shot gets hot."

She laughed. "That's an apt simile."

"Metaphor," he said.

"If you say so. And, McKean, don't flirt with anyone else. I don't care what you say, if you turn all that rakish charm on these foolish women, we'll be here until day after tomorrow because no one will stay their obligatory fifteen minutes, they'll all stay until Rokeby will be obliged to cart them out."

The door opened and Rokeby, without missing a beat, said, "I have carted out Mrs. Van Vooren and Miss Van Vooren. Mrs. Henry Tilghman is calling."

McKean grinned. "Cart her in, Rokeby."

"Yes, sir."

Coming Out into the World

For his very life, McKean Livingstone couldn't remember whose card he had signed for the next dance. As he led Miss Singleton (nice eyes but blushed too much and had an annoying giggle) back to her eagle-eyed mama he furtively searched the crowded floor for a sign. The sign was sure to be another young girl gazing at him expectantly. As soon as he met her gaze, she would blush and drop her eyes.

The problem was, all the debutantes always did that to all the men. McKean sighed inwardly as he caught signs from at least four young women in a single sweep of a corner. He wished he was dancing again with Patience Van Vooren—she met his gaze, smiled pleasantly, and looked away—because at least she didn't moon-eye around and giggle, and she could string together words to make sentences, even complex sentences. But he had danced with her just two dances ago, and he knew he had been careful not to sign anyone's dance card twice. For such a rake, he did have a strong sense of duty. He especially didn't mind this time, though, because it was all for his sister Lorna. He watched as another gangly youth went up to her to claim the next dance. Catching McKean's eye she smiled brilliantly at him. She looked stunning, and she looked happy.

"You didn't think you were going to escape me, did you?"

He turned, already grinning. "Miss Carrollton, of course not. I was just looking for you. I believe this is my dance?"

Charmaine looked up at him with wide-eyed innocence. "Why, yes, I believe it is, McKean."

The first strains of a Viennese waltz and they began, Charmaine smiling a cat's smile. As they whirled by McKean saw Colette staring at them indignantly and then hustle over to her mother in a huff. Narrowing his eyes he asked, "Hey, Char, it is our dance, right? I mean, I signed your card for this dance, right?"

"Mm-hmm," she said angelically.

"Yeah? Then lemme see it."

"What?"

"Your dance card."

"How impertinent," Charmaine said haughtily. "I'm not going to show you my dance card, you oaf. And if you don't even know who you're engaged to—"

"To whom I'm engaged," McKean corrected her, his mouth twitching.

"—to whom I'm—you're engaged for this dance, then I'm certainly not responsible."

McKean watched as Vaughn Pascal hesitantly went to speak to Mrs. Carrollton and Colette. Colette promptly snatched him up—Vaughn looked dazed—and then waltzed him close to McKean and her sister.

"This was my dance with McKean," Colette snapped. "How childish."

"It was?" Vaughn Pascal mumbled. He was taller, bigger, and more handsome than his best friend McKean, but he wasn't much of a match for him—or their other friend Endecott Carrollton—in the brains department. "But I thought it was my dance with you."

"I'm Colette, Vaughn," she said with gritted teeth.

"Huh? Oh. Well, that's all right then. Isn't it?" he said, appealing first to Colette and then to McKean.

McKean shrugged apologetically to Colette. "Sure, Vaughn," he said and whisked Charmaine away.

Charmaine rolled her eyes. "I cannot believe that after all these years Vaughn still can't tell us apart. Your four-year-old brother can tell us apart. Cousin Hattie can tell us apart, and we only see her once a year and she's ninety if she's a day. Even the collier can tell us apart and he's barking mad."

McKean laughed. "Y'know, Char, you're a pain but at least you're never boring."

"Such romantic talk and you might sweep me off my feet," she said acidly. "Look, Trista's dancing with Endecott again. Isn't that three times? They should know better."

"I don't think anyone's going to think anything improper about your brother and my sister."

"Hmph! As if Endecott ever considered doing anything improper, he's such a stick. No wonder Trista looks like she's about to doze off. He's probably boring her to death with torts or ravages or something."

"Ravages?"

"Yes, you know, that legal thing about mortgages—or is it real property?"

"I don't know," McKean said truthfully. "But I doubt Endecott's talking to her about ravages. I'm pretty sure that the reason she looks so tired is because never in my life have I seen such a hoopty-do and hoo-raw over this ball. Females screeching all 'round the house, all hours of the day and night, people ringing the bell and carting in fabrics and shawls and gloves and shoes and bonnets and feathers and lace and who knows what else. Not to mention the carriages lined up on Tuesdays and Thursdays, those afternoons have been like a French rout. Miss Wardwell and I have been hiding in Father's library for the last two weeks solid."

"Lucky Miss Wardwell," Charmaine said coyly.

"Poor thing. She's been terrified, and so have I."

As always, McKean had paid no attention whatsoever to her little flirtation, so she sniffed with disdain. "You are not terrified of anything, McKean Taylor Livingstone, much less a houseful of women, so I don't feel at all sorry for you. Poor Miss Wardwell, though, she is such a shy little bookish thing, isn't she? I did catch a glimpse of her three days ago, flitting like a little gray ghost down the kitchen hallway. Her hair had come out of the comb, and the comb fell out. Colette fetched it and tried to give it to her, but she just melted away. Like Cinderella."

"Her hair comes out of the little whingdings a lot," McKean said in a mystified voice. "Always has. Can't figure it out."

"She needs an expert modiste, I've always told Trista that. Anyway, your father looks well, McKean. Very distinguished. I'm so glad he's here. My father has been worried about him. And Lorna is positively glowing, I'm so envious."

"She does look pretty, doesn't she?" McKean agreed, his eyes softening. She whirled by, a vision in icy pink satin and tulle, on the arm of a sensitive-looking youth with dark soulful eyes and a shock of black hair. "Who is that she's dancing with? I must be getting old, I don't know half of these boys."

"That's odd, since you know all of the girls," Charmaine said tartly. "That's Billy Tilghman, Henry Tilghman's youngest son."

"It is? I thought he was twelve!"

"He was five years ago which was probably the last time you saw him in church, since it was probably the last time you went to church. Anyway he's very intelligent, is rich of course, is going to Harvard Law, and is a virtuoso on the oboe. Or tuba. I forget because they both sound alike."

"Char, they sound nothing alike."

"They certainly do: ooo-boe, tuuu-baa. And maybe that's why Lorna seems so interested in him. They would have music in common, wouldn't they? Like us."

"I can't carry a note in a box," McKean said, "and you don't know the difference between an oboe and a tuba. What does that tell you?"

"That we have much in common, such as ignorance of musical instruments. Oh, come, McKean, dance me over that way, I don't want the waltz to end with us right here in front of Mrs. Andersen and her sisters. I'd have to speak to them and maybe fetch them some punch, though heaven knows I'm no footman, even if this is my house."

Frances Cleveland had sponsored Lorna, as she had promised, but it had not been possible for the ball to take place at the executive mansion, because that would have been tinged with improper personal use of the people's house. Neither Frances Cleveland nor President Cleveland would ever countenance anything of that nature. So Mrs. Cleveland and Lorna's cosponsors, Bettina Pascal and Evangeline Carrollton, had agreed that the best venue for this rather unusual debut was a semiprivate ball at Carrollton Park.

This room was not actually a ballroom; originally Endecott Carrollton had knocked down a wall between a smallish parlor and a smallish music room to make himself a billiard room and card room. But Evangeline Carrollton entertained so frequently and had such large parties that the room had always served as a dining room if more than thirty were invited to dinner, or as a ballroom for cotillions and musicales. It was a little crowded for more than one hundred, and there were exactly one hundred and twenty people here (not counting servants) so the dancers did sometimes come very close to the groups of ladies sitting in side chairs grouped along the walls.

"Shh, Char, they'll hear you," McKean said, quickly twirling her away.

Lightly following his vigorous turns—Charmaine was a very good dancer—she smiled. "What do you care? You call them the Gorges, after all."

"Not the Gorges, the—oh, never mind. I shouldn't be saying stuff like that. And neither should you."

"Oh, fie on them," Charmaine said spiritedly. "They're so—so grim. They never smile or laugh. Did you know that Mrs. Andersen's cards used to read 'Mrs. Senator James Andersen'? When he was a senator of course, and now that he lost his election and wrangled poor Mr. Cleveland out of an appointment to the Carcassees or Batalvia or wherever—"

"Scandinavian Desk," McKean managed to put in.

"—so I thought she would have 'Mrs. Ambassador to Scandinavia James Andersen' printed, but I guess it would have gone all the way 'round to the back. Anyway, all three of them still put their maiden names in parentheses after their real names—I suppose they're proud of being Motts, though I can't think why—and it is kind of sad that that's all one can remember, really, the Mott part."

"I remember all of their names," McKean said with a touch of smugness. "Mrs. James Andersen, formerly Harmony Mott; Mrs. Paul Sandel, formerly Honora Mott; Mrs. Kenneth Oliver, formerly Constance Mott."

"How in the world do you know all that?" Charmaine asked.

"Trista and I memorized them the other day, when they called. Rokeby sniffed all day after we told him to bring the salver in and leave it on the table in the parlor so we could study their cards before they were shown in," McKean said with satisfaction.

She stared up at him. "You were taking morning calls with Trista?"

"Yeah, thought I'd give her a hand with all the ladies."

"If I'd known that I would have—Oh!" She made a jerky misstep. "Oh! McKean, my heel's caught in my—my—a ruffle!"

He grinned. "Yeah? Wanna switch to an allemande, hop around for a while?"

"It's not funny, you big clumsy boor! Stop—no, don't stop—just here, dance me over there, quick!" Charmaine, still making an odd hop-step, headed over toward the far wall. Couples danced closely around them, but McKean threaded them toward the center of a pair of enormous heavy velvet draperies that he knew were drawn over a pair of French doors that led out into a garden.

"Char, the dance is about to end, why don't you just let me take you out to the hall so you can slip out and fix it?"

The great double entrance doors were wide open, but they were all the way across the room. "No, it's too far, and I refuse to trail my petticoat all the way across the room like some drabble-tailed raggle,"

Charmaine hissed. "Here—the knob's right in the center—quick—"
She slipped through and disappeared, and McKean heard, "Well?
Come here, McKean, you'll have to help me! I mean it!"

With a last glimpse around—no one seemed to be watching—he
slipped through the door and outside onto a bricked terrace. "No,
you fool, don't close the door, it'll lock!" Charmaine said, slapping
his hand. "Help me!"

He looked down. The moon was on the wane, so its light was
weak. "I don't see a thing except your train, Char. Are you sure
you—er—damaged something?"

"I heard and felt it rip. I must have a tail hanging out. Don't just
stand there like a big dumb lump, get down there and look."

McKean knelt. Charmaine's dress was a very light blue, and she
had a small train in a waterfall style. "Nice bustle," he said mischievously. "Uncollapsed and everything."

"Shut. Up. Just. Look." She ground her teeth.

"But, Char, your train's all flouncy, I can't tell if all these ruffles
and things are the right—ruffles and things," McKean said helplessly.

"Well—don't you have—something, a light or something?
Some Lucifer matches?"

"Gee, Char, I don't happen to have any lanterns on me at the
moment. Or matches. Too bad, we'd really have a good laugh if we
went back into the ballroom with your train on fire."

The music stopped; the night was very quiet with no wind, and
they could hear murmurs of conversation, the clink of crystal glasses,
a lady's quiet laugh. Then a distinctive voice carried to them, even
through the closed draperies and the very slight crack in the doors.
Evidently the speaker was passing close by.

"—only in mourning for a year, Sister. Scandalous. And you do
know that Lorna Livingstone is not yet sixteen? For shame, Frances
Cleveland should certainly know better, even though the family has
no sense of propriety."

"Well, Sister, what can one expect with that mother? As wild as
the March wind, Phoebe was, and poor Stockton without the slightest

notion of her and that great hulking German. They do say that the husband is always the last to know, and Harmony says that Stockton is so paralyzed with grief that he's all but useless at the law offices and the Foreign . . ." The busy loud whisper faded away.

McKean and Charmaine had frozen, as still as the little statuette of Cupid in the garden. Suddenly McKean stood up, a jerky movement that startled Charmaine. He grabbed her arms and turned her to him. She looked up at him, her great dark eyes filling with tears. "Oh, McKean, I'm so very sorry," she said in a choked voice. "I'm so sorry . . ."

"Never mind that," he said in a guttural voice quite unlike his own. "You just tell me everything. Now."

The next morning McKean paced alone in the morning room, his face grim and showing lines of weariness. His sleep had been uneasy and he had jerked awake at the cruel hour of three-thirty. He'd been up since then, pacing. The sun was barely up, and the June morning was showing signs of being lovely, but it was all wasted on McKean. He'd barely registered the dawn, but he had heard the servants stirring. When the door opened he said without looking up, "Not now, just let me know when my father wakes up."

"McKean? McKean, what's wrong?" Trista came in and closed the door behind her.

"Oh, it's you. I thought it was one of the servants. It's nothing, Mab, I just need to talk to Father before he goes in to the office."

Trista sat down on the sofa and watched her brother's restless pacing. "It's Saturday, McKean, and I doubt that he'll go in today. Or if he does it will probably be after luncheon."

"I know that. I just need to talk to him."

Trista said softly, "What is it, McKean? What's wrong? Can't you tell me?"

"I don't know," he said distractedly. "I don't know if I should."

She waited as he paced, giving him time to work it out. Trista was a fairly patient woman, and she knew that if she didn't nag McKean he would tell her what was bothering him in his own good time.

Finally he stopped, ran his hand through his hair, spiking it up, and threw himself down beside her. He stared off into space, unseeing, and said in a dull voice, "People are talking. Saying ugly things about Mother. And Father."

"What—what do you mean? What ugly things?"

"I made Charmaine tell me." He swallowed hard. "They're saying that Mother and Kruger were involved. Romantically. And that Father can't do his job anymore."

Trista made a peculiar little sound, a little breathless gulping sound, as if she couldn't breathe properly. After a long heavy silence she said in a strangled voice, "Who—who would—"

"I heard the Gorgons. Two of 'em, Mrs. Sandel and Mrs. Oliver. I wasn't eavesdropping, it just happened so that Char and I heard, just a sentence or two."

"I'll never receive them again." Trista's eyes were glittering and her nostrils flared.

McKean shook his head. "Won't help. Char said that the talk's all over Washington, there's no way to tell who started it. You know how things like this are, it's like—smoke. If you cut them, you'll have to cut half the women in town, and even then you don't actually know who's doing the talking and who's not."

"Well—the president—and Mrs. Cleveland—"

"Yeah. Charmaine said everyone knew that was just sour grapes, about Father. The president wouldn't have Father back if he couldn't do his job, even Mr. Cleveland's worst enemies admit that. But about Mother . . . Guess that's why Mrs. Cleveland was so good about Lorna. Kind of a show of support." McKean leaned forward, resting his elbows on his knees, clasped his hands, and dropped his head.

Trista was sitting bolt upright, her hands clasped together so tightly that her fingers were white and bloodless. Two spots of red burned on her smooth cheeks.

After a long silence she jumped up and burst out, "Well, you're not going to tell Father! As if he doesn't have enough to worry about anyway, and he's always had to do all the worrying in this house!"

McKean frowned and looked up at her. "What are you talking about? What does that mean?"

"I mean Mother was so—so careless! So imprudent! She just behaved any way she wanted to and never cared that people might talk."

McKean's blue eyes grew dark and stormy, and he stood up slowly to loom over her. "You can't mean that you think it's actually true. That's crazy, Trista. You know she would never, ever do anything like that. She was the best Christian woman—person—I've ever known, and she—she could never—"

"I know that! Of course I know that she could never think such a thing. But she was so high-spirited, so reckless! Riding, at her age, with a storm coming up, it was just like her, she always was doing something irresponsible like that, and there she went merrily off on that accursed horse, for miles! And left us—and Father—all alone!" Trista's eyes blazed and her mouth trembled.

She and McKean stared at each other.

Then Trista blinked and pressed her fingers to her mouth. "What have I done? What have I said? Oh, McKean, I—I'm so sorry, you know I didn't mean it."

He immediately softened. "Hey, I know that. C'mon, Mab, you're scarin' me. I don't think I've ever seen you so upset."

She sat limply now and shook her head. "I can't think what I was—was—thinking. It's not like me. It's not—right. To be angry at Mother."

"Maybe not," he said quietly. "But I was, too."

"You were? When?"

"On Boxing Day, of all things. I just started thinking about her parties, and how they'd never be the same, that particular day would never be the same without her, and I knew we wouldn't have any more Boxing Day parties. I was in St. Petersburg you know, and even if ol' Vaughn and E. C. were there it wasn't the same. It was a dreary, snowy day. And the more I thought about it, the more I got more and more resentful, I guess you'd call it, and finally I realized I was really angry at Mother."

"Then what did you do?"

He turned then to face her, and he looked sad and very tired. "I was sitting there, brooding, and I remember I thought clearly, 'She had no right, no right to just go off like that and kill herself.' And all of a sudden I felt like I had a hot knife sticking in my brain, and it—kinda hurt—and kinda scared me. So I just fought it, and jumped up and made Vaughn and E. C. go out with me for a walk. And every time after that when I started thinking that way, I just—fought it."

Trista looked down. "I didn't know."

"I never told anyone, of course. I thought I was some kind of monster, being mad at my own mother for dying suddenly in an accident."

"I feel like a monster, too," Trista said in a small voice. "But it certainly helps to know that I'm not the only monster. Oh, McKean, I miss her so much. I still miss her so much."

He took her hand. "I know. I do too. It's hard. But you know, I think you're right, about telling Father, I mean. There's nothing he can do about it—there's nothing anyone can do about it." He grinned raggedly. "I wanted to go challenge the Gorgons to a duel, I was that furious. And it's a good thing that Andersen wasn't in on it, or I would have challenged him, I swear I would have. But what can you do to women? Nothing. Char was a brick. She was sensible and kind."

"Charmaine? Not Colette?" Trista said with disbelief.

"Yeah, Charmaine Carrollton. She calmed me down some and made me see how hopeless it was to fight anything like this. So I asked her why, why hadn't she or someone, our real friends, told me or you? And she said it did no good to know it—was I really any better off knowing it? And no, I'm not. I wish I didn't know it now. And I wish I hadn't told you."

"You forget, I knew Mrs. Van Vooren was hinting at something that first day of morning calls—oh, so that's what Patience's little charade was all about," Trista said, narrowing her eyes. "She didn't want Mrs. Van Vooren to keep simpering on about Kruger. And there have been several hints from some of the other women, the Gorgons and Mrs. Vinton, I remember. You know, questions about Kruger and why Mother hired him and what exactly he does here. And wasn't it a bit unusual for the wife to hire a plantation overseer? They know perfectly well The Cedars isn't a plantation any more, but you know they're so persnickety they can't say 'stud farm.' Of course they're always hoping I'll be vulgar and say it."

He looked at her, his eyes warm and kind. "Hey, Mab, you know Mother never would have said 'stud farm.' She was respectable, and she played by the rules. You know that, don't you?"

"I suppose so," Trista said with some difficulty. "She was just different from other women. She was so energetic and vital, and it made her seem—loose. Like a libertine."

"Oh, Mab, Mab, little fairy queen! Such primness doesn't suit you, you know. 'And in this state she gallops night by night / Through lovers' brains, and then they dream of love . . .'"

"Stop that this instant," Trista said, though now she was getting in a much better humor—McKean could always cheer her up—and it didn't come out nearly as severely as she wished. "You never should have nicknamed me 'Mab.' I'm nothing like that—that bawdy little tart that Mercutio goes on and on about before Romeo has the good grace to shut him up."

McKean laughed, a genuine laugh that made him look young again. "You know when I was seven years old and gave you that nickname I didn't have the slightest idea what she was. I just thought you were so like the tiny little delicate queen of the fairies, 'no bigger than an agate-stone / On the fore-finger of an alderman, Drawn with a team of little atomies / Athwart men's noses as they lie asleep . . .'"

"You most certainly did know exactly what that passage meant," Trista said, fighting a smile. "I don't care if you were only seven. My only consolation is that most people are so illiterate they've never read *Romeo and Juliet* and they have no idea who Mab really is. Colette does, and she smiles when you call me that, and it infuriates Charmaine. Of course, Charmaine thought you were calling me 'Mad' until she was sixteen, and then when she realized it was 'Mab' she threw a blue-faced fit when Colette wouldn't tell her what a 'Mab' was, I don't suppose she knows to this day." The smile now broke out on Trista's face.

"Maybe. But after last night I'm not too sure Charmaine's not putting on that brainless female act. Some of it anyway, but it is fashionable, you know, which brings me back to my point. Mother was unorthodox because she wasn't a vaporish breathless helpless stupid baby-talking weeping female, which for some reason has been considered the ultimate in a lady in this silly country for three decades now. And I'll try to break this to you gently, Mab, but you aren't a fashionable woman either. In your own way you're just as unorthodox as Mother was."

"I am?" Trista said. "But I try so hard to be dignified and respectable."

"I know," McKean said quietly. "Quit tryin' so hard."

Only Fog

*T*he morning was chilly and clammy, odd for June in Washington. Fog swirled outside the window like a wraith searching for a way in. Miles and miles away Trista heard a long low growl of thunder. It would rain today, and then it would clear off and be hot and so humid one's clothes would feel damp.

Trista was sitting in one of the plush armchairs that faced the windows. She had drawn the curtains with the full intention of contemplating the view to induce a meditative mood. But there was no view, only fog.

She heard the door open behind her and didn't turn. Susie said, "Oh, I beg pardon, miss. I didn't know you were in here."

"It's all right, Susie," Trista said distantly, then roused somewhat. "Oh yes, today's Monday. I had forgotten that the morning room was to be aired today." She turned to the maid, who fidgeted in the doorway.

"Yes, miss. Though airing might be a little 'zaggeration today, considering. I did have a mind to ask Mrs. Cross if I might wait till this afternoon, when the air might be drier, like."

"I do think that's a better idea, Susie. Please go ahead and straighten the sitting room first instead. We left a sad mess last night, I'm afraid, with the games and cards everywhere and just about every book in the room out of the bookcases."

"Yes, miss." Susie made her curtsy and started to leave, then turned back hesitantly. "Would we be having prayers this morning, Miss Livingstone?"

Her back turned again, Trista frowned. "No. No, not—this morning." *Or any other morning since—when? We limped along a month or two after Mother died . . . and then we just all sort of stopped meeting here in the mornings, somehow.* With a shock Trista realized that this must mean they hadn't had family prayers for a year or more.

"Yes, miss. Um—I was just wondering—"

"Yes?" Trista said distantly.

"Would you be wanting anything at all? It's still some time until breakfast, and I thought maybe coffee or even tea, you know Mrs. Trimble did get a new box of Twining's yesterday that's so fresh it does smell that good?"

"No thank you," Trista replied automatically. Susie was closing the door when Trista said, "Wait . . . I apologize, Susie, I wasn't attending. Yes, I would love coffee, hot and strong, please. And when McKean comes down would you ask him to join me?"

"Beg pardon, miss, but he's out riding."

Trista swiveled in the chair again. "In this weather? At this hour?"

"Well—yes, miss, not to put too fine a point on it."

"But—oh, never mind. If he comes in tell him I'm in here and"—she managed a small smile—"that I have hot coffee, and I won't mind his muddy boots."

"Mr. Rokeby would never allow that, I'm sure," Susie murmured. "P'raps if I place another, clean pair by the kitchen door . . . oh, will that be all, miss?"

"Yes, thank you, Susie."

Trista had already begun staring out the window. It was a long time—or it seemed a long time—before she managed to gather her thoughts. They were as amorphous and dismal as the swirling fog outside.

"I must call on the Gorgons. I know, I just know it's today."

Morning calls—still called that even though they actually took place from one o'clock until four o'clock—had a complex protocol, particularly in Washington. For some reason it had evolved that, instead of waiting for a proper introduction to call upon a new acquaintance, strangers made their calls first. Mrs. Florence Howe Hall, in her *Social Customs* published the previous year, had noted this curious derangement in the capital city, and had taken the complacent view that any American citizen had the right to social recognition from their elected officials.

Trista's view was that Mrs. Florence Howe Hall would be utterly horrified at a pack of strange females from who knows where and who knows what lineage standing on her exclusive Boston doorstep. But then Mrs. Howe had not introduced the tradition, she had only noted it. Trista supposed that it had actually invaded the societal protocols from the public's long familiarity with the inhabitants of the executive mansion; even now, if one were visibly sane, had clean fingernails, and a printed card, one could present themselves at the executive mansion and gain an audience with the president. Trista supposed it had not been such a wild aberration for newly arrived congressmen's wives to begin the round of social calls instead of waiting for the introductions that might never come.

The problem was enormous for Trista, for she had not been as attentive to all of the city's networks of callers as her mother had been. Also, Trista had gone to Vassar Female College in September 1886, and so had further lost touch with the Washington social scene. Trista had returned to The Cedars in March 1887 when her mother had died and had missed the remainder of her first year. Somehow she hadn't been able to face reenrolling last September. Sometimes she regretted it. Sometimes she just didn't care. And certainly here at home she hadn't cared about brushing up on the latest edition of the Washington *Social Register*.

In the last three weeks since Mrs. Cleveland's unexpected visit, Trista had received dozens of women that she had no recollection of ever meeting. She honestly didn't know if they were first-time callers or if she'd met them and forgotten or if they knew her mother or father and not her. Rokeby had been invaluable, making neat little notes on the back of the calling cards like "Mr. Witt is aide to Senator Dimble," and "Mrs. Penney knew Mrs. L through Pres. Orphan's Aid Society." And Rokeby had helped her work through the calendar, organizing the maze of return calls according to each lady's at-home day.

Trista was certain that today was Mrs. James Andersen's at-home day. "I can't do it. I won't."

But then, struggling to damp down the fires of anger and rebellion, she told herself sternly that she certainly could, and she would.

Trista thought that it was Susie returning with her coffee and moved to one of the chairs surrounding a large tea table. But after some odd scratching noises at the door and some hissing whispers, Miss Wardwell came in, herding three very forlorn children: Merritt, Dolly, and Penn. Even Penn looked droopy, with his head hung and his hands stuck in his pockets.

"Miss Trista, I'm so sorry to intrude on you—oh, are we having prayers this morning?" Miss Wardwell said, looking quickly around the room as if she were surprised to be there.

"No, Miss Wardwell, we are not," Trista said, eyeing her brothers and sister suspiciously. "What has happened?"

Miss Wardwell made flapping motions, and the children moved woodenly to sit like birds on a perch along the sofa. Miss Wardwell was a wispy, shy little woman who often made flapping motions. She had forgotten to take off her reading spectacles and they slid down her nose in her agitation. But Miss Wardwell ignored it and stared over the little square rims, for if she removed them she knew she would lose them, as she so often did.

She had never seemed either young or old, but Trista now noticed, and was surprised to see, some strands of gray in her dark brown hair. Miss Wardwell had been with them for over fifteen years now, Trista recalled with some difficulty, and so she must be thirty-five. She was so much a part of the family—at least, she was like a benevolent family ghost, familiar and dependable, but rarely seen—that it just seemed that she had always been with them.

With her charges seated, Miss Wardwell turned and joined her hands primly in front of her apron as if she were reciting. "Miss Trista, it grieves me to bring this to your attention, but I do feel that it is a matter that should be attended to by you personally. Master Merritt saw fit to take your father's telescope and go out last night—in the falling damps, for shame, Merritt—to view Venus, I understand, which was at some favorable juncture. And he took Penn with him. At least, I assume he did, for both of their boots were fairly soaked and muddy and shoved far under their beds, as if I wouldn't notice that they weren't by the door after Mr. Rokeby placed them there after polishing them. And I must remind you, Master Merritt"—she pushed up her glasses with real distress and then peered over them at him—"that if I had not noticed the boots—or rather the absence of the boots in question—that Mr. Rokeby certainly would have and if he'd found them in that state I couldn't answer for the consequences."

"I know, Miss Wardwell, I'll clean them, I promise," Merritt said in a small voice. "Even Penn's."

"I should think so," she said severely. Miss Wardwell was afraid of men in general and Rokeby in particular, and her extreme indignation had something to do with the fact that Rokeby would likely blame her for the sorry state of the boys' boots. Not that Rokeby would ever say anything to her—Rokeby was always exquisitely polite to the servants and Miss Wardwell—but a single glance from him could make Miss Wardwell take to the schoolroom for hours.

Trista said with exasperation, "Let me make certain I understand this. Merritt, you took Father's telescope without asking, and then crept out of the house in the middle of the night, in the falling damps, and took Penn with you?"

"Well," Merritt said glumly, "that makes it sound so much worse than it was."

"Then tell me what happened and make it sound better," Trista snapped.

He fidgeted, his head down. "Guess I can't, exactly."

"I thought not. Oh, Merritt, what am I to do with you? Aside from everything else, how could you be so careless and thoughtless to go outside on such a dreary night and I'm certain you must have gotten chilled and wet clear through!"

He muttered, "But Venus was supposed to be horned last night, only it was so foggy I couldn't find it, and I watched out for Penn, that he didn't fall down or anything. And I'm not sick."

"But—" Trista began, then everyone, even Penn, stiffened in what might be called a listening posture. "Is that Lorna?" Trista whispered to herself, then looked for the violin case, leaning against the piano bench as it had for so long. It wasn't there.

"It must be," Dolly said. "She's the only one who plays the violin."

Random notes were floating down from the second floor, very faintly. Lorna was tuning her violin. Everyone stayed still and quiet, absurdly gazing up at the ceiling, listening. The sad, sweet strains of some tune in a minor key barely filtered down into the room.

The door opened. McKean came in, followed by Susie with an enormous coffee service and a plate of blueberry muffins. "Hey, you hear that, Mab, Nibbie's playing—" he stopped and looked around. "Oh. We having prayers?"

"Don't I just wish," Merritt whispered.

"No, we are not having prayers, because we are all a bunch of godless heathens it would seem, only now it's not just me and you, McKean, it's also Merritt and Penn," Trista said, feeling exceedingly guilty by now, which made her speak more sharply than she intended.

"Oh no, Miss Trista," Miss Wardwell mumbled, backing a step away from McKean. Even though he was always careful to be very kind to her, he did fluster her so. "No, you'd never be so wicked, and neither would Merritt nor Penn . . . or, of course, you, Mr. McKean . . ." She backed up another step, flapping a little.

McKean turned to frown at the children lined up stiffly on the sofa. "What'd you do, Diggers? You've upset Miss Wardwell, and you shouldn't do that."

"I know," he said. "I did tell her I'm sorry. Lots of times. And your boots are muddy, and nobody's having the vapors over it."

"I scraped them good," McKean said, quickly glancing down at them. "I didn't track in, did I? Where's Rokeby?"

"Never mind that," Trista said impatiently. "Merritt stole Father's telescope, kidnapped Penn, and went out wandering around in the dark last night."

"In the falling damps," Miss Wardwell put in faintly.

"Uh-oh, you're going to catch it but good, Diggers," McKean said gravely. "And you too, Penn. I'll just bet you didn't get dragged out kicking and screaming."

"I made Merritt take me, or I said I'd jus' follow him," Penn said defiantly. "I didn't tell. I wouldn't tell."

"That's true," Dolly put in. Three pairs of grown-up's eyes swiveled to her, and she very much regretted speaking out.

"What are you doing here?" Trista asked, a sort of confused afterthought.

"I didn't tell," Dolly said fiercely. "Mother hates—hated informers. Penn didn't know, he was too little, but I explained it to him. That's why he didn't tell Merritt he'd tell to make him take him with him."

"Wait, say that again?" McKean said.

"What I can't figure out," Merritt said thoughtfully, "is why kids can't inform on kids, and they sure can't inform on adults, but it was okay with Mother for adults to inform on kids."

"I had a hard time with that one, too," McKean said, sighing. Then, with a guilty glance at Trista he went on quickly, "Because adults are concerned with your welfare and morals and well-being, especially yours, Diggers, because you know very well that you shouldn't be out in the damp night airs."

"But I'm not sick," he said pleadingly.

"I'll deal with you later, young man," Trista said grimly. "Now would you please explain, Miss Wardwell, why Dolly is here and why she is now trying to make herself as small and unnoticeable as possible?"

Miss Wardwell pushed up her glasses and took a tentative little step forward out of the corner that she had managed to shrink into. "Miss Trista, I'm so sorry to report to you that I found this child reading Voltaire! *Voltaire!*"

"Yeah?" McKean asked, impressed. "In French?"

"No, only English," Dolly whispered very meekly.

"Voltaire!" Trista repeated, shocked. "Dolly—Dolly—was reading Voltaire?"

"I told you she was smart," McKean said smugly.

Miss Wardwell looked as though she might cry, but she managed to splutter, "But, Mr. McKean—Miss Trista—Mr. McKean—it was—it was Letter XI! *On Inoculations.*" She gazed at Trista and clasped her hands together in a perfectly unfeigned gesture of extreme distress.

Trista shook her head in bewilderment and sank into the nearest chair. She saw Susie still standing there by the tea tray, her eyes alight. "Susie, I want coffee. Now."

"Me, too," McKean said, but he didn't take a seat. Miss Wardwell was still standing—barely—and he would never sit while a lady was standing. "Miss Wardwell, won't you sit down and join us? These little ruffians can just wait until we sort this out."

"Well, I—I—don't know . . ." Very gently McKean took her elbow and led her to a chair. "It's all so upsetting."

"Yes, yes, but Trista and I will take care of it. You did the right thing, you know," McKean said as if he were calming a frightened child.

Susie served them and Trista dismissed her (to Susie's very great disappointment). The adults took some fortifying sips of the still-hot coffee. "Now then, Dolly," Trista said with some sternness but also with some uncertainty, "you were reading Voltaire. Um—did you—perhaps steal the book from Father's study? Maybe while your brother was in there stealing his telescope?"

"Oh no," Dolly said, shocked. "It was in the schoolroom. It's Miss Wardwell's."

Neither McKean nor Trista noticed Miss Wardwell's look of horror. McKean asked curiously, "Did you understand what you were reading, Wortley?"

"Well, most of it," Dolly answered more confidently now. "It was about her, you know. Lady Mary Wortley Montagu."

Trista looked blank. "You know, Trista," Dolly went on impatiently. "*On Inoculation.* McKean said he'd read about her in Voltaire, so I just decided to see if I could find it. So I did, and I read it."

Trista frowned and turned to Miss Wardwell, who shrank back in her chair, even more guiltily than Dolly had done. "But, Miss Wardwell, I don't understand. It's—amazing, yes, that Dolly is reading at such an advanced level, but not really so very wicked. Is it that you particularly value the book and resent Dolly borrowing it?"

"Oh, oh," Miss Wardwell said, her cheeks flaming, "but, Miss Trista, surely you recall—you remember—about Voltaire—"

"I recall very little about him, but I do recall that the Letters are generally of a political nature. Aren't they?" She turned to McKean, who looked as mystified as she did.

"They seemed to be," Dolly said conversationally. "I read XII, too, *On the Lord Bacon,* because I thought that was such a funny name and I thought maybe he invented it. Bacon. But Voltaire didn't say. It was all about great men in England."

Trista stared at her. "Good heavens, it's like talking to a forty-year-old midget."

Miss Wardwell was making peculiar little noises, so Trista sighed and turned back to her. "I'm sorry, Miss Wardwell, I still don't understand why Dolly is in as much trouble as those truant boys."

"The—the Circassians!" she whispered.

"The Circassians?" Trista repeated blankly. "What about them?"

"Uh-oh," McKean said under his breath. He stared hard at Dolly, who wilted again. "Hey, Wortley, so you did read about that? About the Circassian women?"

"What about the Circassian women?" Trista blustered.

"I did," Dolly admitted. "But honestly, McKean, I didn't understand all that about the Turkish sultan's seraglios and the Persian Sophy."

"You know how to say seraglio right," McKean said accusingly. "You looked it up."

"Seraglios?" Trista wailed. "McKean, what have you been telling this child to read?"

"I didn't tell her to read it," McKean said hastily. "I just mentioned that I'd read Voltaire about Lady Montagu, that's all. I didn't know she was some kind of literary genius and she'd go read it! Besides, I'd forgotten about the seraglios."

"What's a seraglio?" Merritt leaned over and asked Dolly.

"Never mind!" Trista and McKean snapped together.

Suddenly Dolly burst into tears. "I don't understand. It's not fair! It's no worse than some things in the Old Testament! Is it?"

The door burst open. Lorna stood in the doorway, her hair all falling down, her face streaked with tears, her eyes wild. She was holding her violin. "I'll never, never play again!"

Trista and McKean jumped up, while Miss Wardwell hurried to Dolly and scooped her up. Merritt and Penn rolled their eyes at each other.

"No, no, Nibbie, don't cry, I can't stand it." McKean said. "What's the matter? Of course you'll play again, you play like an angel!"

She threw her arms around him and said, rather muffled, against his chest, "Oh, McKean, I can't! No, it's not that I can't! It's that I can't bear to, I just can't bear it!"

"Lorna, pull yourself together," Trista said ungraciously. "All this high tragedy so early in the morning."

"What would you know?" Lorna said, now pushing McKean away. "You didn't play duo sonatas with Mother every day as I did!"

"I know! I'm well aware that I'm no musical genius or literary genius or good mother to Penn and Merritt and Dolly and that we haven't had morning prayers for more than a year!" Trista shouted. "So what do you expect me to do about it?"

"We haven't had morning prayers for over a year?" Lorna repeated.

"No, no one realizes, no one cares, no one helps, no one thinks I've read Voltaire!" Trista said recklessly, disregarding everyone's stares. "And I'm the one who has to go make nicey-kissy-talk to the Gorgons this afternoon!"

"What are Gorgons?" Dolly asked, sniffing a little. She had stopped crying to listen to Trista.

Merritt sneezed. Twice.

Stockton Livingstone stepped into the hallway, behind Lorna. "Good morning, everyone. Was that Merritt sneezing?"

Lorna burst into tears.

Dolly started crying again.

Merritt sneezed, then sniffled.

Stockton frowned. "All right, then. Everyone in—no, Miss Wardwell, please stay. It looks as if we'd better start with morning prayers."

Stockton Lee Livingstone prayed for his family and for the entire household. Afterwards he could see that his children were glad—and relieved—at this renewal of the tradition. But he was neither glad nor relieved nor anything else particularly. He only reflected that that did sound sincere. *I must be a very good diplomat; we can say anything and make it sound solemn and heartfelt.*

He looked around at his family. Dolly, Merritt, and Penn were still lined up on the sofa; Trista and McKean were in armchairs on either side of the settee where he and Lorna were sitting. She was still clutching her violin and sniffling. In a far corner Miss Wardwell perched on the edge of a chair.

Stockton decided to tackle Merritt first. He was pale and the first telltale hint of translucent blue marks underneath his eyes were starting to show. "Son, come here," Stockton said gently. Merritt rose and came to stand in front of his father, his head bowed. Stockton felt his forehead, then brushed back his hair. "Are you feeling ill?"

"Yes, sir," Merritt said in a low voice.

Stockton waited.

Merritt fidgeted a little, then sighed deeply and raised his eyes to his father. "I stole your telescope, sir, and then I went out last night. In the falling damps. I wanted to see Venus, because it should— anyway, sir, I took Penn. And got wet. And muddy."

"I see," Stockton said. "Merritt, why didn't you just ask me about the telescope?"

He dropped his eyes again. "I—I did go into your library to ask you, Father. But you weren't there . . . so I just thought you wouldn't mind if I borrowed it."

Stockton's lips tightened for a moment, but he was always careful to avoid showing any distress to the children, so he quickly smoothed out his expression. It was true. Last night, while his family had been gathered in the sitting room, playing games and talking, he had been upstairs sitting in Phoebe's room, holding his head in his hands and staring blankly at the floor.

For several months after his wife's death he had stayed closeted in his library; he had even slept there on the nights when he couldn't face going into the suite he had shared with her. After McKean had gone to university and had gotten his flat in town, Stockton had completely renovated the second floor to make a new roomy boudoir, dressing room, and bath for his wife. It interconnected with the master bedroom, so Stockton had to go through it to get to the bedroom. This was a journey that, many nights, he simply couldn't take. Last night he had, with sheer stubbornness, made himself go up to sit in Phoebe's room. All of her things had been cleared out long ago, of course—her clothes packed away and stored, her toilet articles and perfumes and shoes and hats and silver brushes, everything that she had touched had been removed and stored in the attic. But still, in the enormous bathroom were unopened boxes of her jasmine soap. The scent floated into the room. Stockton had sat down on the canopied bed, put his head in his hands, and stared bleakly at the floor for hours. Just remembering and struggling to find a way to recall the joy and deaden the pain. He had been able to do neither.

Now he said sternly to his son, "You didn't ask when I came in for prayers."

Merritt looked wretched. "No, sir. I had already—already stolen it by then, so I could hardly ask, could I?"

"I suppose not. Merritt, I think you know that I have never minded you using the telescope, because you treat it with respect and you are conscientious in cleaning it and returning it. I think you also know that borrowing anything without asking the owner's permission is not acceptable behavior.".

"Yes, sir," Merritt said glumly. "I did say that I *stole* it."

"Yes, you did. A thief, but an honest, hardworking thief," Stockton said, ruffling the boy's hair again. His forehead felt cool but clammy. Sighing, Stockton went on, "I'm not going to punish you, Merritt, because I can see that you're going to pay a price for this little outing." He turned to Miss Wardwell's corner. "Miss Wardwell, I'll hear about all the details of Merritt and Penn's infamy later. Right now I think you'd better take them—and Dolly—to the kitchen and tell Mrs. Trimble to give them their breakfast."

"Yes, Mr. Livingstone," Miss Wardwell said, standing and taking her three charges in hand again. "I expect I'd better put Merritt to bed afterwards, sir."

Stockton nodded. "I'll come up to the schoolroom before I leave."

They left, and Stockton turned to Lorna, who still sat forlornly clutching her violin. It was a lovely instrument, an Amati that Stockton and Phoebe had given her when she was ten years old. Even now, though she was distraught, she held it in her lap and ran her long supple fingers down the curved sides, then brushed the strings to make soft whispering sounds like wind in leafy trees. Trista and McKean watched her, both of them with a hint of sadness and bewilderment.

Stockton reached over and took Lorna's hand. She gripped his hand tightly. "I heard you playing," he said quietly. "It lifted my heart."

Lorna sobbed a little. Her head was bowed and her long thick silvery hair swung down, hiding her face.

"Child, don't cry on the Amati," Stockton said.

"Oh dear," Lorna said, jerking upright. "Did I?" Anxiously she searched the face of the violin for tear spots.

"Of course, it won't make any difference if you've decided never to play again," Stockton said lightly.

"But I want to!" Lorna burst out. "I just can't!"

"You can. You did. Bach, I believe, wasn't it?"

"Yes, sir," she answered, sniffling dismally. "Umm—I was just trying the Violin and Oboe Concerto, Suite 1600. The largo."

"Oboe, not tuba," McKean muttered under his breath. "I'm glad."

"Ah yes," Stockton said thoughtfully. "I like the violoncello in the largo. Plucked, not bowed."

Lorna bit her bottom lip. "Perhaps we could—try it together?"

Stockton frowned and turned to stare off into the distance. Lorna—and Trista and McKean—waited . . . hoped. Finally he turned back to Lorna. "All right. Tomorrow morning, after breakfast. It'll be good to play again." He smiled, a singularly sweet smile for such a grave and often stern man. "It's your gift, Lorna. You make music."

She nodded, her eyes filling with tears again. "I know. It's just so hard . . ."

"Yes, it is," Stockton agreed, "but maybe if we try it together it will be easier."

"It will be," Lorna said vigorously. Mercurial as always, she jumped up and headed for the door, then turned. "Oh—pardon me, Father—may I be excused? I think I might dust off my flute . . . and I didn't do anything wicked, like Merritt and Penn and Dolly, so I'm not to be punished, am I?"

"Dolly?" Stockton repeated, confused. "Um—no, Lorna, of course you're excused." After she left he turned to Trista and McKean. "Dolly?"

"Oh, she's wicked is Wortley," McKean said, grinning. "Sneaking around and reading Voltaire."

To Trista's amazement, her father only nodded. "Voltaire, I see. *Candide?*"

"Nah," McKean said dismissively. "The Letters. Politics, not romance."

"McKean! It's not romance, but—the sultan's seraglios?" Trista said indignantly. "Circassian women?"

"Ah, that letter," Stockton said thoughtfully. "*On Inoculation.* Oh yes—Wortley. Lady Montagu."

"Exactly," McKean said with satisfaction.

"Father!" Trista sputtered. "I don't recall the letter, but I hardly think that Dolly needs to be reading about Turkish seraglios!"

"It's no worse than the Old Testament," McKean said, his eyes twinkling.

"That's what she said!" Trista snapped, then turned to appeal to her father.

"She's been reading the Old Testament, too?" he said, pleased. "That's interesting."

"But—but—" Trista began, then stopped. Her little Mab-mouth twitched. "I see. That naughty, wayward child. Actually reading the Bible instead of the big storybook with the pictures."

"What can you do?" McKean said. "Voltaire's pretty tame alongside ol' Phinehas, or Solomon and his concubines."

"Stop showing out," Trista muttered. "I don't know who Phinehas is and you know it."

"Bet Dolly does," McKean teased.

"Mmm, I see the problem," Stockton said, frowning. "At least with you, McKean, all we had to do was keep the Balzac and Pepys hidden. We didn't have to worry about you reading the Old Testament."

"I read the Old Testament, Father," McKean said self-righteously. "But you'd better find another hiding place for Balzac and Pepys. Behind the collected works of the ancient Greeks won't work for Dolly, she'll probably be reading them next week."

"Obviously I know now that it's not a very good hiding place since you found them. But somehow I doubt Dolly will be prowling around my library in the dead of night with a candle and set the Turkish carpet on fire and manage to scorch Linnaeus and Descartes."

"Wait," Trista said, frowning darkly. "Wait . . . are you telling me . . . you mean, McKean, you were a—a—prodigy? Like Dolly?"

He grew sober. "No. Not like Dolly." He shifted his gaze to his father. "She's different. She's more intuitive than I was, more insightful. I soaked it all up, yes. But she applies it. Or tries to, anyway."

"How can I remember that you set the house on fire," Trista said impatiently, "but I forgot that you're a genius?"

Ignoring her, Stockton said to McKean, "You mean that she's of a more philosophical bent?"

"Yes, sir. The other day she was talking to me about the higher meaning of *Windy Nights*, which is one of Robert Louis Stevenson's poems in *A Child's Garden of Verses*. Remember it? 'Whenever the moon and stars are set / Whenever the wind is high . . .' Anyway, she explained to me that it really wasn't about a man riding about on a horse on stormy nights; it was about 'fears common to all children of a tender young age,' she said." McKean made a wry face. "And the thing about it was she was right."

"Oh no, not a poet," Stockton groaned.

"I'm afraid so," McKean answered gravely.

"How old was I when you set the house on fire?" Trista said.

"Which time?" McKean asked brightly.

Stockton stood up. His face was thoughtful, his dark blue eyes shadowed. "I'd like everyone to be at dinner tonight," he said to Trista. "Even Merritt, unless he's positively bedridden. I'm going now to see Professor Dodge, and I'll invite him, too. Trista, would you make the arrangements with Mrs. Trimble?"

"Of course, Father."

"Thank you. I have several meetings today, and one that I expect will keep me late. I'll try to be back around seven o'clock. If I'm not, would you be so good as to wait dinner for me?"

"Of course we'll wait for you," Trista said warmly. "If you're late we'll make Mrs. Trimble give us cookies and tea."

"Good, good," he said absently and left.

Trista turned to McKean with an accusing look on her face. "Now then, Mr. Mad Firebug Genius. Suppose you just start explaining to me what we're going to do with Dolly."

He shrugged. "Father's going to see Uncle Cash. Uncle Cash will know what to do."

Logic and Legend

Cashman Wynn Dodge lived in an old stone cottage down on M Street, right on the C & O Canal. Nearby were a foundry, a fish market, a paper mill, two cotton mills, and a power station for the city's streetcar system. Alongside Professor Dodge's house was a tavern whose patrons were mostly stevedores and ferrymen and the women who always seemed to cluster around such places and such men. As the brougham pulled up in front of the little cottage, Stockton told Redmond Kruger, "I may be a while, Kruger."

"It is fine, sir," he said in his thickly accented growl. "I will watch." Professor Dodge's neighborhood required a vigilant coachman, and Redmond Kruger—tall, thickly built, and grim—would guard the carriage and the horses like a wolf. Normally Brock McElhenny, one of the grooms and a good driver, took Stockton into Washington. But when any of the Livingstones came to visit Uncle Cash, Redmond Kruger drove them.

Stockton knocked on the four-inch-thick massive oak door, so old it was black. The knocker was a great brass lion's head with a heavy ring in its mouth. It always amazed Stockton that it had never been stolen, but it had been on this door for as long as Stockton could remember. *How many years is it now that I've been knocking on this door?* he mused as he heard muffled voices inside. *Twenty? No, no, McKean's twenty-four. Thirty . . . thirty-two years . . .*

The door creaked open and Cash Dodge's face broke into a welcoming smile. "Stockton, come in, come in! I see Kruger out there; won't you bring him in for something in the kitchen? That vixen Maymie will likely give him a crust and cold coffee."

"If I let him come in I'll never see that carriage or horse again," Stockton said firmly. "And Kruger wouldn't care about the brougham but he'd spend the rest of his life hunting down the horse thieves. But I'm sure he would appreciate it if Maymie would take him a mug of coffee."

"Of course, of course. Go on in, Stockton, and sit down, I'll hunt down that female . . ." He turned and stomped down the hall calling, "Maymie! Show yourself, woman, don't lurk around like a burglar!"

From the kitchen—which was only twelve feet down the hall— an exasperated female voice called, "I'm right here, sir! In the kitchen! Fancy that!"

Stockton shook his head, smiling, as he watched the old man. Cashman Wynn Dodge was seventy years old now, tall and thin, but still with an aura of vigor. His arthritic knees had started bothering him just this year, and he walked stiffly, leaning heavily on a cane. He had ice-bright blue eyes set in a long gaunt bony face, with sharp cheekbones and jawline. Thick silvery eyebrows bristled over those sharp eyes, and for the last twenty years, in fashion and out, Cash had sported a ferocious swooping mustache.

Stockton turned into the parlor/study/library on the left and reflected that all of the five living rooms in Cash Dodge's house might be called the study/library. There were books and papers everywhere: in this parlor, in the dining room across the hall (stacked on the long dining table that had never been used to dine on), in the actual study behind it, and in Cash's bedroom. There were even books and papers in the hallway, piled on the floor. Stockton wondered idly if the books had invaded the kitchen, but he doubted it. Maymie, a sassy black woman that Phoebe had engaged for her uncle Cash for his fiftieth birthday, would have no truck with such litter in her kitchen.

This room tended to be where Professor Dodge spent most of his time, mainly because it was the largest room and he had been able to cram so many books into it. A long, fat gold velvet camelback sofa (also a gift from the Livingstones for Christmas five years ago) faced the fireplace, with two comfortable wing chairs on each side and a great Turkish ottoman in the middle for tea trays, when Cash could remember not to pile books on it.

Happily oblivious to the design of the room, Cash had bought an enormous library table, old and scarred, and butted it up against the sofa back. He had also bought a rickety old straight chair, but the legs were so uneven that he had to put a book under one of the legs, and he was always scooting back and teetering off to the side. Stockton, exasperated, had bought a fine walnut revolving desk chair and had it delivered to Cash, with the note: *Take it. Phoebe's afraid you're going to tip over and break your head.* Cash had stiffly thanked him for it and had never mentioned it again. It was the only gift he had ever accepted from the Livingstones, aside from birthday and Christmas. Now Stockton saw it, scuffed, the upholstery comfortably dimpled and faded, the arms scarred from ramming up against the table. He moved it slightly, and saw with satisfaction that it rolled smoothly and soundlessly, and the seat revolved easily and quietly. Maymie was good about things like that. It would never occur to Cash to tighten and oil the rollers and the seat.

He came back in shaking his head. He was bald on top, with a feathery fringe. The top of his head was pink. "That woman's going to drive me mad, Stockton. I can't think why I let Phoebe talk me into keeping her."

"Maybe because without her you wouldn't have anything to eat or clean clothes to wear?" Stockton said politely.

Cash stumped to one cozy armchair and waved his cane for Stockton to sit down. Ignoring Stockton's comment he went on, "She fiddled with my books out there"—the cane stabbed toward the hall—"and I had them arranged in order, with my notes marking the pertinent passages. I was studying Marcus Aurelius, contrasting him with Ecclesiastes and Proverbs—and scorching him and his pile of tripe to shame, if I may say so myself—but my Greek text of Proverbs was falling apart, so I put it on the bottom, with my notes carefully inserted in order into it. And I piled Ecclesiastes and that villain Marcus Aurelius on top. And that woman came and picked up the Proverbs and it fell apart and scattered my notes! Said she was trying to sweep under it or some nonsense."

"Professor Dodge, I know we've been stepping over those books for at least a year," Stockton said. "I'm only surprised that Maymie has left them alone this long."

"Well she had, and now look what's happened when she's wrecked them. I'll have to start all over again, I suppose, and Marcus Aurelius is so tiresome, the blackguard self-righteous pompous hypocrite."

"I don't know why you ever study the Stoics, they always irritate you," Stockton said with amusement.

"I don't either. I suppose that's why he's been out there for over a year," he said slyly, his eyes sparkling. "To tell the truth I probably threw the books out the door in a fit of temper and Maymie straightened them. So, Stockton. It's good to see you. How are things at The Cedars?"

"Busy, noisy, and . . . bewildering," Stockton answered hesitantly. "That's one reason I came, sir. I need your help with the children, especially Dolly."

"So I hear," Cash said, chuckling. "How do you educate and inspire a five-year-old girl who's already searching for the world in poetry and God in the Old Testament?" At Stockton's quizzical glance he said, "Trista and McKean came to see me on Sunday afternoon, after church. I wanted to hear all about Lorna's debut, and they told me about Dolly."

Stockton nodded. "I'd really appreciate it, sir, if you'd have dinner with us tonight and talk to Dolly. I know it's asking a lot, but I trust you more than anyone to evaluate her and help me decide how to proceed with her education."

"I'm honored. I'd love to talk with Dolly. With all the children, in fact. You have interesting children, Stockton. You're very blessed, considering that most children are squalling puddingheads."

"Oh, they can be that, too," Stockton said dryly. "I had ample evidence of that this morning. Even Trista lost her temper."

"I'm not at all surprised. Are you?"

Stockton had been surprised; and he was surprised now, by the professor's direct question. He frowned, then stood and went to stare out the window, clasping his hands tightly behind his back. On the street he saw Redmond Kruger, leaning up against the carriage, sipping from a crockery mug, giving narrow-eyed looks at everyone who passed, even women.

"They heard the gossip, didn't they," Stockton said softly. "Trista and McKean."

"Yes."

"You know, it's odd, Professor Dodge. Somehow, worrying about Dolly has made me less angry about all those vicious rumors."

Stockton's voice was very low, but Cash Dodge's hearing was fully as sharp as his eyesight, so he didn't have to strain to hear. Now he matched his quiet, thoughtful tone. "Has it, now. Please explain."

Stockton continued, "I've been thinking about what Dolly's life is going to be like, and I can see that it's going to be so very hard on her. It was different with McKean. A man can do anything he wants, go anywhere he wants, be anything that he decides to be according to his abilities. At least, in this blessed country. But a woman—" He stopped and shook his head. "A woman with any sort of intelligence, spirit, intellectual curiosity—what can she do? Buy another dress, make a pivotal society acquaintance, conduct a popular drawing room . . . and amuse herself by gossiping. It's very sad. Some of the wealthiest and most popular women in our circles are the unhappiest women I've ever seen. Particularly the ones who would say such cruel and stupid things about a lady like Phoebe. And I mustn't neglect to say that it's equally—or perhaps even more vicious—to spread such ugly rumors about such an honest and honorable man like Redmond Kruger. Of course, these pathetic women never think of that. Of him, and his reputation and feelings."

"No, they wouldn't. And of all of the players in this drama, I do feel the most sorry for the gossips. God has an odd way of keeping backbiters in His eye, and it's a fearsome thing to be under God's scrutiny. Still, Stockton, it's magnanimous of you to overcome what must be tremendous anger and bitterness and be able to forgive these people."

"I didn't say I forgave them."

"No, you didn't," Cash said. "But you will. What else is wrong?"

Stockton grew quiet again.

Cash Dodge waited patiently, sitting still, not fidgeting, his gaze on Stockton filled with compassion. He had a gift for waiting, for somehow projecting his patience, his stillness, to the person he was speaking with, to the most awkward and tongue-tied student, to his nieces and nephews, no matter how young. The only time Cash Dodge was impatient and sharp was with adults who incurred his wrath by being insincere or pompous or supercilious.

"Everything is wrong, Professor Dodge," Stockton finally said in a weary voice. "Nothing has been right since Phoebe died."

"I know. Go on," Cash said quietly behind Stockton's back.

"Just this morning I realized how wrenched all of us are, how off-kilter. And do you know how I handled it? Diplomatically. Yes, sir. The calm, judicious consul. Stabilize the situation, normalize the relationship. Then leave and let the aides scurry around worrying about the details."

"You're wrong to belittle yourself in this way, Stockton. The fact of the matter is that you are the bedrock of that family, you always have been. If Phoebe had married a man less solid and grounded than you she would have ricocheted off into space long ago, and so would all of your children. Except for Trista and who knows about Penn yet. At any rate, you are their stability. You are their normality. That's what a good father is."

Stockton was silent.

Cash waited.

Finally Stockton turned, returned to the sofa close to Cash, and leaned forward with his elbows resting on his knees, his hands tightly clasped. "I love my children, and I do try to be a good father. I've been neglecting them, I know, but I'm going to change that. And you're right—I don't think that they're suffering from insecurity, or that they feel the family is unstable. The problem is that I have never been their joy or their laughter or their music or their poetry. Phoebe was. And I don't know what to do without her."

Cash Dodge nodded and then said in a strangled voice, "She lit up my life, too, Stockton. I miss her cruelly, and I can't fathom how you must feel." His face crumpled, his bright eyes dulled and filled with tears. Stockton was shocked; he had never known Cashman Dodge to weep. He hadn't wept at Phoebe's funeral—he hadn't even wept in the consuming tragedies of the War between the States.

Cash pulled out a handkerchief from his jacket pocket and wiped his eyes. "I cry for her less often now. But still I do, sometimes."

He let the tears flow for a while, and Stockton sat in silence. He hadn't wept. Not once. The only time in his life Stockton had cried was when he was four years old, when his mother had died. Since then his spasms of grief—and there had been many—had been heavy weights in his chest, burning in his throat, making his head pound. But he hadn't been able to cry again. Sometimes he wished he would, and now, when he saw Cash Dodge unashamedly weeping, for himself, for Stockton, for the six children who had lost their mother, for the world that had lost such a shining light, Stockton wished again that he could cry. But he didn't. He just sat, stony and heavy-hearted.

Cash wiped his eyes, blew his nose, and shook his head. "Ah, Lord, You sure make it hard on those who are left behind," he said in a low tone, as if he were alone. Tucking his handkerchief away he turned again to Stockton. "So you've lost your joy in the Lord, have you?"

Stockton was taken aback. "No—no, sir. What I said was that Phoebe was the joy and the laughter in our family—"

"I know that's what you said," Cash said with a hint of impatience. "But you know better than that, Stockton. God gives to every man his just and good measure of all those things: joy and laughter and music and poetry. You're not some sort of little mirror, reflecting Phoebe's brightness. You have your own measure of joy that God especially designed for you alone."

"It's gone," Stockton said bluntly. "I have no joy."

"I see. Do you have faith?"

"I don't know."

"Do you pray?"

Stockton's mouth twisted. "I haven't been able to face morning prayers for the household in a long time until this morning. But I've always said my prayers, yes. Did you know I had to make a list? I actually had to make a list, to write down the names of people and things I needed to pray for. I read it to God every morning."

Cash wasn't amused; he was sharply attentive. "And at night?"

Puzzled, Stockton replied, "I say prayers with Merritt and Dolly and Penn. Simple ones. Child's prayers."

"Good," Cash said with relief. "Then you still have your faith. If you actually discipline yourself to make a list and read it to God and if you can still pray like a child, then you have both a deep faith and a simple faith."

Stockton stared at him.

"Don't act as if you don't know what I'm talking about. You know very well. You know what faith is, Stockton, you've been a man of faith all your life."

"But I just feel so—joyless. So listless. Uncaring and dull."

"Oh, so you feel that way and this way, do you?" Cash said, his eyes sparking dangerously. "Well, you know that stupid cat that Maymie lets in every morning to drink up all my cream *feels* deliriously happy then; and he *feels* horribly depressed and joyless when I throw him out every night. And the Lord God Almighty has given that stupid cat a tool to deal with these feelings: He's given him an instinct to show up at the kitchen door every morning, looking pitiful and needy. And because Maymie has grace and mercy, she gives him all my cream. Do you think the Lord God has given you no tools to deal with your feelings? When He even is concerned with that stupid cat?"

"No, sir," Stockton said in a subdued voice.

"No, *sir*," Cash repeated solidly. "I guess you know what tools He's given you."

"Yes, sir, I do. He's given me faith."

"Well then it does appear that you haven't lost all of your ability to think clearly and logically. I thought I might have to brush you up on your Aristotle after all these long years."

Cashman Dodge had been Stockton's teacher at Calvert Academy in the preparatory school from the time Stockton was thirteen until he was eighteen. Then, in that time of great and terrible brotherly bloodshed, Stockton had found himself serving in the Army of Northern Virginia under General James Longstreet—along with Cashman Wynn Dodge. Even more unlikely and surreal was that the eighteen-year-old wretchedly confused Stockton Lee Livingstone became a sharpshooter—along with his forty-four-year-old bookish professor. Of the five men from Georgetown that joined General Longstreet's brigade in 1862, Stockton and Cash Dodge were the only ones to return alive in 1865. Stockton was finally able to move into The Cedars with the young bride he'd married in 1863. Cash Dodge went back to Calvert Academy, and when McKean Livingstone reached the age of thirteen, his favorite professor was Uncle Cash.

In spite of the fact that Stockton had learned about life from this man in a schoolroom and about death with him in the bloody battlefields, Stockton had never been able to call him anything but "Professor Dodge." To Stockton it was a mark of respect; to Cash it was a bittersweet pang. Neither of them, of course, had ever spoken of it.

Now Stockton grinned a little, and it had a touch of the old schoolboy guilt about it. "Too late, Professor. I've read everything in my library two or three times since Phoebe died, including Aristotle, old newspapers, *Godey's Lady's Book,* and Grimm's Fairy Tales."

"Interesting choice of—wait a minute," Cash said, and he narrowed his bright blue eyes and squinted off into the distance. "Grimm's Fairy Tales—yes, yes, I meant to—just a minute—" He stood up and hurried to his littered library table, shuffling papers this way, books that way, finally finding a pen. Turning over an already annotated, underlined, wrinkled, dog-eared piece of paper he wrote, muttering, "Greek *logos,* logic . . . akin to Greek *legein?* Legend? *Legein,* to gather, say, *logos*—speech, word, reason . . ."

Stockton watched him with affection, used to these little flights of scholarliness. Then, when he heard what Cash was muttering to himself—sort of a verbal punctuation of his train of thought—Stockton said, "Logic and legend? That's odd. That's partly—sort of—one thing I wanted to discuss with you, Professor."

"Oh yes?" Cash said, snapping up alertly. "Grimm's Fairy Tales. Legends . . . Germanic legends. Logic . . . German logic. Trying to get into Bismarck's head again, are we?"

"Why—yes, sir," Stockton answered. After all these years and miles, Cash Dodge's astuteness still could surprise him. The old man's brain was just as keen and sharp as his eyesight had always been.

"Samoa?" Cash asked, coming back to sit in his chair, cocking his head to watch Stockton like some predatory bird. "You mean you're actually interested in something outside The Cedars again?"

"To my great surprise, yes, sir, I am," Stockton answered. "As a matter of fact I—I—" He hesitated, his brow wrinkling.

"Just say it, Stockton, you're not some illiterate inarticulate fluff-brained schoolboy."

Stockton swallowed hard. "I've been thinking about accepting the Samoan consulate. Isn't that unthinkable? Impossible?"

Once again Cash Dodge shocked Stockton. The old man's eyes flared up into a glinting blue, he slapped his knee, and threw back his head, and laughed. Stockton stared at him, his expression both concerned and bewildered. Finally Cash wiped his eyes, teary from laughter this time, and said in a booming voice, "Stockton Lee Livingstone, nothing—absolutely eternally nothing—is impossible with God! Thanks be unto Him, great and glorious, you're actually alive in there!"

"Well, yes, sir," Stockton muttered, just a bit ungraciously. "But maybe not quite sane again yet."

"You think not?" Cash said, his cheeks and the top of his shiny head growing an excited pink. "Then wait until you hear this. I'm going with you!"

A Big, Big Decision

Stockton looked down the long expanse of the gleaming mahogany dining table at the stunned faces of each of his children, waited some more, then finally gave up and resumed eating his hot plum tart and sipping his coffee.

On his right, Miss Wardwell looked utterly terrified; on his left, Uncle Cash looked smug. Next to Miss Wardwell, McKean was still blinking, his brow wrinkled; then Dolly, with her little mouth open in a pink *O;* then Penn, who was grinning and shoveling whipped cream into his mouth just as fast as he could. Not plum tart with whipped cream—just the whipped cream. Since Trista, next to him at the opposite end of the table, wasn't paying any attention to him at all, he spooned mounds and mounds of the froth into his mouth. On her right Merritt's eyes were as round as marbles. Next to him, on Uncle Cash's left, Lorna sat, her expression as bewildered as if her father had suddenly started speaking in a foreign language—a really strange, unknowable foreign language such as Finno-Ugric or Etruscan.

"Sir—I'm going," McKean said after swallowing hard. "Right? You want me to go, don't you? I can help you, I can—"

Merritt jumped out of his chair, ran to the dining room door, and disappeared, his quick light footsteps fading as he crossed the entrance hall.

"Wait, Merritt!" Penn shouted, scrambled down from the two volumes of the Oxford English Dictionary propping him up in his chair, and scurried off after Merritt.

"What—" Stockton began, startled.

Dolly jumped up and ran out. They heard her, for a few seconds, tripping lightly up the stairs.

"Oh, dear," Miss Wardwell said, flapping. "Those children know better than to run out without excusing themselves."

"But where are they going?" Stockton blustered. "Are they frightened?"

"Oh no, no, sir," Miss Wardwell said hastily. "I'm sure Merritt's going to your library to get the globe—he and Penn will likely roll it in here like some great India rubber ball in a moment, if someone doesn't stop them."

"But—" Stockton began.

Uncle Cash interrupted him with glee. He was having a very good day and dinner had been excellent. "Let the boys bring it in, Stockton. Even if they roll it with a stick like a hoop they probably won't hurt it. What better toy for children to play with? But, Miss Wardwell, may I ask where might Dolly have gone? She doesn't strike me as a globe-plunderer."

"No, she would never," Miss Wardwell said, slightly shocked. "I'm sure she's gone to get the world map. The Mercator projection. Just yesterday I taught her about it."

"Did you now?" Uncle Cash said alertly. "How did you illustrate to her the conformation?"

Miss Wardwell blushed a little, but she didn't flap. Oddly enough, Uncle Cash and Stockton were the only two men who seemed not to frighten her. "I—I managed to peel an orange, whole, in one single peel so that it would lay flat. Dolly immediately understood. Then we drew sample latitude and longitude lines on another orange, peeled it, and laid it down. It illustrated the necessary projections perfectly."

Uncle Cash smiled with delight. "Why, Miss Wardwell, that's positively brilliant! I never thought of using such a tool to illustrate the Mercator projection to young children. Then again, I probably was never agile enough to peel an orange in one single peel."

Miss Wardwell looked distressed. "Actually, it took me seven practice oranges, and then we used two more. Mrs. Cross was very—er—"

"Cross?" Uncle Cash suggested mischievously.

"Yes. But we did, after all, eat them. It's not as if they were wasted," Miss Wardwell finished with satisfaction.

"You and the children ate nine oranges?" Stockton asked, eyebrows high.

"Father!" Trista called, much too loudly and brusquely from the far end of the table. "Did you say—you really meant—that is—"

"You want to go to Samoa," Lorna said slowly, staring at her father, "and you want us to go with you? All of us? Me?"

"Oh, dear," Miss Wardwell murmured. Her hair was coming out of the comb on the left side and nervously she tried to tuck it up, but was unsuccessful.

"No, Miss Wardwell," Stockton said gently. "I would never ask you to go."

"Oh, thank you, sir," she said fervently.

Shuffling footsteps and loud thumps sounded down the hall. Then Merritt came in, his face red, his nose running, puffing, holding the great globe, still fastened in its cast-iron stand. Penn was manfully lugging the end of the stand. "I found it!" Merritt gasped. "It's all the way out in the middle of the ocean! At the end of the world!"

Penn dropped the stand and clambered back up on his seat. With a careful sidelong glance at Trista, he started shoveling whipped cream again. In a sticky, muffled voice he said, "Miss Wardwell said the world is an orange. But *I* think an orange is like the world."

Stockton couldn't help but smile. Aside he murmured to Cash, "At least there's one of my children that I don't have to worry about being a tortured genius."

"Mmm," Uncle Cash said noncommittally, staring hard at Penn.

Dolly came back in, the enormous map flapping like a train behind her. "I found it."

"I found it first," Merritt said. He and McKean had managed to get the heavy globe upright, and now Merritt stood, pointing to what looked like an empty patch of blue Pacific with a few dust motes on it. "It's there! That's it! Samoa!"

"All right, son, sit down. Dolly, give the map to McKean and please take your seat again," Stockton said firmly. Obediently Merritt and Dolly sat down while McKean rolled the map. "Now I'm glad that you're excited, so we won't talk about the necessity of excusing oneself from the table in a Christian manner right now."

Dolly and Merritt looked crestfallen, though Penn didn't.

Stockton went on in the same firm tone, "And, Merritt, your nose is running. Do you have a handkerchief?"

"Yes, sir," Merritt said, fumbling in his pocket.

"Then use it. And I insist that you calm down, or you really will be bedridden."

"And then we'll all go to Samoa without you," Dolly said slyly.

"Father!" Merritt said, his eyes enormous.

"Of course we won't, Merritt. But aside from going to Samoa, I just don't want you to get overexcited and make yourself ill," Stockton said gently.

"I don't feel really ill, Father," Merritt said. "My nose is running like a leaky pump but my chest doesn't feel funny and my throat isn't sore. Honestly."

Stockton shifted his gaze to Miss Wardwell. "He did rest quietly much of the day, sir, and never developed a fever," she assured him.

"I feel very well, sir," Merritt said stoutly. "Very."

"All right, I'm glad. Very," Stockton said, smiling. "Now before we were so rudely interrupted by heathen children streaming away from the table like a bunch of startled geese, I was trying to tell you that I'm considering taking the consulate of Samoa, that I have spoken to the president and the secretary of state about it, and they have formally offered me the position. I've also spoken to Professor Dodge and he has made a most generous offer to help us work this out, if that's what we decide to do. Because naturally I would never consider such a thing without talking to all of you about it, and, in truth, asking all of you if it's something you would like to consider."

"I'm going," McKean said vehemently.

"Me, too! I have to go, Father," Merritt said, pleading.

Dolly and Penn piped up together, "Me, too! Me! Me!"

Stockton raised his hand. "All of you let me finish, please. Understand that I'm not talking about us just throwing on our pirate clothes, sticking our knives in our teeth, setting our parrots on our shoulder, hoisting the Jolly Roger, and sailing off to a desert island to dig for buried treasure."

"Coo-ee," Merritt said, awed.

Treasure Island," Dolly said smugly.

"*Not* Treasure Island," Stockton said sternly. "That's my point. This is not a holiday. This is my work, and I will be very busy with that work, and I will have to work hard. Otherwise I would never consider going to Samoa, because that is my duty, to do my work."

"Uh-oh," McKean muttered. "I heard the dutiful word."

"That's right," Stockton said sternly, gazing around at each of the children. "And all of you will have your duties, too."

"Aww," Merritt groaned. "School? Even in Samoa?"

"Of course in Samoa," Stockton answered.

Merritt's eyes brightened. "Is that what Uncle Cash is doing here? Is he going to go with us and be our tutor?"

"It's very rude to make reference in third person when the person is present," Uncle Cash said crisply. "Just listen to what your father is desperately trying to say between the interruptions of impertinent young men." This was directed at McKean, and he looked just as guilty and fidgety as did Merritt.

Stockton continued, "Actually he has consented to be Dolly's tutor, and I hadn't thought of foisting the entire gaggle of you—"

"Gaggle of geese." Dolly giggled.

"Gaggle geese," Penn repeated thoughtfully.

"I'll take them all, Stockton," Uncle Cash said expansively. "Three for the price of one."

Doubtfully Stockton said, "You will? That's very generous—and courageous—of you, sir. Now, Merritt, Dolly, Penn, you may be excused to consider while I talk to McKean and Trista and Lorna. The only other thing that I want to tell you is that before we make a final decision, I'll come up to pray with you about it. You know that we must never make any decisions, whether they're big ones or small ones, without first asking the Lord."

"A big, big decision!" Penn said happily as he hopped down. He had a blob of whipping cream on his upper lip.

"Aw, I want to stay downstairs," Merritt protested.

Miss Wardwell rose and took charge. "No, Merritt, your father is right. You may not be ill, but you do need your rest. Dolly, come along and bring the map. If all of you will wash up and get dressed for bed quickly and without complaint, then perhaps we will have time to trace possible routes to Samoa."

After they left—the children's high voices squeaking excitedly all the way up the stairs—Stockton turned back to the table. "Trista, dear, why don't you come up and sit by me? Unless you're too stunned, that is."

Rising and taking Miss Wardwell's vacated seat at Stockton's right, Trista murmured, "Why, no, of course not. That is—yes, I am. Stunned." She searched her father's face, her hazel eyes darkening to a rich olive brown. "Father, I don't want to intrude on you, but you look—almost—happy. More animated than I've ever seen since . . ."

Stockton patted her small hands, clasped lightly on the table. "Since your mother died? Happy . . . I don't know. Animated, yes, that's a good word for it. Today is the first day since she died that I've actually felt something like anticipation, that I've actually been looking forward instead of behind."

A rather awkward silence descended on the small group. Stockton was not the type of man to speak of such intimacies to anyone, and McKean, Trista, and Lorna dropped their eyes. Cash watched them all, his hawklike gaze soft and compassionate.

Stockton cleared his throat and said in a businesslike tone, "Now then, I would like to talk about the situation in Samoa as it affects us, and tell you of the alternatives that I and your uncle Cash have considered for you, Lorna, and you, Trista.

"When the president first approached me about going to Samoa, I only thought of making a short visit as a special envoy, perhaps taking all of you and staying for a month. Right now Samoa does have a capable and competent young consul, Harold Marsh Sewall. But he wants to come back to the States for a while. As I studied his dispatches and some other information I had on Samoa, I realized that because of the particular complexities of Samoan politics, a special envoy on temporary assignment would not be a suitable way for the Foreign Office to deal with Samoa."

Comprehension smoothed McKean's face. "Samoans, they would have a tribal hierarchy, yes?"

"Yes," Stockton said, watching him with interest. "Basically they are more tightly knit than many other Micronesians and Polynesians—the tribes are small family groups. But there is still an overall tribal structure."

McKean nodded. "So a full consul would be considered a tribal chief, but a temporary envoy, no matter how special, would not be viewed as a figure with any real authority."

"Exactly," Stockton said, pleased. "In fact, the Germans made a mistake like this last year. For some reason, they sent a man named Captain Brandeis who is exercising all the authority of both the consulate and the German firm. This firm—it has a long involved German name, but it's my understanding that in Samoa everyone just calls it 'The Firm'—does actually seem to be the representative German government in Samoa, in actuality if not in name. And so this Captain Brandeis was sent by the German foreign office to manage the Samoans; but when they sent him he was instructed to pose as a clerk for The Firm." He shook his head. "The Samoans had no respect for him, and he was obliged to manifest his authority in a military manner and it has caused untold problems."

"Prussians," Uncle Cash muttered. "How could such a brilliant, artistic, valiant people be so thick-brained, childish, and needlessly suspicious?"

"I'm working on that," Stockton said heavily. "But anyway, that's an example of my reasoning in considering exactly what this position would entail. Trista, Lorna, I would have to accept the appointment as consul to the Samoan Islands for at least one year. That means actually moving us to Samoa. Now, Trista, I know—at least, I've finally come out of some of the fog to realize that you would probably want to go back to Vassar in the fall. And you, Lorna. I haven't yet come out of the fog enough to have made any arrangements, but I can see that you might be much more interested in staying here and getting some professional music training.

"So what I propose is that, if you like, you might want to come to Samoa for a month, and then return for the fall terms. You could go back to Vassar, Trista, and of course you could stay with Aunt and Uncle Dodge in Poughkeepsie if you wouldn't like to board at school.

"Lorna, I would either engage a suitable music tutor for you here and you could continue at Miss Darlene's, or if you prefer I would be glad to find you a special tutor in New York. I've already thought of two expert teachers who would take you, one French and one Viennese. Both of them would be excellent tutors. Your cousin Leland Colden would be very happy for you to stay with them, I know. And if you two decide to stay here, Uncle Cash has offered to move into The Cedars and help you and take care of you."

During this long speech, Trista and Lorna never took their eyes from him: Trista with growing horror, Lorna with tears starting in her eyes.

When he finished Trista burst out, "Stay! Here? Go to stupid Vassar instead of to Samoa with my family! Oh no, no, Father, and you can't make me!"

Tearfully Lorna said, "Oh, Father, please don't make me go to the Coldens'! Leland Junior is a terror and Daphne hates me and Fanny sings like a buzzard screeching! And I can't stand Daphne, either!"

Smugly Cash said to Stockton, "I told you."

Stockton sighed and looked at McKean.

"I'm going," he said sturdily, for the third time.

"I'm glad," Stockton said quietly. "You'll miss Barcelona. But then I suppose you could always go in the fall. Winter in Spain is better anyway."

McKean frowned. "Do you have a vice-consul, Father?"

"No. There's a clerk there by the name of William Blacklock, who's been very helpful to Mr. Sewall, I understand. He's the only other member of the Samoan consulate."

"Then you'll need an aide-de-camp," McKean said with satisfaction. "I nominate me."

Stockton said evenly, "That's all fine and good, McKean, but it takes more than that. An appointment by Secretary Bayard, for one thing."

"I'll apply tomorrow. I have really good references; I know a big Pooh-bah on the European Desk that can pull some strings for me," McKean said, grinning.

"Very funny," Stockton said sternly. "It also takes a commitment to a real job. That means work, McKean. Are you sure you want to make a commitment like that? Don't you think it would be wiser to take some time, consider it?"

"Sure," he said, leaning back, crossing his arms, frowning, and staring into space. "Okay, I've considered it. I'm going. And, Father, I know I'm acting like a fool but I honestly have thought about applying to the Foreign Office. You know that Mr. Cleveland promised long ago that he'd give me a chance if I was interested. I didn't think I would be interested until maybe next year." He grinned at his father. Two serious sentences in a row were just about McKean's limit. "But if I have the opportunity to work for the Grandest Pooh-bah of them all—and piddle around on a South Pacific paradise for a year—I would be a fool if I didn't jump at the chance."

Stockton Livingstone had no such limitations. "Good," he said, deadpan. "But if you ever call me a Grand Pooh-bah again I'll fire you before you're hired."

McKean looked absurdly pleased and winked at his uncle. "You're going, too, aren't you, Uncle Cash?"

"Young man," Cash said with satisfaction, "I successfully fooled your father about my sense of duty, but if these girls hadn't decided to go I would have left them high and dry and been beachcombing before you figured out how to tie your lavalava."

"What's a lavalava?" Lorna asked with interest. "Something you wear? May I have one? A blue one, perhaps, or red?"

"No, you may not have a blue one or a red one," Stockton said, "since it is a sort of loincloth. Longer on the bottom, but with no top."

"Oh, dear," Lorna said, then brightened. "But perhaps I could wear it like a skirt? Do they? The women, I mean? Surely they do. Maybe a red one, with bright flowers? To look tropical. Native. Samoan. Oh, dear, will I get tanned? How I hope I won't freckle!"

"You're going?" Trista said. "I'm so glad, Uncle Cash."

"So am I, child. So am I."

Southern Cross

*P*hoebe Livingstone had despised the Victorian trend of filling every room to overflowing with furniture, art, and accessories with absolutely no attention to aesthetics. All of the rooms of The Cedars were furnished elegantly, even extravagantly, with rich velvets and satin brocades and gleaming woodwork and fine art and crystal chandeliers, but none of them glared with the clutter and jumble that had been fashionable for almost two decades.

The only exception at The Cedars was the sitting room, and Phoebe had allowed—even encouraged—this room to accumulate what might very well be called a clutter and a jumble, because this was the room where the family actually lived, as a family. The glass-fronted attorney's bookcases along one wall had long overflowed with books (a staple of every room in The Cedars), so a gigantic mahogany library table had been added, and stacks of books were still usually lying around on the consoles and side tables.

In the sitting room the jumble of books were symbolic of one of the pillars of the Livingstones' lives: all of them loved to read and all of them constantly meandered through several books at a time. The books also illustrated the complicated mosaic of the family, for each person had his own brand of bookmark, and each pile of two or three or sometimes five or six books seemed to be a sort of sculpture with hidden meaning.

For bookmarks, Phoebe had used blank half-sheets of gilt-monogrammed notepaper; Stockton used letter openers. He stole them from everyone and everywhere. McKean, quirky as always, used feathers that he had been picking up around the grounds since he was a child. Trista used small squares of fabric; her books always had neat little reminders of her clothing stuck in them. Lorna laid them down spine-up and splayed, to universal condemnation, but it was not uncommon to see two or three of them lying in a snug pile, spines cozily aligned. Merritt folded corners, but not the top corner of the page as was common in such trespassers; he had always folded up the bottom corner. When he had begun this at the age of five Stockton had tried to break him of the habit, but Phoebe had told him that no letter-opener thief had the right to condemn a corner-folder.

Trista smiled a little to herself at these odd reflections and studied the rest of the room with this new introspection.

The room contained two long sofas, facing each other, with identical Queen Anne tea tables between them; leather club chairs and overstuffed armchairs gathered in nooks in each corner; a Queen Anne secretary; a Duncan Phyfe pedestal-base card table; and assorted console tables, side tables, and pedestal tables all around the room. Here the Livingstones had always gathered each night after dinner (when they weren't playing music or dancing or entertaining) and talked and read and played games and wrote letters. After Phoebe had died, the children hadn't had quite the same painfully vivid associations of her as they'd had with the morning room because, quite simply, that was the music room and Phoebe was their music.

Trista realized that in here, the sitting room, was the solidity and warmth of family, even with the loss of their brightest star.

So here they were, two days after the astounding announcement that they were going to move to a primitive island in the South Pacific. Uncle Cash had had dinner with them and had joined them in the sitting room for what McKean had laughingly called a meeting of the "Samoan Legation." Trista reflected how odd it was for

Uncle Cash to accept two dinner invitations in one week. He rarely would accept one a month and Trista knew that it was because he was poor and couldn't return the hospitality. It had frustrated her mother no end that her (admittedly distant) cousin had such pride that he couldn't make exceptions for family, but Uncle Cash had remained stubbornly aloof. He seemed to feel that he was another of the Livingstones' charity cases, and though all of them had tried everything they could to illustrate to him that they loved him and—perhaps more importantly—liked him and thought him interesting, he had still kept his distance.

Trista reflected that, now that her father had asked for his help with Dolly, Uncle Cash seemed to feel that he had a place with the Livingstones and joined them with no apparent discomfort. She recalled that he had joined the family more often long ago, when he had been tutoring McKean. He took money for that, she knew, but he would never take any sort of loan or gift or stipend or allowance or anything else you could call money from her family. She wondered how he was managing the journey to Samoa, for she knew that he would never allow Stockton to pay for his passage.

Which was what Merritt was excitedly telling her father about now, and Trista turned her attention away from Uncle Cash and Dolly sitting together in a corner, talking quietly, to listen to Merritt. He was standing at the library table. McKean, Stockton, Lorna, and Trista gathered up some side chairs, while Penn sat on the floor, making a card castle on the pedestal underneath the table.

"Across the Atlantic"—Merritt pointed excitedly to the enormous map spread onto the library table—"through the Straits of Gibraltar, in the Mediterranean. And just look—look what's in the Mediterranean, Father: Sicily, Tunisia, Crete—"

"I know, son, I've been there—" Stockton said patiently.

"Then through the Suez Canal—Africa! Egypt! Arabia!—into the Red Sea!" Merritt said, jabbing the map. "And then—and then—the Gulf of Aden, the Indian Ocean, the Timor Sea, the Torres Strait, the Coral Sea, and the Pacific Ocean!"

"You've mapped this route carefully, haven't you, son?" Stockton asked with a little smile.

"Oh yes, sir," he answered happily. "I know all the possible ports of call, the prevailing winds, and I even calculated the sea miles!"

"Did you? And how did you do that?"

"Well, Miss Wardwell helped," Merritt said reluctantly. "She taught me about degrees and nautical miles, and McKean went and bought me a set of dividers, and I worked all last night and today on it."

"And so," Stockton said, amused at the expectant look on Merritt's face, "how many miles is it from Georgetown to Apia, Samoa?"

"It's fifteen thousand seven hundred fifty-seven," he announced proudly.

Dolly, from the far corner, piped up: "Or fourteen thousand eight hundred eighty-nine."

"Well—maybe," Merritt said, crestfallen. "I did keep getting different answers." He brightened. "But McKean said that it was because we don't have detailed charts with precise gradations for meridians and latitudinal lines. With a world map in Mercator projection it was just an estimate anyway."

"That's true," Stockton agreed, then hesitantly, he said, "Son, you did a really fine job mapping out this route. But we're not going to travel to Samoa through Suez. We're going to take the Pacific route."

"What?" Trista exclaimed. She noticed that McKean didn't look surprised, and neither did Uncle Cash. He came up to sit in a fat armchair on the other side of the library table and Dolly climbed up in his lap.

"We are?" Lorna said. "Merritt, show me."

"Well, whaddya think, Lorna," he said, rolling his eyes theatrically. "This is the Pacific Ocean. It's just a straight shot from—from—San Francisco . . . Wait, no, that won't work . . ." His voice faded out as he bent over the map. His dark eyes were brilliant and a lock of hair fell over his forehead.

"Perhaps you might plot that for us, Merritt," Stockton said kindly. "I decided to take the route, but I don't actually have an idea of the mileage."

"Yeah! Hey, McKean, you'll help me, won't you?"

"Sure, Diggers, but later. I think Father's convened this meeting of the Samoan Legation to make some plans. Right, Exalted Effendi?" McKean said mischievously.

Stockton grimaced. McKean hadn't again called him the Grand Pooh-bah, but he had dragged out every odd ambassadorial designation he could think of.

"But what does it mean?" Lorna asked, frowning. "What I mean is, what clothes do we need? Wait—did you say San Francisco, Merritt? Oh, Father, are we taking the varnish?"

A *varnish* was a private railroad car, so called because of its luxurious appointments. Livingstone, Carrollton, and Pascal, Attorneys-at-Law, owned such a car, and the partners used it for both business and pleasure.

"Yes, we are," Stockton answered. "Eight days to San Francisco, then clipper to Honolulu, then south, with one call for water on what I understand is a deserted island, and then to Samoa. It will take about a month and a half, with God's grace in the Doldrums at the equator."

"It would only take about a month to go steamer through Suez," Merritt said half-hopefully.

"I've considered that," Stockton said calmly. "And I've had nightmares trying to envision taking my six children on a voyage that entailed fourteen ports of call in eight different countries and four changes of ship. I can easily foresee reaching Samoa with half the children and no luggage except my hat and stick."

Dolly giggled. "At least you didn't call us the thundering herd, Father. That's what McKean called us when he said you'd never go through Suez."

"And so you are, but since I am a diplomat I wouldn't call you that," Stockton said, his eyes twinkling. "At least, not to your face."

"Did you say a desert island? A treasure island?" Merritt asked alertly.

McKean turned to Stockton. "A clipper? I knew we'd have to sail the Pacific, but is it a real clipper?"

Stockton started to answer, but the convened council of the Samoan Legation sort of went downhill from here.

"I'm taking the Amati," Lorna said decidedly. "I just can't bear to leave it behind for a whole year."

"You'd better not," Uncle Cash warned. "You'd better get yourself a workaday violin, Lorna. A damp tropical atmosphere is not at all good for a work of art such as an Amati."

"Tropical? Is it?" Lorna asked. "Trista, we'll have to have lots of lightweight cottons and linens—and piqué, each of us must have at least two piqués—"

"I'm taking Aristotle, Voltaire, and *Dr. Jekyll and Mr. Hyde,*" Dolly announced.

"You're reading *Dr. Jekyll and Mr. Hyde?*" Stockton blurted out.

From under the table Penn said loudly, "I'm taking my dirk! In my teeth!"

"I don't know about the Aristotle, Dolly," Uncle Cash said thoughtfully. "They are your father's London Excelsior editions. Perhaps we can find a cheap secondhand set in Baltimore—"

"Dirk? Did someone give Penn a knife?" Stockton snapped, staring very hard at McKean.

"Piqué, yes, though it may be rather ostentatious for Samoa everyday wear," Trista said thoughtfully. "Perhaps mousseline . . . dimity, of course, oh, percaline, too. And, Lorna, you must help me with the men, we'll have to have simply miles of lightweight broadcloth for suits for everyone, even Merritt and Penn—"

"I'm wearing lavalavas," McKean decided.

"Me, too," Merritt said eagerly.

"Lavalava," Penn repeated, his high voice rising ghostlike up through the air.

"What about oiled canvas, then felt, then straw?" Lorna said pleadingly to Uncle Cash. "For the Amati, I mean?"

He shook his head. "Rats," he said succinctly.

"Oh, dear," Lorna said, giving up. "Trista, what about satinet? May I have a satinet? Red?"

"Lavalava—"

"Aristotle—"

"Desert island—"

"Taffeta—"

"A *dirk?*"

The only other item of substance brought up in the council of the Samoan Legation was that they were leaving in less than a month.

On July 15, 1888, the Livingstones left The Cedars.

Looking back on the last three weeks, Trista could not frame a coherent picture in her mind of planning and executing the move to Samoa. Every day seemed to her to be much like that first meeting of the Samoan Legation, with a dozen different things being simultaneously flung in her face from breakfast until bedtime. Somehow she had done it, had gotten all of them organized (including Uncle Cash), had assigned everyone different duties according to rigorous timetables, had ordered clothing, had ordered extra luggage and a wild assortment of packing cases suited to everyone's must-have accessories, had accomplished packing and shipping, had kept Merritt healthy, had kept the household fed, had returned calls and written dozens, if not hundreds, of notes to acquaintances.

The varnish was linked with a West Coast Flyer of the Baltimore & Ohio Line, and only required being sidetracked and changed once, to Central Pacific. On the eight-day trip Merritt disappeared twice— on the first and second day. After the first time they knew very well that he would again go all the way up to the engine to torture the engineer with questions. Because Stockton Livingstone was a VIP the engineer and conductor hesitated to ask the inquisitive little boy to leave. But the second time McKean grabbed Merritt by the ear and hauled him back through all thirty-two cars to the varnish, the last car of the train, and he didn't disappear again.

Penn pestered everyone that would talk to him. To Trista's surprise, Uncle Cash took charge of him quite often. Because the varnish was really just a day salon with only four fold-down berths, Stockton had also rented a first-class salon/sleeping car for the girls. Trista slept late every morning, napped in the afternoons, and went to bed rather early. The previous month had exhausted her.

There were other painful incidents on the train. Dolly first baffled, then almost frightened, a shy bookish-looking clerk whom she observed reading *Dr. Jekyll and Mr. Hyde* in the dining car. Unnoticed by the adults, she slipped away and joined the young man at his solitary table and immediately launched into a solemn soliloquy about Aristotle's identification of the soul as the principle of life and how Mr. Robert Louis Stevenson had used the visible, tangible bodily changes of Jekyll/Hyde to illustrate this Aristotelian principle of essence and the effects of corruption upon the soul.

If Uncle Cash had witnessed this little incident, he would have immediately understood that Dolly was simply parroting one of his lectures; she had a prodigious memory. She didn't really comprehend many of the things that he told her—especially Aristotelian philosophy—but Uncle Cash thoroughly believed that many things that children learn by rote do sink in later. It was just that Dolly memorized so effortlessly. For a skinny, blonde, wide-eyed five-year-old girl to start spouting such profundities would unsettle anyone, and the poor little clerk was almost in tears before Stockton rescued him from Dolly's clutches.

On the third day, at luncheon, a steward rolled a three-tiered cart by the Livingstone's table, and Penn somehow managed to grab a whole boiled lobster off the bottom tier and hide it in his lap. When the Livingstones finished lunch and were trying to leave the dining salon in some order (always a difficulty for such a large and generally spirited party), Penn crawled under a table and pinched an unfortunate lady's ankle with the lobster's claw, and then moved to her husband's skinny ankle. Penn insisted that he had just been conducting a "'speriment" to see if the lobster's claws worked properly, and the lady loudly suggested that she might try the lobster's claws on Penn's nose. A sad, noisy scene ensued, with Penn sent to bed immediately—without the lobster—and Stockton obliged to pay for all of the couple's meals for the remainder of the trip.

There was also a very uncomfortable day with a young person named Miss Goodloe who invaded the varnish one afternoon along with her mother. McKean later said that he had nearly knocked down Miss Goodloe—she had inadvertently stepped out of their compartment just as McKean was making his way through second class to the club car—and somehow Miss Goodloe and Mrs. Goodloe had managed to sort of herd him back to the varnish. He hadn't at all meant for them to come plop down and take tea (Mrs. Goodloe ate all of Dolly's marzipan) and then follow along to dinner. They were voluble and eager ladies; Miss Goodloe was eager to exclusively engage McKean's attention, and Mrs. Goodloe was eager and unashamed to ask what everything cost, from the varnish to Trista's satin slippers.

In the dining salon the ladies proudly kept repeating French phrases, but unfortunately they pronounced *menu* as MIN-oo and *entreé* as INT-tray and *aperitif* as uh-PERT-if. Lorna's lips remained pursed, though Trista kept signaling her with warning glances. Even Stockton looked pained as Mrs. Goodloe leaned over to stare at his diamond stickpin and inquire loudly exactly how much a big shiner like that would cost.

Somehow they came back to the varnish after dinner—Trista had great sympathy for McKean now, for she herself felt curiously swarmed and overpowered by the Goodloe ladies—and they played cards and sang (Lorna openly winced at Miss Goodloe's rendition of "Red River Valley" in a painful off-key yodel) and stayed until one-thirty in the morning.

Wearily Stockton said to Trista and McKean and Uncle Cash that night—or rather, morning—"I know that people think that we're in this private car so that we don't have to mingle with the unwashed masses. The truth is that I'm trying to protect the innocent public from the Livingstones."

"I just said that I would stop by their car on the way to luncheon," McKean grumbled. "I didn't propose marriage or anything."

"We have to go right by their compartment to get to the dining car," Trista said. "I may not eat until we get to San Francisco. It's only four more days."

In five more days—they stayed overnight in San Francisco—they sailed out of the harbor on the clipper ship *Air Dancer*.

The first part of the voyage was much like the train trip, with mass confusion and regrettable incidents, including Merritt almost falling overboard and Penn climbing to the maintop before anyone could stop him. But then they fell into a rhythm, a sweet rhythm of dawn risings and ship's bells and to-the-minute regularity of meals and stargazing.

Captain Morgan—it was his real name, he insisted, and he even had an eye patch—was the saltiest sea dog imaginable. As soon as work on the Suez Canal had begun, he had fled to San Francisco from Maine, bought an old clipper, strengthened her with iron braces and knees, reconfigured below decks for passengers, and had even, with fierce regret, installed brace winches and steam donkey engines for managing the miles of sails. Still, *Air Dancer* was a clipper, sleek and fast and queenly. Trista was surprised how much she enjoyed blue-water sailing.

On the evening of August 22 Trista sat alone at the sharp prow, surrounded by webs of rigging, comfortable on a chair one of the sailors had made for her out of folded extra sailcloth. She never tired of sitting here at night, listening to the susurration of water cleanly singing down the sides from the bow, the creaks of the rigging, the continuous rushing sounds of the southeast trade winds in the full-bellied canvas.

But mostly she loved just looking at the sky and stars. She had never realized that the night sky had so many different delicate tints.

On this, the night of the new moon, the color of the sky was a deep blue-black with just the merest hint of purple.

Being a well brought-up young girl, Trista hadn't had many opportunities to be outdoors at night, at least without the shielding glare of street lamps. She wasn't particularly interested in astronomy, either, so the night sky and the stars had never been much in her thoughts. On this long, calm sea journey, however, she had, night after night, hour after hour, looked to the heavens. In spite of her ignorance of astronomy she found it fascinating that she could tell that the southern heavens were different from the northern hemisphere's canvas. She knew no constellations, northern or southern, but always her eyes were drawn to the Southern Cross, with its two brilliant eternal lights, Alpha and Beta, and its poignant evocation of Calvary. But this was the single inspiration she ever found in her search of the heavens. The expanse of delicately hued night with its countless frosty lights seemed cold and impersonal to her.

God took so much care to create this masterpiece; each of these millions of lights are stars specifically designed by Him and live and shine by His will.

So how could He be so thoughtless, so careless, and let my mother die? He didn't care? Or He just wasn't paying attention?

"Do you mind some company?"

Trista was startled but didn't show it. "Of course, Uncle Cash, please join me."

He moved delicately, threading between some complex of rigging to lean against the base of the bowsprit. Like Trista, he turned his face to the sky. For a long time neither of them spoke. But Trista could sense him waiting and that he knew that she wanted to talk to him. Finally she cleared her throat and said in a bloodless tone, "I have been contemplating the heavens, and I see only a distant and unfathomable design. Beautiful, yes, but nothing to do with me and my life. Like a painting that you can intellectually acknowledge is expert, but that evokes no response."

"Ah, so that's what's on your mind?" he said lightly. "I thought you might be thinking about God. Most Christians do when they view the heavens."

Trista grimaced, though he had not turned to her to see it. "I said He was an artist, didn't I?"

"No, you said He was an expert craftsman. There's a difference. But I don't think you were actually considering God, the Creator." He turned to face her and she dropped her eyes.

"No, I wasn't. I was thinking of the God that let my mother die. It just isn't fair. There was absolutely no reason for her to die."

Cash sounded neither startled nor shocked. "I see. So you are questioning the concept of justice."

She was the one who was startled. "What? No, I just—just want to understand why He allowed my mother to die. And I can't. I don't think there is any reason or logic to it."

"That's what I just said," Cash said patiently. "You are questioning whether there is any such thing as justice, what it is, if it exists, and in what realm, either eternal God-given justice or even earthly, naturally occurring justice."

Trista shook her head. "I'm not a deep thinker like you, Uncle Cash. I hadn't thought of these things at all. I was just sad about my mother."

"No, you are nursing the seed of bitterness about your mother, because you feel you have been the victim of injustice. And the fact that you haven't phrased it that way in your own mind, and that I have said the actual words, only means that sometimes all of us need a teacher to clarify what we are really seeking. In other words, a teacher's first obligation is to phrase the question correctly."

"I understand. So, Uncle Cash, do you also have the answer?"

He grinned, and it made him look young. "What was the question again?"

"This isn't funny," Trista said rather sulkily.

"Perhaps not, but I meant it," Cash said, turning back again to gaze upwards.

This confused Trista—Uncle Cash often did—but after heavy contemplation she said slowly, "You mean—it's my question—my own personal doubt—so I have to narrow down exactly what I'm searching for?"

"Precisely."

"But—but that's what I said, Uncle Cash. I want to know if God is really fair—if He is truly just. But I'm not a profound, deep thinker. I can't figure it out by myself."

"Of course you can," he said with the merest wisp of impatience.

Another, heavier silence descended on them. Trista felt awkward and confused. She honestly didn't know how to search out such a question.

When Uncle Cash spoke, he again sounded quiet and kind. "The most famous case I know that tested the evidence of true justice was in the court of one King Solomon, and concerned two women and a baby. Do you know the case of which I speak?"

"Of course," Trista answered. "Both women claimed that the baby was hers, and King Solomon decreed that the baby must be sawn in half, so that each woman would get her fair share, I guess you'd say. But then the real mother spoke up and offered to give up her claim to the baby, so that his life would be spared."

"Yes, that's the test case I'm speaking of," Uncle Cash said. "But aside from the particulars, what is the first thing that was necessary for justice to be served? What is the first thing that King Solomon needed to know before he could make a truly just decision?"

Slowly Trista answered, "Why . . . I suppose he needed to know, first, who the real mother was."

"Exactly," Uncle Cash said with satisfaction. "He needed to know the truth. The truth must be ascertained before justice could be served. Only truth can shed light on justice."

Trista said slowly, "So . . . so . . . Oh, Uncle Cash, this is ridiculous! Men from the beginning of time have gone on the search for Truth—Diogenes and his lamp, Plato, Socrates, Aristotle—it's absurd that I would attempt such a—such a—quest!"

He turned again and smiled. "I can give you a hint, Trista."

"All right, Teacher, sir," she said dryly. "Give me a hint. Just to get me started."

"Jesus said He is the truth. Not that He knows the truth or can teach the truth. He said He *is* the truth. If you know the truth, you can shed light on justice. If you know Jesus, you will know God. If you know the truth about God, you will know whether or not He is just. Go on this quest, Trista. Your reward will be much better than a Golden Fleece or a Holy Grail. It will be wisdom, and that is eternal."

Trista stared up at him, noting the strong line of his jaw, his eyes that burned, even in this uncertain starry dimness, with passion and vigor. Long moments passed.

Finally Trista shifted and stared up at the Southern Cross. "All this because I was missing my mother," she said lightly. She was much like McKean in that way; she automatically deflected intense emotions and deep conversations. "I talk to you for five minutes and suddenly I'm on a noble and courageous quest for truth and justice."

"Sorry, my dear," he said carelessly, taking his cue from her tone. "Your question, your quest. Besides, we're all questing together. At least, your father and I are. And coincidentally we happen to be looking for the same thing: the answer to a question of justice. This political situation in Samoa fascinates me, and this is an example of why the questions you're asking, Trista, are not just airish philosophical speculations. What is the truth about the situation in Samoa? And once we know that, how can justice best be served? These questions exist all over the world, all the time, in situations writ both large and small."

"That's true," Trista said thoughtfully. "It's exactly right. What is the truth of the situation in Samoa? And once we know the answer to that question, what do we do to assure that justice is served? It's the same process, whether you're trying to arbitrate between countries or an argument in the servants' quarters."

"See? You said you're not a deep thinker. You sell yourself short. Don't do that, Trista."

She sighed. "It's hard, you know, Uncle Cash. I'm not a genius like McKean and now Dolly, I'm not wise and knowledgeable like my father, I'm not an angel of music like Lorna, I'm not even curious and clever like Merritt. I'm just—not dumb—but plain, and rather boring."

Cash said sternly, "That is not the truth, Trista. In fact, it is diametrically opposite: It is false. You must find the truth, Trista. And where do you begin?"

She smiled, sweetly this time, and said simply: "Jesus is Truth."

PART III

As the Sparks Fly Upward

Although affliction cometh not forth of the dust,
neither doth trouble spring out of the ground;
yet man is born unto trouble,
as the sparks fly upward.
                    Eliphaz the Temanite to Job, 5:6–7

Whenever the trees are crying aloud,
And ships are tossed at sea,
By, on the highway, low and loud,
By at the gallop goes he.
By at the gallop he goes, and then
By he comes back at the gallop again.
        "Windy Nights," *A Child's Garden of Verses*
                    Robert Louis Stevenson

The Forbidden Land

*I*t was a rich emerald isle set in a turquoise sea, with silver rivers and streams and palms waving gracefully like hula dancers. Apia, the port of the Samoan Island of Upolu, was shaped like a big *C*, and consisted of a string of tiny villages, or settlements, right along the curved coastline. Two rivers in the belly of the *C*, the Mulivai and the Vaisangano, flowed fast and cold out of the interior heights to roar right into the bay. Behind the town the mountains, verdant and misty, soared to a perfect cloudless cobalt sky.

The Samoan Legation—which was, of course, the Livingstone family and their uncle Cash—crowded into the prow of *Air Dancer*, hungry to see their new home. Merritt lifted his face to the hot sun and sniffed appreciatively. "Smells like fish and hot sand and flowers and there's even that green earthy smell on the wind," he said to his father. "Wonder if I'll be able to go botanizing and get samples of rocks and flowers and bugs and grass and the soils and—and—I wonder if they have orchids?"

Stockton smiled down at him and ruffled his thick dark blond hair.

Mr. Ailes, the first officer (who had shown a marked, almost reverential awe for Lorna), huddled near her and explained the geography. "To the west—no, Miss Livingstone, that would be to your right—that little skinny finger of land is Mulinuu, where The Firm's offices and settlement is located, all along the coast to that next little huddle of buildings, which is called Matafele. Then there you see the Mulivai River; that's like a border, I guess you'd say. Past the Mulivai are the English settlements and houses and consulate. Then down east—to your left, that's very good, Miss Livingstone—is the American portion of Apia, pretty much past the Vaisangano River."

"And where would the Samoan portion of the town be?" Trista asked politely.

The young seaman, who was staring goggle-eyed at Lorna as she glowed in the early morning sunlight, said in some confusion, "The Samoan—oh, you mean, where do the natives live? Oh, see, scattered around here and there, the *fales*. The open houses, thatched-like. They live in them."

Trista and McKean exchanged glances. The settlements lining the coast were clapboard houses, usually two stories, with nice wide-roofed verandas. The fales were huddled humbly behind. "I see," Trista murmured, but Mr. Ailes was pointing out something else to Lorna.

The tiny bay buzzed with all kinds of craft—deep-sea packets, cargo transports, island schooners, fishing trawlers, native skimmers. Looming over all, however, were the grim warships: the German corvette *Adler,* bristling with armaments, and the smaller American gunboat *Adams.* The two glowered at each other across the small expanse of the idyllic bay.

As *Air Dancer* sailed proudly into the narrow entrance with her miles of canvas billowing, deep-throated booms of big guns tore through the air. As *Air Dancer* passed the USS *Adams,* all hands lined the deck and saluted and the American flag was hoisted as the gunboat gave the envoy of the United States an eight-gun salute. Stockton Livingstone, standing tall and straight at the prow, touched the brim of his hat as they sailed by. He was now the living, breathing embodiment of the United States of America in Samoa.

As was usual with the Samoan Legation, much confusion ensued upon disembarkation. Lorna's violin had been misplaced; Merritt and Penn disappeared; Dolly was asking so many questions of Uncle Cash in her high, thin, excited voice that he could barely acknowledge his introduction to Mr. Blacklock, the clerk who had been temporary American consul in Samoa since Mr. Sewall had left; Stockton, already deep in conversation with Mr. Blacklock, ignored Trista's pleas for help to establish order; McKean dashed off after Merritt and Penn.

So Trista was left with the responsibility of checking to make certain that the sailors had indeed collected all of the mountains of luggage and packing cases that the Samoan Legation had brought, and finding the lost violin, and soothing Lorna, and saying their thankyous and distributing tips to the crew of *Air Dancer,* and arranging for a cheerful German man with a handy cart to transport all their belongings to the American consulate.

It was a nice white two-story house with a long shady veranda, right on the beach, only two houses down from the British embassy. They all trooped into the cool shady interior—McKean had returned, dragging Merritt and Penn—and immediately Stockton and Mr. Blacklock went into a rear living room, talking all the way. Trista said, "Dolly, dear, you really must come help me get everyone settled in. Merritt, Penn, come upstairs right now and wash up. What did you do, roll in the sand? Lorna, do please be quiet, I'm sure the violin is all right . . ."

She took them all upstairs, so Uncle Cash and McKean were able to join Stockton and Mr. Blacklock in the combination study/library, a smallish room, comfortably furnished with a Chesterfield sofa and a huddle of manly leather armchairs.

William Blacklock was a sturdy, solid man, with a straightforward, no-nonsense manner of speaking and a wit as dry as the Sahara. "I have kept the embassy white book updated to the minute, Mr. Livingstone," he said with satisfaction. "The last entry I logged, as a matter of fact, was just an hour ago, when *Air Dancer* was saluted in port."

"Thank you, Mr. Blacklock, and I intend to read all embassy logs and dispatches at the first opportunity," Stockton said. "But for now, please just summarize the situation here, in your own words, giving me your own personal views."

"Very well. The German firm, in hand with the German consulate, has effectively annexed Apia—in fact, the entire island of Upolu, and some of the other islands' properties as well," Mr. Blacklock said. "After they exiled poor old Laupepa, the former king, and set up Tamasese as king of Samoa and effectively placed themselves as his 'protectorate,' they are in the position to make laws, to enforce them, to conduct the courts, and to impose taxes, all in the name of the High King Tamasese."

Stockton asked, "What about the tripartite agreement? That Apia shall be governed by the three powers—United States, Great Britain, and Germany? And that Apia proper is supposed to be neutral territory?"

"Ah yes, the Neutral Territory," Mr. Blacklock said dryly. "Germany still insists that it is Neutral Territory. However, what that has come to mean to the Germans is that no Samoan—except King Tamasese's men—may bear arms within the Neutral Territory. As for the other two sovereign nations—America and Britain—they may bear arms, for whatever it is worth; but they must pay their taxes to High King Tamasese of Samoa."

"I see," Stockton said. "And the High King Tamasese does all this with the force of the German navy behind him, I suppose."

"Exactly," Mr. Blacklock answered. "As you know, Mr. Sewall protested formally whenever the opportunity presented itself. And Mr. Moors, who owns much Samoan property and the big general store you saw in the American quarter, has refused to pay his taxes. But so far, he is the only one. Captain Brandeis has spoken with him, but the captain gave Mr. Moors no cause for alarm. The Germans aren't quite prepared to threaten physical harm to a United States citizen."

"Thank heavens for that," Stockton said. "What about the British?"

"Colonel de Coetlogon, the consul, is a military man of some wealth and lineage, I understand," Mr. Blacklock said thoughtfully.

"My impression—and this is a personal observation, sir—is that the British government is not happy about this German takeover of these islands, but they are not contemplating a direct confrontation with Germany. I believe Colonel de Coetlogon's general program is to try, if at all possible, to salvage the Crown revenues, but not to get into a posture of open hostility with Germany." Mr. Blacklock, who was a direct and forceful man, stared hard at Stockton Livingstone.

With a half smile Stockton said quietly, "As I'm certain that you had a good understanding with Mr. Sewall on the position of the United States here, Mr. Blacklock, I wish to assure you that my instructions are exactly the same as his."

Mr. Blacklock looked relieved. "That's—good to hear, sir. I am aware that you are a personal friend of the president's. And of course, I know that he is already unhappy with the kaiser over the tariff issue. And this is an election year, after all. So I had hoped that our formal position had not changed."

Stockton shook his head. "No, it has not. Mr. Cleveland is the kind of man that works hard to find a just and fair solution to any problem, and does not allow—shall we say—peripheral matters to cloud his judgment. He truly believes that Samoa can thrive and be a more prosperous and healthier nation with contacts with Western countries, and he insists that the United States be perfectly fair in all their dealings with Samoa. Or any other country, for that matter."

"Of course, the problem here is not America's dealings with Samoa," Mr. Blacklock said. "The problem here is America's dealings with Germany."

"Yes, and that is why I'm here," Stockton said quietly. "To evaluate the situation with Germany, and to offer recommendations to the president. Do you, Mr. Blacklock, believe that the Germans would actually go to war with America and England over these islands?"

Mr. Blacklock frowned and was silent for a long time. Stockton, Cash, and McKean waited patiently. Finally the clerk sighed. "I just don't know, sir, and that's the honest truth. I don't understand the

Germans at all. I don't know if they're just bluffing and saber-rattling, or if they are truly aggressive enough to go to war, or if it's just, if you like, their way. Their manner. They're proud as the sky above, they're touchy and sensitive to the slightest hint of an affront, they're bluff and militaristic, but yet they're also secretive, and even sly. It just doesn't make sense to a plain man like me."

Stockton said intently, "Please explain. What gives you this impression of the Germans?"

Mr. Blacklock shifted in his chair. "Well, take an incident that happened just a couple of weeks ago. A British lady who came over from Australia on one of the German mail packets made a comment that the parasites on the boat had almost eaten her alive. The German sailors—who are not even military men—took great offense. 'This is a German ship, madam,' they said, outraged, and repeated the story here on Apia. It was regarded by the Germans as a personal insult to the kaiser and almost caused an international incident.

"And then, sir, of course you know about Captain Brandeis. We now see that he is to be a sort of governor, military commander, and law enforcement officer all in the person of one man. But he was brought here, ostensibly, as a clerk for The Firm, and when he first arrived he was seen by all Apia, sitting there on a stool, counting coconuts or whatnot. Then he was the one who engineered the coup against Laupepa, set Tamasese on the throne, and started issuing royal proclamations and decrees about the laws, the taxes, the courts, and all. It was no end of confusion to the natives, for they have a hard time understanding why some two-bit clerk should suddenly hop up and be the big boss over them, even over their high king. And I happen to agree with them. What was the purpose of inserting him secretly, as it were, and then he openly takes over the governance of Upolu? It was a furtive and secretive thing to do, and I can find no reason for it."

McKean spoke up for the first time. "What is he like? Captain Brandeis? What kind of man is he?"

"I admire him, in many ways," Mr. Blacklock said. "He is a strong man, with strong ideas; and I think he honestly does love this island and these people, and wants the best for them. And if you look at it one way, his first decree was that they stop mortgaging their lands and pay off all existing mortgages, first the personal ones, then for the province, then for the island, and in that way Samoa would be out of debt in a year. That might have been a little idealistic, but it would be very good for the natives.

"He's taught them to grow cacao so they won't be dependent on the single copra crop. He's tried to form an island army so that they might have a sense of esprit de corps, instead of the old warlord mentality. The taxes and oppressive courts came later, and he did go along with them, but I think they were Consul Becker's ideas, not Captain Brandeis's."

The four men sat quietly for a while, considering. Finally Uncle Cash spoke up quietly, his eyes boring in on Mr. Blacklock. "Sir, I appreciate your honesty and clarity. And I must here stress that I am not employed by, and do not represent, the United States government in any way; so that means I can say what I like. You've spoken at some length about the Germans and the British, but you have yet to say anything about the Samoan view of all of this maneuvering by the Three Great Powers. What about them? What do they think?"

Mr. Blacklock looked a little surprised. "The Samoans? I'm not sure what you mean, Professor Dodge."

"I mean, what are your observations about them? What do they say to you? How do they view the Germans, the British, and us?" Cash said with a hint of impatience.

Mr. Blacklock shook his head. "Sir, if I could find that out, I would have to be a mind reader. They rarely say anything at all to white people. If you ask them a direct question, they will answer; but the answer is usually so obtuse and general that it means nothing at all."

Uncle Cash sat back in his chair and studied him. "I noticed, as we walked here from the ship, that I didn't see one native on the beach. Not a single one. I saw merchants in fine linen suits, and sailors, and priests, and ladies in nice dresses, and children in Western clothes. But not a single Samoan have I seen."

Mr. Blacklock frowned. "Is that right? I must admit I didn't notice. But generally you don't see many Samoans on the beach, in Apia proper. After all, we call this the Neutral Territory, and all three of the great powers are about to come to blows over it, and that just illustrates the confusion we Westerners feel. Can you imagine how the Samoans feel?"

"No, I can't," Stockton said softly.

"Neither can I," Mr. Blacklock sighed. "And they won't tell you. Do you know what they call the Neutral Territory?"

"What?" McKean asked with interest.

"*Eleele Sa*. It means Forbidden Land. For so long now to Samoans, Apia has been the Forbidden Land."

Stockton sighed. "Well, Mr. Blacklock, while I am here to try and evaluate the Germans' thoughts and intentions, I'm also determined to try and understand the Samoans—what they think, what they want for their country, how they would like their foreign relations to be conducted. And in my opinion, the first thing to do to immerse oneself in a culture is to learn their language. Do you, by any chance, speak Samoan?"

Mr. Blacklock looked bewildered. "Speak Samoan? Oh no, sir. And I don't mean to tell you your business, sir, but there's really no need to learn the language. Most all natives speak English. Because of the missionaries, sir. Most of them are British or American. And the Samoans are generally very devout and dedicated Christians, sir, and they revere the missionaries."

Stockton nodded. "Yes, so I understand. But my point is, Mr. Blacklock, that I wish to learn about the Samoan mind-set and culture, and so I would very much like to learn their language. Could you, perhaps, recommend someone to teach me?"

"It'll probably take him a week or so at least," McKean said dryly. "My father picks up languages easily."

"Is that so?" Mr. Blacklock said with interest. "That's a gift indeed, Mr. Livingstone. I never had the knack with any lingo, especially Polynesian. I almost never got down *hic haec hoc*. Now, let me see . . . a native couldn't teach you, they'd never be able to understand that you want the meat of it, so to say, and not just the names of coconuts and flowers and trees and such . . ." He frowned and pursed his lips. "Well, there is a—a person, sir, who can speak not only the common lingo, but also has even learned the high chiefs' courtesy language, which is another can of worms altogether."

"That would be perfect," Stockton said eagerly. "Who is he?"

"Well, that's just the thing, sir. He's not a man. It's a woman. A lady, I mean," Mr. Blacklock added hastily. "She's gone a bit native, but she's a lady just the same. A missionary's daughter of the name of Thoroughgood."

Stockton looked shocked out of all proportion at Mr. Blacklock's words. After a few moments he repeated, "Thoroughgood? You say—is she Roger Thoroughgood's daughter?"

"Why, yes, sir," Mr. Blacklock said, puzzled. "When Pastor Thoroughgood died, we thought that she might go back to England. But she never made a move to, and we—well, we didn't like to intrude on her and ask her why. So she stayed here. You knew Pastor Thoroughgood?"

"I did," Stockton said softly. "And I knew he had a daughter, but—I, too, just assumed that she had gone back to England. Yes, Mr. Blacklock, Miss Thoroughgood sounds like she would be perfect as a language teacher. Would you be so kind as to tell me where she is, and how I might get in touch with her?"

———

Trista installed everyone in the four bedrooms upstairs: her father in the master bedroom suite, Uncle Cash in the second largest, with McKean and the boys in another and herself, Lorna, and Dolly in the smallest. Leaving Lorna in charge of unpacking and sorting out beds and cots, Trista went downstairs to introduce herself to the staff, which consisted of a British couple named Armbruster. Mr. Armbruster was butler, gardener, and footman; his wife was cook and housekeeper. Trista was already happy with them, for the embassy was spotlessly clean, the silver candelabras polished to mirror gleams, the draperies and ever-present mosquito nettings over the windows dusted and in good repair.

Mr. Armbruster was tall and cadaverously thin, while Mrs. Armbruster was short and chubby. As Trista introduced herself to them, she made a mental note to threaten dire punishment to the children—and McKean—if a single word was said about Jack Spratt and his wife. "My father and I hope that the adjustment from caring for bachelors to caring for our family won't be too difficult," Trista said lightly. "The children are fairly well behaved, but they are high-spirited."

Mrs. Armbruster nodded, which gave her three chins instead of two. "We had six, Miss Livingstone," she said. "Mr. Armbruster and I can handle this lot, don't you worry. I've fresh milk and cookies out in the kitchen for the children, and tea is on for you, ma'am."

"Bless you, Mrs. Armbruster," Trista said gratefully. "I am rather wilted."

"Miss Livingstone, we have received many cards," Mr. Armbruster said, looking down his long thin nose at her. "May I show you into the parlor? I've taken the liberty of putting all the cards in there, on the secretary, and stocking it with the consulate stationery. I'll be happy to bring your tea in there."

Trista sighed. "Oh, dear, I didn't anticipate this quite so soon. Yes, of course, Armbruster."

He led the way into a smallish room at the front corner of the house, with windows looking due east. It was a rather formal room, with red velvet Queen Anne chairs and ornate walnut tea tables. In one corner, by the window, was a fine upright Queen Anne secretary, indeed well stocked with notepapers, envelopes, and cards. Trista, in the preparations for moving to Samoa, had managed to order cards, printed with both the U.S. Foreign Service logo and her father's name, shipped directly from New York to Samoa, and she was gratified that they were of fine quality and had reached the embassy in time. She began work on the surprisingly large number of calling cards the consulate had already received, and started her calendar, just as Rokeby had taught her.

Her tea was cold and untouched when her father came in later.

"Armbruster told me you were closeted in here, toiling away," he said, leaning over her to look at the piles of note cards and invitations.

"You know, Father, we have calling cards and invitations from many of the Americans here, and some of the British subjects," Trista said thoughtfully. "And Colonel de Coetlogon and Mrs. de Coetlogon have sent their cards and intend to call tomorrow, and have invited us to the British consulate for dinner on Wednesday night. But there is not a single card or invitation from any of the German nationals."

"And the German embassy?" Stockton said rather sharply.

Trista shook her head. "Neither from the embassy nor any personal greeting from Consul Becker."

"I see," Stockton said and seated himself, rather precariously it seemed, on an armless side chair with spider-thin legs.

After watching carefully to make sure her father wasn't going to end up on a pile of splinters—and making another mental note never to let McKean sit on the delicate side chairs in this room—she asked, "Should I, perhaps, send our cards and a note with our at-home days?"

Stockton had agreed with one idea that McKean had put forward: that he and Trista would represent the family's social base, receiving and making calls and responding to invitations. In that way Stockton could differentiate embassy business contacts and purely social contacts.

"Perhaps that would open the acquaintance on a less—um—political footing," Trista went on.

Stockton thought for a moment, then shook his head. "No, rules for diplomatic receptions and contacts are very clear, and in this case those are the rules that apply. It would seem that the German Empire is declining to diplomatically engage the United States of America, and so we must nod wisely and log it and include it in our white book. In any case, I intend to call upon King Tamasese, and I must apply to the German embassy to do that, so that must be the next contact formally made."

"The next contact?" Trista asked. "When was the first one?"

"It was what we in the highest diplomatic circles call an initial non-contact," Stockton rasped. "If I were just a man I'd call it a petty childish insult; and indeed, I'm not certain that's not precisely what it is, and not at all representative of the kaiser's attitude toward America."

"Well, this is a perfect example of why you're the consul and not McKean. He would have already dashed off to stand outside the embassy and bawl out a challenge to Consul Becker for a duel at dawn. He may still, when he finds out."

Stockton smiled. "No, he won't, not if he doesn't want to be shipped back to the States via the next cockle boat to Sydney." His smile faded. "You do see, don't you, Trista, how these things seem so petty and insignificant, but when you are dealing with men who represent nation-states you must be very careful to analyze every word, every nuance, every small event, in light of national significance? That you cannot afford the luxury of viewing men and their actions only as it affects you personally?"

Trista nodded. "Yes, I see, Father, and I promise you I'll do my best to be a help to you and represent not just you but also your office."

Stockton reached over to pat her hand. "I know that, Trista. And I would like to tell you how very proud I am of you. I realize what an immense task this was, moving all of us here, and it's mostly due to you that it went so smoothly and happily. Thank you, Trista."

"Don't thank me, Father, for it's a great and exciting adventure, too," she said calmly, but her cheeks colored pink with pleasure. "For all of us."

"Yes, it is," he said with satisfaction. "But for now, back to work. I have a rather sticky social situation, and I need your help."

"You do?"

"Yes." He shifted in his chair and stared into space for a few moments. "I suppose I'd better tell you the story. In 1845 my father, your grandfather John Ed, met a young British missionary couple at the general synod that year. He was very impressed with them and especially liked Roger Thoroughgood, a cheerful, energetic young man from Northumberland. Their provincial synod had decided to send them to Samoa, and because John Ed and Roger became friends, he paid close attention to the couple's ministry."

Trista smiled. "I can already guess the rest of the story, Father. Soon Grandfather John Ed was supporting them personally, and after he died, you continued to do so."

"Basically, yes," Stockton said, a little uncomfortably. His father had deeply ingrained in him the reluctance to make any part of his philanthropies public. He disliked even mentioning them to the family. Of course he and Phoebe had worked together to make certain that their monies always went to godly causes, and Phoebe had come to be of the same mind as her husband: that doing your alms before men did no good to the giver and could possibly do great harm. Therefore they continued John Ed's philanthropies, and their own, in complete anonymity.

"The problem came to be that the Presbyterian synod did not support them very well, for one reason and another," Stockton said quietly. "It is true, Roger never had a large congregation and he never made the natives pay tithes, of which any denomination is bound to take a very dim view. At any rate, Roger did have much success with a particular family here in Apia, and he made it a lifelong commitment to minister to them, all of them, from birth to death. He and Adelaide taught the children, advised the high chief, nursed the sick, shared the hardships, worked alongside them, and all day, every day, taught them what it means to be a Christian."

"Past tense," Trista said thoughtfully. "They're dead?"

"Yes, but their daughter evidently is not. Adelaide died many years ago; in 1877, I think it was. But Roger just died last year." Stockton stopped, cleared his throat, and continued in a deeper tone, "He died, in fact, less than a month before your mother did. And I didn't get the news until—if I'm not mistaken, just about the time that Phoebe died. I barely noticed it," he said with a trace of bitterness.

"Father, you can't blame yourself for that," Trista said solidly. "No one would ever think of condemning you for it."

"Maybe not, but I do regret it. You see, Trista, I knew, of course, that Roger had a daughter, for we corresponded for many years. In fact, now that I think of it, of course it was she who wrote me to tell me of her father's death," he said, frowning. "But I think—if I thought at all—that I assumed she—the daughter—would just return to their home in England after Roger's death. But she didn't. She's still here."

"Is she? Is she married?"

"No, that's the rather sad part. I knew she never married," Stockton said thoughtfully. "Let's see, I believe she would be around thirty? Thirty-five? I'm not sure. Anyway, it seems that she's been here without any support from her family. And of course after Roger died I stopped sending money."

"But, Father, you couldn't have known. And besides, how could the daughter make a claim on you? It just—wouldn't do, you know."

"I know that, and obviously she does too. She never mentioned in her letter that she was staying on in Samoa. Certainly she never asked for money; in fact, she never wrote me again. But she is here, and as it happens, I do need to call on her, which is why I need your help."

"But why do you need to call on her?" Trista asked.

"Because I want to offer her a job," Stockton said, smiling a little. "As a linguistics teacher. Evidently she is the only English-speaking Samoan linguist on the island. And also, of course, we should include her among our acquaintance, Trista. Mr. Blacklock says that she's gone 'a bit native,' whatever that means, but says that she is perfectly respectable, and highly regarded among the natives as a virtuous woman and Christian lady."

"Then of course we must make her acquaintance," Trista said warmly. "And the way to do that is to send her our cards, with a note that we hope to be received—when?"

"Tomorrow," Stockton said firmly.

"So soon? All right. With the hope that we will be received early in the afternoon on Tuesday, to renew the family connections," Trista finished with satisfaction. "How does that sound?"

"Stuffy and boring." Stockton sighed.

"Then she will be surprised when she meets us," Trista said, smiling. "The one thing I may say is that the Samoan Legation is anything but stuffy and boring. But, Father, please answer me this: Would the United States of America in Samoa have any such practical thing as a courier? Armbruster told me that there are normally hordes of little native boys to act as runners, but that for some reason there hasn't been a single boy at the kitchen door today, begging for errands or Mrs. Armbruster's cookies."

"The United States of America reposes the great responsibility of embassy courier in its aide-de-camp in such cases," Stockton said, his eyes alight.

"McKean? We're doomed," Trista groaned, and they both chuckled. "No, no, he'll be perfect to take this note, in truth. Women do love him so, and I must admit that he does treat them all with respect and can make any woman feel at ease. I'll explain to him that the lady may feel awkward, and I know he'll hit exactly the right note. By the way, what is this lady's name?"

"Her name? It's Mavis," Stockton answered. "Miss Mavis Thoroughgood."

The Sky Bursters

*M*isi Too-Good! Misi Too-Good!"

Mavis Thoroughgood lifted her head, blinked in the first red rays of the dawn, and called back through the window, "Yes, Lita, I'm awake." Pulling aside the mosquito netting, she leaned out to smile at the twelve-year-old girl with the fat baby boy slung on her hip.

"Your lordship wants pig today, for *umu?* Tui asks."

Mavis shook her head. "No, my plans have changed, Lita, I won't be cooking today. Tell Tui thank you, but no pig today."

"Your lordship sick?"

"No, I'm having visitors."

"*Afemoeina?*" Lita asked sympathetically. The Samoan word was, significantly, translated both "a long call" and "to come as a calamity."

Mavis smiled. "No, dear, these are welcome friends from America. I'll be very glad to see them. I'm going to bathe in a little while. Would you like to come with me?"

Lita's dark eyes lit up. "Oh yes, Misi Too-Good. To feed Vigo his breakfast I will go and come up?"

"Come back," Mavis corrected her. "Very well then, off you go."

Giggling at the phrase—one of the syntactic oddities that the natives could never fathom, but which they always found amusing—

Lita dashed off toward her home, the three fales of *Matai* Nifo Sisi and his *aiga*—extended family—of forty-three people.

Yawning and stretching, Mavis contemplated her reflection in the small age-darkened mirror atop the chest. Now thirty-one years old, she had thick straight almost-black hair, regular but not particularly pretty features, no wrinkles yet but small sun-and-smile creases at the corners of her blue eyes. She was tall and slender, but did not give the impression of fragility that feminine thinness generally did; rather she was athletic-looking, almost wiry.

"And I'm as brown as a coconut," she said under her breath. *It's odd that I didn't notice until that young man, Mr. Livingstone, delivered their cards yesterday. I'm so rarely with white people that it's quite a shock to realize that except for my eyes, I look just like a native woman.*

That wasn't exactly true, for Mavis's skin tone was much more of a golden tint than the dark bronze of the Polynesians. But there was no doubt that she was scandalously tanned. Though she wasn't aware of it, it made the rather average color of her blue eyes look like aquamarine jewels, and the whites of her eyes and her teeth glow. If one could get past the cultural prohibition against white people—actually white women—having any tint to their skin, Mavis would have been seen as an exotic beauty. But of course, she would never have thought such, and that is certainly not what she saw when she looked in the mirror.

And when McKean had found her little cottage the previous afternoon, he had mistaken her for a native woman, for good reason: She had been on her knees, barefoot, wearing a blouse and a lavalava, digging in the flower beds that fronted the cottage. McKean had just walked up to her and greeted her cheerily, but he would never have been so offhand with a white woman, and Mavis had been very embarrassed. He had not seemed to be, however, and that had helped her bruised self-image somewhat. But it was hard to receive gold-embossed visitor's cards from the American embassy with filthy hands, standing in a muddy flower bed with bare feet.

Mavis shrugged philosophically as she gathered her toiletries for her bath. At least today, to receive her visitors, she would be properly clothed. "And in my right mind," she laughed to herself. "I hope."

———————

At precisely two o'clock the knock came on the front door. Mavis received them, graciously introducing herself, receiving their introductions, and invited them in. Cashman Dodge, Stockton Livingstone, and Miss Trista Livingstone went into the tiny parlor and seated themselves on the only furniture Mavis had—wooden frames handmade by natives, with pillows made by Mavis and her mother, stuffed with their own chickens' feathers.

Mavis made quick assessments of her guests as they settled in. Stockton Livingstone was a tall, athletic-looking man with a surprisingly ingenuous and warm smile; Cashman Dodge was openly curious, looking around the shabby little room with penetrating blue eyes; Trista was tiny, delicate, but with a direct gaze and manner.

Social niceties first: Mavis expressed her sorrow for Phoebe's death, which she had only found out when the news of Stockton's appointment to Samoa had reached the island. Then she went on to ask about their journey; commented on sea travel; asked after Lorna, Merritt, Dolly, and Penn by name.

"I see you know of the entire entourage," Stockton said with a hint of surprise. "Would that be because of my letters to your father?"

Mavis answered softly, "In my father's house we prayed for the Livingstone family every day, by name, and gave thanks for you always." This was met with a stunned silence from her three guests. Mavis inwardly sighed, thinking that her native lack of sophistication and polish, which constantly warred against the British reserve strictly ingrained into her by her mother, had again interfered with her comportment with white people. She smiled, a little ruefully, and added, "But I must tell you that not only I, but everyone on the island, knows all about your entourage, Mr. Livingstone. That is one trait all Samoans, whether native-born, German, American, or British, have in common. We all tell everyone everything we know."

"Believe me, Miss Thoroughgood, rampant gossip is not limited to Samoans," Trista said, smiling reassuringly at her, which made Mavis immediately feel more at ease. She had been subjected to much disapproval from white ladies in her life, and she had expected Miss Livingstone to be cut from much the same cloth—only worse, perhaps, since the Livingstones were extremely wealthy. Trista continued, "I had always thought that Washington was the capital city of gossip, but perhaps every city, town, and village could be the same."

"Or fale," Mavis added.

"Fah-lay," Stockton pronounced carefully. "Interesting. Often your father used native words when writing to me, but I am only now learning the correct pronunciations."

"Certainly reading a new language is different from speaking one," Mavis said. "I myself am trying to learn German, and I find that I can learn the words and the grammatical rules fairly easily from the textbook I have. But the pronunciation is something else altogether."

Eagerly Stockton leaned up closer to her; he was seated in a plantation chair next to Mavis, while Uncle Cash and Trista were on a small settee opposite them. "You're learning German, Miss Thoroughgood? May I ask why?"

Mavis dropped her eyes to her brown hands, gracefully folded in her lap. "I'm afraid I'm something of a bluestocking. That is, I love to read, and I love to learn, but my—my resources are very limited. I managed to beg a secondary school grammar textbook from the German schoolmaster, and he also gave me a dictionary. I have no real application for learning the language, but I do enjoy the study, limited though it is."

"So you enjoy learning the language just for the intellectual exercise?" Stockton asked eagerly. "How very interesting. As a matter of fact, one reason I was determined to call on you, Miss Thoroughgood, was to beg your help with a language study of my own."

"Oh? You're interested in language studies, sir?" Mavis asked, looking up to regard him with interest.

Uncle Cash laughed. "He speaks six languages fluently. Picks them up as easily as kiss my hand."

"Not quite," Stockton said. "Anyway, Miss Thoroughgood, as I was saying, as soon as I accepted this post I determined to learn Samoan, but there were no resources to be had in Washington. I inquired of Mr. Blacklock for a linguistics teacher I might engage, and he recommended you. Would you be interested in teaching me Samoan?"

Mavis struggled to maintain her composure, but now, like a flood, the reality of her situation overwhelmed her and a succession of mental images made her cheeks burn a hot copper color.

She was wearing the one skirt she owned which was not visibly mended; her buttoned high boots were eleven years old; her blouse was of cheap cotton and clumsily made; her cottage was tiny and shabby; she was an old maid, conveniently dismissed by her family connections; and she could not bear being an object of pity, particularly from this powerful man or his privileged daughter. The Livingstones had supported her family for years, and Mavis had been grateful for their charity. But that was because her father was a true missionary, dedicated to his calling, and his brothers and sisters in Christ had supported them, rightly according to Scripture.

But she was no missionary, and she hated the thought of being perceived as piteous. Naturally, as she had talked with her guests, she had watched carefully for the signs of distaste for poverty that the wealthy could not hide, no matter how well-bred or well-intentioned they may be; but she had seen none, not even from the elegant, splendidly dressed Trista. Still, this offer from Mr. Livingstone must be made from pity, and pity almost always had an element of condescension in it. Mavis's bronzed face suddenly closed down, losing all expression. "I'm not certain that's feasible, Mr. Livingstone. I'm sure there are others who would be better suited."

"Are there? Mr. Blacklock couldn't think of anyone but you," Stockton said easily. "Would you mind giving me a name?"

"Um . . . I can't think of anyone—at this particular moment," Mavis said stiffly. "But I'm sure I shall."

Stockton asked, "But why won't you consider it, Miss Thoroughgood?"

"I didn't say I wouldn't consider it, sir," Mavis answered, frowning. "It just presents some difficulties . . ." Her voice trailed off uncertainly.

Uncle Cash, who had listened to the exchange with open amusement, said, "Miss Thoroughgood, do you know why my nephew sometimes allows me to come along with him on social calls?"

Mavis answered, "Why—why, no, Professor Dodge, I suppose I don't."

"Because I am old and impatient and have no social standing to preserve and I can if needed speak plain English and not this milquetoast fumble-mouthed flittering and twittering that is called polite conversation," Cash said with satisfaction. "So I'm going to translate the conversation you two have just had. My nephew truly does want to learn Samoan, and you have come highly recommended, and that recommendation had nothing to do with the fact that you are a woman, alone, in Samoa, without any visible means of support. When Mr. Blacklock recommended you to Stockton—and I witnessed the conversation—there was no mention of your circumstances, only of your linguistic skills. And Mr. Blacklock had no intimation of Stockton's connection with your family either, for my nephew is more closemouthed than any clam about his tithes and offerings."

"Oh, Uncle Cash," Trista said faintly.

"Don't have the vapors, Trista. I say it's a great shame when a man can't speak plain truth without someone getting all delicate about it," Cash said with irritation. "At any rate, my point about my nephew's offer, Miss Thoroughgood, is that it was made disinterestedly, with no element of pity, but was merely a business proposition."

"I see," Mavis said, her eyes shining with mirth. She liked Uncle Cash already.

"And furthermore, don't let some misguided sense of pride keep you from accepting the offer, my dear," Cash went on, eyeing her so sternly that she dropped her eyes. "We all know that Stockton supported your family for so long, and now that he doesn't—can't—support you, you must be feeling very awkward. I do, at times. I'm very poor, you know. It's my own fault; when I was young, the Lord blessed me with riches, and I was a terrible steward, so now I am reaping what I sowed. You, however, don't have that constraint on you. And finally, I might add that though I refuse outright charity from the Livingstones, it does not embarrass me a whit to take money for tutoring Dolly. I'm a teacher; that is one gift with which the Lord has blessed me, and I properly regard it as the means that He has given me to earn money. As I see it, you could provide a valuable service, and as a good steward you should extract a fair return for providing it."

Mavis stared at him blankly for a long time, and then she suddenly giggled, a sound that was much younger than her years. "You mean, Professor Dodge, that I should drive a hard bargain?"

"Of course," Cash said with satisfaction. "Stockton's got more money than King Solomon. Make sure you get your fair share."

To Mavis's vast relief, Trista seemed amused at her uncle's bluntness. Though Trista did not smile—she had a very still, composed manner and expression—her eyes were alight with amusement as she said, "Miss Thoroughgood, in spite of my uncle's declaration that he and only he is the true oracle, I would simply have assured you that my father employs not one, but two ladies at the State Department, as typewriters. He has always said that a lady will get twice as much work done in half the time, with much less lolling around for cigar breaks and the Exchange and the trotting races."

"Oh? Ladies do work now, in America?" Mavis said, turning to Stockton.

"They do," he assured her. "As a matter of fact, I saw some statistics just last month which indicated that there are about sixty thousand ladies working as typewriters and stenographers in America now. It has dramatically changed American culture and social mores, and I personally thoroughly approve."

"He means they're respectable women," Cash said. "'Working girl' now means just that."

"Uncle Cash!" Trista blurted, appalled.

But Mavis, who had no notion of any other meaning of "working girl," turned eagerly to Stockton. "Then, sir, I would be happy to accept a position as your language teacher. When would you like to begin?"

"Now," Stockton said, smiling. "You'll find that I don't just want to learn the language of Samoa, Miss Thoroughgood, I want to learn Samoans. Do you understand?"

"I think so," Mavis said cautiously. "You don't just want to learn how they talk, but how they think."

"Exactly."

"That is difficult, for white people. They are very different, in all ways, not just their outward lives, but also their inner lives. Their thoughts, their wishes, their dreams, their longings, their fears, are all very different from ours. I'm sure you realize this, Mr. Livingstone?"

"I do, and believe me, Miss Thoroughgood, I don't have any delusions of grandeur—that I'm going to be some kind of great white father to the Samoans, or that I hope to be high king."

Mavis smiled. "That's a very difficult posting indeed, these days, Mr. Livingstone. I would imagine that sometimes even poor old Tamasese wishes he could resign."

"Do you really think so, Miss Thoroughgood?" The question sounded merely polite, but Stockton's expression was intent.

A hint of wariness crossed Mavis's face, but her answer was off-hand. "I know very little of the affairs of kings, sir."

"Neither do I. Particularly of Samoan kings. I have not yet had an audience with Tamasese, but I have requested a state visit tomorrow. Do you know him, Miss Thoroughgood? Personally, I mean?"

"I have met him, yes."

"Oh? And what kind of man is he?" Stockton asked curiously.

Mavis frowned. "That's a difficult question to answer, Mr. Livingstone, because the answer means different things to different people. For instance, do you mean what kind of king is he? And do you mean what do the Samoans think of him as high king? Or as you say, as a man? What does a British subject think of him? Or a German? Or a consul?"

Stockton looked slightly taken aback, and then he grinned. "Yes. That's what I meant."

Cash chuckled, and Trista gave Mavis a sympathetic look. "My father is insatiably curious. It makes him good at his job, but it can be hard on his advisers."

"But that's my point," Mavis said, smiling. "I'm not qualified to be anyone's adviser, particularly an official of the American government."

"It matters little what you say, Miss Thoroughgood, my nephew will pick your brain about all things Samoan anyway," Uncle Cash said. "So it seems to me that you're accepting a position not only as a language teacher, but as a consular adviser. Ask for more money, Miss Thoroughgood."

"Uncle Cash, you are incorrigible," Trista said lightly. To punctuate her words, she snapped her fan open and fanned crisply, eyeing him with mock severity.

It is hot in here, Mavis thought. *It's so silly, sitting in this little cramped stuffy box when it would be so pleasant out in the fale, with the afternoon breeze. Lord, what silly pride, what senseless vanity I do have.*

Abruptly she said, "I would love for you to stay and have tea with me. I always have tea out in the fale. Might I persuade you to join me?"

Stockton jumped to his feet. "I thought you would never ask, Miss Thoroughgood. I've not yet had the pleasure of actually seeing a fale, and I'm very curious. And thank you, I'd love tea."

Trista, who looked momentarily nonplussed at her father's boyish eagerness—and his very warm response to Miss Thoroughgood—quickly smoothed out her expression and stood, and Uncle Cash stood along with her. Miss Thoroughgood took Stockton's arm and Trista and her uncle followed out the back door of the cottage.

"I'm sure you noticed that the cottage has no kitchen," Mavis said. "We—I—have always followed the Samoan tradition of cooking outside. Even making tea."

"In such a warm climate, I'm sure that's much more amenable," Stockton said. "Good heavens, what lush gardens! And what a delicious scent." The hot air was laden with the spicy scent of herbs and the heavy sweetness of old English roses.

"My kitchen garden, my herb garden, and my cutting garden," Mavis said with pride. "Neither I nor my mother could ever make the Samoans understand what a cutting garden was. And when you think of it, if you live in a house with no walls, it does seem odd to cut the flowers—which kills them—and bring them into the fale—out of the sun where they are most beautiful—when you can see them perfectly from every room." She trilled girlish laughter again and Stockton found himself grinning along with her.

The Thoroughgood fale, which had been built for them by the family of Chief Nifo Sisi, was typical of the native house: sturdy pillars topped by a conical roof thatched with palm leaves. Beams ran along the roof in a grid, so that the woven mats the natives had made for centuries could be hung so as to form rooms in any configuration. Mavis's fale was not strictly native, for she had a permanent room blocked off with mats, where a hammock was hung. She slept there most nights, and like the wise natives, took afternoon naps there with a wet cloth wrapped around her head. In fact, she felt a little sleepy now, but she reflected wryly that, like most white people, the Livingstones didn't seem to know that too much exertion in the afternoon tropical heat could make one ill. Of course, having tea in a fale was not like working in the garden or cooking a pig over a white-hot brick umu. Mavis had learned long ago never to do her chores in the afternoons.

"How far is it to the river?" Stockton asked curiously. Mavis's cottage was a half mile behind Apia proper, close to the Vaisangano River.

"It's just out of sight, over there," Mavis answered, pointing to her right. "Sometimes you can hear it rushing along merrily. But only when the bay is quiet, and that's not often."

"No, you can hear it thundering even now, can't you? A half mile from the beach, and it's not even high tide," Stockton observed.

"On Upolu you can hear the sea even at the top of the mountains," Mavis said softly. "The few times I have been away from this island, I kept listening for the sea . . . Well, here is my fale, over there are my chicken coops, this is my umu. Tui, one of Chief Nifo Sisi's sons, keeps the oven stoked for me." An enormous heavy iron tea-kettle sat atop the umu, steam already wisping from its narrow spout.

The four reached the fale, and Mavis indicated that they seat themselves at a long, wooden table, with benches on either side. A tea service, of chipped and mismatched crockery, was on the table, and as they talked Mavis prepared the tea.

Stockton said, "I know that you and your parents were very close to one of the families here, the aiga of Chief Nifo Sisi. In fact, your father wrote me much about him and also his wife, Pana, and the talking chief, Laki, and the young men and women. There were, I believe, about forty in that family?"

"Forty-three," Mavis said. "They are well, all of them. Chief Nifo is very old and sometimes is fatigued, but he seems never to be ill. All of the family, at the moment, is in good health, thank the Lord."

"Amen," Stockton said. "I would very much like to meet them. I don't wish to seem too curious, but I had the impression that generally there were some of them here, with you. The children, in particular. If I understand these family units—the aiga—correctly, the children seem to feel free to go from one fale to another within the family unit."

"Yes, my family has, over the years, come to be considered by Chief Nifo Sisi as part of his aiga. Naturally the children are often here, because my father was actually the young men's schoolmaster, and my mother and I taught the girls. I still do have classes for the young girls early in the morning, but there are only three of them now that are too young to work."

Mavis prepared tea, all the preferences were noted, and she served with a quick, sure grace.

Stockton continued, "I have been looking forward to meeting some of the Samoan family that your father had written my father and me about for so long. Would you, Miss Thoroughgood, consider introducing me to Chief Nifo Sisi? I thought I might meet at least some of the children today, but since they're not here, perhaps we could walk over to their fales?"

Mavis seemed startled, then quickly busied herself with the tea service, arranging little bits of sugared fruits on a tray. "Um—I— I hadn't thought of calling on the chief—today—sir. He—he might be quite startled—or—surprised by three strange *palangi* coming in unexpectedly. Palangi, you know that's their word for white people. It means 'sky bursters,' because when the white men first came, the Samoans thought they were very great beings that burst upon Samoa from the sky. Perhaps some other time would be more—appropriate."

"Of course, you must instruct me in the etiquette," Stockton said easily. But he, Trista, and his uncle exchanged quick puzzled glances as Mavis's head was bowed. She was not, perhaps, quite as sympathetic to the palangi as she seemed.

The Samoan Legation

here, it's the thundering 'erd," Mrs. Armbruster said to Mavis. "Won't be a moment's peace in this here kitchen until Mr. McKean comes to fetch them."

Merritt, Dolly, and Penn all seemed to come through the swinging door at once, arguing about whether or not Mrs. Armbruster would give them a cookie before breakfast. When they saw Mavis, seated on a high stool at the worktable, all three stopped talking and eyed her with comical round-eyed expressions of surprise.

Merritt recovered first. "Hullo," he said, stepping forward boldly. "Who are you?"

"Here, now!" Mrs. Armbruster said sternly. "Where are your manners, Master Merritt? Just you remember how you speak to a lady!"

"Oh, are you a lady?" Merritt asked, while Penn shoved up beside him and Dolly peeked from behind. "I thought you were a Samoan."

Mavis smiled. "And so I am, in a way. My name is Mavis Thoroughgood. And you are, I believe, Master Merritt Livingstone? And Master Penn? And Miss Dolly Livingstone? I am so happy to make your acquaintance."

Recalled to his duty by Mrs. Armbruster's glare and by Mavis's cultured British, Merritt made a slight bow and poked Penn in the side until he bobbed, too. "It's our pleasure, ma'am," Merritt said formally.

Dolly piped up, "So pleased to meet you, Miss Thoroughgood. What a lovely name. Have you, by chance, ever read Aristotle?"

"Aw, Doll, she doesn't want to talk about dumb old Aristotle," Merritt said scornfully. "Who are you, Miss Thoroughgood? What did you mean, you are Samoan? I mean, I thought at first that you were, you know, because your skin looks like theirs. At least, I think it does, but I haven't even seen one. I was hoping you were one."

"Save us all—" Mrs. Armbruster groaned, but Mavis put up a hand to quiet her.

Amused, Mavis said, "I meant, Master Merritt, that I could be considered a Samoan because I was born here, and Samoa has always been my home. And yes, my skin color is very like the natives', but I am actually British. And no, Dolly, I have never had the pleasure of reading Aristotle. I would very much like to, but it's not possible."

"Why not?" Dolly asked, making a small face of triumph at Merritt. "I do."

"She's such a showboat," Merritt grumbled to Penn, who agreeably mumbled "showboat."

"Because books are very difficult to come by here," Mavis said gravely. "No books are printed in Samoa, you see, and we have no libraries. So books must be shipped in, and that makes buying them very expensive."

"Economics," Dolly said knowledgeably. "My father knows all about that."

"So I hear," Mavis said.

Elbowing to the front again, Merritt demanded, "Do you know anything about bugs, Miss Thoroughgood?"

Dolly gave a theatrical groan.

"Bugs in general or Samoan bugs?" Mavis asked.

"Samoan bugs."

"A little," Mavis answered. "But only because of my botanical studies. I had to learn which bugs were repelled by which herbs and plants, for on Samoa one must find ways to keep bugs out of your food, and mattress ticking, and pillows, and away from your fale."

"Coo, do you live in a fale?" Merritt asked.

"Sometimes," Mavis answered thoughtfully. "In fact, most of the time."

"May I come visit you? In your fale?" Merritt asked eagerly.

"And me?" Penn said.

"And I," Dolly corrected him. "And I, also, Miss Thoroughgood?"

"Certainly," Mavis said warmly.

"When?" Merritt demanded.

"Whenever your father gives you permission."

The children's faces fell. "He probably won't, you know," Merritt said. "Unless you ask him."

"Then I shall certainly ask him."

Three faces brightened. "Would you? Would you really?" they chorused.

McKean came in, yawning. "Heavens, you're swarmed, Miss Thoroughgood. Good morning. What are you doing here in the kitchen?"

"Begging coconut-gingersnaps from Mrs. Armbruster, as is everyone else," Mavis answered. "Good morning, Mr. Livingstone. I have an appointment with your father, but Mr. and Mrs. Armbruster are good friends, so I came a little early to give myself the pleasure of a visit. I hope you don't mind."

"Me? 'Course not. All are welcome in Mrs. Armbruster's kitchen, right, Mrs. A?" McKean said, poking in some pots and bowls hidden under linen cloths on the sideboard.

"No cookies before breakfast, Mr. Livingstone. I have never seen the like of grown men begging for sweets before meals. Here now, drink your coffee, hot as hot and black as sin, just as you like it." She rolled her eyes at Mavis behind McKean's back, a clear signal from one Englishwoman to another: Americans and their muddy coffee.

"Oh, dear, you haven't served breakfast yet, Mrs. Armbruster?" Mavis cried with distress. "I didn't realize—"

"Of course I have. Isn't the sideboard in the dining room loaded down with a good hearty breakfast and Armbruster standing by?" Mrs. Armbruster said, almost but not quite slapping McKean's hand as he continued peeking in her pots. "So why would there be four Livingstones in this little hot kitchen and not in there eating their breakfast, is what I say, when I've said no cookies for breakfast?"

"Miss Thoroughgood had one," Dolly said accusingly. "I see the crumbs."

"Miss Thoroughgood is an adult and may have whatever she likes for breakfast," Mrs. Armbruster retorted.

"I'm an adult," McKean protested.

"That's as may be," Mrs. Armbruster said, lips pursed. "Now get along with all of you. Mr. Livingstone will be asking for Miss Thoroughgood presently, and I'd like to have a civil word or two with her without her having to answer a lot of questions from impertinent children about Aristotle and rocks and bugs."

"I didn't get to ask her about the rocks yet," Merritt said faintly.

McKean said, "That's it, ducks, Mrs. A has spoken. Come on, before she gets the wooden spoon to us."

"Like Mrs. Cross does, at home," Penn said in an aside to Mavis.

"Oh, dear," she said sympathetically.

He gazed at her with clear blue eyes. "You will ask Father, won't you? You promised."

"So I did. I try to always keep my promises."

He nodded, satisfied, and McKean swept him up, tucked him under his arm like a sack of flour, and the four Livingstone children—the three small ones and the big tall one—left the kitchen.

"Whew!" Mrs. Armbruster sighed, fanning her round red face vigorously with her apron. "Americans! They're so—so—energetic!"

"Lovely children," Mavis commented. "One can't help but like them. They're precocious, yes, but they don't seem spoiled."

Mrs. Armbruster floured one end of the table, briskly smoothed it in a circle, dumped a huge lump of bread dough on it, and began kneading. "No, they aren't what you'd call spoiled," she said thoughtfully, her strong hands working quickly and efficiently. "They're obviously privileged, and I guess you'd say they've been indulged. But it hasn't made them bratty. Miss Lorna is the only one who's a mite temperamental, but I'm of the mind that it's because she's an artist, you know. She plays the violin—oh, it would break your heart, it would! And me not knowing a whit about that high-hat music."

"As I was saying before the children came in, Professor Dodge came with Mr. Livingstone and Miss Livingstone yesterday when they called. So I suppose now Miss Lorna is the only one I haven't met."

"That Professor Dodge, he's a caution. And smart! You ought to hear him talking away with that little Dolly. Bizarre, I'd call it. The little girl, knowing about such things as Aristotle and that French-man Volter," she finished with a very British sniff of disdain.

"Ah yes, Voltaire," Mavis said, hiding a smile. "She's obviously a prodigy. Mmm . . . what do you think of Mr. Livingstone?" she asked very casually.

"A fine gentleman, for an American. Kind and patient to a fault with the children. Generous, too. Armbruster said that he saw the rental agreement with that usurer MacArthur, and Mr. Livingstone is paying the rent on that cottage next door for me and Armbruster out of his own pocket. Now you've seen the lot of them, you'll under-stand why Armbruster and I lost our rooms here in the consulate. Howsomever, I'd like to see the day that a consul paid one penny out of his own funds for anything and didn't dock the government for it, but Mr. Armbruster says he heard Mr. Livingstone tell Mr. McKean not to enter it in their expense report. That's how rare a gentleman he is, is Mr. Livingstone."

The paragon himself stuck his head in. "There you are, Miss Thoroughgood. McKean just told me you were hiding in the kitchen, but that the children found you anyway. Have you had breakfast?"

"Cookies," Mavis said guiltily.

"Oh? Are there any left, Mrs. Armbruster?"

"For tea," she answered sternly.

"Oh. Yes, of course," Stockton said quickly. "Miss Thoroughgood, I'm ready for my first lesson in Samoan, if you are."

"Certainly."

Clutching a bulky parcel wrapped in brown paper, Mavis followed him across the hall to the study. They settled into deep leather club chairs, and Mavis awkwardly thrust the parcel toward him. "Mr. Livingstone, I've brought you something that I think will be of use to you," she said, coloring slightly. "I—I hope you—I think you'll appreciate it."

Stockton opened it and found a thick stack of papers, unbound, written closely in a fine hand. "It's your father's handwriting—is it—why, yes! A Samoan-English dictionary!"

"The only one in existence, I presume," Mavis said with some diffidence. "He worked on it all his life. There's also an appendix, with some grammatical rules."

"But surely you must treasure this," Stockton protested. "Not only for the wealth of information, but because it was a life's work of your father's."

Mavis looked down at her faded skirt. "I do, of course, Mr. Livingstone. But I would like you to have it. *He* would like you to have it."

They were silent for long moments. Finally Stockton murmured, "It's curious how hard it is to accept gifts; and the more precious they are, the more difficult it is to accept them gracefully. But I do accept with my most heartfelt thanks, Miss Thoroughgood."

"It's my pleasure, sir." She still did not meet his eyes.

He stood up and said as he fetched two books from a nearby bookcase, "Well, in contrast, my gifts may seem very superfluous. But I did mean to give you these, Miss Thoroughgood, and though they are not so dearly bought as your father's work, perhaps you may enjoy them."

Mavis took the two books Stockton held out to her. One was an English-German dictionary and the other was a beginner's-level German language study. "Why, how did you come to have these books? I know you didn't go out and buy them when I told you I was studying German, because you can't buy such things in Samoa."

"No, they are—were—my books," Stockton answered, settling down again opposite her. "I had no idea that Professor Dodge was going to pack up and bring my entire library, but now I'm glad he did. Please accept them, Miss Thoroughgood, with my sincerest thanks for agreeing to help me. All considerations of filthy lucre aside"—he gave her a crooked grin—"I need your help very badly, and I would be in a sad position if you hadn't agreed to teach me."

Mavis searched his face intently. "It is that important to you, then? To learn about Samoa, and Samoans, and not just to gain some sort of advantage over the Germans?"

Stockton looked puzzled. "I'm sorry, Miss Thoroughgood, I don't understand your question. Do you mean that you think I want to learn to speak Samoan for purely political reasons? Of course learning the language will be advantageous for me in the political context. But I also have, shall we say, a more charitable interest in the language and the people of Samoa. I want what's best for them and their country, and I want to learn firsthand exactly what that is."

"Yes . . . yes, I see that," Mavis said slowly. "I believe, Mr. Livingstone, that you do have the best interests of the Samoans at heart. You truly do," she finished as if she were speaking to herself. She straightened her back rigidly and continued, "I'm afraid that I misled you yesterday, Mr. Livingstone. I didn't tell you an outright lie, but I didn't tell you the entire truth, either."

He became very still. "Please go on, Miss Thoroughgood."

She swallowed hard. "When you asked yesterday if I would take you to visit Chief Nifo Sisi and I just passed it off as a sort of social inconvenience, that was not quite true. You see, the reason I didn't want to take you to visit the chief and the aiga is because they are not there."

"I don't understand. What do you mean?"

Mavis shifted to the very edge of the chair, her hands, clad in old mended gloves, fidgety. Stockton waited patiently until she finally answered with difficulty, "I don't know exactly what it means, Mr. Livingstone. But I will tell you what I do know. The only time I have known the men to leave the aiga for long periods of time, they have gone to a chief's camp in the forest. There they make plans. Military plans. They strategize, and form themselves into military units, and store up food and supplies."

Stockton sat up abruptly. "And then?"

"And then," she said softly, "they go to war."

Stockton's indrawn breath was sharp. "I see. Miss Thoroughgood, as you know, I have only been in Samoa for three days, and I am sadly ignorant of the situation here. Will you tell me everything you know and help me to understand?"

"Yes, sir, I will—now."

"Good." He rose and went quickly to the door. "Please excuse me, but I want my son McKean to hear this." Without waiting for her leave he hurried out.

Mavis felt a vast sense of relief. She knew she had done the right thing in trusting Stockton Livingstone on such a quick acquaintance. To reinforce her decision, she carefully reiterated to herself her reasoning: *Mrs. Armbruster likes him. I've known her all my life, and she's a woman of good judgment and hard common sense.*

He certainly is a generous man. Father and Mother and I never wanted for a single necessity because his support was so generous that we could often afford luxurious things like beef and imported cloth and fresh produce.

He's meticulously honest with money, and that is a rare trait.

He's a good father ... I wonder ... I wonder if he was as good a husband ... ?

Suddenly self-conscious, Mavis quickly looked down, her cheeks flushed, and smoothed her ancient brown velveteen skirt. She knew that there was more to her sudden decision to trust Stockton Livingstone than any list of reasons. She thought that perhaps her heart was telling her that he was honorable and honest, and she blushed, but then sternly composed herself. In spite of this emotional turmoil—

not at all characteristic of Mavis Thoroughgood—she did realize, deep down, that because she was a woman alone in a hostile world the Lord had given her a special insight into people, a wisdom beyond her years and certainly beyond her experience. She simply knew that Stockton Livingstone was a man that she could trust, believe in, and depend upon.

Stockton returned with McKean in tow. They settled in the armchairs directly across from Mavis.

"McKean, Miss Thoroughgood has just told me that some of the natives are in the bush, preparing for war," Stockton said.

McKean's face grew grave, and Mavis was struck again by how alike the two men were, for their basic dispositions to be so very different. McKean was quick and seemed always to be brimming with secret laughter, while Stockton had a calm and thoughtful manner.

Clearing her throat, she began, "First you must understand that I know nothing of actual plans for a rebellion. I don't know anything about numbers or strategy or timing. Mr. Livingstone," she said, turning to McKean, "all I have told your father is that I know that Chief Nifo and his men have been gone from the aiga for most of the month, and that usually means that they are in some camp, preparing for war. I have not spoken with any of the natives directly about this, and they have not given me any concrete information."

"I understand," McKean said. "But my father and I haven't had time to figure out the works here, if you get my meaning. You can help us with that. Won't you?"

Smiling a little, she said, "Yes, I will. And I must tell you that the other consuls and The Firm and the other governmental agencies— the post offices and the crown surveyor and such—are perfectly ignorant of this, too. And they don't have the excuse of only being here for a few days. They don't know anything because they haven't noticed that the men are gone. It did, at least, come to your attention that there were no natives in Apia. That is more than any other governmental officials have noticed."

"I realize, Miss Thoroughgood, that you are a British subject. Do I assume that you haven't alerted your own embassy?" said Stockton.

She answered coolly, "No, I have never been introduced to Colonel de Coetlogon or Mrs. de Coetlogon, and I am not acquainted with any of the staff. As I said, Mr. Livingstone, if they take so little notice of the Samoans, then I feel it is hardly my place to advise them. And no British or American citizen is in any danger, because the Samoans are childlike and unsophisticated, yes, but they do understand that these two countries are trying to put a check on the German aggressions without declaring an all-out war. That is—true, isn't it?" she finished, faltering a little.

"I can't speak for Great Britain," Stockton said, smiling a little to ease the tension in the room, "but it is true of the United States of America."

She looked relieved. "So as I was saying, the Samoans understand that. So you and your family, and the embassy, and my embassy, are in no danger, sir. That much I do know."

McKean asked, "Perhaps we are not a target, but what about simple geography? Is Apia the strategic goal? Do they want to take over the town?"

"Just a moment, son, we have to get this information in order," Stockton said mildly. "You're already asking about the end of the rebellion, and we don't know the beginning yet. Miss Thoroughgood, I am not ashamed to admit that I don't even understand the factions yet. Who are the rebels?"

"Mr. Livingstone, Samoan politics are complicated. But you must understand them if you are to understand the situation, so please bear with me if I seem to be overexplaining. Before The Firm and the German consulate started their bid to take over Samoa in 1881, there were three prominent chiefs in Samoa: Laupepa, Tamasese, and Mataafa." She stopped when she saw the light of comprehension dawn on Stockton's face.

"Laupepa . . . the first puppet king the Germans set up. They exiled him when he couldn't control all the natives. Now they have Tamasese for their pet high king, but I hadn't spared a thought for Mataafa. I honestly hadn't."

"Neither has anyone else," Mavis said dryly. "That is precisely what I meant when I said that none of the Three Great Powers pays the slightest attention to the Samoans themselves."

McKean said, "So—so the Samoans are rallying around Mataafa? Does this tell us what they want? I guess what I'm trying to grapple with, Miss Thoroughgood, is the image of Samoans in armed rebellion against Germany. I just don't understand what they foresee as their goal."

She smiled ruefully. "That's because you're trying to predict the outcome based on a false premise. The Samoans aren't rebelling against Germany. They're rebelling against Tamasese, because he insulted them. They won't directly attack a German warship or German marines; they understand that would be foolish and suicidal. But Tamasese has his own force, you know, Tupua men who are loyal to him."

"No, I didn't know," McKean said. "Guess I'd better keep my mouth shut and let the smart people talk."

Stockton grinned, while Mavis looked a little surprised at McKean's self-deprecating humor. Generally wealthy, privileged, important young men were not so amused by their own foibles.

Stockton asked, "All right, it's the Mataafas against the Tamaseses. What is the grievance? How did Tamasese insult them?"

"Again, it's a cultural matter that I'm afraid will be incomprehensible to whites," Mavis said, unconscious that she was white. "But I'll try to explain. In Samoa, the royal lines are attached to certain provinces, which bestow certain names upon the heirs. Think of it sort of as England bestows titles to the aristocracy. So Laupepa was Malietoa, or of Malietoa blood and title; Tamasese and Mataafa are both of Tupua blood, but have different provinces, or titles.

"The problem first began last year, when Tamasese appropriated the Malietoa title and began signing himself so. Then, just this month, he usurped the title 'Tuiatua,' which is Mataafa's title. So Tamasese managed to insult both the Malietoas and factions of his own blood—the Tupuas who belong to Mataafa."

"What did the Germans have to say about this?" Stockton asked, frowning.

"Nothing. They evidently had no notion of what it meant, if they even ever noticed the way Tamasese signs all their proclamations," Mavis scoffed. "And then, just this month, too, Tamasese began collecting Malietoa mats. I know how silly that sounds to you, but I assure you it is no light thing to a Samoan. Some of the mats that the Samoans make are rather like heirlooms, but they are more than just, for instance, the family jewels or diaries of ancestors or such things as that. The closest analogy I can think of is, suppose your family was of an ancient lineage, and you still had in your possession a tapestry handmade by your ancestress in the fifteenth century. Suppose that your king, who also had an ancient lineage and honors of his own, decided that he wanted your tapestry, too, and came and took it, and then claimed that it was actually his heirloom and the honors of your ancient lineage were actually his own. That's as near as I can get to trying to illustrate to you what a deadly insult Tamasese has inflicted on the Malietoas."

"I do understand, I think," Stockton said. "All right, I believe I see the grievance; I know who the warring parties are. Here is the big question: What is their strategy? What will they actually do?"

"I don't know, Mr. Livingstone," Mavis answered firmly.

The three sat in silence for long moments. Then McKean asked, tentatively, "Do you think you could find out, ma'am?"

She looked at him, considering. "I—no, I don't think they would tell me their military strategy, Mr. Livingstone. I could go to the camp where I know Chief Nifo and his men are and speak with them, I suppose. The women go back and forth all the time, though it's generally the men's wives, and I would be—rather—out of place. They wouldn't be insulted, but neither would they tell me anything of substance, such as their numbers or dispositions or battle plans. They don't even tell their wives such things as that. And here I may add, Mr. Livingstone, that women and children are never involved in the tribal wars. They are allowed to come and go through the camps, and if they should happen upon a battle, all firing ceases until they get out of the way. Also, any pastors, priests, preachers, or seminary teachers or students are never touched."

Stockton sighed. "Very civilized rules of engagement for what we think of as barbarians."

Mavis smiled. "Oh, I suppose they might be called barbarians. For instance, they do take trophy heads. Once a missionary asked a chief how they could do such things, and he replied, 'Is it not so that when David killed Goliath, he cut off his head and carried it before the king?'"

Stockton and McKean looked taken aback and then chuckled. "Wonder what the minister answered?" McKean said.

"That part is not known in Samoan lore," Mavis said primly, but her blue eyes were sparkling.

Stockton grew serious, and he leaned forward intently toward Mavis. "Miss Thoroughgood, I cannot thank you enough for giving us this information. And I understand that you can't answer all the questions we have. But I do have one pressing question, and I must ask you to take your very best guess: Are my children in danger here at the embassy?"

Mavis answered evenly, "Sir, I can assure you that your children are in no danger from any Samoan. But if you will permit me to make a rather impertinent observation, I should say that the only potential danger is from the Germans; and I cannot assess that risk. You, Mr. Livingstone, are the one who must make your best guess about that."

He nodded, then frowned and went into a dark reverie.

McKean glanced at him, then said lightly to Mavis, "Well, ma'am, you sure seem to know a lot more than you let on; it's just that you don't know you know it, if you catch my drift. Would you mind if I asked you a few thousand questions?"

"I suppose not," she said, smiling. "As a matter of fact, I'm very glad to see that you are so interested in the Samoans and their well-being."

"Oh, all of us are, I can assure you, Miss Thoroughgood. We're nosy like that. We're the Samoan Legation, don't you know. Hey, you want to join? You've already been in our first council of war."

"Have I?" Mavis said. "Oh, dear. I'm beginning to feel like a traitor to the queen and crown and John Bull and all that rot."

"Only if old Colonel de Coetlogon declares war against us."

"Unlikely. There, I feel better. But about joining the Samoan Legation, I promised that I would ask you, Mr. Livingstone, if the children could come visit me."

Stockton, who was still deep in thought, looked up. "Hmm? You want my children to come visit you? You are a courageous woman, Miss Thoroughgood."

"I think they are charming. No, actually, I think they're interesting. That's even better. It would be my pleasure, sir."

"All right. I think it would be wonderful for them, Miss Thoroughgood, and I thank you. But for right now, I would like to ask you to stay and have dinner with us tonight, and then, perhaps, we might have another council of war after dinner? If you've decided to join the Samoan Legation, that is?"

Mavis blushed. "I—I would be honored, sir. Would there, by chance, be any ribbons or garters or scepters given to new members?"

"Nah, you just get the honor of running with the thundering herd," McKean said. "But, Miss Thoroughgood, I think you're just the lady for it."

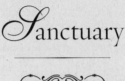

Sanctuary

They prayed now.

Stockton reflected, as he closed morning prayers, how much the Livingstones' world had changed—and how much he had changed. Before, in the dreary dimness that shrouded him after Phoebe's death, his prayers had seemed to be so artificial, so lifeless. Now the family's morning prayers were alive and sincere and the Lord seemed, in this time and place, to be making His presence known to them in a special way. Stockton smiled to himself at the thought. *The Lord was always with me, lighting my way. I'm the one who chose to walk in the darkness . . . but now, at last, I've come home.*

The Livingstones and the Armbrusters, with much ado, left the parlor on their daily business: Uncle Cash and the children to lessons, the servants to their daily tasks, Lorna to her violin. McKean and Trista stayed behind. Trista served coffee that Mrs. Armbruster always thoughtfully provided for after prayers, before breakfast; McKean, of course, had dubbed it APBB coffee.

After everyone else had left, McKean grimaced at his father. "I tell you, we are just about the sorriest spies that ever were. I think the Samoan Legation needs a new secret service division."

Stockton gratefully took a cup of steaming coffee from Trista. "I agree. I've met, or had dinner with, or had meetings with, or had tea with, just about every white man on this island. So far I haven't heard a word about any Samoan uprising."

"What about you, Mab? What about your Mr. Herrington-Carruthers?" McKean asked innocently. "He seems to know everyone and be everywhere all the time, when he's not squiring you around. Doesn't he have a job or something?"

Trista settled into an armchair and sipped her coffee. "In the first place, he's not *my* Mr. Herrington-Carruthers. In the second place, he does know many people here, because, after all, Apia is a very small town and he was born here. In the third place, you know perfectly well he works in his father's land-surveying office."

"I have seen him there. But I never noticed him actually *working* there. Guess those pencils and things would get those lily-white aristocratic hands dirty."

Paul Herrington-Carruthers was British, foppish, and languid; but he had certainly shown a lively interest in Trista. He and his father had called on the Livingstones shortly after their arrival in Apia five days ago, and Mr. Herrington-Carruthers had called every afternoon since then, taking Trista—and usually the children and Uncle Cash, as chaperones—for a walk.

"You don't have much room to talk, dear brother," Trista said. "It seems all you do is run around with Commander Leary and get into trouble."

"I haven't been in trouble!" McKean protested. "We haven't done anything. Besides, that is my job. I'm the consular aide-de-camp and he's the commander of the only U.S. warship in the bay. I'm the naval liaison," he said with sudden inspiration.

"You call you two playing cricket for six hours—with native girls, I may add—and hitting Mrs. Nussbaum's poor pig with the cricket ball your work? And you think Mr. Herrington-Carruthers doesn't work much?"

"Onerous duties of my profession," McKean said gravely. "Father asked me to try and keep Commander Leary occupied so he won't attack the Germans."

Stockton sighed. "I have great faith in Commander Leary as a naval officer, but he's a bit high-spirited. I think if I didn't hold him in check, he'd challenge Captain Fritze of the *Adler* to a ship-to-ship duel, just like in the last century, with great ships of the line thundering broadsides bow to stern. Of course, the fact that the *Adler* is almost twice as big as the *Adams* and that it outguns her by three to one makes no difference to him. Please, McKean, keep him playing cricket."

"See?" McKean said to Trista, almost but not quite making a face. "Anyway, Father, he seems to have no inkling that there's any revolution in the making. But as you say, he is a good naval commander, and his job here is to be a check on the German navy. He keeps his eye on them and is always aware of the movements of the *Adler* and the German marines. He does say that most of the marines are actually in Mulinuu, ostensibly guarding King Tamasese. The contingent at the German consulate is nominal, usually four men for show on the front veranda."

Stockton nodded. "I've thought about putting the *Adams* on alert, but it just doesn't seem feasible. After all, there is no naval threat. If there is a native uprising, I cannot see that our navy would have any place in it."

"Unless the *Adler* takes part," McKean said quietly.

"Yes," Stockton said. "That would change the position, of course. But I can't see a foundation for any kind of preemptive action at this time."

"I agree," McKean said, then gave an exaggerated sigh. "Guess I'll just have to keep on playing cricket."

"Father, I did hear something—yesterday," Trista said tentatively. "I don't know if it's actually important or not. Anyway, Mr. Herrington-Carruthers and I took the children to Mr. Moors's store for licorice. You recall their clerk is that charming little old man named Kipu. A young boy came in and was buying rifle cartridges. They were speaking Samoan. But I did hear Kipu ask him something, and I caught the words 'Mataafa' and 'Tamasese.'"

"As in, 'Are these for Mataafas or Tamaseses?'" Stockton asked alertly.

"Ye—es, I think so," Trista answered.

"What did the boy answer?" McKean asked curiously.

"I couldn't tell, because he laughed and said several things with both names in it," Trista said, more confidently. "As if he were saying, 'Oh, I wouldn't buy a single cartridge for X, but I'll fight to the end for Y . . .' and so on."

"Interesting," Stockton mused. "By the way, how much are rifle cartridges in the store?"

"Twelve cents currency," McKean answered quickly. "Between nine and ten cents gold. Each."

"Good heavens," Trista exclaimed, "that is horribly expensive."

"Yes. As usual, the arms dealers are making the money," Stockton said. "But what I find even more interesting is that Mr. Moors gave no hint of any rise in arms sales to Samoans when I visited with him yesterday. The American merchants are not exactly pleased with the United States government right now, but that is not my primary concern. At any rate, Trista, that was valuable information. It is the single piece of what you might call corroborating evidence of Miss Thoroughgood's information."

Trista nodded, but then frowned. "Father, I must say, it seems so—unlikely. Are you certain . . . that is to say, I don't mean to imply that Miss Thoroughgood is misleading us, but is it possible that she has simply misread the situation? Apia seems so—so lighthearted. So peaceful."

"It does," Stockton agreed. "And it is entirely possible that Miss Thoroughgood is mistaken. She readily admits that she has no concrete knowledge of any Samoan uprising. She merely gave me her opinion of the situation, and though I happen to think she is right, I do know that we are merely surmising. That's precisely why I've decided to take no official action right now."

"But unofficially, Mab," McKean added, "keep your eyes open."

Three days later, on the last day of August, it began.

A soft knock sounded on the kitchen door of the American consulate at two o'clock in the morning. Stockton came instantly wide awake, alert, knowing. He threw on his dressing gown, lit a candle, and ran to the back door.

Mavis Thoroughgood stood there, her eyes brilliant in the dim candlelight. "It's begun, Mr. Livingstone. The woods behind Apia are full of Mataafas, and Captain Brandeis has just marched many Tamasese warriors up the Siumu Road into the bush."

"Please come in," he said calmly. "The children will awaken, and I would appreciate it if you would help."

"I will," she said quietly. "That is why I came here."

The entire household awoke when the noise of men shouting, and a few scattered shots sounded in the woods behind the town. Uncle Cash and Mavis took charge, making cocoa and tea and occupying the children, which mostly took the form of keeping Merritt and Penn from sneaking out. Lorna and Trista sat together, talking in low tones—Lorna nervously and Trista calmly as always. McKean left to go to the *Adams* and confer with Commander Leary while Stockton dressed and went to the British consulate, whose lights were, by now, burning bright.

Day came, with only a few distant shots heard all night. At dawn smoke hung over the mountain. The people gathered on their verandas if they had one, and if they didn't, they gathered on Apia's single main street along the beach.

At about eleven, three or four heavy volleys were heard, and then silence. Soon the victorious Tamaseses, about six hundred strong, came marching back in with one dead body and one wounded man. Behind came Captain Brandeis, striding along, his handsome Nordic face grim and pale, a cigar clenched between his teeth. Stockton stepped up to talk to him.

"Captain Brandeis, I hope there have not been too many casualties?"

Brandeis shook his head. "Three of the enemy, sir, and one of my men wounded. My men took two heads, which I do solemnly regret, but I didn't allow them to bring them in."

"Where are they?" Stockton asked.

"The bodies? In Tanungamono, I suppose," Captain Brandeis answered, obviously distracted. "Poor people, it's the worse for them! It'll have to be done another way now."

Stockton wanted to continue the conversation, but Captain Brandeis hurried on. Stockton told Mavis that there were two dead in Tanungamono, a small bush village about a mile north of Mavis's home. Together they hurried there, unmindful of the oddity of the two of them—the widowed Samoan consul of the United States of America and Misi Too-Good, the British old maid gone native—attending to such things together.

They found the sister of one of the dead, wailing and kissing her brother's cold face. Mavis knew the two dead young men and their families; and she wept unashamedly with them as she helped them wash and prepare the bodies and then the two boys' heads.

Two small graves were dug, and at their memorial service, Stockton quoted, "O death, where is thy sting? O grave, where is thy victory?" Then to the surprise and comfort of the families, he quoted Psalm 23 in Samoan, a work that he and Mavis had just perfected the previous day.

Night soon came, and Stockton realized with dull sadness that the first day of the Battle of Matautu was over.

This small skirmish was, of course, merely a prelude. The only reason the Tamaseses had succeeded in disarranging the Mataafas was because the Mataafas had been betrayed to Captain Brandeis, who had been told of the imminent attack during dinner and had managed to form a preemptive strike force. However, High Chief Mataafa, with a keen military sense, had realized he had lost the offensive and simply withdrew his forces and scattered them into the bush. Hence the small number of casualties.

But the Three Great Powers knew that this small engagement between two Samoan warlords had changed the realities of the positions of their countries. Consular dispatches flew to the capitals. Messengers ran back and forth between the three consulates. The two warships bristled at each other across the ever-turbulent waters of Apia Bay.

Stockton and Mavis had agreed that for propriety's sake, she would come to the consulate every weekday morning for his language lesson. The night of the skirmish she offered to put off the lessons until Stockton was free and could send for her. He said with surprise, "Why? No, please, Miss Thoroughgood, your help has been so valuable to me already, I would much prefer that we keep our business arrangement. Under the circumstances, we may not speak in Samoan very much; but your opinion of and advice on events as they unfold will help me immensely."

And so Mavis was at the American consulate every morning, sometimes talking with Stockton, but more often visiting with Mrs. Armbruster or even sitting in on the children's lessons with Uncle Cash. Often in the course of the day Stockton would come looking for her to ask her about things pertaining to the Samoans, though she never, of course, sat in on his meetings or made any kind of official contacts. Three afternoons she and Uncle Cash took the children, and once Lorna, to Mavis's fale for tea, and Mavis took the children out for long walks along the Vaisangano River. She was a great help to all of them in this time. On his part, Stockton (when he had time to think of it) was somewhat surprised at how much Mavis Thoroughgood had become such an important part of his Samoan quest.

On September 1, the day after the skirmish, Captain Brandeis sent the *Adler* along with King Tamasese's "fleet"—sixteen native canoes with men armed with rifles in them—to shell the single village on the tiny Samoan island of Manono. Then he fortified the finger of land of Mulinuu at the isthmus and extended his lines of armed natives all the way around the shoreline of the *C* to the bottom point, Matautu.

And then he waited. Naturally during these days the consuls were very busy, both with the other consuls and with their own concerned countrymen.

On the afternoon of the eleventh Stockton was closeted in the study, composing his latest dispatch to Washington, when McKean and his friend Commander Leary came in.

"Sir, we have just walked toward Matautu," McKean said gravely. "We saw young boys digging trenches and some warriors in the bush, their faces blackened."

"Where?" Stockton asked.

"Just beyond the Vaisangano, sir," Commander Leary answered. He was a man of medium height and unremarkable appearance, except for bright blue eyes that sparkled with alertness and, most often, mischief. Always resplendent in his commander's uniform, he had a military bearing, and was quick and lively in speech and gesture. "Some of the Tamaseses are arranged right across from them, behind breastworks, but they just watched with interest. I'll never understand this polite drawing-room type of warfare. Just take your stand and start shooting, first if possible. That's my idea of winning a war."

"Commander Leary, once again I must order you not to start shooting at the *Adler* unless you are fired upon," Stockton rasped.

"But, sir—"

"No," Stockton said. "There are enough rifles on the beach and in the bush without having naval artillery flying about. Aside from that, I do believe that your mischief has almost driven the Germans stark raving mad anyway. I had two more letters from Consul Becker today, complaining about, among other things, your"—he shuffled some papers on the desk—"'malicious and aggressive insults to the kaiser, his representatives, and to his Imperial Navy.'"

As Mulinuu, at the top of the *C*, was the central command of the German disposition, they often shot rockets as signals to their forces strung along the curved shoreline down to Matautu, at the bottom of the *C*. Commander Leary amused himself at night by sitting on the poop deck of the *Adams* and shooting off rockets of his own to confuse the signals. And every day for the past eleven days he had composed a note to "High Chief Tamasese" (not High King Tamasese) in Mulinuu and had taken it to the German post office and insisted it be delivered. The rather humorless Germans had been irritated beyond measure.

"Aw, rot," Commander Leary scoffed. "I'm simply employing time-honored tactics of peaceable resistance to an aggressor."

Stockton hid a smile. "Oh, is that what it is?"

"Yes, sir," Commander Leary said, then he asked, "You aren't going to order me to stop, are you, sir?"

Stockton did smile then. "No, as a matter of fact, I'm not, Commander Leary. What you do on your own ship with your signal rockets, sir, and your own personal correspondence, is no concern of mine."

Both Commander Leary and McKean beamed. Leary said, "Thank you, sir."

Stockton now grew grave. "So I suppose what you're telling me is that you believe battle is imminent?"

McKean and Leary exchanged glances. Then McKean replied, "Sir, that is our considered opinion."

"Very well. McKean, go to the British consulate and speak to Colonel de Coetlogon. Tell him what you've just told me, and ask if we can assist them in any way. Commander Leary, report back to your ship, cancel all shore leave."

"Yes, sir. I would like to suggest a detachment of marines to guard the consulate," Leary said. "It's not as if this attack is a secret. If we know it, certainly the Germans know it; and the consulate should have a visible military presence."

Stockton thought, then nodded. "All right, but just an honor guard. I hope the consulate won't be in the line of fire, and I don't want it bristling with a regiment, because that may appear that we are establishing a fortified beachhead."

"I agree, sir," Commander Leary said. He was high-spirited, but he was not a fool.

McKean looked worried. "But, Father, it's all very well to *hope* that the consulate won't be all shot up but—"

"Don't worry, McKean," Stockton said. "The children and Professor Dodge won't be here."

The knock on the door of the cottage startled Mavis. It was evening, and she wasn't accustomed to callers. She opened the door to see Stockton Livingstone standing alone on her doorstep, his face lined with worry.

"Please come in."

He came in, taking two steps, and she turned to face him.

"I've come to ask a favor—no, I've come to ask for your help, Miss Thoroughgood."

"I'll help you," she said quickly.

He nodded. He towered over her, even though she was tall for a woman. He seemed uncomfortable.

She took a step closer to him. "What can I do, Mr. Livingstone?"

He swallowed. "I'm afraid for my family, Miss Thoroughgood. I believe there is going to be a battle, and I believe they are in danger at the consulate. Would you take them, Miss Thoroughgood? They would be safe here. With you."

Her eyes widened, then she said simply, "Yes."

He reached out and grabbed her hand, grasping it warmly between his own. "I don't know how to thank you. I know it will be an immense bother for you. But let me assure you, Miss Thoroughgood, that I prayed long and hard about this, and I do feel that this is what the Lord is directing me to do. So I have placed my family in His hands for safekeeping, and I know that His will will be done. I don't wish you to be burdened with thinking that I will in any way hold you responsible for their safety; all I am asking is that you give them sanctuary. Do you understand?"

She nodded. "I understand. I do think they will be much safer here than on the beach, because my fale is behind the lines. And since you have made me understand that you're putting them into the Lord's hands—not mine—then I know that He will watch over them. And besides, I'm very happy to have your family here, sir. I like them."

"All of them?" he asked with a faint smile.

"Every one of them."

They stood still. Stockton was aware that he still held her hand, but somehow he just didn't want to let go. The moments, and the silence, heavy and thick, stretched out. He searched her face hungrily; her features were unremarkable except for the golden glow of her tan, and the extraordinary deep blue of her eyes. She met his gaze, startled a little, perhaps, but still and composed.

Stockton cleared his throat. "I—I don't know what else to say."

She smiled. "That is a very grave situation for a diplomat to find himself in, sir."

"Well—" he said awkwardly, letting go of her hand and stepping back. "I thank you, Miss Thoroughgood. In the short time I've—we've—known you, you've become a very good friend, of mine and my family's. I wish you to know how much I appreciate that."

Gracefully she inclined her head. "I just hope that the sentiment is returned, sir."

"Oh, it is," he said fervently. "It certainly is."

Quarrels of the Gods

*T*here will be storms tonight," Mavis said softly as she saw the red dawn. The sun, barely arisen, was blood red, and dark wispy clouds flitted around it. She stood on the eastern side of her fale, sipping her first cup of tea.

The night had passed uneventfully, for the island was eerily quiet. Uncle Cash had, after much argument, slept in Mavis's parents' bedroom; Lorna and Trista had taken Mavis's bedroom; and Mavis and the children had slept in the fale, to their delight. The children had awakened when Mavis got up, and they were propped sleepily in their hammocks, sipping the hot sweet tea Mavis had served them.

They had, however, heard her quiet observation, which was spoken much to herself. Behind her she heard Merritt ask in a small voice, "Will there be a war today?"

"Probably so," Mavis said, turning to them. "You're not frightened, are you? You're safe here, you know."

"I'm not scared," Merritt said stoutly.

"I'm not scared, either," Penn echoed in a little-boy growl.

"I'm not really," Dolly said tentatively. "But what about Father, Miss Thoroughgood?"

Mavis smiled and knelt so that she could speak to Dolly face-to-face. Mavis was one of those rare people who could see the world through a child's eyes, and knew how intimidating it was to crane one's neck up to see an enormous adult looming over you. "The Lord watches over your father all the time. He will take care of him."

Dolly looked down and whispered, "My mother died, you know."

Mavis swallowed hard. "I know, Dolly. But she is in heaven with the Lord Jesus, and she is very happy. And you mustn't be afraid for your father, for the Lord has taught us that we don't ever have to live in fear. If you will just talk to Him and tell Him about being afraid, He will comfort you."

Dolly nodded, and then as children will, perked up. "May we bathe this morning, Miss Thoroughgood?"

Mavis rose. "I am certainly going to, but we must ask your uncle Cash for permission for you children."

"Hurray! Hurray!" they all cried, running into the cottage. Mavis thought that Professor Dodge may not be so happy to have the children awaken him at dawn, and so she quickly made American coffee. Before dawn Tui or one of the other boys had, according to her instructions, brought a pig and made a fire in the umu to begin the daylong process of roasting, and had thoughtfully filled the iron kettle with clean water and set it on the grate, so she already had gently steaming water. When the coffee was almost boiling and was the consistency of thin mud, she took in a tray with cups and saucers and coconut-gingersnaps donated by Mrs. Armbruster.

Uncle Cash and Lorna and Trista were up, sitting in the tiny parlor. The children danced with impatience, talking excitedly.

"It's a grotto," Merritt was explaining importantly. "Miss Thoroughgood showed it to us."

"With a waterfall, like a shower of cool rain," Dolly put in quickly.

"And rocks to sit on, if you'd rather have a bath," Merritt added, "in the little pool at the foot of the waterfall."

"Coffee," Uncle Cash mumbled, and with a slight smile Mavis served him. He glanced up at her and in spite of his apparent grogginess his eyes were keen and bright. "Anything?"

"Not yet," she answered.

Trista frowned. "Excuse me, Miss Thoroughgood, but is this true? You actually—you bathe in this—this—grotto?"

"Every morning," Mavis said cheerfully. "It's very secluded, you know; and anyway, it's my private property. No one would dare intrude."

"I see," Trista said rather frostily. "Penn, put that cookie down. It's not suitable for breakfast."

"I'm sorry," Mavis said contritely. "You see, I always bathe first thing in the morning, before breakfast. I intend to prepare breakfast for all of you when I return, but I thought that just one cookie wouldn't hurt for the wait."

"It won't," Uncle Cash said sturdily. "Trista, the children won't suffer any dire effects from one cookie. In fact, I intend to have one myself. And then, once all you women are finished, I'll take Merritt and Penn and we'll bathe too. No sense in being filthy savages in such genteel company."

Trista managed a small smile. "You're right, of course, Uncle Cash. I didn't mean to be so thoughtless, Miss Thoroughgood. I think I shall just wash up here, but if you would show me the—the arrangements, I'll be glad to start breakfast. Certainly we don't expect you to be our maidservant and cook."

Mavis laughed. "Miss Livingstone, I'm afraid that I truly start meals from scratch here. The first step is gathering eggs, and I'm hardly going to send my very welcome guests out to the chicken coop to do that. Please, allow me to take care of breakfast; but I warn you, it will be so long that it will be a cross between breakfast and lunch. And dinner, such as it is, will be late this evening, for today I am roasting a pig."

"A whole pig?" Penn asked, his eyes wide.

"Mostly," Mavis answered with a smile. "Do you like roast pork?"

"Yes," he said thoughtfully, "but I don't know 'bout eating a pig."

"Silly." Dolly laughed. "Pigs are pork."

"Pigs are pork," Penn repeated, obviously liking the words without really catching the meaning. "Pigs are pork."

Lorna stretched and yawned like a sleepy kitten. "I'm going to bathe, too. What does one wear?"

Mavis answered, "I wear a chemise and a lavalava; and then bathe in the chemise, and use the lavalava as a towel."

"I don't have a lavalava," Lorna hinted, her eyes bright.

"You may borrow one of mine," Mavis said. "In fact, I have a lovely red one with white flowers that I've never worn. Perhaps you would like to have it."

"Oh, I would! But surely you mustn't give it to me. I'll be glad to pay whatever you paid for it."

"Actually, I and the women of Chief Nifo's family make all of my lavalavas, and we all stocked up last year when Captain Brandeis ordered that the Samoans may not buy cotton but only use their own tapa cloth. All of us made many lavalavas then. I have several that I've never worn, and I would be very happy for you to accept the red one as a small gift."

The thought of a person actually having to make their own cloth from the bark of a tree in order to make their own clothes struck all of the Livingstones—even Uncle Cash—dumb.

In the awkward silence that followed Mavis went on hurriedly, "Very well then, ladies, everything we need is out in the fale, and we'll collect it and go bathe. Miss Livingstone, please, just relax and do your morning toilette at your leisure. Professor Dodge, I wish you to be as comfortable here as you would be in your own home. We'll be back soon."

Mavis, Dolly, and Lorna went outside, and found Lita, with the baby Vigo as always slung on her skinny hip, poking the coals of the umu and eyeing the great bulk of the leaf-wrapped pig on the grate. "Is it a good morning to you, Misi Too-Good." She bowed her head as Dolly and Lorna eyed her curiously.

"It is a good morning, Lita," Mavis said gently. "Lita—here— look up, child, don't be shy. Lita, I wish to introduce you to Miss

Lorna Livingstone and Miss Dolly Livingstone. Miss Lorna, Miss Dolly, may I present Lita to you? And this is Vigo."

"I'm very pleased to make your acquaintance, Lita," Lorna said, inclining her head gracefully.

"I'm very glad to meet you, Lita," Dolly said formally, but she cocked her head and edged up to the girl, who watched her with lively curiosity, her eyes round at the bright yellow aura of Dolly's hair.

"I am so happy to make the acquaintances of your lordships," Lita said. "Misi Living-Stone, Misi Living-Stone." Mavis had already taught the girls the names of her new friends at the American consulate, including teaching them how to spell the name. The Samoans carefully pronounced it as it, indeed, was: living stone.

"We're not lords," Dolly said absently. "Whose baby is that?"

Lita frowned. "His name is Vigo."

"Yes, I know, but whose is he? Is he your brother?" Dolly persisted.

Lita looked despairingly up at Mavis, who stepped up and explained, "Actually he would be—let's see—Lita's third cousin by marriage, I think. You see, in Samoan families, the little girls take care of the babies while the women work on the plantations, or go fishing."

"Oh. Is he a good baby?" Dolly asked.

"Most of the time he is good," Lita said with a world-weary air. "But he sometimes is bad when he is ready for sleep."

Dolly nodded with understanding. "My brother Penn gets grumpy sometimes too when he needs a nap. We're going to go bathe. Can you come with us?"

Lita looked up at Mavis, who nodded. "Yes, I love to bathe with Misi Too-Good," she said eagerly. "Her bathing place is best on all the island."

The little company gathered their toiletries and lavalavas and headed off for the grotto.

Dolly asked, "Why do you call her Misi Too-Good?"

Lita laughed. "She says because we don't say English words right. And she says she is not too good, at all. But we always call her that; and we called her mother that and her father that. We think they are all very, very good."

Overhearing the conversation, Mavis said, "Dolly, you've noticed Lita slightly slurs her *r*s in conversation? That's because there is no *r* sound in the Samoan language. That's why they sort of soften that consonant and why they pronounce my name the way they do."

Dolly looked up at her and blinked in the lurid red morning sun. "Maybe," she said shrewdly, "but maybe it is because you are good."

The baths took an unconscionably long time, because Misi Too-Good's bathing place was indeed the best on the island, surrounded by palms and enormous ferns, and the pool lit by the hot tropical sun, and the waterfall splashing coolly down. When at length they made their way back to Mavis's cottage, it was already late morning.

The morning wore on, with the large party at Mavis's fale seemingly on holiday, but still they all at times stopped to listen to a sound in the bush or a far-off shout or even when the birds fell silent altogether for a moment, as sometimes happens.

Finally, early afternoon, the first volley was heard, some distance away toward the bay; then the answering volley; then continuous firing like thunder rolling near and far, all day. Though the simple wooden walls of Mavis's cottage would actually afford them little more protection than an open fale, they all huddled in the cottage. Mavis went out several times to speak to natives who occasionally passed by along the river. The reports she received were vague, with no details of the lines or conquered territory or casualties.

All day, and most of the night, volley followed volley. It stormed deafeningly and rained like a flood. The children slept fitfully, sometimes sitting in the chairs, sometimes curling up on Uncle Cash's or Mavis's lap.

At dawn McKean came, disheveled, his boots filthy, his face lined. "Father's fine," he said first, and the Livingstone children visibly sagged with relief. "The consulate took one stray bullet in a pillar on the porch. The harbor's all shot up and it seems that one German seaman was wounded on the *Adler,* and a white man, master of a schooner from Fiji, was killed, but both of these were by stray shots. The warships took no part in the battle."

"And the outcome?" Uncle Cash asked in a harsh voice.

McKean answered, "The Germans have been routed; they are besieged on Mulinuu. The Mataafas are parading the streets of Apia. The German warship *Adler* has drawn up to the isthmus of Mulinuu in a defensive position, but as yet they have made no aggressive moves toward the *Adams.*"

Mavis, standing next to him, laid her hand on his arm. "What about native casualties, McKean?"

His mouth tightened. "Quite a butcher's bill for Samoans, I understand. The Germans have taken the Tamasese wounded to Mulinuu, so we're not sure about their numbers. The Mataafas have about forty wounded, including three women."

Quickly Mavis asked, "Where are they? There's no hospital here, not even a town doctor."

"Colonel and Mrs. de Coetlogon started taking them as soon as they were brought in. My father offered the American embassy, but the British embassy is so much larger, and Colonel de Coetlogon insisted that they may stay there, if the Americans will help with supplies. The doctor from the *Adams* is there, and Mrs. de Coetlogon and her helper, Miss Taylor, are nursing."

Mavis nodded. "I have some herbal remedies, and I'll make up some more. They are not prescriptives and no doctor would likely use them, but the natives often come to me for medical help, and if nothing else it would comfort them. I'll—I'll make arrangements for them to be delivered." Mavis had met Mrs. de Coetlogon once, in MacArthur's store, and the lady had given Mavis a rather cool reception. Mavis Thoroughgood was not exactly in their social circle. Mavis noticed that Trista seemed to be eyeing her knowingly.

"I'm sure we would all appreciate your help, ma'am," McKean said warmly, bowing a little. "But for now, my father sends his most gracious compliments, and begs your hospitality for the children just a while longer. He will try and come tonight, if circumstances permit."

"All of the Livingstones are welcome in my home," Mavis said. "Always."

The rest of the month of September, and then October, were, for Stockton Livingstone, a rackety confusion of days and nights filled with war and rumors of war. Tensions escalated, then eased; small things grew portentous, large events receded in importance; loyalties waxed and waned; pleas, threats, plans flew about like moths caught in a hurricane wind.

The Germans, as always, were valiant, stubborn, and ruthless. In spite of Stockton's and Colonel de Coetlogon's repeated attempts to reestablish a fair tripartite neutrality in Apia—where no armed groups would be allowed to occupy it with a military force—the German Consul Becker issued a proclamation from King Tamasese that declared that indeed, Apia was Eleele Sa, and that meant that no armed natives may invade the territory. Armed German soldiers did, however, patrol the town "to protect German interests."

Mataafa, victorious with his four thousand loyal warriors, humbly withdrew from Apia.

"I don't understand it," Stockton said to Mavis in one of their private daily meetings. Each day, either Mavis came to the consulate, or, when some of the Livingstones were at her home, Stockton came there. It just became a sort of understanding between them, to have a private talk at least once a day. Stockton valued her advice, and he felt completely at ease confiding in her, as long as it did not compromise his consular responsibilities, of course. He found her to be stable, not at all excitable, and she had an insight into the Samoan mind that he found invaluable.

Besides, he liked her.

"Mataafa is victorious," he went on, "Tamasese is besieged on Mulinuu; Mataafa outnumbers the Germans at least ten to one; and Tamasese's forces are deserting by the dozens every day to join him. I honestly don't believe that Germany would try, with arms, to enjoin battle with Mataafa if he stayed in the—I won't call it neutral territory, that's a bad joke—in the Eleele Sa."

Mavis smiled, a little sadly. "You still don't understand the Samoans, Mr. Livingstone. No native, however intelligent, determined, and clearheaded, as you have seen Mataafa is, would dream of defying Western powers. White men burst through the sky and rule Samoa now, with titanic ships that have incomprehensibly powerful weapons that can throw death for miles. Palangi have powers, riches, and weapons unthinkable to mere mortals. Though the Samoans are a Christian people, the palangi look and behave suspiciously like gods to them. They constantly give inconsistent orders, and if the poor Samoan can't sort out those orders and obey them quickly enough to suit, then they may be banished forever, beyond the sky, beyond the eyes of men, like poor King Laupepa. No, Samoans have no wish to become involved in the quarrels of the gods."

Stockton sighed deeply. "Yes, I suppose that is how we seem to them. I had hoped to change their view—of Americans, at least—but it's obvious that none of us palangi are exactly endearing Samoans to us."

Such was the disjointed situation of the little town at the end of October: all government extinct; the German consul issuing proclamations as if he were high king; armed German marines patrolling the streets; England and America openly defying Consul Becker's orders (though not with force, not yet); and Mataafa and his victorious army sitting outside an odd fairy-tale boundary drawn by the palangi, as if they would fall off the end of the world if they crossed it, as ancient mariners believed of the lands beyond their maps' borders: *Here there be dragons.*

They all seemed to ricochet through November and the first of December, again, with almost daily changes in the situation that, taken piece by piece, would have had no immediate significance, but which served to slowly increase the aggressive postures of the Three Great Powers. To Stockton's regret, Grover Cleveland lost his bid for a second term as president, but Stockton was also acquainted with Benjamin Harrison, who had won the election. Stockton knew that for many months at least he would have no new instructions from Washington.

The German consul, Mr. Becker, was replaced by a new man, Dr. Knappe. At first Stockton had high hopes that the new consul would be a little less hostile to the United States. But when Stockton attempted to call on him, he was turned away without an audience. Dr. Knappe did not return the call.

Commander Leary, irrepressible as always and full of mischief, bluffed setting up a military post in very close proximity to Mulinuu. The poor addled king, along with Captain Brandeis, who remained loyal to him (against the wishes of his own consul), fled to the bush. Immediately the Mataafas besieged him, and the typically ceremonial Samoan battles began.

In November, the British warship HBMS *Calliope* arrived. She was escorted by a small but menacing gunship, HBMS *Royalist*. And as per the new president's instructions, the screw steamer USS *Nipsic* and Commander Mullan arrived in Apia Bay to replace the smaller *Adams*.

Commander Leary and McKean stood on the beach in front of the consulate. It was a fine sparkling day; the wind gusted merrily in, bringing the blunt smell of salt and the complex musk of seaweed and fish. The bay, as always, was tossing restlessly, heaving the small vessels around as if they were toys, slapping temperamentally against the sides of the great warships. The water was a luscious deep aquamarine. It reminded McKean of the color of a great square-cut ring he had seen on the finger of a Russian lady's hand.

"What are you grinning about?" Leary demanded. "I'm not amused." He was a little peeved that he and his beloved *Adams* had been replaced.

"Oh, just remembering a lady," McKean said. "This bay reminds me of her. Beautiful, treacherous, mysterious . . ."

"I tell you what, bucko, this hussy of a bay is going to turn on all those sailor boys out there someday," Leary said. "She's going to turn on them and make them pay for taking liberties. I've spent a lot of time fighting to keep my nose above water in this little corner of the sea. She's treacherous, all right, and she's got some tricks she'll pull on you, even on fine days like this." He shook his head. "Maybe me and old Miz Adams are better out of it after all. This bay has sure enough mistreated her, knocking her around for the last year. She needs a nice soothing overhaul. And I expect we'll meet again in Washington. You'll probably be president, and I'll be Admiral Leary, Secretary of the Navy."

"Next year, you think?"

"Maybe." Leary sobered, then swept his arm out in an all-encompassing gesture. "Seriously, McKean, look at the armory out there. You don't think the Germans are going to let themselves be outgunned for long, do you? You know better. You'd better watch yourself, my friend. Some day there's going to be a big noisy bloody war. If this sea siren don't sink you all first."

"Mmm," McKean said noncommittally. But secretly he did think Leary was right. "Too bad you're not going to be here for all the fun. Commander Mullan's a good man, but he's an awful cricket bat."

"True," Leary agreed. "You're going to miss my bat, bucko. And my impish cheerfulness. And my dry, but energetic, sense of humor. And my creative ideas for noncombative hostile engagement. And my eternal optimistic—"

"I get it, I get it, Admiral," McKean interrupted, grinning. "And Consul Knappe and Captain Fritze will miss you so much, too. They're probably having a big party to celebrate the end of your tour."

"Nah," Leary grunted. "Those Huns don't ever have that much fun."

He was right about that, for though the Germans were very glad to see the back of Commander Leary, they had no party. And Leary was right, too, about their naval dispositions. The Germans did not long let the uneven balance of naval power stand. In December two more German ships of war sailed defiantly into Apia: the *Eber* and the *Olga*. All three warships started menacing patrols around the island, occasionally shelling Samoan villages. The bay bristled with great guns. The town grew increasingly restive, and the first small dark hints of real fear began to creep into the minds of the powerful palangi. It seemed the quarrels of the gods had only begun.

This Time and This Place

An emergency again in the middle of the night, a dismal ink-black night of the new moon, at the haunting hour of three o'clock. But this time, instead of Mavis Thoroughgood's soft knock at the kitchen door of the American embassy sounding the portent, Stockton Livingstone stood outside her fale, right by the mat that he knew shielded her hammock, and whispered, "Miss Thoroughgood, may I speak with you, please?" One could hardly knock on a mat.

Instantly she whispered back, "I'm coming . . . one moment."

He heard rustling. He turned to look up at the sky, lacy with stars, and as he always did, he picked out the Southern Cross. But the sky seemed at this moment more foreign, more cold and uncaring, than ever before.

She came around to the side of the fale and motioned for him to follow her. Merritt, Penn, and Dolly were asleep in the fale, and Lorna was asleep in the cottage. In the last few months hardly a night went by that some of the Livingstone children, and often Uncle Cash, did not stay with her. Trista never did, but Mavis knew that she was very taken with young Mr. Herrington-Carruthers, and, like the de Coetlogons, Mavis was not in his "circle." McKean, of course, stayed at the consulate, but he came to see Mavis often, sometimes when the children were there, but sometimes even when they weren't.

Mavis led Stockton to a small wrought-iron bench in her cutting garden, a gift from a grateful merchant captain that Robert Livingstone had led to the Lord many years ago. Mavis, who slept in a chemise and lavalava, had quickly thrown on a skirt and blouse and used the lavalava for a shawl. This gloomy hour of the night was chilly, even in a tropical paradise. The eternal sough of the restless bay was loud in their ears. One part of Stockton's mind recorded that light wafts of Mavis's roses were sweet to his nose, along with the dark aroma of moist rich earth and faint sea-and-salt tang carried on the cool breeze.

They seated themselves on the bench and Mavis lifted her head. "I hear the firing now."

Stockton nodded. "Armed German marines have landed at Fangalii."

Startled, she said, "But—how many? What can they possibly be doing? Mataafa has four thousand men around Laulii . . ."

"I don't know," Stockton said, and he sounded very weary.

The warring factions of Tamasese and Mataafa had gathered about two miles to the south of Apia, Mataafa's camp in and around the village of Laulii, Tamasese's lines south of them concentrated in the village of Lotoanuu. Around there, for the last three months, there had been assorted sieges and skirmishes, and also two set-piece battles. The territories of each camp had ranged north to the village of Fangalii, and south to Saluafata Bay. But in Apia there had been no more open warfare, only political tensions and warships posturing. Though the Americans and British had been arming the Mataafas, and the Germans had been arming Tamasese and his followers, no whites had done any shooting.

Until now.

Stockton reached out and took Mavis's hand. She was startled, but she warmly returned his clasp. Both of them looked up, contemplating the heavens, listening to the far-off din of war.

After a long time of silence, he turned to her. "I didn't have to come here, you know. You—and whichever of my children are here, I can never quite keep up with who is intruding on you at any given time—are not in any danger at all. Fangalii is far away, and I know that, whatever happens, the Germans would never harm any women or children."

"I know that, too. I'm not afraid."

"Are you ever afraid, Mavis?" It was the first time he had ever used her given name and her heart leapt.

But her voice was steady. "'For God hath not given us the spirit of fear; but of power, and of love, and of a sound mind.' Whenever I feel the least bit of fear, or confusion, the Lord speaks that verse in my heart, and I immediately know that it is truth."

He bowed his head and spoke so softly that Mavis had to strain to hear. "Fear . . . now I feel fear. Again. I fear for my children, and I wonder just how sound my mind really is. How could I have brought them here, endangering them by bringing them to Samoa in the middle of a war? Whatever could I have been thinking?"

Evenly she asked, "What were you thinking?"

"I—I beg your pardon?"

"I mean, how did you make the decision to come here? How did it come about?"

"Why—Mr. Cleveland offered me the post, and after thinking about it, I decided that I was qualified to deal with the diplomatic tangle here with the Germans," Stockton said thoughtfully. "And then I—of course, I prayed about it. And I felt so strongly that the Lord was directing me to come to Samoa."

"And the children? Did you understand the Lord to say that you should bring your family?"

"Yes, of course," Stockton said, but he still sounded uncertain. "It was unthinkable for me to leave them after my—after Phoebe died. But I certainly didn't know that I was setting them down right in the middle of a war."

"And you think the Lord didn't know it, either?"

He stared at her. "Of course, He knew it. Knows it. But—but it's not that simple. What if I was mistaken? What if He really didn't mean me to come here or to bring the children?"

"We are the sheep of His pasture, and we know the Shepherd's voice. It *is* that simple."

He watched her as she spoke. She was dark, mysterious in the night, with only the shimmer of her eyes and the star's glints on the ebony cascade of her unbound hair. In his eyes she was beautiful, and in his mind a wisp of a contrast between his beloved Phoebe and her flitted by . . . Phoebe, vibrant gold and dancing sunbeams and laughter, and Mavis, as rich as the earth herself, wise and calming and restful . . .

He kissed her, and she abandoned herself to him with a passion that surprised both of them. He murmured against her fragrant hair, "Mavis, Mavis, what a time and place for me to do this to you!"

"Just kiss me again, once more," she said fiercely. "Before you have to leave. That's all I want, and that's all I expect right now, in this time and this place . . ."

He kissed her again, encircling her in his arms, clinging tightly to her. Then he stood, smiled down at her, and walked away.

Dawn came, and Uncle Cash appeared in the garden and found Mavis Thoroughgood still sitting on the bench, staring with half-closed eyes at the first golden light over the eastern mountains, humming to herself.

"Well," he grumbled, painfully settling himself next to her, "you look like a pixie just risen from the river."

"Pixies are tiny little delicate fairies," she said in a lilting voice. "Water sprites rise from the streams and rivers, and they are generally held to be wand slender, with greenish blond hair and green eyes and pale skin."

"Oh. Then I suppose you look like a Samoan sprite," Uncle Cash decided.

"Thank you," she said with a dreamy smile.

They sat in silence for a while, Uncle Cash blinking owlishly at the growing brightness, Mavis with a continuous smile playing on her lips.

"You know that the Germans attacked the Samoans last night," Uncle Cash finally said, with obvious reluctance to break the spell.

She sighed and turned to face him. "Yes, I know. What happened?"

"The Mataafas—of course—prevailed. As far as we can tell, the Germans only landed about a hundred and forty men. The Samoans say there were fifty-six killed and wounded. The rest managed to fight their way to the beach and board the *Eber*, which had pulled into Letongo Bay and shelled the beach. The shelling killed five Samoan men, but they seem to have been the only Samoan casualties."

"Foolish, foolish Germans. I cannot fathom their intent. But whatever the plan, they have stumbled into war, and have suffered a defeat." She shook her head. "Only this kind of folly would ever have brought the Samoans to a point where they would shoot a palangi. What could the Germans have been thinking? To land such a small force, with such stealth, and with obvious intent to engage?"

"I have no idea. And neither does Stockton, and he understands them as much as a civilized, commonsensical man can. But I suppose by the end of the day he will have gathered enough information to comprehend the situation clearly. He is gifted that way, you know."

"Oh yes, he certainly is," Mavis agreed with perhaps a little too much fervor.

Uncle Cash gave her a shrewd sidelong glance. "You look very fresh and pretty and pleased with yourself to have sat on a cold hard bench in the falling damps all night."

She turned to him with surprise. "How did you know I've been here all night?"

He grimaced. "I'm not in my dotage yet, Miss Thoroughgood. I have a fairly good idea of what goes on in my family, though I work very hard at not interfering with it because it's none of my business."

"Oh."

"And furthermore, Stockton was like a ghoul walking around blank-eyed and mindless and bloodless until he got here and then he was even better when you came into his life. Our lives. And I'm glad for it, and I hope that neither you nor Stockton will be mindful of certain people who stick their noses into what is none of their business. Not everyone adheres to the rule never to interfere with what is none of their business, such as you and Stockton and whatever you are doing, of which I have no idea."

Mavis laughed with delight, and then, to Uncle Cash's surprise, she threw her arms around him and hugged him hard. "Professor Dodge, you are truly a wonderful, wonderful man!"

"Hmph," he grunted, but his old sharp face was alight with pleasure. "Just you remember, Misi Too-Good. There are people who aren't as wonderful as I am. You just stay strong and know the Lord's will." He patted her hand. "You and Stockton have some rough waters ahead, and I don't just mean from the war and riot and destruction all around us. Speaking of that, isn't it time to awaken the thundering herd?"

———————

The Fangalii Affair, as it came to be called by the British and Americans—the crushing defeat and shame was never mentioned officially by the Germans—took place on the night and early morning of December 19. Stockton made a quick call to Mavis's fale that evening. The children and Uncle Cash were at Chief Nifo's fales. Uncle Cash and Chief Nifo had made fast friends, and Merritt and Penn were practically inseparable from Tui, his sixteen-year-old son. Dolly and Lita, too, seemed to enjoy each other's company. Lorna was down at the grotto, bathing before tea, which Mavis was preparing.

Stockton had brought Trista—and her bags. She didn't seem to be pleased to be exiled to Mavis's, but she greeted Mavis politely enough and disappeared into the cottage.

"The Germans are planning to start shelling villages, and this time they're not going to be so polite about it," he said, his face pale and grim. "This time they're not making a point; they want revenge. I must stay at the consulate, for some of the people are seeking asylum. And I have that fool John Klein there; the Germans want to arrest him. He has contracted some sort of marsh fever, wallowing around in Mataafa's lines. So I don't want any of the children there, especially Merritt.''

John Klein was a reporter for the *New York World*, and he had been deeply involved in the Fangalii Affair; the Germans believed he had actually been a combatant. He was a young, impulsive, sometimes blowhard young man that Stockton had been at some pains to try and tactfully keep calm, without actually attempting to censor the press. To Klein's credit, he had for months been in the bush with the Mataafas, living with them, eating with them, faithfully sending informed (if somewhat melodramatic) dispatches about their plight to his newspaper.

But now, somehow—Stockton still could not get a straight story from the excitable young man—he had appeared in the guise of a U.S. citizen in open warfare against Germany. It was a sticky situation, indeed, for Stockton.

Sympathetically Mavis said, "You know that I love having all the family here, and the children do seem to enjoy staying with me as much as I enjoy having them. Please, Stock—Mr. Livingstone, attend to your duties and be assured that we're all very well and safe here."

Stockton nodded and gave her a wan smile. "Once again, Misi Too-Good to the rescue. Thank you, Mavis. I expect I won't be able to come again for a few days, but one thing I do promise: I am going to have Christmas with my family, and we are all going to attend church that morning. I'll see you then."

"Until then," she said in a lilting voice, her eyes alight.

They saw nothing of Stockton or McKean until early Christmas morning, but then they did come with two little native girls happily acting as bearers for all the gifts, for which they each received a ten-cent gold piece. The entire family had chipped in—even Penn, from his allowance—and bought Mavis a small blue Wedgwood cameo mounted on a black velvet band. Stockton fastened the choker for her. No one but Uncle Cash noted the stormy expression on Trista's smooth face, which quickly disappeared.

Mavis had prepared small gifts for each of the family, too. For Stockton and McKean she had tatted bed sets of mosquito netting, fine and filmy as a cloud. Merritt, Penn, and Dolly each received lavalavas sized especially for them, the boys' in the black and white geometric patterns favored by Samoan men, and Dolly's pink flowered. Merritt and Penn swore that they were going to wear theirs to church, but Stockton quickly squashed that.

"As soon as I can, we will go to Chief Nifo Sisi's when he has a gathering of the aiga for a dance, if Miss Thoroughgood can possibly wrangle us an invitation. And you may wear your lavalavas."

"Really? Truly?" Merritt asked, his eyes shining.

"Truly," Stockton promised.

"May I get a tattoo? Like Tui's?" Merritt said hopefully. All young Samoan men got tattooed in oddly beautiful patterns from their waists to their knees.

"No, you may not," Stockton said sternly. "And if you knew how they gave them their tattoos, you wouldn't even ask."

"I do know," Merritt said. "They take things like combs, only with sharpened teeth, and pound them into their skin with little hammers. It's really the bomb."

"Horrors," Trista said faintly.

"You think so," Uncle Cash rasped, "until they start hammering on you. Better just stick with your lavalava, young man."

"I've been thinking I'd get tattooed," McKean said, his blue eyes dancing. "But now I know how they do it, I've suddenly decided against it."

"You're all reprehensible," Trista said, and she didn't appear to be joking. But they were merry and paid little attention to her.

For Lorna and Trista Mavis had made her special cocoa butter and coconut oil preparation for hair and skin. It was her mother's recipe, researched over many years of experimentation; and it was the reason why Mavis's hair was shiny and healthy, and her skin, even though she had been exposed to so much tropical sun, was fresh and soft.

Lorna was effusive in her thanks, for she had—oddly enough—become interested in Mavis's herbal teas and remedies. Lorna had taken special interest in this preparation, because the quality of Mavis's hair and skin were extraordinary for the climate, and also for a woman of Mavis's age. Mavis had a few gray hairs, yes, but her hair was as full and glossy as a young girl's. Lorna had begun to discern the women around town who secretly bought Mavis's preparation, for their hair and skin were noticeably better than the other women whose skin and hair dried out quickly in the sand, sun, and salty air. Mavis had joked to her, "My mother only gave this to women that she liked. Soon word got around, and my mother sold it to women she didn't like. And so I have followed in my mother's tradition. It's been a nice little source of income for me."

It was very difficult to make, and as, of course, it had no preservatives, it wouldn't keep any length of time in the tropical heat. Lorna knew how precious this gift was and thanked Mavis effusively. Trista expressed her gratitude, but she was unmistakably cool.

The family and Mavis all went to the Wesleyan chapel that Mavis had attended all her life. Her father had been the only Presbyterian minister that had ever been to Samoa; and he had, typically, never been comfortable with making the Samoans pay a tithe to build a Presbyterian church. He had said, "There are over forty churches and chapels on this tiny little island, and I can't see that the Lord needs another earthly house for us Presbyterians to compete for attendees' numbers." This was, of course, why the Presbyterians had quickly reduced their support of the Thoroughgoods—and why John Ed Livingstone had finally ended up being their main source of financial support.

They trooped to the chapel, and Stockton quickly took his seat beside Mavis. Trista could hardly hear the sermon for she was so conscious of her father's warm glances at Mavis Thoroughgood and their easy nearness.

The next day was Boxing Day. Trista awoke from a dream of her mother. She couldn't remember anything of the dream, only her mother's face. She felt depressed and was irritated at having to stay at Mavis Thoroughgood's tiny and inconvenient cottage. Mr. Herrington-Carruthers never called on her here. Once he had drawled, "Misi Too-Good the barefoot native certainly seems to make herself at home at the American consulate these days. Mrs. de Coetlogon has never received her, you know."

Later that afternoon, after a day of slowly growing anger because none of the rest of the children seemed to remember that this day had been one of Phoebe Livingstone's special days, Trista asked Mavis if they might have a private talk.

"Of course," Mavis said with only an instant of surprise, immediately concealed. "Shall we walk down to the grotto?"

Trista remained silent, her face pale, her eyes red, her steps hard and uncompromising. They reached the grotto, and Mavis sat down with natural grace on a wide flat rock by the pool. But Trista remained standing, pacing, as she spoke.

"I cannot fathom what you think you are doing with my father, Miss Thoroughgood," she said angrily.

Mavis recoiled a bit from shock, her face suddenly drawn and tight. In her raptures and dreams, and in spite of Uncle Cash's veiled warning, she had not seen this coming at all. She was aware, of course, that Trista was not as friendly and open to her as the rest of the family; but she had seen that Trista had a natural reserve that was much like Stockton's, and she had believed that Trista's cool treatment of her was a natural outcome of this. Now, with Trista's harsh words, her own doubts and insecurities came crashing in on her. She swallowed hard and struggled to remain calm. But when she spoke, her voice was thick and strained. "Miss Livingstone, I'm sure I don't know what you mean."

"Don't pretend you don't understand. I can see the—the—regard that my father has for you. And I can see that you invite it, encourage it. How can you?"

Mavis struggled to remain calm, to quickly pray, to quiet the din of anger, confusion, and resentment that beat in her brain and against her temples like hammers. She was a Christian woman, utterly surrendered to the Lord Jesus Christ, and her life had been filled with His love, flowing into her and also from her to others. Of course, as soon as she realized that she was falling in love with Stockton Livingstone, she had prayed fervently, seeking the Lord's will in this, as in all other things in her life. She had half-disbelieved the goodness of His gift to her: a man that she had so quickly, so helplessly fallen in love with—and he was falling in love with her, too! Of course she had realized that there were chasms of difference between them—their social standing, the Livingstones' wealth, her own life of poverty, her upbringing in an environment and culture utterly alien from his—but none of that had affected her certainty that, at last, God had given her the most precious earthly gift of all: a fine Christian man to love, and who, He had assured her—was learning to love her.

But now she had the taste of ashes in her mouth. How could Stockton Livingstone possibly risk his beloved daughter's wrath for a woman like her?

A dullness, a heavy feeling of defeat, settled on Mavis. As she had taken hardship and disappointment all of her life, she grew calm and detached. "Miss Livingstone, in good conscience I cannot discuss your father's personal relationships, or state of mind, or his private confidences, with you or anyone else. Have you by any chance spoken to him of your concerns?"

"Of course not," Trista retorted. "It is not my father who is in error here, Miss Thoroughgood. It is you. Don't you understand that he is vulnerable, he is still struggling with the pain of my mother's loss, and you have taken advantage of a business association that represents a simple convenience to my father to—to entice him into an unsuitable relationship?"

"You seem to have a very clear and concise view of your father's state of mind, and intentions, and standing with me, considering that you haven't spoken to him of these matters. All I can say, Miss Livingstone, is that I wish only for your father's—indeed, all of your family's—happiness and well-being. Including yours."

Trista straightened tensely. "Then you will understand that I believe that your relationship with my father is not only harmful to him, but to the children. There is Merritt, begging my father to get tattooed like the Samoan boys! And Dolly, and even Lorna, have taken to wearing lavalavas and going barefoot!"

"Of course I know it, since they only do such things when they are here, never at the consulate," Mavis said in a broken whisper. "And as for Merritt's tattooing, I can assure you that I did explain to him how unsuitable it would be."

"This is exactly my point, Miss Thoroughgood. It is your influence, which in my view is a rather low, uncivilized influence, that has subjected the children to these outlandish ideas anyway. And it is the same case with my father. Don't you understand that in Washington he is a highly esteemed minister in the Foreign Service, a man of influence and even fame, now that the eyes of America are turning to Samoa? How do you think it will affect his career, his standing, his entire life, if it becomes known that he is cavorting about with a native woman?"

Mavis abruptly, awkwardly stood. "Miss Livingstone, you must excuse me. I think that you are saying things you will regret; and I— I feel a little ill. Please don't say anything to your father, or let him know that you are so upset. It will only hurt him. When I have recovered, we will continue, if we must. But for now I—I—simply can't bear to listen any more." She hurried off, one hand in front of her, as if she could not see her way.

Behind her, Trista suddenly sagged, feeling bruised and somehow soiled. And then she burst into hot, bitter tears.

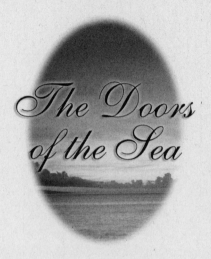

PART IV

The Doors
of the Sea

Then the Lord answered Job out of the whirlwind, and said . . .
Who shut up the sea with doors, when it brake forth,
as if it had issued out of the womb?
When I made the cloud the garment thereof,
And thick darkness a swaddlingband for it,
And brake up for it my decreed place,
And set bars and doors,
And said, Hitherto shalt thou come, but no further:
And here shall thy proud waves be stayed?

Job 38:1, 8–11

Sky red at morning, sailor's warning;
Sky red at night, sailor's delight.

Old Proverb

Stutters and Lies

"Why isn't Misi Too-Good coming?" Penn demanded.

Merritt frowned. "You've done up your waistcoat buttons wrong. Come here, I'll help you." Obediently Penn stood in front of his brother and allowed Merritt to unbutton and then rebutton his blue satin waistcoat. They were dressing for dinner, the first family dinner the Livingstones had had at the consulate together for over two weeks. The date was January 2, and the occasion was a celebration of the new year of 1889. The children had only returned to the consulate from Mavis's home two days previously, so they had just now settled back in enough for Trista to organize a celebratory dinner.

"Misi Too-Good?" Penn insisted.

"I'm not sure," Merritt said slowly as he neatened up Penn's floppy tie, "but I think Trista didn't invite her."

"Why?"

"I don't think Trista likes her."

"Why?"

After a hesitation Merritt replied, "I don't know. Don't say anything to Trista about it, Penn. Okay?"

"'Kay," Penn said reluctantly. "But can we go see her tomorrow?"

"We can ask, but I don't think Trista will let us."

Penn thought, then said slyly, "We could ask Uncle Cash."

A grin slowly lightened Merritt's face. "Good idea, Penn. Really good idea. I didn't know you were that smart."

Trista came in then, her face set in stern lines. She had come to the boys' room to fetch them downstairs for dinner and had stopped outside the door to listen when she had heard Penn say Misi Too-Good. As is always the case with eavesdroppers, she had heard nothing that helped her; she had only injured herself, for she was now angry and resentful. *Silly little boys have no idea of what it's like to have adult responsibilities . . . don't like Misi Too-Good, indeed! And what a stupid nickname! As if my dislike of her had anything to do with it. And besides, I don't dislike her!*

But Trista could hardly say any of this to the boys, or indeed say anything that hinted that she had been eavesdropping. Stockton and particularly Phoebe Livingstone had always been very strict against invasions of privacy, such as listening in on others' personal conversations. Trista now passed off her momentary feelings of guilt with the thought, *I'm not their mother, I have to use every opportunity to learn about them so that I'll be able to bring them up correctly.* But it still didn't make her feel any less irritated with Merritt and Penn.

"Hurry up," she snapped. "We don't want to be late."

"We're ready, Trista," Merritt said meekly.

"Merritt tied my tie, see?" Penn said, pointing to it with both forefingers. He looked angelic, with his bright silvery blond hair and wide innocent blue eyes and sweet smile. Trista's heart softened.

"Yes, and he did a good job, too. You look like very elegant gentlemen. Both of you." Merritt and Penn had replicas of adult suits— black broadcloth, long pants, satin waistcoats, silk ties—for formal dinners with the family. Phoebe had always believed that allowing children to wear decorous formal clothing, instead of cutesy costumes, on appropriate occasions helped to teach children dignity. It was true, Trista reflected as they went downstairs. Even Penn, irrepressibly high-spirited and energetic, did try to be calm and grown-up at formal family dinners.

The dining room was the largest and most elegantly appointed room of the consulate, since commonly state business was done at state dinners. It was a simple room, painted a creamy white, with two wide windows facing west. A brand-new Turkish carpet was centered underneath an eighteenth-century French refectory table that Armbruster polished lovingly with lemon oil every single day. Ten Louis XV cane chairs had been painstakingly imported. A massive bibliotheque of the same period served as a dresser and sideboard, displaying a heavy beaten silver set given to the consulate by the firm of Moors and Company for service to the merchants of Western Samoa.

At each place setting was a menu written on a small parchment half-sheet, with place cards inserted. Trista had an elegant hand and her calligraphy was pure artistry. Phoebe had always asked Trista to make the menus and place cards for her dinners, and while Trista was doing these she had cried a little at the memory.

Everyone sorted themselves out, with Stockton at the head of the table and Trista at the foot. After a gracious blessing by Stockton, Armbruster served the first course, a creamy asparagus soup. Penn picked up his menu and turned to Dolly, his neighbor on his left. "Whassat, Dolly?"

"Bonito mousselines," Dolly read patiently.

"Bonito fish?"

"Yes."

"Whassa mousseline?"

"I don't know," Dolly admitted.

"You'll see when they're served," Trista said with amusement. "You've had the dish before, only with salmon."

Penn, satisfied, pointed to the next course on the menu. "I can read this one. B—braised beef and veg—ables with a yellow b–b–"

"Béchamel," Dolly said.

"B—béchamel sauce," Penn finished proudly. "Sugared yam pie. Chocolate bread pudding. Mmm, yum. And—whassat, Dolly?"

"Macadamia."

"Macadamia nuts, dried fruits, sharp cheddar cheese for the—the—I forgot the name of 'em," Penn said, frowning.

"The savories," Trista said.

"Yeah. But, Trista, where's the *pisupo*? Aren't we having pisupo?"

"What's pisupo?" McKean asked.

"It's real good," Penn said earnestly. "Misi Too-Good has it every day."

Uncle Cash laughed. "Boy, you're a caution! With this menu and you want pisupo?"

"I like it," Penn said.

"What is pisupo?" McKean asked again.

"Samoan for pea soup—sort of," Uncle Cash explained. "At least, the first tinned food on the islands was pea soup—pisupo. But then they got tinned corned beef, and they love it so much it is a staple part of their diet. But they still called it pisupo."

Stockton laughed. "Well it's a comfort to know, Penn, that if we ever fall on hard times, you won't complain about the food."

"What's fallin' on hard times?" Penn demanded.

"Being poor," Dolly said matter-of-factly. "Like Misi Too-Good and Chief Nifo and Tui."

"Are they poor?" Penn asked, astonished.

"Of course they are."

"Do they know it?"

This was too hard for Dolly, and she hesitated.

Trista said tightly, "Yes, they know it, Penn. And it's embarrassing to be poor, so don't say anything about it to them."

"That's not quite true—at least, *they* aren't embarrassed by it," Stockton said lightly. "Anyway, Penn, don't you worry about Misi Too-Good and Chief Nifo. The Lord takes good care of them." He took a sip of the soup. "Trista, this tastes fresh. Is it?"

"It is," she said with satisfaction. "I happened to be in Moors's store when the produce came in, so we have fresh vegetable dishes tonight." Since the family had been shuttling back and forth between the consulate and Mavis's home, and since shipments of fresh produce to the islands were scarce, it was difficult to buy enough, at the right time, for the Livingstones.

"Delicious," Uncle Cash said. "We must be certain to give Mrs. Armbruster our best compliments. And what a coup, Trista! I know that organizing these dinners is a lot of trouble. I, personally, would never attempt it, not even for family."

Any formal dinner was, of course, an undertaking. Trista had decided upon the menu; had gathered all the foods and ingredients and supplies; had assisted Mrs. Armbruster with the cooking; had designed the table settings and had created the centerpiece: a grand silver epergne with an arrangement of hibiscus flowers, breadfruit leaves, and vines.

She smiled at her uncle. "You know very well, Uncle Cash, that I would help you any time you would care to give a dinner. I believe that the drawback here is not that you don't know how to do it, but that you just don't care to do it."

"True. Your mother always said the same thing. Once I tried to deny it, but she told me I was a terrible liar and either should practice enough to get better at it or just stop it altogether. I decided to stop it altogether."

Everyone laughed—except for Trista. She still missed her mother horribly; the merest mention of her pained Trista. She couldn't fathom how the family could be so cold, so callous, as to stop mourning Phoebe. She sat frowning, looking down, dipping her spoon pointlessly in her soup while everyone reminisced of how Phoebe had, at times, said much the same things to each of them, except for Penn, of course. But he understood the gist of the topic.

"Misi Too-Good told me that I shouldn't lie 'cause when I do, I stutter," Penn announced. "An' so I tried to tell Merritt and Tui some lies, but I stuttered. So I guess I won't do that any more."

More laughter greeted this, and Penn looked absurdly pleased.

"Oh, Pips, what lie did you tell Misi Too-Good?" McKean asked, still chuckling.

"I told her I shot a journamiss for the president," Penn said reluctantly. "It was almost true. But I stuttered anyway."

"You shouldn't lie, whether you stutter or not," Trista said harshly. "It's not cute, Penn."

Penn flushed deeply and hung his head.

Stockton said gently, "I'm sure you understand that, don't you, Penn? That Christian gentlemen don't tell lies?"

"Yes, sir," he whispered.

"Good," Stockton said. "You're a good boy, Penn, and I'm proud of you."

Penn lifted his head and grinned. "Thank you, Father. I'm proud of you, too."

Though Stockton didn't so much as glance at Trista, she was aware of his disapproval. But because Trista was filled with bitterness, it only made her feel a dull rebellion and a stubborn determination to go through with her plans. She managed a weak smile at her father. "What are those horrid Germans up to now, by the way? I've been so busy since we all came home that I'm not aware of the latest."

"The last few days have been relatively quiet," Stockton said. "Since the Germans seem to feel that they had avenged their honor in some way by shelling Mataafa's camp and some of the villages, they haven't had such an openly aggressive posture. At least, they haven't been shooting for the last week."

"But surely, Father, you aren't lulled into some delusion that we're safe, are you?" Trista cried, her voice shrill. "Just because they haven't shot our heads off yet? It was just a week or so ago that the *Olga* shelled Mangiangi—while we were at Miss Thoroughgood's! How can you possibly forget that?"

After the unfortunate Fangalii Affair, Dr. Knappe had dispatched the *Adler* to mercilessly shell Mataafa's camp at Laulii. When Stockton had realized it, he had sent Commander Mullan of the USS *Nipsic* to intercept the *Adler* and request a delay so that the women and children might be evacuated. Captain Fritze of the *Adler* had agreed, so Commander Mullan had sent a lieutenant to warn the camp. Naturally, all of the Samoans had evacuated Laulii, so that when the mighty battleship hurled shell after shell into the small village, it was with impotent fury, for it was empty. This had not endeared Commander Mullan or Stockton Livingstone to Dr. Knappe.

Mataafa and his men had moved to Mangiangi and Tanunga-mono, villages about two miles behind Apia and about a mile and a half beyond Mavis's home. Three German shells from the warship *Olga* had sailed majestically over the beach, over Mavis's fale, over the Vaisangano River, over Mangiangi, to land deep behind in the river valley.

"They sounded like loud singing," Penn said excitedly. "Show them, Merritt!"

Merritt began making a shrill, buzzing whine to illustrate the shell's song, but Trista snapped, "Stop it, Merritt!" When she saw her father's eyes narrow slightly, she immediately said, "I beg your pardon, Merritt, I didn't mean to speak so sharply. But that noise does set your teeth on edge, doesn't it, Uncle Cash?"

He shrugged. "What amazes me is how much he sounds like the shells. It does rather set your teeth on edge when they're sailing over your head, screeching like banshees."

Trista said, "Father, I never understood how that happened. That the Germans shelled Mangiangi, and there we were at Miss Thoroughgood's, right in the line of fire. They didn't give warning that time?"

Stockton grimaced. "Yes, they did. But due to my ignorance of island geography I didn't know exactly where Mangiangi was. If I had discussed it with Miss Thoroughgood, she would have been able to warn me, and of course I would have brought you all back here. But you recall, Trista, that in the days directly after the Fangalii Affair things were happening so rapidly and tensions were escalating so quickly that I barely had time to visit you, and I certainly didn't have time to confer much with Miss Thoroughgood. By the way, did she come by today? Did I miss her?"

"She didn't call," Trista said shortly. "But, Father, about the Germans. Now that they are engaging in open warfare, it is such a dangerous position for the children. Perhaps it would be better if we all stayed here, instead of moving to the bush every time the Germans rattle a saber."

McKean said lightly, "Mab, you overestimate the danger of ship's artillery. They missed Mangiangi by a mile. Attempting a bombardment of an inland site—particularly where you don't have good maps indicating the position of the target or a visual bearing—is not a very efficient way of waging warfare. The Germans know that, of course. I'm surprised they attempted it at all."

"I think it was Dr. Knappe's idea," Stockton said. "It certainly wasn't any naval officer's plan. When we last met I could see that Dr. Knappe is ill with some sort of tropical fever. It is likely affecting his judgment."

"These fevers! They're rampant in the tropics, I suppose," Trista said. "You know that Colonel de Coetlogon also suffers from a recurring fever. That's another reason, Father, that I think we had better keep Merritt from roving about the bush quite so much. If he contracted yellow fever or malaria it could be devastating for him in his delicate state of health."

"But I feel fine!" Merritt protested. "I haven't been sick since we got here! You just don't want us to go to Misi Too-Good's!"

Penn's eyes grew huge. "You told me not to say anything about it and look what you did!"

Stockton said carefully, "What do you mean, Merritt? You know that your sister is always concerned for your health, rightly so."

"But—" Merritt began, but then he saw Trista's face, and in it he saw his defeat. "I know," he murmured. "I didn't mean anything, especially."

Trista said evenly, "Actually, Father, Merritt is right in a way. Of course it's not that I don't want them to go to Miss Thoroughgood's per se. It's just that it's not convenient, for many reasons. Merritt contracting some fever in the bush, or from some native, is one of them. Penn is getting rather wild, you know. Dolly is neglecting her studies—"

"Excuse me," Uncle Cash said pleasantly, but his blue eyes sparkled with warning as he gazed at Trista, "but you are mistaken, Trista. Whether we are here or at Miss Thoroughgood's, fevers or not, shells or not, war or not, Dolly studies. And most of the time when we are at Miss Thoroughgood's Merritt and Penn and Lorna join us for language studies at least. Did you know that Merritt and Penn and Lorna can speak a good amount of Samoan? No, I thought you may not be aware of that. And also, Lorna practices her violin and flute faithfully."

"But she——" Trista turned to her sister. "But just look at your lovely creamy skin, Lorna! You're getting tanned! It just won't do, and I'm surprised that you can bear it!"

Lorna shrugged. "I know it, Trista, and I know it's because I don't wear my hat and gloves all the time when I'm gardening with Misi Too-Good. But that's my fault, not hers."

"But if you weren't there, you wouldn't be out barefoot in a lavalava with no hat and no gloves."

"Maybe," Lorna said, her mouth set stubbornly. "But maybe I would start a garden here and go barefoot and wear my lavalava and not wear a hat and not wear gloves. I'm fairly sure the sun is the same here as it is at the fale."

"This sure is a silly argument," McKean grumbled. "Just like girls."

"What is the argument?" Stockton asked. "Is what Merritt says true, Trista? That you just don't wish the children to visit Miss Thoroughgood?"

Trista took a deep breath. When she answered, she mustered all the calm and reasonableness she could. "Father, please consider it. We haven't been *visiting* Miss Thoroughgood. We have practically been living with her. In spite of all of our jokes about the thundering herd, the fact remains that we are a large family, we are basically strangers to Miss Thoroughgood, and her house is not at all convenient to accommodating several guests. In addition, her life, as I understand it, is somewhat solitary, and she seems to me to be a private person. I'm just afraid that we are intruding on her."

Trista watched her father's face change as she spoke. She could see his suspicion wane and a dawning uncertainty come over him. It is a measure of how deep in darkness Trista was that she actually felt a sense of surly triumph.

Stockton murmured, "You know, I hadn't quite looked at it that way. I've been so busy . . ."

The children, including Lorna, watched their father with dismay. McKean frowned but said nothing.

After a long silence Uncle Cash said firmly, "All of your speculation may very well be true, Trista. But it is, after all, only speculation on your part. I know a fact. A real, true, solid fact. Miss Thoroughgood said, 'All of the Livingstones are welcome in my home. Always.' That's what she said, and I happen to believe that she is a truthful person."

Stockton studied his uncle. "You're right, Professor Dodge. But perhaps she has, considering the extreme circumstances, been more tactful than truthful. After all, after the Fangalii Affair everyone stayed with her for almost two solid weeks."

Uncle Cash shrugged. "Ask her. She doesn't lie."

"But she may be tactful, as Father says," Trista interposed quickly.

"He'll know the truth," Uncle Cash said with peculiar emphasis to Trista, who immediately dropped her eyes. "Your father will know the truth."

Mavis sat at the table in her fale, staring into space. Ever since Trista had confronted Mavis about her relationship with Stockton, Mavis had suffered agonies trying to see the truth. That she loved Stockton Livingstone deeply, passionately, was certainly the truth; that he was beginning to fall in love with her, Mavis sensed, was also true. But that didn't mean that Trista was wrong about them. Mavis had hardly slept, tossing and turning until she felt raw, endlessly repeating the things Trista had said in her tortured mind. During the day it had been a herculean task to keep her attention on the present. Like some awful carrion bird, the same dark pieces of worries would dart through her mind and pick tirelessly at her as she cooked, bathed, played with the children, visited Chief Nifo's aiga, did lessons with her three students, gardened with Lorna.

Stockton kissing me—low influence—selfish—"after Phoebe died"—cavorting about with a native woman—poor one at that—enticed him—unsuitable—my fault, my fault, Phoebe lost, lost Phoebe, lost . . . lost . . . lost . . .

With an effort Mavis pulled her mind out of the exhausting ever-present endless loop and stared down at her first cup of morning tea. It had grown cold.

It's been eight days since the children left, she told herself bleakly. *And he hasn't come . . . it must be a good thing. It must be because he, too, has realized the truth . . . It must be the truth . . . that we're not at all suited to each other, that he doesn't really care for me, that we were just caught in one crisis after another and that sort of thing tends to promote false intimacies between people . . .*

He was there. "Hello, Miss Thoroughgood," he said gravely. "I hope we aren't intruding?"

"Oh my—no, no, not at all," she said nervously, jumping up from the bench seat with a clatter of crockery. "Good morning, Mr. Livingstone, Professor Dodge. Please, won't you join me? Sit down, I'll get you some tea . . . no, really, it's quite all right, of course I remember how you both take it . . ." She chattered on until Stockton and Uncle Cash had seated themselves on opposite sides of the table. Then she served their tea and sat down with Uncle Cash.

After some niceties and finishing his tea, Uncle Cash said easily, "I believe I'll go over to visit Chief Nifo. I haven't seen him in a week or so."

Mavis said quickly, "I'll go with you. I mean to say, Mr. Livingstone, wouldn't you like to go visit Chief Nifo? I'm sure he'd love to see you."

"Not particularly," Stockton said, smiling a little. "Not right now."

"But—" Mavis began, but could think of nothing else to say as Cash rose, bowed and tipped his hat to her, and made his way off toward the river.

She looked down, fidgeting with her empty teacup. Stockton said nothing and finally she looked back up at him. He was watching her, frowning slightly. He didn't look angry, she thought, but he was obviously troubled.

He's an honorable man, he knows he needs to—to—distance himself from me, and he doesn't want to hurt me. Mavis tried desperately to think of something clever, something pointed and final and dignified to say to get this painful scene over with, but her mind was utterly blank.

Finally Stockton said, "You know my wife and my uncle taught me the value of saying the plain, simple, unvarnished truth if the situation is appropriate. I think this is one of those times. Mavis, I'd like to know: Have I intruded on you?"

"What?" Mavis said in confusion.

"Have I or my family just—overrun you? Intruded on you, on your life?"

"Why—no, I—it's—not like that."

Stockton narrowed his eyes. "Have I made you uncomfortable in any way?"

"Uncomfor—no! That is, no."

"You look uncomfortable," he said gently.

She took a deep breath and closed her eyes for a moment. When she opened them he was still staring at her intently, his blue eyes dark with some emotion she didn't understand, refused to understand. Mavis, after days of thought and worry, had decided that Trista Livingstone, while too angry and brusque, had basically been right.

Mavis Thoroughgood was not at all the kind of woman that Stockton Livingstone needed in his life, in any way. She was too far away from him, too removed from his life, his thoughts, his upbringing, the things in his life that had shaped him. He needed to find another woman like his first wife had been: polished, elegant, accomplished, from a family of long solid social standing, with wealth of her own so that she could be his equal.

Not like Mavis, the poor church mouse, always dowdy, eccentric, more Samoan than Anglo, a "low influence" as Trista had said.

The problem was that in these past days when Stockton had not called on her, she had convinced herself that he, too, had come to understand all this about her. Now, however, she sensed that he had not seen this as clearly as she (and his daughter) had, and that he was genuinely hurt.

But Mavis, in her own particular pain that had caused her blindness, steeled herself to do the right thing. For Stockton, for his family, for his career, for his life.

She smiled brittlely at him. "I'm not uncomfortable, Mr. Livingstone. It's just that I am a little tired. These last few months have been tense and very busy, for all of us."

"Trista said that we had intruded on you. That I had intruded on you, fobbing the children off on you as I have."

"No, no, it's not—that at all!" Mavis cried quickly. "I do care about the children, Mr. Livingstone. I enjoy having them here, I always have. It's just that—I—have been—spending too much time with them, and with—um—at the consulate, and I've been neglecting my—my real family. Chief Nifo and Tui and Lita and the rest."

"I see. You don't want to continue our language lessons, then?"

"You don't need them any more, anyway. You speak Samoan as well as I."

"But you don't speak German as well as I," he teased, a little hesitantly. "Wouldn't you like to come at least once or twice a week, and we could continue your German studies? And Mav—Miss Thoroughgood, you know that I—I value our time together very much. Our private time, I mean. Just to talk, and other times, too."

She dropped her head quickly, to hide the tears growing in her eyes. With a supreme effort she blinked them back, then tossed her head up defiantly. "I don't think that's wise, Mr. Livingstone. People have begun to talk, and I don't care to risk my reputation any further. It's tattered enough as it is."

A spasm of pain crossed his face. Stockton had always been exquisitely careful to maintain all the proprieties with Mavis. He had never called on her by himself, except that one time last August, when the Livingstones had first arrived, when Stockton had come to Mavis's fale in the middle of the night before the first battle between the Mataafas and the Tamaseses. When she was at the consulate they were always with either McKean or the children. The quiet talks they had, just the two of them, had been in the study with the door open, and generally with Armbruster serving them tea or coffee, and with the children coming in and out.

"Please forgive me," he said dully. "I honestly didn't realize. But of course, I should have. Apia is, after all, only a small town, and in this charged atmosphere people gossip even more viciously than usual. In fact, I see now that I shouldn't be alone with you here."

He jumped up with a rattle of crockery. She put out her hand to stop him, but quickly withdrew it. He didn't see.

Stiffly he said, "I'll be going now, Miss Thoroughgood. Thank you again for all you've done for me and my family. And please accept my sincerest apologies for any inconvenience I've caused you." He bowed deeply, then turned and walked away.

Tensions and Trials

I have been a stupid fool," Stockton said bitterly.

"You *have been?*" Uncle Cash repeated with an innocent air. "But you're not now?"

Stockton ignored him. Uncle Cash struggled to keep up with Stockton's hard fast walk back to the consulate. Stockton had come to Chief Nifo's to fetch him, and as soon as Uncle Cash had seen his nephew's face he had come along without a word.

"I can't believe how arrogant I was," Stockton went on. "I'm so much older than she, for one thing!"

"She's not a dewy-eyed giggling squealing child," Uncle Cash retorted. "You are thirteen years older than Miss Thoroughgood, but it is not at all unseemly."

Stockton didn't appear to hear his uncle. "And just think! I thought I was such a prize, such a catch! But I've got all those children!"

Uncle Cash couldn't help but chuckle. "Yes, you do indeed have all of those children. And Miss Thoroughgood loves them. At least, she loves the children, which is only natural, since she doesn't know McKean or Trista very well."

"She does? But I thought—oh, hang it all! She just doesn't love—I mean—I just—assumed—because—she—that is, I—we—"

Uncle Cash sighed. "That last sentence was fragmentary and vague, Stockton. Try again."

Stockton shook his head vigorously, but then said in a rough voice, "She's been a Christian all her life, living for God, she's pure, she's wise, she's good. How dare I—just—what kind of fool—dashing in there and—and—oh, forget it!"

"I think you'll have trouble forgetting it, Stockton. Sure you don't want to go back and try again?"

"No!"

"Why not? If you spoke to her in the same disjointed clauses as you've been speaking to me, she probably had no idea what the topic actually was."

"It's not funny," Stockton growled.

"I suppose not." Uncle Cash sighed. "I know I do have a sort of quirky sense of humor . . . Oh no, Stockton, what is that?"

They had walked the path along the Vaisangano River, which was thickly wooded right up to the mouth where it spilled into Apia Bay. Now they had reached the beach and could see up and down Apia clearly. To their left—the west—was a column of ugly black smoke.

"Fire," Stockton said, narrowing his eyes.

"Do you know what it is?" Uncle Cash asked, straining to see.

"I think so," Stockton answered. "But I'm not sure. Can you go faster, Professor Dodge? I need to get to the consulate."

"Yes, I can keep up; lead on, Stockton."

They hurried down the main street, passing many people standing on their verandas staring speculatively down toward the western end of Apia, which was, of course, the German quarter. Some people asked Stockton questions as he and Uncle Cash hurried by: "Do you know, Mr. Livingstone? Have you been there? What is it?"

"I'm afraid I don't know anything yet," he answered. "But I'm sure the Germans will get it under control quickly."

When they reached the consulate, McKean and Mr. Blacklock were standing on the veranda. McKean had his father's glass, and as they neared, he closed it with finality and said, "It's the German consulate, Father."

Stockton nodded. "I thought so. How long has it been?"

McKean shrugged. "We were in the study, and Armbruster just came and told us a few minutes ago. What do you want us to do?"

Stockton thought for a few moments, then answered, "Go on down there, McKean, and you, too, Mr. Blacklock. Offer your assistance in any way—from a bucket brigade to temporary asylum for German nationals here at the consulate, if needed. Just do what you would do for anyone. Offer your help."

McKean and Mr. Blacklock left, and Stockton turned to his uncle. "You know, any other time I would ask Mavis to find out if any Samoans had anything to do with this, or at least what they're saying about it. But now . . ."

"She'd still help you, Stockton," Cash said firmly. "You're just not thinking clearly."

He shook his head. "No, I honestly don't wish to intrude on her good graces any more. So, Professor Dodge, please come into my study, if you would do me the honor of conferring with me on some matters. By the way, how is your relationship with Chief Nifo Sisi these days?"

"I am nowhere near as good a spy for Stockton as you were," Uncle Cash grumbled. "All Chief Nifo will talk to me about is questioning me about the etiquette of Western rules of engagement. He keeps asking me if they are prosecuting the war correctly. He's not so worried about winning it as he is that they aren't rude and offensive as they do."

Mavis replied, "But that's a grave concern for all Samoans. You must understand, Professor Dodge, that warfare, for Samoans, is very much like ancient tournaments. The flair, the pomp, the feasts before and after, the traditional dances, the spectacle, is all much more substantive than the importance attached to inflicting a high number of casualties on the enemy."

"I know. But that's why I have such trouble communicating with Chief Nifo. He doesn't understand that we are primarily interested in butchering more of the enemy in the most efficient way possible. He's really very dense that way."

Mavis laughed with delight, and Uncle Cash couldn't help but join her, not because he thought he was all that funny, but because her laugh was girlish, joyful, and infectious. "Yes, all Samoans are stupid that way, I think. And I thank the Lord for it."

"Amen."

They were sitting in Mavis's fale, late in the afternoon of January 18, ten days after the German consulate had burned. Uncle Cash had called on Mavis just about every day as he visited Chief Nifo Sisi, and Mavis had assured Uncle Cash that she would very much like for the children to come to the fale whenever it was convenient for him to bring them. Taking her at her word, he brought them almost every day, and continued Dolly's morning classes in the fale. Merritt, Penn, and Lorna joined in for a Samoan language class that Mavis taught, an informal time of fun for all of them, including Uncle Cash, as they walked around, naming things, and talking—a relative term—to the Samoans in their native language.

Just now Merritt sat quietly at the other end of the fale, making botanical drawings. He and Mavis collected specimens from all over the island. Mavis had showed Merritt how to press them to preserve them, and Merritt had shown a great talent for drawing as he made sketches of the plants, and then graduated to delicate and detailed watercolor paintings. Now Uncle Cash smiled as he watched the boy, sitting cross-legged on a mat, a small study table in front of him, his tongue sticking out the side of his mouth as he drew.

Just beyond the fale, in the shade of towering palms by the river, Dolly and Penn played with Lita. She had woven them a ball out of palm leaves, as Samoan children had been doing for centuries. Even Vigo, who was still too young to walk, was allowed to crawl around and join the game.

In the distance they heard the first sweet strains of Lorna's violin. She played every day. Sometimes she did rigorously formal exercises, but sometimes—like now—she just played bits of music that came into her head: dreamy, airy strains that enchanted everyone within hearing. Uncle Cash recognized two phrases from Bach's Violin Concerto No. 2, the first movement; Lorna played them over and over again, sometimes fast, sometimes slowly, sometimes bridged with her personal otherworldly music. Uncle Cash and Mavis sat quietly for a long time, just listening.

Finally there was a long silence, and then Lorna began the concerto from the beginning, obviously now playing by the score. It broke the dreamy spell. Mavis sighed. "It seems so peaceful, doesn't it? Sometimes I have a hard time believing that the things that have happened in the last few months—no, actually years—are real. But I know that those long years of quiet, of peace, of innocence, are gone now."

She shifted her position so that she could see Dolly and the other children better. "By the way, Professor Dodge, I've been trying to remember to tell you that I have nothing to tell you. About the German consulate fire. As far as I can ascertain, none of the Samoans know anything at all about it. Of course I don't want you to break any confidences or compromise any information that belongs to the United States of America," she said, smiling a little, "but I am very curious if you have found out anything about it."

He looked surprised. "I didn't realize that I hadn't told you. I'm old, and I don't know what I've told to whom. That's why Stockton would never entrust any big secrets to me, I would probably just dodder around and tell all the wrong people."

"Nonsense," Mavis interrupted. "No—what is it the Americans say? Hogwash, that's it. Hogwash. You're extremely intelligent, and one of the most intuitive and perceptive men I've ever met."

"Thank you," Uncle Cash said, genuinely pleased. "Anyway, McKean and Mr. Blacklock went right to the German consulate to offer any help they could. Marines had surrounded it, and they were warned to get off the property or risk arrest. Dr. Knappe has been arresting Samoans and interrogating them right and left ever since then—but I suppose you know that."

Mavis nodded. "But they do protest their innocence, and I believe them. Not because such a thing is beneath them—they've been known to burn a rival warlord's crops and fale—but because they are such abysmal liars. They simply cannot tell a direct lie effectively."

"I believe them, too," Uncle Cash agreed. "Though I can't get anyone to address it directly. They just look blank and start talking about other things and pretend they didn't know there was a fire, and then they didn't know it was a consulate, and then they didn't know it was the *German* consulate . . . and so on. You know what I mean. They may not be good liars, but they can certainly dance around a question for hours.

"At any rate, I believe them because that is the information we managed to glean, too. You see—I know you already know this, so I'm not breaking anyone's confidence here—you recall that McKean has developed a sort of cordial professional contact with Captain Fritze of the *Adler*. This sort of thing is very common in diplomatic circles, I understand; the principals can only maintain contact under the strictest rules of their government's positions, but the underlings keep a sort of back door of communication open. And so McKean spoke with Captain Fritze about the fire, and he indicated that it was just an unfortunate accident with the cooking stove."

"I see," Mavis said thoughtfully. "But Consul Knappe obviously doesn't share his naval commander's view. Arrests and interrogations right and left, and actually boarding a British ship to search for armaments of war? They're really coming it the high hat now, aren't they." The Germans had boarded the British merchant ship *Richmond* on the fifteenth and had ostensibly found armaments to "aid and comfort the enemies of the kaiser and the Imperial German Navy."

"Yes, and I know that once again, if you can just get off the beach, you're in a haven," Uncle Cash said, waving with an all-encompassing gesture. "But in Apia it's very tense, particularly since Dr. Knappe declared the island under martial law yesterday. People are running in and out of the consulate all hours of the day and night. It's like a lunatic asylum."

Mavis bit her lip. "You know, I would be so happy to have the children stay with me for a while, if it would help."

"It would," Uncle Cash said casually. "Why don't you come to the consulate and speak to Stockton about it?"

She looked away quickly. "I can't do that."

"Then I don't suppose it will happen."

"But—I thought that perhaps you might speak to him about it," Mavis said, watching the children playing and laughing.

"I'm afraid not."

"Oh."

"Yes, just so."

She frowned at him. "But he hasn't come to see me or ask me to take the children."

"No, he won't do that."

"But—I can't go talk to him."

"Why not?"

"Because it—because I—that is, it wouldn't—somehow—"

"You know, Stockton's been talking in that same moronic pidgin English. Why don't you two try speaking in Samoan? Maybe you'd be more articulate."

"It's not funny," Mavis said darkly.

"He said that, too," Uncle Cash said. "But I find it rather amusing myself."

Mavis dropped her eyes. "You just don't understand, Professor Dodge. I—I honestly believe that we almost made a very grave mistake. Stockton and I."

"Fine," Uncle Cash said shortly. "Except that Stockton doesn't believe that. But at any rate, one reason that I never interfere with people's private affairs is because even when I can see who is right and who is wrong, there is rarely anything that I or anyone else can say or do to remedy the situation or solve the problem. Only when the parties involved recognize the true problems and work together to find solutions can the situation be resolved."

"But I *know* the problems," Mavis said. "I *am* the problems."

Uncle Cash's mouth tightened. "Your singular verb doesn't agree with your plural predicate nominative, but aside from that I only have one thing to say."

"And that is?"

"Hogwash."

"Seven warships in the bay," Trista said tightly. "The islands under German martial law for six weeks now. How can you say that we're not heading for war, Father?"

After the Germans had declared martial law, tensions, particularly between the Germans and the British, had risen sharply with the Germans' insistence on searching all ships in Apia. Stockton had reluctantly sent word that America should increase her naval presence in the islands. On February 5 the USS *Trenton,* carrying the flag of Rear Admiral Lewis A. Kimberley, had arrived; on February 22 the USS *Vandalia* with Captain Schoonmaker had reached Apia Bay. The seven enormous warships, plus all of the normal shipping and pleasure craft in the bay, made for constant tensions, with the jostlings and maneuverings required to keep accidents from happening. Even so, on the tenth a German brig had wrecked, a high tide slamming her into a dock; and on the fourteenth the same thing had happened to an American brig and a small schooner. These types of accidents were not at all uncommon in the restless bay, but they caused flurries of accusations and counteraccusations among the citizens of the different nations.

"I didn't say war was impossible, Trista," Stockton said. "I said that it's not imminent. That means I don't believe it will begin today."

"Perhaps tomorrow or the next day. Or next week. Father, we cannot stay here."

Stockton studied her, then turned to search McKean's face, and then Cash's face. Both of them looked grim. He turned back to Trista. "I didn't know you felt this strongly."

"I do."

Trista was determined to get her family away from Samoa. Though she had seen that her father and Miss Thoroughgood were estranged, the children were still constantly at Mavis Thoroughgood's. Uncle Cash or Lorna ran back and forth between the consulate and Mavis's, dragging Merritt and Penn and Dolly with them all the time. Many nights they stayed with Mavis. And though her father no longer formally "made calls" on Miss Thoroughgood and she no longer came to the consulate, Trista knew they saw each other occasionally. Sometimes, if McKean was unavailable, Stockton was obliged to go to the fale to fetch the children. Trista tried to make him let her do it herself, but for some reason he flatly refused to let her go to Mavis's. Also Trista knew that Stockton and Miss Thoroughgood often met by chance when Stockton and Uncle Cash went to visit Chief Nifo Sisi.

In the back of Trista's mind, she knew that her father's look of distant regret and sometimes even loneliness was her fault. But she ignored—even smothered—these uncomfortable thoughts. Now she could hardly bear the thought of her father and Miss Thoroughgood meeting, even by chance.

"We simply cannot put the children in more danger," she went on firmly. "It's irresponsible of us."

Stockton rose from the armchair to clasp his hands behind his back and pace a bit. There wasn't much room for pacing in the small study—really just six steps to the door and six steps back to the armchairs grouped about a tea table—but he took several turns anyway. McKean, Trista, and Uncle Cash were respectfully silent.

Finally Stockton sighed and resumed his seat. "All right, Trista. I'll book passage for all of you on the next available passenger vessel to Sydney. You know you will likely have to make the arrangements yourself from there?"

Trista looked shocked. "But—what do you mean? You must come, too!"

Now Stockton looked shocked. "Trista, I can't do that and you know it. I accepted a tour of duty for at least one year, which means that I must remain here in Samoa for at least another five months. I can't possibly leave."

"But—but—I hadn't contemplated going alone. We can't do that, Father. We need you. How could you think that Uncle Cash and I could manage the children all by ourselves?"

"Your pardon, Trista," Uncle Cash said easily. "But that would be *you* managing the children all by *yourself*. I'm not going anywhere."

"Whoa, Mab," McKean said, now grinning. "You and the thundering herd going back to the States? On who knows how many ships? And how many ports of call? You'll lose Diggers in the first five minutes of the first shore leave, I predict."

But Trista ignored him; she stared at her uncle with outrage. "What! What do you mean, Uncle Cash?"

"I'm not leaving Samoa," Uncle Cash repeated. "Unless, of course, you ask me to, Stockton."

"You don't think the children should leave, Professor Dodge?"

"What difference does it make? It's not my responsibility, so I don't believe I should air my opinion too lightly," Cash said, staring very hard at Trista. She dropped her eyes. "What I will say is that I think that's a decision that you alone should make, Stockton. After all, you alone bear the responsibility. That gives you the right to make the decisions."

"Well, I can't possibly manage them alone," Trista snapped. "So I suppose the question is moot now."

Stockton said thoughtfully, "You know, Professor Dodge is correct, as usual. It's my decision, Trista; it always has been. I believe that it was the Lord's will for us to come here, and I believe it is the Lord's will for us to be here now. I forgot that for a few moments, I suppose because I didn't realize you were so frightened. But don't be afraid. I do know that we are in the Lord's hands, and He will care for us now and always, no matter what comes."

"I'm not afraid," Trista said with ill humor. "At least, I'm worried about the children. But I'm not afraid."

"And are the children afraid?" Stockton asked.

"Yes," Trista said quickly.

"No," Uncle Cash said, his bright blue eyes fixed on Trista's face. "They're having the finest vacation any child could ever have. They're in a tropical paradise; their lessons are light and tailored exactly for them; they have all the delicious food they can eat; they have friends and music and dancing every day from dawn to midnight. None of them show the least apprehension, not even Dolly."

"Also, they get to swim as much as they want. And wear lavalavas," McKean said regretfully. "Lucky pups."

But a couple of days later they weren't so lucky—at least, Merritt wasn't. It was March 2, with a full moon so bright that Stockton's bedroom seemed lit by a blue heaven-lamp. He awakened slowly, barely coming back to reality after a dream of silently sailing alone on a moonlit sea. It was a sad dream, and he was sad when he awoke. But then he heard his son's wracking cough in the bedroom down the hall, and all thoughts of the dream dissolved.

Merritt was very ill, his temperature raging. Immediately Stockton awakened Trista, and they moved a very sleepy Penn into the girls' room. Stockton sat up with Merritt all night, and Trista took over in the morning. Still Merritt was no better.

Stockton called in Dr. Runyan of the *Trenton*, who prescribed aspirin and quinine. The aspirin brought down the fever a bit, but Merritt still was a sick little boy requiring constant attendance. Trista and Uncle Cash took turns, for Stockton and McKean were extremely busy dealing with the day-to-day crises arising from the hostilities in Samoa.

Three days later Stockton was slowly climbing the stairs, going very quietly so as not to awaken Merritt in case he was napping. As he neared the door he heard Merritt talking in his weak invalid's voice: "I just thought I would like to have my specimens and my drawings . . ."

"That would be fine, I will send Armbruster to fetch them," Trista said crisply.

"You don't think maybe Misi Too-Good could bring them to me? I thought she might visit me . . ."

"I told you, Merritt, she can't come; she has a life and responsibilities of her own and she can't be worried with a stranger's sickly child. Why would you want Miss Thoroughgood, anyway? Aren't Uncle Cash and I taking good care of you?"

Stockton came into the room. Both Merritt and Trista started guiltily. "Go on, Merritt. I would like to hear why you are asking for Miss Thoroughgood, too."

Merritt looked down at the light cotton coverlet and picked at it a little. His face was chalky, but he had two scarlet patches on his thin cheeks. His forehead was sweaty, and his hair clung to it. He had purple shadows, like great bruises, under his eyes. "I—I don't know, exactly. Something about Misi Too-Good . . . it's like when you can hear Lorna, far-off, down by the grotto, maybe, playing something sweet. Misi Too-Good's voice is quiet and doesn't hurt your ears and her hands are always cool and soft. I can go to sleep when she reads to me."

Stockton's normally calm face was now as dark as thunder, but his voice was soothing. He bent and kissed Merritt's forehead and smoothed back his hair. "I'm going to sit with you for a while, but first I need to speak to your sister in private. Will you excuse us for a few moments?"

"Sure," Merritt said, his dull eyes growing big. "Are you going to talk about me?"

"Of course," Stockton said, smiling. "We're just going to step outside here and whisper about how you're lazing about pretending to be sick just to get attention. So you just lie there and pretend to rest, and I'll be back in soon to pretend to watch you."

Stockton wasted no time as Trista followed him down the hall to the head of the stairs. "Have you asked Mavis to come?" he said bluntly.

Trista swallowed hard and dropped her eyes. "No, sir."

"Why not?"

It was the sharpest tone Trista had ever heard her father use. She flinched. "I—I—didn't want to impose upon her."

"Ah, the old mantra. I see," Stockton said in a harsh half-whisper. "At least, I think I do. Trista, I want you to go to Miss Thoroughgood's and ask—no, *beg*—her forgiveness that I have not called on her to ask her help. Then you will humbly ask her to come to see Merritt, and to bring his specimens and his drawings and his art supplies."

"But—Father, I have no escort—"

"McKean is downstairs. He will *accompany* you. You will not send him."

"Yes, sir."

"Now, Trista," Stockton ordered.

"Yes, sir." Trista ran down the stairs, her cheeks crimson, angry tears in her eyes.

It was two hours before they returned, a seemingly eternal time for Stockton. He sat with Merritt and talked and watched him, for he wandered in and out of a feverish daze, but in the back of Stockton's mind was a boyish excitement to be seeing Mavis again. He heard her quiet step on the stairs, and rose, his eyes alight.

She came in, smiled perfunctorily at Stockton, and immediately went to Merritt's bedside. "Hello, Merritt," she said softly, laying her hand on his forehead. "What's all this?"

"I've got a fever. I asked for you, Misi Too-Good. Did you bring my samples? And my sketches and my paints?"

"Yes, I did," she said soothingly. "But for now I'm going to fix you some tea, and then maybe you can take a nap."

"You won't leave if I go to sleep, will you?"

"No, I'll stay. Until tonight."

He stirred, then turned his head and closed his eyes. "Thank you for coming to see me, Misi Too-Good."

"You're very welcome, Merritt."

She and Stockton stepped out to the hallway. "His fever is high," Mavis said worriedly. "I'm going to make a plaster and fix him some tea. Will you sit with him until I can prepare everything?"

"Of course."

She turned to leave, but he reached out to touch her lightly on the shoulder. She flinched a little, but turned back.

"I can't thank you enough, Mav—Miss Thoroughgood, for coming," he said warmly. "I know you—I know that I have made you uncomfortable with my—importunities, but I want to assure you that I wouldn't dream of continuing to—to—"

"Stop," she said harshly and turned away. "Just—please excuse me." She hurried to the stairs.

Stockton stood staring after her, mystified. He could have sworn that he saw tears in her eyes before she had fled, but how could that be? She cared nothing for him, except as a friend, so his gratitude and apologies couldn't possibly have upset her, could they?

With frustration he shook his head and went back to Merritt's bedside.

That evening, after a busy day of dealing with the arrest of two Samoan chiefs and one American citizen by the Germans, Stockton wearily went upstairs to check on Merritt. He heard Mavis's soft voice speaking, and Stockton simply couldn't resist the temptation to just listen, just let her voice soothe him, just let the blessed sound wash over him, and pretend that the gentleness and warmth he heard was directed toward him.

"This is called a dreaming pillow," she was telling Merritt. "It's for good dreams." She leaned forward and lifted him, then slid a small square of satin underneath his head.

"I have nightmares when I have fever," Merritt said wearily. "Sometimes I even—sort of—hear things. Scary noises."

"I know. I remember when I was a child, and I had fevers and bad dreams. My mother fixed me dreaming pillows and they work. Would you like to hear how they work?"

"Yes," he said sleepily. "It smells good . . . not perfumey or flowery like girls. Like . . . home . . . in springtime . . . maybe after it rains . . ."

"Yes, that's what I hoped you'd think of when I made it for you," Mavis said. "You see, for dreaming pillows you must find the scents that make you think of home. So for you, Merritt, I thought it would be the smell of grass and rich cool mud and old trees and cool evenings. And do you know what else a dreaming pillow must be like? It must be like a safe place, so that the bad dreams can't get in. And so you see this dreaming pillow, for you, is like a pasture. You just imagine that you are a little, sleepy lamb, and you are in a green pasture, just drifting off to sleep. And you know you are safe because your Shepherd loves you, and is responsible for you, and will take care of you."

"The Shepherd? Like Jesus is the Good Shepherd?" Merritt asked, his eyes closed and his face composed.

"Exactly like that. He not only loves you, Merritt, but He is your Shepherd, and the shepherd always feels an obligation and duty to protect and care for his sheep. Like David, who killed a lion and a bear to protect his lambs, do you remember? And so Jesus will protect you from all the bad dreams, all the scary noises, all the frightening things you think of when you have fever. You just breathe deeply and remember that you are in a very safe place, and you are protected, always . . ."

Merritt slept.

The days wore on, and Merritt grew no worse, but his recovery was very slow. Mavis came every day, usually in the afternoon. She always slipped in the kitchen door, so Stockton never knew when she came or left. And true to his word, he never sought her out. He only spoke to her if she was there when he took a moment or two from his tense, busy days to go upstairs and check on Merritt. Sadly, he tried to keep his contact with her to a bare minimum, only formally thanking her whenever he chanced to see her.

That was why Stockton was so astounded on March 15, that Mavis came to the consulate very early in the morning; and she came to see him, not Merritt. For all of his life, Stockton recalled the shock—and pleasure—he experienced when she appeared at the door of his study that lurid dawn, for that day changed all of their lives forever.

Red and Lowering Sky

*H*ave you seen the sky this morning?"

At the sound of Mavis's voice Stockton jumped up too precipitately, scattering papers all over the carpet of the study. "Good morning, Mav—Miss Thoroughgood! How—how good to see you. Have I seen the—no, I haven't, perhaps you would be so kind as to—er—accompany me—er—onto the veranda to—to view it?"

He struggled to bow to her, to retain some semblance of dignity, to speak calmly and directly to her, and to kneel to gather up his papers. She knelt with him and their eyes met. Mavis's sparkling blue eyes twinkled and then they both laughed. It was the first easy, natural moment between them in months.

"Please forgive me for ambushing you in this way," she said as she helped him gather the scattered papers. "But the Samoans are—not alarmed, they take these things as a matter of course—but they are quite sure a bad storm is coming. And the sky is red and bloody-looking."

"I see," Stockton said, taking her hand to help her to rise. He grasped it a little too long and then dropped it too quickly.

A shadow crossed Mavis's face and she stepped back, putting more distance between them.

"Well, they may not be alarmed, but I can see that you are," he said a little stiffly. "Or perhaps not alarmed, but wary."

She sighed and waved one brown hand nervously. "I feel—apprehensive. Haven't you ever noticed that one feels a bit touchy, or high-strung, before a storm? I've particularly observed it in children and animals. And so I wanted to check on Merritt, you see, and—and—to let you know that the Samoans are preparing."

Gallantly he offered her his arm. "I thank you, Miss Thoroughgood, for your concern for my son, and for the timely warning. Now, perhaps, you would accompany me out onto the veranda to see your red warning sky? So that next time I may be a little more sensitive and observant myself."

She took his arm. "I believe that you are sensitive and observant, Mr. Livingstone."

"Thank you," he said with surprise. "Compliments are much more meaningful coming from a person whose opinion I respect so much."

They went out onto the veranda. The consulate faced due north, directly out to sea. It was barely dawn. To the east the roofs of the village of Matautu were red-tipped, as if touched with blood. A bloated sullen sun hung just above, a crimson fireball. There were no clouds, and no wind. The sky was orange-red in the east, darkening to a purple still-night sky in the west.

"It does look strange," Stockton muttered. "But there are no storm clouds, no wind."

Mavis's hand on his arm tightened just a little. "I know it doesn't seem too ominous. But believe me, the Samoans know. They always know."

He nodded and turned to look down at her. His clear eyes were warm, appreciative as she gazed hungrily back up at him. It seemed that she was starving for his touch, just to look at him, just to talk to him. She was recklessly glad that a storm was coming. It had given her the perfect excuse to be with him.

"Would you do me the honor of having coffee out here with me?" he asked lightly. "Sometimes, on fine mornings, McKean and I sit out here and enjoy the fresh air, instead of hulking about plotting darkly in the study." He pointed to a wrought-iron table with four chairs on the east end of the veranda. The sun cast a lurid light on it. "It'll be in the shade in a few minutes, but we have a fine shading mat that Chief Seumanu gave McKean for assisting him and his wife with some legal advice when he was arrested." Talking lightly, Stockton moved to loosen the ties that bound the heavy mat up. "If you'd like, why don't you go check on Merritt? I'll instruct Armbruster to serve coffee out here, and if McKean's up—and if he's had his first cup of coffee—I'll invite him too. So please join us back here as soon as you can, Miss Thoroughgood."

As he so matter-of-factly took her assent for granted, Mavis gratefully allowed herself to relax and not try to resist, as it seemed that she must do each moment that she was anywhere near Stockton Livingstone. She loved him so much, and she fought valiantly not to.

Half an hour later she, Stockton, and McKean sat at the table on the veranda. It was hot and sultry, even in the shaded corner of the porch.

"Not a breath of air stirring," McKean said. "It's bizarre. Look at the bay."

Apia Bay was full of short, vexed chops, with little whitecap tops that slapped each other in no pattern of wind or wave.

"Did you know," Mavis said, "that Apia Bay is much like a great flask with a narrow neck? For large ships, that is. The coral reef forms a barrier at the harbor entrance—that's why you often see breakers out there—and it also traces the inside of the harbor, forming the floor. In places the reef is close to the surface and forms a sort of tabletop with the deeps underneath; in other places it sinks down deeper, but never deep enough for great ships, though the Samoans say that the sand bottom of the bay is quite deep."

"You said the Samoans are preparing for a storm," McKean said. "What do they do to prepare?"

Mavis answered, "They take down their good, light mats, roll them, and anchor them securely inside the fales. If they think the storm will not be too strong, they have heavy-weather mats they hang. If the storm is very bad, then they go inland, to the river valleys, where typhoon winds never reach. They aren't going inland today, by the way. But they are bringing in their boats."

The harbor had perhaps two dozen native craft pulled up onto the beach. Natives busily filed along, the light skimmers on their heads. Some of them were small enough for two men to carry; others required a dozen men. They were all heading inland.

The harbor had, along with the seven warships, about a dozen other craft dotted along the shore all the way from Mulinuu to Matautu. There were two American brigs of five hundred tons or more, half a dozen schooners, and some island hoppers and fishing trawlers. The only other sign of activity in the harbor was two lighters busily off-loading one of the brigs and transporting goods to Moors's store.

They all looked searchingly at the crowded harbor. In the bottleneck fairway the American ships *Trenton* and *Vandalia* lolled on the restless chops. Inside the harbor were the American *Nipsic*, the German ships *Adler, Olga,* and *Eber,* and the British ship *Calliope,* all huddled perilously close together.

Mavis said, "They all hurried out to sea last month, on the two blows that wrecked the German brig and the American brig and schooner."

"Yes, on February 14 and 22," McKean said. "And just last week, on the seventh, came another blow that ran them out of the harbor. I had vaguely noticed that they have to sail out of the bay in single file, though I hadn't considered why. Now, since we have your very clear and concise description of what's under those restless waves, ma'am, I realize that the fairway entrance between the reef must be tight."

"It is, they tell me, only three cables wide," Mavis said in a low voice.

"How wide is that, in English?" Stockton asked. He was a hopeless landlubber.

"I have no idea," Mavis said. "I just have heard about the 'three cables wide' all my life. Seamen always say it in dark portentous tones."

"It's a little over two thousand feet," McKean answered. "Not much leeway."

Mavis said in a low voice, "Well, they aren't lining up to sail out today, it seems. Mr. Livingstone, do you think that perhaps you should warn them?"

Uneasily Stockton answered, "I would hesitate to try and dictate to a naval officer how he should manage his ship. And after all, Rear Admiral Kimberley, who is our commander of the Asiatic Squadron, is on the *Trenton*. He's an experienced naval officer with a long and distinguished record. I couldn't presume to tell him his business."

"Of course not," Mavis said. "A foolish suggestion. I—I'm just concerned, because the Samoans, as I said, are never wrong. But a blow that would wreck their light canoes might have no effect whatsoever on these mighty warships."

"I hope not," Stockton muttered. Then he turned to her. "Miss Thoroughgood, would you do me a favor—again—and stay here, at the consulate today? I would be so much more eased in my mind if you were here to see to Merritt."

"Of course I'll stay," Mavis said softly. "Tui and the other boys have already secured the fale and my cottage. I'll stay until the storm is over."

At 2:00 P.M., Stockton and McKean anxiously checked the barometer in the study for at least the dozenth time. It had been falling all day and now stood at the ominous low pressure of 29°11.

"Father, why don't I just go out to the *Nipsic* and talk to Commander Mullan?" McKean asked. "He and I haven't made such good friends as Leary and I did, but we still have a cordial relationship. I could just ask him if he's at all concerned."

Stockton thought for a few moments, then nodded. "Go ahead, McKean. Just don't appear to be trying to advise him. You know how the navy is. And I can't say I blame them; I would imagine a dumb landlubber trying to tell them what to do about sailing a ship is perfectly infuriating to the most patient of seamen."

McKean grinned. "Diplomatic as always, Father. I promise I'll be good."

One of the *Nipsic*'s boats was on the beach, for Commander Mullan's steward had come ashore to buy some oranges that had just been delivered to Moors's store from the six-hundred-ton American merchant brig *Musketoon.* McKean hitched a ride back out to the ship.

Commander Mullan, a somber, dutiful man, received McKean as soon as he boarded and took him into his day cabin for a glass of iced mango punch. They talked for a few minutes of the Germans' latest search of a British merchantman, and then McKean asked casually, "I noticed that you're striking your topmasts. My father and I have seen that the barometer has fallen sharply in the last few hours. Are you expecting a blow?"

"Yes, though we haven't spotted any storm clouds from horizon to horizon," Commander Mullan answered. "The bay is just too restless. Must be a blow out there somewhere."

McKean nodded. "But you have no plans to go out to sea to ride it out?"

A short silence ensued. Commander Mullan was not the type of man who was easy to read; his features were always calm, but to McKean he seemed to be struggling with his answer. Finally he said quietly, "I haven't heard from the flag, and my standing orders are to keep to my anchorage here, Mr. Livingstone."

"I understand," McKean said, and rose to leave the cabin. "Godspeed, my friend."

Captain Fritze of His Imperial Majesty's ship *Adler* stood on the quarterdeck and watched the *Nipsic*'s boat head back toward the shore. He could see McKean Livingstone—a man he considered honorable and even likable, though he was an enemy of his country, according to his consul Dr. Knappe—turning this way and that in the boat to observe the crowd of ships jostling each other in the restless bay. McKean, catching sight of him, tipped his cap, and Captain Fritze gave him a sketch of a salute in return.

His first lieutenant came close and said, "Sir, the *Nipsic,* the *Vandalia,* and *Trenton* are striking topmasts and battening down their hatches."

Captain Fritze nodded. "Strike topmasts, ready the ship for a storm. Signal same to *Eber* and *Olga.*"

"Aye, sir." He hurried to the signalman.

Captain Fritze turned to the north and focused on the American flagship at the entrance to the harbor. *The* Trenton *and the* Vandalia *are still blocking the entrance. I should overrule the consul and sail the squadron out to sea, but perhaps he is right. We shouldn't let the Americans make us blink first . . .*

———

Captain Wallis of the *Eber* cursed under his breath as he watched the signals from the flagship. "Strike topmasts, make storm preparations," he growled. "I can't believe the squadron is staying in this little hole; we're going to batter each other to pieces if there's any sort of wind at all!"

His signalman asked woodenly, "Any reply, sir?"

"Acknowledge the orders, Lieutenant," the captain said with resignation. "And send over a midshipman to the flag, reminding Captain Fritze that our screw is still being repaired, so we have no steam power at all." The *Eber*'s screw propeller had been injured in the blow of February 14—over a month ago—and the men were still struggling to repair it. It was very difficult without dry docking the ship.

Normally when a steamer rode out a storm at anchorage, the captain would carefully lay out two anchors, port and starboard, and gently steam between them to create just enough tension to keep the ship able to ride the billows, but still securely anchored. Captain Wallis was having great difficulty positioning his injured ship, and even now the wind was rising, and the swell was getting more troublesome.

"Tropical storm coming, little crowded anchorage, and no steam," Captain Wallis growled to himself. "Not that steam is going to do any of us much good anyway. We're just going to toss around like toy ships going down the bathtub drain anyway, steam or no steam."

———————

Captain von Ehrhardt of the *Olga,* the easternmost ship in the bay, eyed Matautu through his glass. The captain, a cautious, stubborn man by nature, decided to edge a little farther east. Matautu had the best anchorage in the bay, and he thought that he might—with a lot of luck and skill and providential help—he just might be able to ground the old girl on the gentle slope of beach with only minimal loss of life.

That, he judged, was their best—their only—hope.

———————

Aboard the royal navy ship HBMS *Calliope* Captain Kane sipped tea in his spacious, airy salon. A discreet knock sounded at the door.

"Come in."

A nervous first lieutenant stepped in and saluted snappily. "Lieutenant Taylor reporting, sir. The natives are saying that a storm is definitely coming, though Mr. MacArthur, the British resident who has lived here for over twenty years, says that he does not believe it to be any more than a summer storm; certainly not a typhoon or hurricane."

"I see," the captain said. "Any sighting of a possible storm front anywhere?"

"No, sir."

"The glass?"

The sweaty young lieutenant frowned. "Mr. MacArthur's barometer showed 30°, sir, but our own is not falling at all; it has been steady all morning."

"Mmm," the captain said noncommittally. "Anything else?"

The lieutenant frowned. "Just that the Americans are striking topmasts, sir, but have sent no messages to us."

The captain eyed his first lieutenant with barely concealed amusement. "Americans," he said, taking a sip of tea. "Excitable young puppies."

"Yes, sir," the first lieutenant agreed, swallowing hard. "Shall I double-check the barometer with the *Trenton*'s readings, sir?"

"Nonsense. We are the royal navy, after all, Lieutenant. We've been reading ship's instruments for about four hundred years longer than the colonists. Our barometer isn't wrong."

But it was.

Rear Admiral Lewis A. Kimberley, standing on the quarterdeck of the light frigate *Trenton*, watched as his seamen did the dangerous, difficult work of disengaging the topmasts and lowering them down to the deck. His steward brought his afternoon coffee and he noticed that the swell was getting bigger and more temperamental. The coffee sloshed in his lidded mug.

Just across the fairway he saw Captain Schoonmaker of the *Vandalia*, also observing his men working. The captain sighted his admiral and saluted formally; Kimberley returned the salute and went on down to his cabin for a nap before dinner.

It was the last time that Admiral Kimberley saw Captain Schoonmaker alive.

By 10 P.M. the small fitful breeze that had flitted in from out of the north had grown into a gale. Rain crashed against the wooden storm shutters covering the windows of Merritt and Penn's room. Sitting between their two cots, Mavis paused in her reading of *Treasure Island* when a particularly violent crash of thunder made the house vibrate. She studied Merritt's, then Penn's face.

"Are you frightened?"

"No, ma'am," Merritt answered calmly. He was much better, though he was still pale and thin and tired easily. Normally he was fast asleep by dark, but tonight he lay quiet, his eyes closed, his thin hands relaxed outside the light cotton coverlet, just resting and listening.

Penn grinned puckishly at her. "Storms are not as scary as when in the wars the chiefs chop people's heads off and peoples get their fingers shot off." The boys' special friend Tui, Chief Nifo's favorite son, had gotten his ring finger shot off in a wild skirmish in the Fangalii Affair. Tui had proudly kept it and dried it to mummification and Penn and Merritt sneaked looks at it whenever possible.

Mavis said, "But you boys have never seen a Samoan storm. I suspect that they don't have storms like this in Washington, D.C."

"We live in Georgetown," Penn corrected her carefully. "Our house is called The Cedars. What do you call your house, Misi Too-Good?"

"Generally only very grand houses have names," Mavis said. "Mine does not."

"Is The Cedars grand?" Penn asked Merritt curiously.

Merritt answered absently, "Guess so. Misi Too-Good, I'm not at all sleepy and I feel very, very well. Do you suppose I could go downstairs to see Father and McKean? Just for a bit?"

"Me too!" Penn shouted, bouncing up.

Mavis considered the boys. Merritt's eyes were not fever-dulled, and though he wasn't his usual vibrant self he didn't seem ill. Penn, like most little boys, was usually sound asleep by this time. Mavis smoothed back his satiny hair and searched his face carefully for signs of nervous energy that children get when they've been without rest for too long. But even Penn seemed not frightened or agitated . . . merely alert. Perhaps this was a night for watchfulness.

"I'll ask your father," Mavis finally said, rising.

Penn and Merritt waited breathlessly, their eyes round and their fingers crossed until Mavis returned. "Very well. Everyone is keeping watch in the parlor. But stop—Merritt, put your slippers and robe on. I know it's warm, but at night one has a tendency to get chilled. Penn, you too."

The entire family was gathered. Trista had realized two hours ago that Dolly was never going to go to sleep, so she had allowed her to sit up with them. Now Dolly and Uncle Cash played chess in a corner of the room. On two facing sofas, Trista read—or pretended to read—while Lorna slowly took her flute apart and cleaned it. Stockton and McKean sat in two armchairs that were placed side by side across from a settee. Mavis and the boys sat on the settee. Merritt said, "Thank you, Father, for letting me and Penn stay up. We truly do feel fine."

"Fine," Penn echoed.

Stockton smiled. "So I see, and I'm glad. Truthfully, I could hardly expect anyone to sleep with all this din."

"Din," Penn solemnly agreed.

Slowly the sound of the wind changed. Before, it had been a series of shrill shrieks, with gusts that rattled the shutters and doors as it first pushed them in and then sucked them outwards. Now the tone deepened to a roar and became a steady thunder that neither rose nor fell, but was one continual battering. Everyone raised their heads to listen. Reading or concentrating on chess became impossible. Mavis and Trista went upstairs and collected coverlets and pillows for the children. The only conversation Trista had with Mavis was one frosty question: "Are you certain you shouldn't have advised my father to go inland?"

Mavis answered, "Your father always does what he feels is best for you."

As they had done on several nights of crisis, Uncle Cash and Mavis made cocoa for the children and roused out some of Mrs. Armbruster's cookies and gave the night a sort of odd holiday feel. Dolly, Penn, and Merritt dozed a little, but as the hours wore on all of them began to feel more and more on edge.

By 2:00 A.M. the storm had risen to a terrifying tempest.

McKean stood up, his face grim. "Father, I would like to go outside and see if I can tell anything about the ships."

"No!" Trista cried. "McKean, that's insane! You'll be just—blown away like a speck in a whirlwind!"

Mavis said, "I don't think so, Trista. Have you noticed we haven't heard anything hitting the house? Before when we've had hurricane winds on the islands, the shrubs and small trees are uprooted and crash around. Also, none of the shutters is loose. I've seen hurricanes where even when the shutters were closed the wind was so strong it would cut in through the seams and break the windows. It's nowhere near that strong now."

Stockton listened intently.

"I believe you're right, Miss Thoroughgood. All right, McKean. Take my glass. And see if any other houses along the beach are lit, particularly the British consulate. I'm curious if we're the only ones who are concerned, or if everyone else is just having a good night's sleep in the soothing rain," he finished drily. The rain was so heavy that the sound of it was more like a gigantic waterfall than the scattershot of raindrops.

McKean put on his heavy canvas overcoat and wide-brimmed hat. He and Stockton had a struggle to open the front door; the wind screeched maniacally as they managed to crack it. Then, as if with malice, it flung open, almost throwing Stockton to the floor. McKean stepped outside and began pulling it shut. Stockton and Uncle Cash together managed to close it.

Everyone stood in the hall, simply waiting and watching, until McKean returned. The puddle on the floor from the water running off his coat and clothing was wide as the hallway and ran down toward the kitchen like a brook. He took off his streaming hat, then took off his coat and just let it drop to the floor. Shaking the water from it would have soaked everyone. In the dim lantern light his face was grim. "There's trouble."

Stockton nodded. "Go on upstairs and change into dry clothes, son, and then come back down."

"Begging your pardon, sir, but I don't think so," McKean said evenly. "I've got to go back out, as soon as I have your leave, and there's no sense in getting another set of clothes wet. Anything you wear is going to be dripping within seconds, and no overcoat's going to prevent it."

"All right," Stockton said. "Then come into the parlor, for there's no sense in all of us huddling out here in the hall." Mavis quickly folded two thick woven cotton coverlets and put them on one of the armchairs so McKean could sit down. But he was too agitated to sit, so he paced, scattering water drops all along his path.

"Is anyone else out there?" Stockton asked.

"Captain Wendt from the *Musketoon* and his crew of seven," McKean answered. "There are lights in the British consulate, and also Mr. Moors's house, and a few others. But that's all."

"And the ships?" Stockton asked, visibly steeling himself.

McKean grimaced. "As I said, sir, they look to be in real trouble. Some of the waves are topping out at thirty feet high! I caught a glimpse of the *Eber*—that's all you can see, really, is just snatches of them between the sheets of rain—and it was nose-up to the sky and almost broached to backwards!"

"What about the other light craft in the bay?" Stockton asked.

"Sir, Captain Wendt's *Musketoon* was that big brig that was anchored up close to Mulinuu. He said that he and his crew have been in Helder's Tavern all day today, drunk. They just woke up a little while ago and went out to see how she was riding out the storm. Captain Wendt said he just knew that all the heavy warships would

leave the bay for the open sea. But they didn't, as we know."
McKean stopped and swallowed hard. "About an hour ago the *Nip-sic*, dragging her anchors, crashed into the *Musketoon* and she went
down, a mass of splinters. The *Musketoon* was the heaviest merchant
ship and the last one afloat."

Stockton's indrawn breath was sharp. "But there were thirteen
merchant craft in the bay this evening."

Mutely McKean shook his head.

A long heavy silence ensued. Finally Stockton said, "I'm going
out with you, McKean. We need to talk to Captain Wendt and any
other seamen here in town. I have no idea how to organize sea rescues, but it sounds as if we need to start getting everything in place."

Trista cried, "But, Father, surely there's no need for you to go?
McKean can do whatever must be done!"

Gently he took her hands. "I know he can, Trista. But it's my
responsibility and my duty."

Her face fell and she sank back onto the settee.

"I'm coming, and just don't even open your mouth, Stockton,"
Uncle Cash growled. "I'm coming. Period."

Mavis said, "I'm coming too."

"That's not necessary," Stockton argued.

She smiled. "You forget yourself, sir. I hardly think you're in a
position to give me orders. I am a British subject, and the United
States of America cannot dictate to me."

"But—oh, hang it, come on then," Stockton said. "I'm not going
to waste my breath arguing with you. I think I'm going to need all
the breath I've got out there."

"That's the truth," McKean agreed heartily. "You hafta kinda
hold your mouth sideways and suck in a breath whenever the water
falls out of your mouth."

Penn frowned. "But what about your nose?"

"Forget it, Pips, no noses are breathing out there, except fish's
noses," McKean said, stooping to tweak Penn's nose. "You're not

scared, are you? 'Cause you and Diggers are going to have to be the men of the house while we're out dashing around in the storm."

"I'm not scared," Penn asserted, throwing his chest out. "We'll take care of these little ladies."

Sounding ludricrous in her little-girl voice Dolly said acidly, "Oh, wonderful. I feel so much better now."

His Wonders in the Deep

To the Livingstone children it seemed as if an enormous crowd came hurtling back out of the storm into the consulate, but actually it was only seven people. Stockton, McKean, Mavis, and Uncle Cash had met the Armbrusters making their way to the consulate, and Stockton had asked Captain Wendt of the doomed *Musketoon* to come in. It was very difficult to talk outside; the gale force winds and hammering rain were deafening.

Gazing at the river flowing down the hall from their rain oilskins and macs, Stockton called out, "First order of business: Take up the carpet in the parlor, Armbruster, McKean. Mrs. Armbruster, never mind the furniture. People are going to have to be coming in and out tonight, and they're going to be wet, and they're going to have to have a place to rest. We'll worry about little things like the furniture later."

"Yes, sir, I'll just go along to the kitchen and get hot coffee and tea started," Mrs. Armbruster said, whisking out of the room.

They got sorted out. Trista, Lorna, and the children huddled in one corner of the room, all together on two armchairs by the gaming table. Oddly, all the adults stood. They were grim and tense.

Stockton began to pace, and the others stood in a loose circle around him. "I couldn't see a thing out in the bay. Captain Wendt, what is the situation with the warships?"

Captain Henry Wendt was an enormous man, tall and portly, with a low rumble of a voice, dark curly hair and beard, and a deep chest and belly. A strong smell of whiskey hung about him, and his eyes were red. But Stockton suspected it was not just from a hangover or from the sting of the salt wind. He was taking the loss of his ship very hard. Pieces of the *Musketoon,* including Captain Wendt's great-great-great-grandfather's ancient very large-bore musket, for which the ship was named and which had hung in the captain's cabin, had washed up onto the shore in two pieces.

Now he shook his head, scattering water from his long dark hair like a shaggy dog. "Can't see out to the fairway at all, Your Excellency. You'm can catch glimpses, like, of the five tossing around in the bay proper, but I can hardly tell of 'em which is which. 'Course, I don't have my glass," he said softly, mournfully. "It were on my ship."

"But they are in trouble," Stockton said, a half question.

Captain Wendt answered, "Sir, they're in about the biggest trouble a ship can be in. All on 'em."

"Then we need to get some kind of rescue operation organized right now," Stockton said. "I don't know how to do a sea rescue. Can you tell me, Captain Wendt?"

Mavis spoke up and stepped close to Stockton. "Mr. Livingstone, the Samoans are the ones who need to be attempting rescues. If anyone can manage a lifeboat in those seas, they can." She turned and looked back at Captain Wendt questioningly.

He grimaced, then nodded. "She'm right, Your Excellency. These here natives can do miracles in those little canoes of theirs."

Stockton asked Mavis, "Will they help?"

"Of course."

"All right, then, McKean—"

"I'll go," Mavis said firmly.

Stockton hesitated, then said, "It would be best. Are you—all right?"

"Of course," she said over her shoulder, as she was already halfway to the hall. "Don't worry about me. I'll be back with Chief Nifo and the men very soon." She threw on her mantle, and McKean managed the door for her. It took a strong man to open and close the door.

Stockton continued, "We're going to need all the cables, ropes, and chains we can gather. Armbruster, McKean, why don't you go up and down the beach and stop at every house. Tell them to bring any rope—also any other supplies like—like—"

"Lanterns, oilskins, boots," Captain Wendt put in helpfully.

"Yes, and anything else they can think of that might help," Stockton continued, pacing. "Tell everyone to muster at whichever of three stations is nearest to them: here, or the British consulate, or the London Missionary Society Chapel. But tell anyone who has a boat that's not at the bottom of the bay and that might serve for a lifeboat to come here and report to Captain Wendt. Armbruster, you go east—and tell Pastor Wetherington that I've volunteered his chapel as a rescuer's station. I know he'll help any way he can. McKean, you go west and go first to the British consulate. We need to keep Colonel de Coetlogon updated as much as we can."

The colonel had come out to speak to them when they were on the beach, but he was an older man and was ill. He had not tried to stay long in the tempest, and had no illusions that he could help with any rescue attempts. He had returned to the consulate after assuring Stockton that they would be happy to be a hospital again, or would help in any other way Stockton could think of. "For now," he had said firmly, "I and my family will be gathered together to pray."

Armbruster and McKean were putting on their rain gear again when Captain Wendt said to Stockton, "With your permission, Your Excellency, mighten I suggest that the gents ask everyone to put a light in a window that faces out to sea?" He swallowed hard. "Me and my crew, we was trying to signal, but it weren't possible. No lantern will stay lit out there in that. It mighten help, though, if even one sailor out there sees even one light on shore. It sure mighten help."

"By all means," Stockton said. "Tell everyone who has a house on the beach, McKean, Armbruster. Some might object and want to leave up their storm shutters, but at least tell all the Americans that those are my orders. In fact, McKean, take the shutters off our front windows before you leave. Trista, get lanterns to put in the windows."

Trista jumped up and fled. McKean and Armbruster, their faces set and grim, left.

Stockton spoke to Captain Wendt and Uncle Cash, who were the only ones left in the room except for the children. "That was my next question, Captain Wendt. About signaling. How could it be done?"

The captain shook his head. "I couldn't keep any lantern lit out there, sir. The rain's just too strong."

"Behind something, under something," Stockton muttered, resuming his pacing. "We must think of a way . . ."

"Excuse me, sir," Merritt said, jumping up and coming to stand boldly by Captain Wendt. The captain, still in dripping black oil-skins, stared bemused down at the pale young boy. They looked like David and Goliath.

"Hmm? Yes, Merritt?" Stockton said, frowning.

"Sir, I—I might know something we could do," he said hesitantly. "To signal."

The captain snorted—it sounded like a mad bull—but Stockton said, "Son, this is important. Make it quick."

"Yes, sir. It's just that I've been up in the attic and there are two windows up there that would be perfect to signal from," Merritt said, talking fast, the words tumbling over each other. "We could set up four or even six lanterns in a square and move a black cloth in front of them in Morse code."

Captain Wendt's eyes went wide. "Why, that just might work. You're a smart boy, ain't you, son?"

"Sometimes," Merritt said with relief.

"Very good, son," Stockton said warmly. "Captain, would some of your men be able to get up there and get the storm shutters off the windows? And I'm sure you know Morse code, if you would—"

"I know it, Father," Merritt said, pleading. "I could code some signals. And Penn and I can manage setting up the lanterns, and then we could maybe signal a little bit. I know we couldn't do it long. But maybe we could until some of the Samoan boys get here to help." Merritt knew it would take strength and stamina to move even just a stretched cloth back and forth in front of the lanterns to make the dot-and-dash signals.

"That would be very good of you, Merritt. Just let me see the signals before you send. And get Trista and Lorna to help you with the lanterns and be careful."

"I could help with that," Uncle Cash said impatiently. "I know I'd be no use out on that beach, Stockton, but I am determined to do something to help."

Stockton said, "Sir, I do have something I would like for you to do. It will be hard, but I think you are better suited for it than anyone."

"Just tell me what it is, and let me get to it," Uncle Cash grumbled. "I can hardly bear this standing about feeling like an old helpless codger any longer."

"No one would ever think that of you," Stockton said firmly. "Professor Dodge, I know that your eyesight is still as sharp as it was twenty years or so ago, when we were sighting down sniper's sights at Yankee bluebellies."

"Closer to thirty years now. And I can see as good now as the day you and I joined up."

"I know. Sir, I think you are the logical choice for a lookout. With my Congreve telescope, I think you might be able to sight the ships. Unfortunately, the only place I can think of for a good post is the belfry of the Catholic church. It's the highest structure on the beach."

"Oh, fine, perched up in the very trappings of idolatrous popery. You know once I get up there I won't be able to come down."

"I know, sir. And I know you will be cold and wet and miserable and your legs will ache. And I also know that you will stand your watch faithfully and without complaint, as you always have."

"God willing," Uncle Cash said.

"God willing," Stockton agreed. "Before you go, sir, will you pray with me and my children?"

"Of course. Captain Wendt, will you join us?" Uncle Cash said, sliding his arm along the man's enormous shoulders.

The captain bowed his shaggy head and spoke so low that the other two men could barely hear him. "I'm not a prayin' man, you know, sirs. But I'd be mighten grateful if you would pray for me and my crew, along with all them men out there in that devil sea tonight."

"Not the devil's sea, Captain Wendt," Uncle Cash said steadily. Merritt slid quietly up and took his great-uncle's hand, and Stockton took Merritt's hand. The three men and the child bowed their heads. Uncle Cash quoted from Psalm 107 in a strong voice:

> They that go down to the sea in ships,
> That do business in great waters;
> These see the works of the LORD,
> And his wonders in the deep.
>
> For he commandeth, and raiseth the stormy wind,
> Which lifteth up the waves thereof.
>
> They mount up to the heaven,
> They go down again to the depths:
> Their soul is melted because of trouble.
> They reel to and fro,
>   and stagger like a drunken man,
>   and are at their wit's end.
>
> Then they cry unto the LORD in their trouble,
>   and he bringeth them out of their distresses.
> He maketh the storm a calm,
>   so that the waves thereof are still.
> Then are they glad because they be quiet;
> So he bringeth them
>   unto their desired haven.

Mavis finally found Stockton on the beach; the night was so dark, the rain so dense, that visibility was measured in inches. Stockton, McKean, Captain Wendt, and his men were down at the edge of the water. Stockton was trying to use his glass to see, while McKean and the sailors were working their way up and down the beach, trying to see which—if any—of the docks were still intact. So far they hadn't found a single board foot of a dock standing, but they had found four pilings anchored in cement, the only pieces of Moors's dock that was left. Captain Wendt and his first mate were trying to figure if they could rig lines and pulleys to run out to the ships.

If the ships ever managed to anchor.

Mavis grabbed Stockton's arm. In the tempest one had to shout to be heard, and water flooded into the mouth and nose. She cried, "Chief Nifo and Chief Tutua and their men have come with me, about thirty. Some of the boys are running to the other camps, and more men should be here soon."

She could see him nod and motion toward the consulate. Slowly, for it was a struggle against wild wind and flooding stinging rain, they made their way inside. Gasping, they stood in the hallway, fighting to catch their breath.

Finally Stockton said, "McKean and I went up to the German consulate. Their guard of fifty men are at full alert on Mulinuu. Dr. Knappe refused to see me."

Mavis shook her head regretfully. "They actually think that Mataafa would use this storm to attack them?"

"Yes, they do, and Dr. Knappe probably thinks that Colonel de Coetlogon and I are planning an attack along with Mataafa." Stockton sighed. "So you'll have to send someone back to tell Mataafa and his chiefs not to come into Apia. Knappe would probably have them arrested."

"All right," Mavis agreed, then asked, "What could you see, Stockton? Can you see anything at all?"

He shook his head, scattering water droplets everywhere. "I can hardly see anything. The rain is like opaque sheets, and none of the ship's lights are lit. I did get one report so far from Professor Dodge. He's our lookout up in the belfry of the Catholic church." Stockton licked his lips and looked pained. "He said that *Olga, Adler,* and *Nipsic* had evidently crashed into each other at some time in the night. *Olga*'s port quarter is injured, *Adler* has lost her bowsprit. *Nipsic*'s smokestack is gone; every once in a while you can see a shower of sparks out there. It's eerie. Professor Dodge says she's still making steam, but the stump of stack spits out live sparks that run along her deck."

"Are they—are they under steam? I mean, are they steering at all?"

"Not really. Professor Dodge says they're just being tossed like toys out there. Especially *Eber*. She had an injury to her screw in a blow last month, and Professor Dodge said it looked as if she were unable to manage any power at all.

"And as for the others, *Trenton* and *Vandalia* are still out in the fairway, but *Vandalia* is being tossed inshore. *Calliope* is under steam and seems to have the best control, but it's so crowded and the bay is so wild, my guess is that the best they can hope for is the dawn, so that they might be able to just try and keep from ramming and sinking each other."

"All right, Stockton, listen to me," Mavis said sternly. "I'm going to advise the rescue stations about treating the rescuers. Beginning right here. Everyone should try and come inside, dry off, and get warm every two hours at least. I'm going to instruct Mrs. Armbruster, Miss Taylor at the British consulate, and Pastor Wetherington at the chapel to give everyone who is out in the storm for more than an hour a tonic of honey, lemon, and whisky or brandy. It's going to be a long night, and if all of the rescuers get chilled and sick it won't do any of those poor sailors a bit of good. And so I'm going to begin with you. Go in the kitchen, warm up, dry your feet, and warm your hands while I mix up some tonic."

"Yes, Misi Too-Good," Stockton said obediently as he followed her down the hall. "But wait, Mavis, I would rather that you would go first to the Catholic church to make these arrangements for Professor Dodge. He's up there alone and it was necessary to take down some of the siding to set up the telescope. He's bound to get wet and chilled."

"I stopped by the church on the way back, to ask Father Dimitri if we could use the church as a hospital. He said he would pray that we'd need one," Mavis said sadly. "Anyway, he told me that Professor Dodge was up in his belfry—actually, he said that 'that old Protestant heretic' was up there. Evidently he and Professor Dodge are friends."

"Yes, they are," Stockton said with relief. "I didn't know if Father Dimitri was at the church or not. I know he'll take care of my uncle."

"So he will," Mavis said. "Tonight we're all taking care of each other."

Tui and four other Samoan boys were in the kitchen, having carried in several boxes of lemons and jars of honey. They had been sent to Moors's store, MacArthur's store, and Helder's Tavern to collect supplies. As soon as Mavis came in they started speaking all together to her in Samoan. She held up her hand for quiet, then Tui said in broken English, "Misi Too-Good, Misi Moo-es and Misi Mac and Misi Held-ue won't give any whisky to us."

"I'll send Captain Wendt," Stockton said darkly. "He'll get you all the whisky they've got, Mavis. Meanwhile, I believe we have some brandy here. Go ahead and use whatever you need."

Mavis nodded and spoke rapidly to the boys. Stockton, who did understand what they were saying, nevertheless had a lag time in comprehension, a not unusual occurrence in using a language that was not native to one and that one rarely used in daily conversation. Mavis turned and said, "I've told Tui that the older boys should help with the boats out on the beach, but the boys under twelve should go up to the attic and help with the signals. To see the lights and the steady signaling even heartened me. That was a very good idea of Merritt's, Stockton. You should be proud."

"I am proud of my children," Stockton said. "All of them. But listen, Mavis, I think you would be of more help out on the beach, with me. I know it's brutal but I must stay out there, organizing. And we need the Samoans desperately. It would help so much if you could interpret. I'm just not quick enough in Samoan, and though they all understand English well enough for polite everyday usage, in this crisis it would go so much smoother if they could communicate in Samoan."

Mavis nodded. "Mrs. Armbruster, you know how to make this tonic, don't you?"

"Don't I, though? And don't any mother who's ever had a child out in the rain too long and come in with croup?" Mrs. Armbruster sniffed. "You just go on about your business, Mavis, and I'll tend to the fires and tonics."

Men and boys came and went in the consulate kitchen, looking for hot coffee or tea, arranging for shifts of men to come in and warm up, Samoan boys begging to do anything to help, to be runners or to fetch anything or just to stoke the fires or help make tea. After a short rest Mavis and Stockton went back out on the beach.

The night, interminable and impenetrable, wore on. Mavis and Stockton stayed close—most of the time by necessity clinging to each other in the maelstrom—with Stockton organizing the rescue parties, assigning men to attempt to rig lifelines, teams to help the Samoans with their boats, teams to help clear the beach, which was littered with the flotsam and jetsam of lost craft, broken coral, and shrubs and small trees. Some bigger trees started washing up, and Mavis told him that both the Mulivai and the Vaisangano had swollen to raging torrents and were washing down trees uprooted from far upstream. The bridge of the Vaisangano was out.

They got updates from Uncle Cash every half hour or so. Stockton had assigned two Samoan boys as runners for him, and Mavis had instructed them that they continuously take him hot sweet coffee and tonic every hour, and try to take him into some shelter and dry him off every hour or so.

Alo, one of the boys assigned to him, shook his head and said, "No no, Misi Too-Good. Misi Dahj, he says nobody can watch or touch his magic tube. Only him."

"Fine," Mavis said darkly. "You tell him Misi Too-Good says no one is going to fiddle with his old tube, but if he doesn't do as I say, I'll personally come up and have a talk with him."

With delight on his face, Alo nodded and dashed away. But within a few minutes he was back, his face pale and his eyes huge. Wordlessly he handed the oiled pouch to Stockton and hurried back into the darkness. He and Mavis went into the consulate to read.

It was evil tidings, indeed.

Eber just foundered, it read. *Crash stopped, went aback, crashed into the reef again, went nose up, and slid down and disappeared. Think I see men in the water opposite MacArthur's store. Try rescue. Hurry.*

Mavis and Stockton ran.

Samoans were already frantically working; evidently they had seen the wreck. Tying ropes to six of the strongest, sturdiest men, three other men held the line and played it out as the men tried to swim out. It was impossible. There was so much debris in the water, and the chops—even close to the shore—were topping out at around ten feet. Gamely the men went out again and again, floundering, fighting, hoping, with logs and small trees and pieces of broken boats and ships crashing into them. One man had a three-foot splinter driven into the meat of his thigh. Another Samoan man leaped to take his place as he was carried off to the Catholic church.

The rescuers did find one man struggling toward shore, and him they helped. Three more survivors of the *Eber* washed up, barely alive.

Mavis and Stockton joined Seumanu Tafa, High Chief of Apia, as he stood looking out to the east. It was a little past five o'clock in the morning. Dawn would come in about an hour. But there was no lightening of the terrible night yet.

The Germans had oppressed the high chief and his aiga in forcing them to their will. They had, in fact, arrested Chief Seumanu twice and had even detained his wife, Fatuila, once. Men from Chief Seumanu's aiga formed the rescue party on this particular stretch of beach.

"Did you see it, Matai?" Stockton asked the chief.

He nodded sadly. Lifting his left arm, he bent his elbow and propped his forearm at an angle. Then he flattened his fingers straight out. He spoke in Samoan, and Mavis translated.

"Here the coral reef is like a table. A table, with the surface only a few feet under the water. The legs of the table are deeply undercut. The ship crashed into the edge of the table head-on, the nose flew up into the air, and she slipped down . . . down . . ." He had illustrated the ship with his right hand. With curiously graceful gestures he hit his flattened left hand, upended his right hand, and then made sinking, flowing motions down his left arm. Tears stung Mavis's eyes.

"How many men were on that ship, Your Lordship Misi Living-Stone?" Seumanu asked Stockton.

"Seventy-eight," Stockton answered. "But there were four souls saved because of you and your men, Matai. God will bless you and your men for your courage and valor. And God will especially bless High Chief Seumanu for his charity. The Bible says that no man has greater love than this, that a man lay down his life for his friends; but it is the true charity of the Lord Jesus Christ when a man loves his enemies and risks his life for those who despitefully use him."

Humbly the old man bowed his head, then turned and went back to his men.

"You're looking pinched and cold," Stockton said, taking Mavis's arm. "We've been out on the beach for over an hour. Let's go back to the consulate and you can take some of your own medicine, Misi Too-Good."

As they fought their way back up that doomed beach, they noticed that they could see their way a little better. It was not as if there was light; there was not. It was as if the darkness had changed from flat black to charcoal gray. A bleak dawn, indeed.

Mrs. Armbruster was alone in the steamy kitchen. Towels hung from a makeshift clothesline set up just over the hot stove, and seven pairs of sandy, muddy, soaked boots were lined up in front of it. The scent of hot coffee and hot cotton hung on the air.

Tears were rolling down Mrs. Armbruster's face. She had known some of the sailors from the *Eber* personally, as she and Mr. Armbruster were Lutherans and attended the Lutheran chapel. Most of the German citizens of Apia and the sailors attended there too. But her voice was strong and steady.

"Armbruster has set up the rescuer's station, with tea and coffee and tonic, in the parlor, sir. Everyone was gathering in here, but there's just not the room. And I know you'll be happy to hear that Mr. McKean just left; he's been coming in to warm up a little and dry off regular. Dolly, Penn, and Merritt were that worn out, and I gave them a swallow of tonic and sent them to bed. Miss Lorna's looking after them and she says they're sleeping as soundly as little babes."

"Very good, Mrs. Armbruster, it's a blessing to have you and Armbruster here to look after my family," Stockton said. "What about Trista? Where is she?"

Mrs. Armbruster shot a quick glance at Mavis, then answered in a bland voice, "She got that upset at the news of the poor old *Eber*, sir. She burst into tears and ran upstairs and slammed the door behind her. She won't let Miss Lorna nor me in."

Stockton's eyes widened. "Trista? Trista behaved that way?" He shook his head. "I just don't understand what's been wrong with her. It's so unlike Trista to be weak and teary. She's always been such a strong child. I was going to ask her to go to the Catholic church; we should have someone there to help Father Dimitri." He turned to Mavis and took her hand. It was damp and cold, and gently he rubbed it between both of his. "Would you go speak to her, Mavis?"

"I? Speak to Trista?" she said, startled.

"Yes. Would you, for me? And for Trista's sake, too."

"I—I don't know . . ."

Quickly he said, "I do think it will help, Mavis. She likes you and trusts you, you know. In spite of some silly things she might have said in the past few months," he went on, his eyes steady and knowing on Mavis's face, "Trista is a very good judge of character, and she knows what kind of person you are."

"Do you think so?" Mavis asked quietly.

"I know so."

"Then I will go speak to her."

She went upstairs and knocked on the door of the bedroom that the girls were using. Trista flung open the door without warning. When she saw Mavis her tear-sodden face grew pale, and then, oddly, a rueful half smile played across her lips. "Please, come in."

Mavis came in and stood watching Trista questioningly.

"Will you sit with me?" Trista asked, seating herself on one of the small cots and patting it.

Mavis sat, rather stiffly, her hands clasped tightly in her lap.

Trista looked up at her and her features were twisted with pain. "Ever since my mother died, I've been—lost, you might say. First I simply refused to believe she was really gone forever; no matter what I did, I still kept looking for her in the next room, expecting her voice on the stairs, half-waiting for her call in the mornings . . . and then, when the realization truly set in, I grew angry. At her. At the children. At my father. At my brother. At the servants. It seemed I was always trying to control my temper."

"I went through something similar when my mother died," Mavis said. "Though it wasn't such a shock as I know it must have been for you and your family. My mother had been ill for a long time. Your mother—"

"Just died. Between one moment and the next." Trista's voice caught, but with an effort she straightened her shoulders and spoke calmly. "But after those initial highs and lows were over, I—I just sort of shut down. I don't know how to explain it. Nothing, it seemed, touched me deeply. No emotion. Not joy, not happiness, not love, not anger, nothing. I was calm."

"Numb," Mavis said.

"Yes, I suppose I was," Trista said wearily. "But my mind was churning, always, beneath the surface. I—I felt that the world, and God Himself, was horribly unfair. I was world-weary and cynical and truth to tell, tired of everyone and everything. Even God."

"That's not at all unusual, Trista. Have you ever read Job? He didn't sin in all his mourning, you know. But he did grow weary of life and even of God."

"Yes, I read it over and over. Although there are not really any answers to our questions in Job, I came to realize that, if you know God at all, you must know that He is good. And if He is good, then He is just and fair. So although it seemed unfair that my mother died, I knew I just had to trust the Lord. There just is nowhere else to go . . . so . . . I was starting . . . starting to come back to the Lord . . . to seek the truth . . . but then—"

Trista swallowed hard. "Then I began to see my father's esteem and growing attachment to you. All of those violent emotions came back like a flood. I was angry, and resentful, and—malicious and cruel. And now—now all those men have died . . . and many more may die . . . and all of my petty spite and temper seem so childish. Such a waste of myself, of my soul, of my God-given, precious, rich, full life on this earth." She turned and took Mavis's hands in her own, and her big hazel eyes were brimming with tears. "I have wronged you so much, and I am truly sorry. Will you forgive me?"

Mavis threw her arms around the girl and drew her close. "Oh yes, Trista, I forgive you freely and happily. Thank the Lord for His goodness and mercy, that He has healed you of this grievous hurt that wounded only you, my dear. Now, tell me. Your father needs you to be strong. Can you do a difficult and trying job for him?"

"Anything," Trista said quickly. "Anything at all."

"Then you must go to the Catholic church and represent your father with all of those poor men who are hurt and wounded tonight. If you can do this he will be much eased in his mind and his heart."

Trista nodded and jumped to her feet. "I will go. For the first time in many months, now I know I can pray for someone else. Please go tell my father—that I'm well and will hurry."

"Good," Mavis said, going to the door.

"Misi Too-Good," Trista called.

"Yes?"

"Thank you, with all my heart."

"Misi Living-Stone," Mavis said lightly, "you are heartily welcome."

Water, Blood, and Spirit

ᴛ he Catholic church had two bell towers at the corners of the
portico. By dawn of the sixteenth, Uncle Cash had been in the
west tower for about four hours. It was simply a tall wooden box with
decorative slats at the top bell chamber. Uncle Cash had been obliged
to knock out three slats to stick the telescope through and rain continually sloshed in through the opening; sometimes, with the wild
gusts of wind, it also came slashing through the other slatted por-
tions on the other walls. He was soaked, chilled, achy, and, after wit-
nessing the loss of the *Eber,* heartsick. But still he doggedly swept
the bay over and over, continually sighting on each of the six warships left, documenting their positions and status every fifteen minutes in a journal and sending short statements to Stockton every half
hour or so.

Every hour either Alo or his other runner Fua had brought him
a swallow of tonic or hot tea or coffee. But after they had both run
up and down the beach with the news of the *Eber,* Uncle Cash had
sent them to the American consulate to get something hot to drink
and something to eat. Father Dimitri and Trista had called up a
couple of times to him, but he had seen the stream of men coming
into the church—four men from the *Eber,* eight men injured on the
beach—and Uncle Cash knew that his niece and the priest were
very busy with the injured men. No one had come for the last hour
since dawn.

But now he heard a heavy slow tread on the small wooden stairs that wound around three sides of the tower, and the trap door in the floor opened. Captain Wendt's shaggy bear's head popped up. "Hullo, Your Excellency," he said, maneuvering his great bulk through the small opening. "I've come to relieve you, sir."

"I'm not a minister or a diplomat," Uncle Cash said tiredly. "My name is Dodge, Captain. Most people just call me Professor Dodge."

"Yes, sir," the captain said, standing and staring down at the older man with narrowed eyes. Uncle Cash's eyes were red, his sharp cheekbones jutted out starkly, his face was a sort of gruel-colored gray. "Mr. Livingstone said I was to relieve you, sir, and that I was not to take any nonsense from you. I'm to watch for four hours while you rest, Your—Professor, and then if you feel up to it, you're to relieve me."

Uncle Cash sighed. "I don't feel as if I've done anything at all useful. It's very hard, just sitting here . . . seeing it happen."

Captain Wendt took off his watch cap and slowly crushed it between his hands, his eyes downcast. "You've bore witness, sir. That's a very important thing. To bear witness."

Uncle Cash gazed up at him, his blue eyes suddenly sharp and bright. "Yes, it is. You think about such things, do you, Captain?"

The man nodded, then looked out the opening toward the bay, squinting his farseeing seaman's eyes against the slashing rain coming through. "I've been at sea all my life, since I was just a little raggedy boy snatched off the Kristiansand docks and put to work on a Norwegian herring buss. I've been all over the world, on all the seas, at one time or another in my life. Everywhere I go, I wonder about the deeps . . . if they hold men. Lost seamen. Men who just sail away from their homes and never come back. The ones who have no witness." He swallowed hard. "I try to be their witness."

"You pray for them?"

He frowned. "I don't know, exactly. I don't know anything about God. I—I sure liked that bit of poetry you said back at the consulate, sir. Would you tell me that bit again about the deeps?"

"'They that go down to the sea in ships, that do business in great waters; These see the works of the LORD, and his wonders in the deep.'" Uncle Cash repeated the lines in a full, strong voice. "That is a psalm, written by a very great king named David."

Captain Wendt nodded slowly. "I've seen His wonders in the deep, I surely have."

"A man called John wrote this about the Lord: 'This is he that came by water and blood, even Jesus Christ; not by water only, but by water and blood. And it is the Spirit that beareth witness, because the Spirit is truth.'"

"Water, blood, and the Spirit bear witness," Captain Wendt said thoughtfully. "I'm not an educated man, you know, sir. But I do think about such things. I—I catch the meaning, sir, about the water and the blood, the stuff of life . . . and my spirit bears witness that it's the truth."

"I see that you understand, Captain Wendt," Uncle Cash said. "John goes on to say, 'For there are three that bear record in heaven, the Father, the Word, and the Holy Ghost: and these three are one. And there are three that bear witness in earth, the Spirit, and the water, and the blood: and these three agree in one.' I think you understand exactly what these words mean, Captain Wendt. I think you know, in your spirit, that the water and the blood and the Spirit bear witness to Jesus Christ, the Son of God, because he is the Spirit, and the Spirit is truth."

Captain Wendt nodded and tears filled his eyes. "I know. I've always known. I just didn't know what to do about it."

"Just pray and ask Him to forgive your sins. You already understand that His blood was shed for your sins, and the water and the blood rushed out of His side as He was stabbed by the sword for your sins. And His Spirit bears witness, now and forever."

Captain Wendt bowed his head and prayed, "My Lord and Savior Jesus Christ, I have sinned, and I ask You to forgive me. I have witnessed Your wonders in the deep. Now my spirit bears witness of You, and I ask Your Spirit to come into my heart. Amen."

He looked up. "Thank you, Your Excellency. And now, sir, you really have to let me relieve you."

Uncle Cash smiled ruefully. "I—I'm willing, Captain Wendt. But to tell the truth, I don't think I can get down those steps."

The captain smiled, an unexpectedly sweet and shy smile for such a big gruff man. "That's all right, sir," he said softly. "It would be an honor for me to carry you."

And so he did.

One by one, the sea conquered them all.

Full dawn came at about 6:00 A.M., but brought no hope of the storm lessening. Though no structure or tree had been harmed in the least by the wild winds, the bay was still a maelstrom and the rain was still torrential. The beach was piled high with debris, and it took dozens of men just to keep spaces cleared to work in.

Samoan boys salvaged wreckage from the sunken ships, taking any identifiable item up to one of the rescuer's stations. They also worked endlessly dragging the mounds of debris out of the way of the dozens of men who worked doggedly trying to launch rescue boats and rig lines. Most of the men working the beach were Samoans; the white men had realized the superiority of the natives in dealing with this accursed bay and mostly stood around helplessly, staring out, struggling to see the tormented ships.

McKean worked with Chief Nifo and his men, trying again and again to rig lines to launch rescue boats, but the sea constantly fought them back to shore. Stockton and Mavis walked up and down the beach, encouraging the rescuers, arranging for needed supplies, seeking out the men who were obviously suffering ill effects from exposure to the savage weather and making them go inside for hot drinks and food and to dry off and warm up for a time. Curiously, the white men seemed to suffer most from the chill and damp; the Samoans, barefoot and bare-chested, clad only in thin lavalavas, could last much longer out in the storm before they grew weak and exhausted.

Stockton tried to speak to each man and boy and thank them for their tireless efforts.

Of the six warships left in the bay, the American ship *Nipsic* and the German *Adler* were closer inshore. The German ship *Olga*, HBMS *Calliope*, and the USS *Vandalia* were battling it out in the rear; still holding on out in the passage was the American frigate *Trenton*.

At about 7:00 A.M., Stockton, Mavis, and McKean, having just come out from a hot tea break in the consulate, were trudging back up the beach when they saw, through fitful breaks in the continual sheets of rain, a warship rear up on the billows, close to shore. It was the USS *Nipsic*. She thrashed and turned, and they thought surely she would broach to and sink; but suddenly, jarringly, she crashed to a full stop and settled slightly awry. Chief Nifo joined them as they ran to the stretch of beach directly opposite from the beached ship. He shouted something in Samoan to Mavis.

"It's a sandbar," she told Stockton, panting with exertion. "Commander Mullan must have known of it. Chief Nifo says he's been watching the *Nipsic* for the last hour, and he says the ship has been working hard to drive up on that little spit of sand."

When they arrived on the beach, they could see that the crew was already deserting the ship, floundering toward shore; and though the sandbar itself was only waist deep, the violent swells threatened to drown them. Immediately Chief Nifo's men and McKean started tying lines to the strongest swimmers—and McKean was one of them—and swimming out to rescue the sailors.

Mavis and Stockton stood on the beach, out of the way of the men who were working so hard to rescue the crew of the beached ship, holding hands, just watching and praying. Stockton held Mavis's hand so tightly that it ached for hours afterwards, though she wasn't conscious of the pain at the time.

About an hour later, the mighty *Adler* came up out of the maelstrom. She was close to the reef, very close to where the doomed *Eber* had smashed against it. As Uncle Cash reported to Stockton later, he could see that as she was flung by the last killing wave, Captain Fritze, with courage and miraculous seamanship, slipped her moorings to ride the fatal wave. The sea tossed her up in the air like a boy's discarded paper ship, heaved her over, and threw her upside down. She did, however, manage to land on the "tabletop" of the reef, instead of crashing against the edge and slipping under. It was, miraculously, a winning gamble for Captain Fritze. Twenty sailors were killed when she broached to and crashed keel-up on the reef. But the other crewmen, and all of the officers, survived.

About nine a quartermaster managed to swim ashore and reported this; it redoubled the rescuer's tremendous efforts. But the sea was simply too angry and unforgiving. One of Chief Seumanu's men did manage to get a line all the way out to the *Adler,* but the reef immediately sawed it in two. Still, the men on the beach struggled on, hoping against hope.

The next few hours were just a blur for Mavis.

Sometimes, standing as always with Stockton, she found herself pulling on a rope with all her might; she had no idea what the rope went to, or why they were killing themselves pulling on it, but she pulled. In graphic horrific detail, sometimes the furious curtain of the storm was pulled aside and she saw the poor *Adler,* belly up on the reef, and could even see men moving around on it. For some reason the sight of these men filled her with more horror than any other sight all those terrible two days and nights.

Once she found herself in the offices of the German firm, listening to a conversation between Stockton and Dr. Knappe. They were speaking rapidly, urgently, in German. Mavis had become very proficient in German, but she looked from one man to the other in stupid wonder, for she could make nothing at all of the noises that were coming from their mouths. It was as if they were hooting like apes or making chittering noises like crows.

Twice she awakened from a sound sleep on the settee in the consulate. Once the parlor was full of men, some Samoans and some of Captain Wendt's sailors. She had fallen asleep with her head on

Stockton's shoulder, and he slept on until she roused him and they went out in the storm again. The second time she, Stockton, and McKean all sprawled on a red velvet sofa that was so water-stained it was of about five different colors. They all fell asleep, collapsed against each other in a heap. This time McKean had to awaken her and Stockton.

During that nightmarish day, the *Olga,* the *Calliope,* and the *Vandalia* all smashed against each other again. Desperately, at a speed later calculated at only one knot per hour, the HBMS *Calliope* managed to sail out of the bay. As she passed the wounded *Trenton,* Rear Admiral Kimberley and his men assembled as well as they could on the decks of the flagship and cheered the Brits as they finally made their way to the open sea and safety.

The *Olga* retained some small portion of control with her fully functioning steam engines and Captain von Ehrhardt's superior seamanship. At about 4:00 P.M., as her captain had hoped, the *Olga* finally managed to beach in Matautu.

The *Vandalia* and *Trenton,* the two American ships, seemed to have their destiny written together. As the *Vandalia* tried to maneuver away from the other ships, Captain Schoonmaker was washed overboard and lost. She was against the reef, getting pounded to pieces, and they lost several more men trying to get a lifeline ashore. But the *Vandalia* was rapidly settling, and desperately her men finally climbed up onto the masts—forty-three of them. The *Trenton* was helplessly blown right up against her and smashed into her quarter. But the flagship did manage to rescue the exhausted men in the tops of the *Vandalia.* The two ships settled to the gun decks, writhing together all night against the barrier reef.

Then it was night again and the rescuers had not been able to reach the *Adler.* Stockton and Mavis stood for hours with Dr. Knappe, on the beach with his marines. Words failed them. Tears ran down the German's craggy, handsome face.

In the morning, the seas were calmer.

Chief Seumanu led the rescue of the men and officers of the *Adler*. McKean Livingstone and Chief Nifo Sisi's men finally sailed out to the American ships and brought all the Americans home with only the loss of one Samoan, who was killed when an enormous piling, uprooted in the storm, rolled over him.

McKean finally came to stand before Stockton and Mavis on the beach, and said, exhausted, "We're finished. We've done it."

Without a word Stockton turned to Mavis, took her in his arms, and kissed her long and lovingly.

Tonight Samoa Dances

To Samoans, the highest form of art is the dance. All Samoans dance. Young, old, dignified, childlike, graceful, agile, clumsy, jesting; it doesn't matter, as long as your dance is the truth. Even the very young children understand this principle.

A week after the storm that changed their world, Chief Nifo Sisi and his people decided to have a great feast and celebration at his fale. The Livingstones and Mavis Thoroughgood were the guests of honor.

"You're wearing your best cream satin evening gown?" Lorna asked Trista in amazement as they began the long arduous work of getting ready for an evening out.

"Yes. I haven't worn it since we arrived in Samoa." Trista dug through her jewelry box for her pearl earrings. "I've been saving it for a very special occasion."

"Ah. By the way, is Mr. Herrington-Carruthers going to be at Chief Nifo's party tonight?"

"No, he isn't. I haven't seen Mr. Herrington-Carruthers lately. As you very well know."

The elder Mr. Herrington-Carruthers had come down to the beach several times during the storm to volunteer for rescue work, but as with the rest of the white men, Stockton had thanked him but told him that they and he were generally just trying to stay out of the way of the natives.

But his son, Paul Herrington-Carruthers, had stayed warm and pampered in his father's great plantation house during the storm. He had refused to assist the rescuers. The following day he had called on Trista and said fussily, "After all, the natives are practically fishmen themselves and they don't mind losing a half dozen or so; they're just primitive barbarians after all. So I calculated that there was no sense in white men catching their death standing about in a storm when there's nothing to be done."

"No, of course not," Trista had said shortly. "I'm very sorry to cut your visit short, but I have some pressing matters to attend to, if you'll excuse me."

"Mmm, shall I call later?"

"Yes, much later; perhaps next month. Or next year," Trista had called over her shoulder as she swept out of the parlor.

Now Lorna teased, "But, Trista, he's such a fine British gentleman. Stiff upper lip and dashing walking stick, wot?"

"Oh, do be quiet, Lorna, anyone can make a mistake," Trista said, but her eyes were dancing. "Even a terrible, disgusting, horrible one. Now. Why don't you wear your green watered silk, Lorna? And, Dolly, you're wearing your pink tulle, aren't you?"

"All right," Dolly said agreeably. "Trista, would you do my hair up? Please, please?"

Trista smiled. "I believe I will, just tonight. And come to think of it, I'm going to send Armbruster down by the Vaisangano to get some of those lovely hibiscus and white *pua* blossoms. I'll use the golden hibiscus for my hair, and for you, Lorna, I think we'll have the coral color, and of course the pink ones for you, Dolly."

Both Trista's and Lorna's gowns were of the latest fashion: a deep rounded neckline, cinched-in waist, big bustle for evening wear, and a long train. Dolly's pink tulle was frothy and trimmed with lacy ruffles made from fine Veronese lace.

Stockton, McKean, and Uncle Cash were all splendid in evening wear and top hats, but Trista—in her newfound lightheartedness—had relented and allowed Merritt and Penn to wear lavalavas with white dress shirts. She had not loosened up enough, however, to allow Merritt to get a tattoo, even though his pleas were heartrending.

In grand style they promenaded to Mavis's fale.

Mavis had dreaded this evening, for Trista and Lorna had laughed about sitting cross-legged on Samoan mats in their bustled finery. Mavis Thoroughgood had no satin evening dress, no Veronese lace, no bustle form, and no roomy skirt with a fine long train to wear over it if she had. She had one good silk blouse with lace cuffs that had belonged to her mother. Years ago, when it had been new, it had been snowy white, but it had yellowed with age. As Mavis had always done, she made the best of it, dyeing it a gentle beige color with tea and wearing it with her old faithful dark brown velveteen skirt. She had a cameo—also her mother's—that she wore pinned at her throat. When she looked at herself in her dressing mirror, she sighed. The tan color was all wrong for her—it made her skin look coppery—and her clothes were indeed very drab.

But when she remembered that Stockton Livingstone couldn't care less what she wore, she brightened. Then, defiantly, she loosened several long thick locks from her upswept hair and curled them, and tucked two enormous scarlet hibiscus flowers behind her left ear. "I'll tell him," she said, staring at her now-dramatic reflection, her eyes dancing, "that flowers behind your left ear means you're unmarried."

Finally all of the Livingstones arrived.

"You look lovely," Stockton said quietly, kissing her hand. And then she felt that she did.

They made their way to Chief Nifo's fale, which was a very large oblong pavilion. After eating for what seemed like hours, they gathered to watch the dances. Tui, Chief Nifo Sisi's favorite son, was first. He leapt and grinned and wheeled.

Sitting next to Stockton, cross-legged on a mat, Mavis explained, "The Samoan *siva* is jubilant, lively, athletic, unlike the dreamy hula of Hawaii or the grim death dances of the Maori warriors. It is an expression of the dancer's emotions, or an acting-out of an event in his life, or a combination of both."

Stockton watched Tui as he alternately grimaced, wheeled, leapt with jubilation, clapped, stamped. He was a graceful dancer. "I think," Stockton said slowly, "that he is acting out his part of the battle in the Fangalii Affair, when he was wounded. I think that the stately, proud parts of the dance portray the Germans. I can see how the Samoans see them as grim and terrible giants, without feeling, unaware of pain, a remorseless enemy. And that Tui, in battle, feels jubilation and triumph, even when he is wounded."

Mavis nodded. "Stockton, you have truly learned much about the Samoan soul. I can't believe a palangi could be so sensitive and insightful."

"You're a palangi," he reminded her.

"Mm," she said nonchalantly. "I forget. Anyway, I don't believe the Samoans see the Germans in quite that light any more. I think this dance is a very good portrayal of the way things were then. But now, after the storm . . ."

"Everything is different," Stockton said. "Everyone is different."

The Three Great Powers were at peace. Washington, Berlin, and London had all agreed to a conference in June in Berlin. Until then a placid tripartite administration of Apia had just sort of crept back into being. Apia was recovering and all of the inhabitants of the tiny island of Upolu were helping each other in thousands of ways, small and large, each day. On Sunday every church had been filled to capacity, and each day at least one prayer meeting was held on the beach, for a memorial or thanksgiving or just for prayer.

After a couple of hours of dancing by Chief Nifo's children and grandchildren, McKean stood up and clapped his hands. "My family and I have so much enjoyed watching and learning of your dance, even though we know that to have the charity and valor of the Samoan heart would take a lifetime of learning. But now I wonder, would you like to learn a palangi dance? Long ago I promised to teach my sister Dolly a Russian waltz. My sister Lorna has consented to play for us. Would you—"

His question was drowned out in shouts and applause.

McKean went to where Dolly sat on a mat with all of the ten smaller children of Chief Nifo's aiga. He bowed elegantly and extended his hand. "May I have the honor of this dance, Wortley?"

"Of course, sir," she said excitedly, and took his hand and stood.

Lorna stood and began tuning her violin, those atonal random notes that are somehow so pleasing to the ear.

"My family and I will demonstrate the Russian waltz," McKean announced solemnly. "All Livingstones are called to duty." Gamely Uncle Cash stood up with Trista; Merritt asked Lita to dance; Penn cockily asked a lovely eight-year-old girl to dance; and, of course, Stockton turned to Mavis, his eyes alight.

"Do you waltz?"

"I have never even seen a waltz, much less danced one," Mavis answered.

"It's simple. ONE, two, three; keep turning. Would you like to dance?"

"Yes, very much." They stood, giggling like children.

McKean announced, "All Russian ladies dancing a waltz always have a long train. It's a rule. Does everyone have a long train? No? How remiss of you, Dolly, Lita, Misi Too-Good. I insist upon long trains."

Lavalavas were brought, selected, and tied around the un-trained ladies' waists. Gallantly McKean bent down and swept up the very end of Trista's train, and she took it elegantly with her left thumb and forefinger, her pinky lifted slightly. "See? This is how the grandest of ladies do it," McKean said, winking at Trista, who winked back.

"How do ladies pick up their trains at balls?" Mavis asked Stockton curiously. "Surely they don't go bending down and grabbing for it themselves."

He grinned; he looked about twenty years old. "Not hardly, my dear. No, generally at grand balls there are servants posted at the doors of the ballroom and around the floor, whose job it is to hand up the ladies' trains to them."

"You're joking."

"I'm not."

"And you—you personally, Stockton Lee Livingstone—have actually paid some person cold hard cash to do this job?"

"I have. And if I had a powdered, bewigged, stockinged footman here tonight, my dear, I would gladly pay him just to follow you around and hand up your train. As it is, may I have the honor?"

"Certainly, sir," Mavis said, blushing a little. Stockton elegantly swept up the tail of her lavalava and handed it up to her. Mavis carefully copied Trista's graceful pose in holding it.

"Now, here are your positions, ladies and gentlemen," McKean said. "Ladies, put your right hand on your partner's right shoulder. Hold your train behind you, at your waist, bending your arm gracefully. Gentlemen, stand just a bit to the side of your lady. Place your right hand on her waist; bend your left arm behind your back. Very good—no—Diggers, you're already standing on poor Lita's toe and we haven't even started yet; stand back a little and let her breathe. Better, much better. Now—maestro?"

Lorna began the first slow introduction of "The Waltz of the Flowers" by Tchaikovsky. The dancers stood poised, ready; and as the waltz began, they—miraculously—all swept together in time. McKean waltzed as elegantly as if he were partnered with an imperial princess. He was holding Dolly three feet in the air, by her waist. She laughed, her pale thin cheeks flushed with delight.

Mavis never missed a step. She waltzed as if she had done it all her life.

"You are a wonderful dancer," Stockton said.

"As are you, sir."

"As a matter of fact, you are just wonderful."

She looked up at him and said simply, "I have dreamed of you, Stockton. All my life I've dreamed of a man just like you. But in these dreams I never dared to imagine that I would be here, like this, with you."

"Will you marry me, Mavis?" The smile never left his face.

"Yes. It's my dream," she said softly.

They waltzed.

"The Lord is good," Stockton said thoughtfully. "And His mercies endure forever. I never thought He would be so kind, so loving, as to give me another woman to love as I love you, Mavis. I know that Phoebe is glad. She would never have wanted me to shrivel up and wander in darkness as I did. You know, she would have liked you, very much."

"Do you think so?" Mavis asked eagerly. "I—I've wondered if she would have. You know, Trista has had a very difficult time. And I did think she had some valid reasons for worry. About me and you, I mean."

"Oh? Such as?" Stockton said carelessly.

"Such as—such as—I don't wear shoes all the time," Mavis said finally, her eyes alight. "And I'm so tan your pale, soggy Washington friends may think I'm a wild Samoan woman."

He shrugged. "I've noticed that all of my children, except perhaps for Trista, have gotten more tanned than even you, Mavis. They look like a bunch of Indians, even Lorna. Who cares what people think? I don't. And now I don't think Trista does, either."

They watched as Uncle Cash expertly wheeled Trista around. Though she was still small and frail-looking, she had color in her cheeks and her hazel eyes shone. She said something to her uncle and they both laughed.

"No, I don't think she does now," Mavis agreed. "Still, we have a lot of problems to work out, Stockton."

"Not tonight, dearest."

"No?"

"No. Tonight—" He threw his arms around her, picked her up, and whirled her around and around, to startled laughter and thunderous applause. "Tonight we dance. Tonight Samoa dances!"

Author's Note

Any time you insert fictional characters into a historical event, the real heroes of the piece must suffer. Here I would like to offer an apology to the memories of such real persons as Mr. William Blacklock (who actually was the clerk who served so nobly as American consul during the great hurricane of 1889); the High Chiefs Tamasese, Mataafa, and Laupepa, may their lines live forever; and the German consul Dr. Knappe and the British consul Colonel de Coetlogon, who both played much larger parts in this tragedy than they did in my fictional account of it. For a true and poetic account of the hurricane and its significance to the Three Great Powers, I urge the reader to read Robert Louis Stevenson's excellent *A Footnote to History: Eight Years of Trouble in Samoa*.

Apia Bay is troubled no more; in 1962 Western Samoa gained her independence. But the memory of the years of trouble still remain. In the bay, the great skeleton of the German warship, the *Adler*, can still be seen.

We want to hear from you. Please send your comments about this book to us in care of zreview@zondervan.com. Thank you.

GRAND RAPIDS, MICHIGAN 49530 USA

WWW.ZONDERVAN.COM